Holy Rollers

Holy Rollers

by

Rob Byrnes

A Division of Bold Strokes Books

HOLY ROLLERS

ISBN 13: 978-1-60282-578-9

This Trade Paperback Original Is Published By
Bold Strokes Books, Inc.
P.O. Box 249
Valley Falls, NY 12185

PRINTED IN THE U.S.A.

Credits
Editor: Greg Herren
Production Design: Stacia Seaman
Cover Design by Sheri (graphicartist2020@hotmail.com)

Acknowledgments

If I thanked everyone who deserved to be thanked, these acknowledgments would read like a phonebook. So I'm trimming the list down. If you don't see your name, know that you're in my thoughts. Unless I just forgot to mention you, that is.

Thanks to my agent, Katherine Fausset of Curtis Brown, who's stood by me for a decade; to my partner, Brady Allen, who puts up with me as I pace and talk to myself whenever a deadline approaches; to my Writing Posse for their support and wisdom; and to my Non-Writing Posse for keeping me more or less grounded, even if they don't always appreciate that it's All About Me.

Thanks to everyone who let me turn them into a fictional character, not that any of them had a choice.

Thanks to my friend and—now—editor, Greg Herren. In fact, thanks to everyone at Bold Strokes Books—especially Len Barot—for making me feel at home. It has been a wonderful experience to become part of the Bold Strokes family.

Finally, thanks to Becky Cochrane: editor, proofreader, cheerleader, and awesome friend.

To everyone who uses religion as an excuse for intolerance, hate, and greed…thanks for making this so easy.

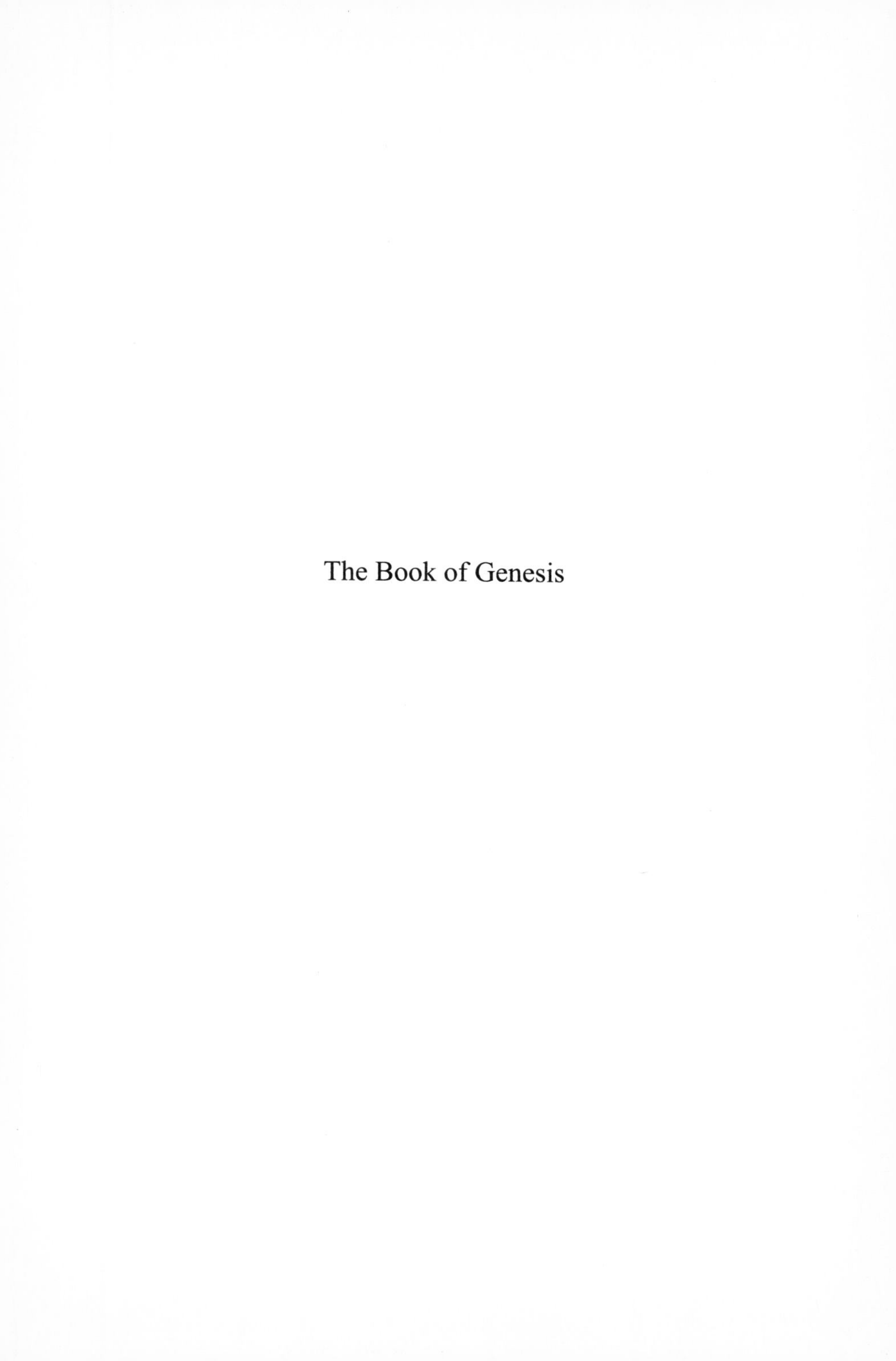

The Book of Genesis

1

In the beginning, there was a 2008 Ford Taurus traveling north at a few miles per hour over the speed limit on the New Jersey Turnpike, piloted by a prematurely grizzled man in his mid-forties as another man—also in his forties, but wearing it better—rode shotgun.

"North Carolina," said the passenger.

"Already have it."

Chase LaMarca, who was the man riding shotgun, leaned forward in his seat, straining to make out the rear license plate on the car they were passing. "New York."

"Already have it," grumbled Grant Lambert, the man behind the wheel, without looking across the seat at Chase.

"Hard to make out the new blue and gold New York plates. I got used to the white ones. You know, with the Statue of Liberty on 'em."

"I grew up with the blue and gold ones," said Grant. "Glad they're back. Makes me feel like things are back to normal."

Chase shifted slightly in his seat. "If you're only a few years older than me, how come I don't remember them?"

"Sometimes a few years are all that matter." It sounded like a reasonable answer, although Grant had wondered the same thing. "It'd be helpful if you kept your eyes on the road. And I don't mean just on the license plates."

Chase shifted again until he was almost parallel to Grant. "I can keep track of the cars while I'm watching the plates."

"And don't forget—"

"*And* yes, I can keep track of the cops, too." Chase turned back until he was facing forward. He was silent for a moment, and then said, "New Jersey."

"You don't have to keep saying 'New Jersey.' New Jersey license plates are not a novelty on the New Jersey Turnpike."

"Sorry." Chase blew away a wisp of hair that had fallen over his forehead. "Just trying to keep things interesting."

"Things are interesting enough."

Chase started to say something but backed off. It was scorching hot, even with the Taurus's air conditioner struggling to keep them comfortable. They'd also been driving for hours. Between the heat and fatigue, Grant was cranky. Chase had offered to take the wheel, but Grant would have none of that. The car was his—at least *now* it was—and he'd be doing the driving.

They fell silent, the only sound inside the car the hum of the tires against the Turnpike for several minutes that felt longer than they were, until Chase finally said, "Bingo! Just ahead in the center lane. Ohio plates."

"I told you, we're not playing that game anymore."

"No, it's a Lexus. And if I'm correct, it's a late nineties Lexus."

Grant focused his eyes on the dark green Lexus with Ohio plates in front of them and allowed himself a tiny bit of hope. "Looks like what we're shopping for." He concentrated on the silhouette outlined through the rear windshield. "And unless someone's taking a nap, it looks like the driver's alone. That's good, too."

"Plus," Chase added as they drew closer to the Lexus, "I think that's an automobile club sticker on the bumper."

Not that it meant anything…or at least not *every*thing. Grant knew professional mechanics who were members of the auto club. Still, it slightly increased the chances that whoever was driving that Lexus was a rookie under the hood, which was another positive sign.

They followed the car awhile until they passed a sign reading OZZIE NELSON SERVICE AREA 3 MILES.

"Time to get to work," Grant said, flashing the Taurus's headlights to signal the Lexus.

It took most of the three miles to the service area to get the attention of the other driver, and even then Grant had to pull up next to the car and motion to him. A round, hairless face looked back at him through thick glasses. The driver was uncomprehending at first, but finally seemed to decide maybe something was wrong because the Lexus's right directional came to life as they approached the service area exit ramp. Grant followed, tailing the car until it braked to a stop in the parking lot.

"I'll talk to him," said Chase, opening his door.

"Cap!"

"Oh, right." Chase reached down to the floorboard and found a baseball cap, pulling it over his spiky, freshly highlighted hair. He liked the look—it took years off him—but he also knew that the hairstyle would make him more much memorable to the guy in the Lexus. And Chase LaMarca had no desire to be remembered that well.

Cap in place, he left the car and approached the dark green sedan parked next to them.

The driver powered his window down. He was a large man—large in every direction—and bald except for a thin fringe of hair ringing his scalp. Despite the lack of hair, Chase made him out for late thirties, although the weight in his face kept the skin tight and gave him a somewhat boyish appearance, even as he sweated through his shirt in the sticky heat despite the air conditioning Chase could feel blasting from the interior.

"Is something wrong?" the man asked.

Chase nodded. "You're leaking something."

"What?" The driver looked perplexed. "What am I leaking?"

"Couldn't tell. But whatever it was, you were leaking a lot of it."

The man unstrapped his seat belt, and with effort, heaved himself out of the car. Chase motioned toward the front wheel well and they both crouched. It was an easy effort for Chase; a more laborious one for the heavy man next to him, who had to prop himself against the car with one hand, his knees creaking under the weight.

"Looked like it was coming from around here," said Chase, pointing at nowhere in particular.

The man wheezed from heat and minimal exertion. "I don't see anything."

Chase looked around and finally saw a damp spot on the pavement, where he pointed next. Behind him, he heard Grant get out of the Taurus and close his door.

"What about there?"

"That doesn't look like a leak. It looks like someone spilled something." He turned his head toward Chase, his expression showing both distrust and confusion. "I really don't think anything was—"

"Here it is," said Grant from somewhere they couldn't see.

"Where are you?" asked Chase.

"Back of the car."

Chase and the Lexus driver dropped to their hands and knees—again an easy maneuver for Chase and major exercise for the other man—and looked along the undercarriage to where Grant's finger pointed to a large, fresh puddle of dampness below the tailpipe. "That's transmission fluid."

Chase popped back up to a crouch and duck-walked a few feet to where Grant knelt at the rear of the car, leaving the man no choice but to follow. Although for him, duck-walking was not an option.

"That doesn't look like transmission fluid to me," he panted when he finally joined Grant and Chase.

"Trust me." Grant dipped his index finger into the liquid. "That's transmission fluid."

"Definitely," Chase agreed.

The man's eyes narrowed and he regarded them warily. "Is this some sort of scam?"

"Scam?" asked Chase. "What do you mean? We're just trying to help."

The man wiped the back of his hand across his damp brow, knocking his glasses askew. His shirt was now completely soaked through. "I've seen this sort of thing on TV. You two convince me I've got a leak, then steer me to a garage where you rip me off for repairs."

Grant shook his head and smiled his most sincere smile, which could almost be passable at times like these when it was good to look sincere. "Listen, buddy, we don't have a garage. We're just two Good Samaritans who saw a fellow driver leaking *gallons* of transmission fluid all over the Turnpike, is all. If you don't want our help..." He stood, followed by Chase, and they took a few steps toward the Taurus.

"No good deed goes unpunished, eh?" Chase said ruefully to Grant, just loud enough to be heard by the Lexus driver.

"Ain't that the truth," said Grant.

Behind them, a voice called, "Guys, I'm sorry."

"Happy travels," Chase replied, not looking back.

"Hope you don't seize up," added Grant.

"No, really. I'm sorry. Please!"

Chase finally turned to face him; Grant followed a few seconds later.

The man, relieved they hadn't abandoned him, forced a smile. "It's just that I'm not always as trusting as I should be."

Grant lowered his gaze to the puddle of transmission fluid on the asphalt, letting the man see exactly how hurt his feelings were. "It's good to be cautious...I suppose."

"Yeah," Chase agreed, tugging absently at the brim of his cap. "There's a lot of bad eggs out there. But you don't want to lose faith in humanity."

The man shook his head and wiped his brow again, and his glasses slid a half inch down his nose. "No, no. Of course not."

"Okay, then." Grant raised his head, squared his shoulders, and nodded toward the bay doors at the other side of the Ozzie Nelson Service Center fuel tanks. "In that case, why don't you pop over to the garage and see if maybe they got time to take a look at your car so you can get back on the road." His eyes traveled back to the large puddle near the tailpipe. "It looks bad, but I figure it'll probably be a quick fix."

The man blinked away sweat from his eyes and pushed his glasses back up his nose. "Yeah, I should have them take a look."

"Also," said Chase, "it'll get you out of the sun for a while. Brutal out here today."

"Brutal," Grant agreed.

The man opened the Lexus door, a ping announcing the keys were still in the ignition. "Thanks a lot, guys."

"Not a problem," said Chase, with a short wave, until he saw the man attempt to force his rotund body back behind the steering wheel. "Wait! You can't *drive* over there!"

"I can't?"

"You can't! You want to ruin your engine?"

"But it's just a few hundred feet…"

Chase looked at him sternly. "A few hundred feet that could *destroy your car*."

"Yeah," said Grant, with a somber shake of his head. "Better safe than sorry."

"Maybe you're right." The man lumbered back to his feet, his pudgy right hand dragging a blue blazer from the passenger seat. The pinging stopped as he removed the keys from the ignition and dropped them in the blazer pocket before slamming the door closed. "Thanks again, guys."

As he struggled into his blazer, Chase leaned close, resting one hand on his shoulder while the other gently patted him reassuringly. "One last word of advice: *We're* not ripping you off, so don't let them"—he indicated the garage—"rip you off either."

"You see *that* all the time on TV, too," said Grant.

"I won't," said the man. He turned and walked toward the garage, offering them a slight wave in parting. As he did, Grant and Chase returned to the Taurus, opening the doors but not quite getting in.

"No one trusts anyone these days," said Chase with a sad shake of his head.

"It's a shame," said Grant. "Makes life tougher, that's for sure. It'd be very good for business if people started trusting other people again."

They watched until the man was almost to the garage and his large frame seemed almost normal-sized.

"Now?" asked Chase.

"Not quite." Grant waited until the man opened the door to the service station office. "Now."

Chase, having lifted the other driver's keys from his pocket while delivering his one last word of advice about not putting too much trust in the garage, was quickly behind the wheel of the Lexus. Twenty seconds later both cars were on the ramp heading back to the New Jersey Turnpike, leaving nothing behind but an empty bottle of transmission fluid where they had been parked.

As he drove north toward New York City, closely following Grant, Chase first removed the EZ-Pass box from the windshield of the Lexus, then finally took the cap off his head and tossed it on the floor before running his fingers through his hair, bringing the styling back to life.

It's too damn hot for a cap on a day like this, he thought, and he cranked up the AC.

$ $ $

They had been in Philadelphia on a day trip—for them, helping some associates clean out a foreign money exchange office in a different city counted as a day trip—when Grant figured he should check in with Charlie Chops, proprietor of an occasionally legitimate garage in the Hunt's Point neighborhood of the Bronx, to see if he might have use for the car they'd stolen for transportation. Chops hadn't needed *that* car, but tipped them off that he needed a late-'90s Lexus, which led them to the dark green number Chase was now taking off the New Jersey Turnpike, figuring that'd be the first place the state troopers would be looking for it.

He followed surface roads through Jersey City and up the west side of the Hudson River to the Lincoln Tunnel, where he paid the toll in cash. He hated dipping into his own pocket for toll money, but using the EZ-Pass would have left an easy trail to follow.

Somewhere along the way he'd lost Grant, but that was fine. It was more than fine, really; it was ideal. Better they split up and take two different routes—he knew Grant was partial to the George Washington Bridge, while Chase had always been a tunnel fan—than parade a caravan of stolen cars the entire distance between the Ozzie Nelson Service Area and Hunt's Point.

Grant is a bridge fan, and I like the tunnels. Chase LaMarca laughed at that thought. Ten words that just seemed to sum up their long relationship.

They were opposites in personality, appearance, and almost every other trait except sexual orientation and criminal proclivity. Grant was abrupt and ill-tempered; Chase was sunny and charming. Grant didn't particularly care how he looked; Chase was a slave to the mirror. Grant was old school, right down to his preference for license plates; Chase was the only one of them who could boot up a computer.

No one who didn't know them would figure them for a couple. Yet they had made it work—and work *well*—for almost seventeen years, and neither of them was going anywhere.

It helped that they had some shared interests. Couples who didn't share interests generally didn't last for almost seventeen years. That their particular shared interests included auto theft, burglary, picking pockets, and even a little blackmail every now and then was beside the point.

Chase didn't see Grant again for another half hour, when he finally pulled the Lexus to the curb outside Charlie Chops's garage and saw him already standing out front, arguing with an older, dark-skinned man who was none other than Chops himself. Apparently the bridge had been the faster route today. Point to Grant.

Chase got out of the car, not bothering to lock it for any number of reasons, starting with the fact that it'd probably be disassembled by the end of the day. As he closed the door he heard Grant say, "C'mon, Chops, this is bullshit."

"Sorry, Lambert," said Chops. "But I only need one Lexus, and Farraday got here first."

Chase looked across the parking lot littered with cars and pieces thereof, spotted the considerable bulk of Paul Farraday scowling on the periphery, and figured out the situation pretty quickly.

"So what do I do with this?" Grant asked, gesturing toward the dark green Lexus.

Chops nodded a silent hello to Chase before returning his attention to Chase's partner. "Take it back where you stole it, I guess."

"How 'bout," said Grant, "I come back tonight after you've closed and park it at your curb. I know this is New York, so the cops wouldn't usually notice for a while, but maybe they get a call. So they come to investigate, and when they do, this Lexus…it'll be sitting right in front of this chop shop. Kind of awkward, right?" He waited until Chops offered the tiniest frown on his weathered, seen-it-all face. "Now, are we gonna negotiate?"

Chops rubbed his eyes and thought for a moment. "Eight hundred."

"Make it a grand, and figure it's a bargain 'cause you'll already have late-nineties Lexus parts on hand the next time someone needs late-nineties Lexus parts in a hurry."

The older man rubbed his eyes again before looking into Grant's own watery eyes. "Okay, a thousand. Just to get you out of here, Lambert."

"Whatever it takes."

But Charlie Chops wasn't done. As he started peeling grimy fifties out of the wad he always kept in his front pocket—because this aspect of his business was conducted exclusively on a cash basis—he said, "You know, Lambert, it's hard enough running a small business these days without dealing with unreasonable suppliers."

Grant ran a hand through his bristling, rapidly graying hair. "C'mon, Chops, I ain't unreasonable. I just want what's mine."

"One of these days, you and people like you are gonna put me out of business. And *then* where will you be? Oh, you can probably find another chop shop, but no one who'll treat you like I do, Lambert."

"And that will be a sad day in my life," Grant said, taking the bills when Charlie Chops finally offered them up. "A very sad day."

Chops looked at the blue Lexus delivered to him by Paul Farraday, then at the dark green Lexus deposited at the curb by Chase, and finally at the late-model Ford Taurus Grant had arrived in.

"This hot, too?" Chops asked, indicating the Taurus.

"What do *you* think?"

"It a local car?"

"Nah. We had to go to Philly for a job, so we grabbed a car in Manhattan last night. But we dumped it in Bala Cynwyd, Pennsylvania."

"So this is from…Bala whatever?"

"No, we left the Bala Cynwyd car in Philly." Chops began to speak, but Grant stopped him. "The Philly car, we left in New Hope…"

"New Hope?"

Grant shrugged. "Heard a lot about it. Always wanted to see it."

Chops shook his head. "So this is the New Hope car?"

"No, this is the car we got from the Ikea parking lot in Elizabeth."

Chops chuckled. "You sure get around, Grant Lambert."

"I try," said Grant, not smiling as he shoved the cash deep into his front pocket without counting it. He trusted no one except Chase—and sometimes he didn't even trust Chase one hundred percent—but knew that Chops would be square with him. "You want the Taurus?"

Chops laughed. "I wouldn't have minded adding those parts to my inventory, but…" His head took in the parking lot. "Got no room now. Gotta get both these Lexuses into the bays before they start attracting the wrong kind of attention."

Grant took another look at the Taurus. "I've been driving it since Ikea, and I really don't want to press my luck."

Chops put a hand on his shoulder. "When you leave the parking lot, make a left and drive four blocks. Leave it outside that high school with the key in the ignition and I can guarantee you'll never see that Taurus again." He leaned a bit closer to make sure the conversation was just between the two of them. "Best watch your boyfriend, though. That hairstyle, well, he's lookin' sorta…" He wobbled his wrist. "You know *I* don't care, Lambert, but I can't say the same for everyone in this neighborhood."

"He can take care of himself." Grant made a half turn until he could see Chase. "Ready to hit the road?"

Chase was, and was about to say so when Farraday was suddenly standing between them. Chops backed away, disappearing into his garage.

"You guys got a minute?"

"Ordinarily," said Grant, "I'd say 'maybe.' But I figure you just cost me a thou or so by beating me to Chops with your Lexus, so now I'm not so sure."

"What, now you don't believe in the free enterprise system?"

Grant shook his head. "I got you lecturing me on free enterprise, and Chops lecturing me on the problems of being a small businessman. Did I miss something and accidentally enroll in an economics course?" When Farraday didn't answer—which he knew he wouldn't—Grant crossed his arms and impatiently said, "Okay, you've got one minute. Make it good."

Farraday straightened his frame. "I got a cousin who got himself into some trouble."

"That's what cousins do. Get in trouble. Cousins and brothers-in-law."

"Believe me," said Farraday, without a trace of a smile, "if this was my brother-in-law in trouble, I wouldn't be coming to you—or anyone—for help."

Grant figured that Farraday's long-ago ugly divorce was still an open wound, so he stayed quiet and let him continue.

"Anyway, my cousin Leonard was working for this big church—one of them mega-churches, I think they're called—and got fired because they thought he was gay."

Grant raised an eyebrow. "And *is* he gay?"

"Well…yeah. That's why I wanted to discuss it with you and Chase."

Grant didn't really like being the go-to guy whenever one of his acquaintances had a gay-related problem, and it came out in his voice.

"Sounds like he needs a lawyer. And we're not lawyers, Farraday. Remember? We're criminals. Which is not the same thing, at least mostly. So how could *we* help?"

"Grant," Chase whispered in his partner's ear, just loud enough for Farraday—but no one else—to hear. "He said his cousin got fired from a mega-church. Which means a *big, big* church, like the ones on Sunday-morning TV. A lot of those places have money."

"Yeah," Grant agreed. "But we're not lawyers."

"You're not getting what I'm saying."

Farraday stepped forward. "Chase is right, Lambert. This ain't about the law. It's about the money."

Grant considered that. "I think I'm beginning to follow."

"Figured you would eventually. Anyway, he's talked to lawyers, and they can't do a damn thing. Or maybe they don't want to. So now Cousin Leonard wants to get back at the church, and since he can't do it legally, he's willing to do it illegally."

"He knows how to get his hands on their money?" asked Chase.

"Some of it," Farraday confirmed. "Enough to make this worth our while."

"You're sure?"

"He's sure. Or at least he says he is. And he was the bookkeeper before they fired him, so I figure he knows what he's talking about."

Grant was silent for a few minutes while he pondered the situation. Finally he said, "Okay, Farraday, let's talk."

2

After Farraday's divorce—the details of which were unknown to anyone but Farraday, not that anyone wanted to know the details because even the generalities were ugly—he'd been forced to abandon his modest apartment for an even more modest furnished basement studio in a part of Brooklyn that would probably never gentrify. In short order, the man and the apartment had become a good fit, equally gloomy and rough around the edges.

It hadn't always been that way. In the increasingly distant past, Paul Farraday had been a legend—and an anomaly—among New York City cab drivers: honest, courteous, and seemingly born with a sixth sense that guided him effortlessly through even the worst traffic tie-ups. But he'd also had a weakness for hard liquor, a problem that grew more severe in the wake of his divorce, and soon the time came to hand in the keys to his cab. It was that or quit the bottle...and Farraday was not a quitter.

But he still had to make a living, which was how, in time, he found himself doing odd jobs like boosting cars for Charlie Chops and occasionally working with people like Grant Lambert and Chase LaMarca when they needed a wheel man. He liked the flexibility—he could pretty much set a work schedule around his handful of non-drinking hours in the day—and he also liked the fact that the income was entirely off the books. Meaning there was no way his bitch of an ex-wife could get her greedy claws on it.

That was why, a few days after encountering Grant at Charlie Chops's garage, he was gruffly welcoming him at the door of the basement studio, blinking at the daylight in a way that made Grant think he hadn't been aboveground for several days.

"Where's Chase?" Farraday asked.

"At the Gross."

Farraday shook his head. "I don't know how he does that."

The Gross was officially known as Groc-O-Rama, a small supermarket chain that earned its nickname honestly, but everyone—except Chase—just called it the Gross. Chase had worked as an assistant manager at The Gross in Elmhurst for the better part of two decades, which Grant figured meant he started about five years after the last time anyone bothered to clean the place, but when times were lean it was nice to have a regular paycheck coming in. And the Gross *did* have some sentimental significance. It was, after all, where Grant and Chase first met, on the night they both separately tried to break into the safe.

"Your cousin here?" asked Grant as he followed Farraday down the narrow, musty stairway.

"Yup."

That cousin, Leonard Platt, was sitting on a threadbare couch in Farraday's tiny apartment, distractedly bouncing one leg and playing with the knot in his tie. Grant wondered why he'd bothered wearing a tie at all, let alone on a hot day in an apartment without air-conditioning, but let it slide. It wasn't the quirkiest thing he'd ever seen on this side of the law. Or on the other side, for that matter.

Farraday introduced Grant to Leonard and asked if anyone wanted a drink.

"It's not even noon," said Grant.

The ex-cabbie looked up from where he was pouring amber liquid into a rocks glass that—true to Farraday's norm—contained no rocks. "What's your point?"

"Okay, then give me a beer."

Leonard Platt was, Grant noted, a nervous man, although that could have been due to his discomfort sitting in a room where every other person was a professional criminal. He sized him up: late thirties, thinning hair, pale, and looking like he wanted to change his mind and flee. The springs Grant could see poking just beneath the surface of the couch fabric probably didn't do anything to improve his comfort level.

While Farraday poured, Grant got down to business. "So what's this job you're suggesting?"

Leonard seemed to jump a bit at Grant's no-nonsense tone, but quickly settled back on the couch and cleared his throat. "Up until last week, I was the bookkeeper for the Virginia Cathedral of Love. I'm sure you've heard of it."

"Don't be."

Leonard laughed nervously, which annoyed Grant. "You're joking, right?"

"Nope."

"It's a huge church, about an hour west of Washington, and—"

"Which Washington?"

Leonard started at him. "Huh?"

"The state? Or DC?"

"DC, of course," said Leonard. "If it was an hour west of Washington state, it'd...well, it'd be in the Pacific Ocean."

"Could be on an island."

"Well, I suppose, but..." Leonard paused, thought, and then said, "I mentioned this is the *Virginia* Cathedral of Love, right? Virginia? As in the state next to Washington, DC?"

"Just checking," said Grant. "In this line of work, you can't take things for granted." He took a swig from the beer bottle. "Why don't you continue with your story. Let's not get bogged down with the details just yet."

"Yes, but..." Confusion clouded Leonard's face, but he managed to shake it away. "The Virginia Cathedral of Love is huge. There are almost twenty thousand members and the church holds twelve services each week. The Sunday service alone brings in an average of eight thousand worshippers. People have to park in a lot a mile away and get shuttled in." He swallowed. "And I was the chief bookkeeper for seven years until, well...until they fired me."

"Farraday told us they fired you because you're gay," said Grant. "That true?"

"Unfortunately."

"Unfortunately what? That you're gay?"

"No. Unfortunately, I got caught. You see, one of the associate pastors was driving through DC a few weeks ago. Spotted me walking into one of the gay bars in the Dupont Circle area. The church launched an investigation and followed me for a few days, until they caught me doing it again. I was called into the chief operating officer's office, and... that was it. Fired on the spot."

"Hope you at least found what you were looking for at the bars," said Grant, forcing a slight grin.

Leonard pursed his lips and held his silence.

"Let me ask you a question. Why us?"

"Because you and your partner are criminals. *Gay* criminals. Right?" He looked to Farraday for confirmation and received it in the form of a slight nod. "I figured as gay criminals, you'd want to help me get justice."

"A lawyer can help you get justice. We're not lawyers. We're the *other* kind of crooks...the kind who aren't especially interested in justice."

"Forget lawyers," said Leonard. "Half an hour after the Cathedral fired me, I was on the phone to a lawyer and spent the next few days talking to a dozen more. And not *one* was interested in the case."

Grant shook his head. "You'd think a discrimination case would interest them."

"We're talking about Virginia," said Leonard with a rueful laugh. "It's not like the rest of the world. Also, we're talking about the Virginia Cathedral of Love. They're huge and have everyone running scared. I couldn't even get the Gay Republican Club to support me."

"There are gay Republicans?" asked Grant.

"Sure."

"Huh. Guess I'm even less political than I thought I was."

Leonard adjusted his tie. Again. "For what it's worth, I've given up on the legal route. When I use the word 'justice'..."

"You mean revenge."

Leonard said, "Yes, that's what I mean."

"Good. Revenge I understand. Justice...I'm not so crazy about justice. How much you figure they have in assets?"

"Billions," said Leonard, his hands having moved from the knot in his tie to absentmindedly fiddle with the tip of his collar. "But forget their assets. It's impossible to touch most of their money. Those bank accounts are iron-clad, and their books are clean enough to eat off. I should know, I kept them. However, I *do* know where they keep the petty cash."

"Petty cash?" Grant was unhappy.

"Petty cash."

Upon confirmation that he'd heard what he'd heard, Grant was beyond unhappy. This was shaping up to be a waste of time; time that could have been better spent swiping laptops from coffeehouses. "I haven't been desperate enough to steal petty cash in twenty years or so, and I'm not gonna start again now."

Leonard smiled his thin smile and stopped playing with his collar. "But cash is good in your business, isn't it?"

"Cash is very good. *Petty* cash is not good. Petty cash is...petty."

"How does petty cash to the tune of seven million dollars sound?"

Grant didn't think he heard him correctly, which he made clear to Leonard. So Leonard repeated himself.

"Seven million—give or take—is sitting in a safe in the Cathedral."

"Seven million? In cash?"

"Seven million. In cash."

"Dollars?"

"Dollars."

"You're sure?"

"I'm sure."

Grant thought about that for a moment. "So let me ask you a couple of questions, like…how do you know about this cash?"

"Remember, I was their bookkeeper for seven years. I know a lot of things they'd prefer I didn't know." He began playing with his shirt cuff. "In this case, I know that almost every piece of United States currency that's donated to the Cathedral goes straight into that safe and never appears on the books. And let me tell you, a lot of true believers walk in with their fists full of cash, just *begging* for the church to take it from them."

Grant wasn't sure he was buying it. "Here's another question: If you were the bookkeeper, but the cash wasn't on the books, how do you know how much cash is in the safe?"

Leonard leaned forward. "I always knew there was cash in the safe, but I had no idea how much. I figured maybe twenty thousand dollars or so. Then one day a few months ago I happened to overhear Hurley and Merribaugh…"

"Who?"

"Dr. Oscar Hurley and his chief operating officer, the Reverend Mr. Dennis Merribaugh. Hurley founded the Cathedral, and Merribaugh came along a few years later and together they started the Moral Families Coalition. Anyway, I heard them talking, and that's how I got the seven-million-dollar figure. It's their number, not mine."

"I still don't get it," said Farraday, finally adding himself to the conversation. "What do they need with all that cash lying around? Why not bank it?"

"Banks have paper trails, Cousin Paul. Everything else they do at the Cathedral goes beyond the legal requirements. Every dollar is accounted for, and they're independently audited twice a year. Everything is clean… *except* the cash donations."

"Yeah, but…"

"Let me explain a bit more. The Cathedral and the Moral Families Coalition…"

"What's this Moral Families Coalition?" asked Grant.

"It's a political organization attached to the Cathedral. Anyway, they account for everything but the cash. The money goes for…oh, you name it. Everything you'd want to spend money on, but don't want a paper trail. Mostly it supplements the income of Hurley and Merribaugh, but I'm pretty sure it's also used for bribes and things like that." Leonard Platt's hands went back to the knot in his tie. "Things they want to keep off the books."

"Okay, so how come you want help?" asked Grant. "If I was you, I'd have grabbed it and kept it for myself."

Leonard smiled, and for the first time it seemed natural. He was finally on solid ground in this apartment full of thieves. They were all now thinking alike…and Leonard had been thinking it *first*.

"Maybe if they had given me a few days to pull it off, I would have. But all of a sudden they were escorting me off the cathedral grounds, so I didn't have enough time. Heck, I didn't have time to react to being fired, let alone rip them off. And now getting back in and grabbing the safe, well…I'll need associates."

"Because you can't go back. Because you've been fired."

"Exactly."

"Just one safe?"

"Just one safe," Leonard confirmed. "You'd be surprised how small a space you can stuff a lot of cash into."

"No, I wouldn't."

Leonard's face flushed. "No, of course not."

Grant was still having a hard time wrapping his head around the concept that people would just keep seven million dollars in an office safe, where anyone—him, for example—could steal it.

"I still don't get it," he said. "What do they need with all that cash?"

"The Cathedral is near Washington, of course, and the Moral Families Coalition is gaining a lot of prominence on Capitol Hill. I doubt Oscar Hurley is making friends with senators and congressmen due solely to his winning personality."

"You're talking bribes?"

"I'm talking bribes."

Grant looked at the floor, and distaste was etched in his face when he finally looked back at Leonard. "So we'll have to go to Washington?"

"I doubt it. Maybe *through* it, but the money isn't in DC. The church—and the safe—is about forty miles west, in Northern Virginia. Ever hear of a place called Nash Bog?"

Grant frowned. "There's really a place called Nash Bog? No. But already I like it more than Washington, DC. I hate Washington, DC."

"So you said. But wait until you get a taste of Northern Virginia." Leonard's hands left his tie and began doing half the talking. "They call Nash Bog 'Cash Bog.' It's one of the richest communities in Loudoun County, which is one of the richest counties in the nation. And one of its richest residents is Dr. Oscar Hurley. Does that give you any idea of the potential?"

Grant settled back in his chair. "I don't know about this. Sounds like the stakes are bigger than I'm used to. And I don't know from Virginia." He turned back to Leonard. "So let's talk turkey. Say we manage to steal this money. What do you expect?"

Leonard's face went blank. "Expect?"

Farraday, standing at the bar refreshing his drink, interpreted for him. "He means, how much do you expect for your share of the haul?"

"Ah!" said Leonard, and he placed a finger thoughtfully on his chin. "I would think *half* would be fair."

Grant let the suggestion hang in the air for a moment. Then he said, "You should think again."

Leonard was perplexed. "But I'm the guy who brought you the job."

"You're also," Grant reminded him, "the guy who can't do it without us. Now, if you'd like to shop it around and try to get yourself a better deal…"

"Maybe I should."

Grant looked at Farraday, shaking his head with disappointment. Leonard did not understand their business. "No, maybe you *shouldn't*."

"Lambert's right," Farraday told his cousin. "First of all, you don't know any other crooks except the ones in this room, do you?" Leonard frowned. "I didn't think so. But even if you did, the more people you start telling about this seven million, the more people who'll want to get their hands on it."

"With you," Grant added, "or without you."

Leonard's shoulders slumped. "Okay, so what do *you* think my share should be?"

"A million five," said Grant with an abrupt finality.

It was better than Leonard thought Grant was going to offer, so he pretended to mull it over for twenty seconds or so. Finally he said, "I guess I'll have to live with that."

"Beats unemployment."

Farraday cleared his throat. "While we're discussing shares…"

"A hundred thou as a finder's fee and for any driving we'll need. I pick up the expenses. If we have to steal a car or two, you can keep *those*, too."

"C'mon, Lambert. You can do better than that."

Grant shook his head. "I think I have to remind you both that Chase and I will be taking almost all the risk, doing all the planning, picking up the expenses, and using our professional expertise. You wouldn't try to shortchange a plumber or electrician, would you?"

"As a matter of fact…" Farraday stopped when he found himself on the receiving end of one of Grant's scowls.

"A million and a half for Leonard; a hundred thou for Farraday. You guys wanna renegotiate between yourselves to keep peace in the family, feel free. Any way you divvy it up is fine with me, so long as you get one-point-six between the two of you. The rest goes to me and Chase. That's the deal. Take it or leave it."

"Take it," said Farraday—he could always lean on Leonard for another hundred thou or two later—and his cousin offered a slight nod of agreement.

"And, of course, it's all conditional."

"What do you mean?" Leonard asked, suddenly alarmed. Farraday tried to *shush* him.

"You only get the money *if* the job is successful."

"And if it isn't?" asked Leonard, ignoring another *shush*.

"In that case, no one here is going to have to worry about money for a long time, because the government will be providing our room and board."

"I don't understand."

"He means prison," snarled Farraday. "Meaning, you'd better be right about this safe, Cousin Leonard."

Leonard smiled, finally relaxed, and for the first time in weeks seemed as if he didn't have a care in the world. "Oh, I am, Cousin Paul. I am…"

3

The Reverend Mr. Dennis Merribaugh, a manila folder tucked under one arm, rapped three times, rapidly and lightly, on the half-open door, and when there was no response, rapped twice more with slightly more force. When there was still no answer, he pushed the door fully open but didn't step into the room. Instead, he waited at the threshold, and his voice a light tenor, whispered, "Dr. Hurley?"

There was still no response, so he took one tentative step across the threshold. "Dr. Hurley?" Nothing. He dropped his voice a half octave. "Oscar?"

A response finally came, in the form of a muffled flush. Merribaugh took a step back to the other side of the threshold, pulling the door to its original half-open position. When he heard Hurley open his bathroom door, he repeated the light rap.

"Dr. Hurley?"

"Come in."

Now properly invited, Merribaugh pushed the door open and walked into Dr. Oscar Hurley's office. Hurley glanced up at him before returning his attention to paperwork spread across his desk.

Even though he'd been in this office several times a week for the nine years in which he'd been affiliated with the Virginia Cathedral of Love, the Rev. Mr. Dennis Merribaugh still marveled at its opulence. Calling it an office, he thought, did it a disservice. It was 750 square feet of luxury. A fireplace dominated one wall, while valuable tapestries depicting Biblical images hung from the others, which were lined with bookcases and credenzas. Atop those bookcases and credenzas were dozens of gold-framed photographs of Hurley with an assortment of dignitaries, including more than a few United States presidents and foreign leaders. Positioned in a semicircle in the center of the room were three overstuffed couches, their frames gently curved inward to align with the edge of a white circular carpet.

That carpet depicted the official seal of the Virginia Cathedral of Love: a representation of the Crucifixion on a towering cross, encircled by dozens of pink and red dogwood blooms, with single red and blue stripes circling the outer edge. The dogwood blossoms represented Virginia; the red and blue stripes represented the United States of America.

Jesus, Virginia, America. That was what the Virginia Cathedral of Love was all about.

And then there was the centerpiece of the room, placed exactly halfway between the couches and a set of floor-to-ceiling French doors opening onto a terrace overlooking scenic views of the Northern Virginia countryside.

The Desk of Christ.

Not that Christ had actually owned it, of course. It had been well-established over the past two millennia that Jesus Christ did *not* hold a desk job.

In fact, this ugly, imposing, eight-foot-long desk was considered by most people to be unworthy of its surroundings until they learned of its provenance. Only then did they believe.

The Desk of Christ was made of cedar, pine, and cypress: the woods used in the True Cross, according to Eastern Orthodox Christianity…and more importantly, according to Dr. Oscar Hurley. The symbolism gave it a beauty to believers that went deeply beyond its surface ugliness; there was even a worn spot on its veneer where Cathedral parishioners were known to touch the desk to be closer to Christ.

Still, even the Desk of Christ wasn't the highlight of the room. Not now, at least. That honor went to the tall, trim man in his mid-sixties who was seated behind it, silver pompadour shining in the sunlight cascading through the windows.

Dr. Oscar Hurley.

He finally looked up from whatever he'd been doing and beckoned the Rev. Mr. Dennis Merribaugh to take a seat on the center couch. Merribaugh did as he was told, his plump frame settling comfortably into the cushions. Only then did Dr. Oscar Hurley tent his fingers across the bridge of his nose, and—in a deep baritone with just a honeyed hint of Southern accent—ask, "How are our talking points trending, Dennis?"

Merribaugh opened the manila folder and rustled through some papers until he found the one he wanted, pulling it out and setting the folder in his lap. He read from the sheet.

"New World Order is down eight points over the past month. That one doesn't seem to have much traction among the congregation."

Hurley hiked an eyebrow. "Really? That surprises me. I thought that one would frighten them."

"You'd think so," said Merribaugh with a slight shrug. "But they don't seem to buy into it."

"That is an unfortunate result of our modern world. The more it's globalized by the elites, the less people are frightened of globalization by the elites. Not unlike in the days of the Romans…" He really wanted to stoke fears of a New World Order, but if the public wasn't interested… He shook the unfortunate thought away. "Next."

Merribaugh glanced at the sheet of paper. "Abortion's still strong. There's been a slight downward tick, but it's still a hot topic."

"They may like it, but *I'm* bored with it. I spent most of 2010 on abortion, and it was like treading water. Blah, blah, blah…Maybe next year I'll have that old enthusiasm back. Next."

"Socialism polls high numbers. I think as long as Obama's in office, it'll stay strong."

Hurley leaned back and his desk chair gave a slight groan. "Maybe. Of course, those are the same people who elected Obama in the first place, then decided they didn't like him…so they elected a Republican Congress, then decided they didn't like *them*. Who knows what they'll think when they wake up tomorrow morning." He again tented his fingers over the bridge of his nose. "I'll play that one around the edges. No sense in getting too far ahead of the flock. Next."

"The new trade treaty with China…"

"Bored. Move on."

Merribaugh looked up from his sheet of paper. "Are you sure? My polling shows the congregation eighty-one percent opposed."

"Eighty-one percent of the idiots who make up this congregation can't even balance their checkbooks. Next."

"But—"

"Next!"

Merribaugh's eyes returned to the paper. "The gay issue is still a winner."

"Always has been, always will be."

"It polls at ninety to ninety-four percent."

Hurley considered that. “Should be one hundred percent.”

“And we have the Project Rectitude conference at the end of the month, so there’s a nice tie-in.”

“Hmm.” Hurley was silent for several long moments. Finally he rubbed his eyes. “And how *is* your little conference shaping up, Dennis?”

Merribaugh felt his stomach flutter but suppressed it. The conference had been his own idea—Hurley had not been enthusiastic—and it hadn’t been going as well as he had hoped. No need to trouble Hurley with the details, though.

“Fine, Oscar. Just fine.”

“Only fine?” There was a sneer to Hurley’s voice.

“The hotel is booked, we’ve confirmed most of the speakers, and the applications are flooding in.”

“Flooding?” There was that sneer again.

“Well…maybe not ‘flooding.’ But there’s been a steady flow and—”

“*Mr.* Merribaugh,” Hurley said abruptly, half rising from his chair and stopping Merribaugh in mid-sentence, his mouth still open. It was never a good sign when Hurley called him “Mr. Merribaugh”; they’d been partners too long for that formality. “I hope I don’t have to remind you that this conference was *your* idea.”

“No, Oscar, you don’t have to…”

Hurley leaned back against his chair, not quite sitting. “And you can imagine how embarrassing it would be to the Virginia Cathedral of Love if it failed.”

“Yes, Oscar, I know it would be…”

“So *don’t fail*.” Hurley dropped back into his chair—it groaned again—and began drumming his fingers on the Desk of Christ as he stared at his second-in-command.

“I won’t, Oscar.”

After a few seconds—seconds that felt like hours to Merribaugh—Hurley ran one hand through his silver pompadour. “Okay, it sounds like I’d better make July ‘Sodomy is Sin’ month. I just hope the congregation doesn’t get bored.”

With an audible sigh of relief, Merribaugh held the sheet of paper aloft. “They never seem to get bored with the gay issue. Ninety to ninety-four percent. The numbers are strong, but you can also see it in their faces. Adults even bring along their impressionable young children to hear your moral message! Gay marriage…gays in the military…gay pride marches with bare-breasted lesbians and men in skimpy thongs having sex right out on the street where *decent* people and children can see it…Our congregation will *never* accept that sin!"

"I suppose you're right," said Hurley. "Of course, I said the same thing about Congress just a few years ago, and now look what's happening."

Merribaugh bravely ventured to correct Hurley. "*Was* happening. I think we've got that under control now."

Hurley sniffed. "I don't trust any of them. Not a one."

"The issue is still a winner. It still trends strongly. And the Project Rectitude conference…"

"We'll discuss the Project Rectitude conference later." There was finality in Hurley's voice. "When your trickle of applications has finally become that flood you anticipate, I'll be happy to talk about the details."

"But—"

"Dennis, *please*!" Hurley saw the chastised look on his second-in-command's face, and for a moment, remembered to love his neighbor. Especially his neighbor who knew, figuratively, where the bodies were buried. "I'll tell you what; I'll talk about it during my sermon on Sunday. Send me an e-mail with a few details and maybe I'll be able to drum up some business for you."

"Yes, Oscar." Merribaugh didn't like Hurley's dismissive attitude but knew he'd come around. Eventually. Hopefully.

Hurley leaned back and tented his fingers again. "Speaking of the Sodomites, we have a more important item to address."

"We do?"

"Leonard Platt."

"Addressed. One hundred percent addressed." Merribaugh chuckled. "We'll never hear from Leonard again. I've taken care of that."

"I hope you're right, Dennis. But it still concerns me that he knows…some things I'd rather he not know."

"You mean the existence of the safe."

"I mean the existence of the *contents* of the safe."

Both men vividly remembered the day they'd found Leonard Platt standing behind a file cabinet moments after they'd been throwing numbers like seven million dollars around. It hadn't been their best moment…although it had been worse for Leonard. He hadn't known it, but that marked the beginning of the end for him. Discovering he was a homosexual was a fortunate accident; they would have found some other reason to fire him—embezzlement would be easy to cook up—soon enough.

Merribaugh bounced the manila folder on his lap. "Leonard Platt really doesn't concern me." When Hurley started to object, he kept talking. "Leonard's been fired, and Cathedral security is under strict orders not to let him back on the grounds. I suppose he could go to the authorities, but then what? Who will take the word of a disgruntled, fired employee—a *homosexual* disgruntled, fired employee—over the founder and the chief operating officer of one of the nation's largest churches?" He smiled. "In any event, the contents of the safe can always be easily explained."

Hurley nodded silently. "It still makes me very uncomfortable. I don't trust Platt. Not one bit."

Merribaugh tried to be reassuring. "Don't concern yourself with him, Oscar. I'll take care of whatever needs to be taken care of."

Past that topic, Hurley returned to a related concern. "There's another thing we need to focus on. Now that Leonard Platt is no longer with us, we need a new bookkeeper."

"I'm sure we can find volunteers from the congregation to help us out. At least in the short term. As far as a permanent replacement, well… you know that will be difficult. We can't hire just anyone."

"Agreed." Hurley laid his palms flat on the Desk of Christ. "We've already made the mistake of hiring the *wrong* person."

Merribaugh fidgeted on the couch. "In fairness to Leonard, he was a good bookkeeper. Hardworking, honest…"

"Nosy."

Merribaugh nodded. "Too bad he turned out to be a Sodomite."

"You hired him, Dennis."

"I did, Oscar." He leaned forward. "*And* I fired him."

Hurley couldn't argue with that. And it wasn't really Dennis Merribaugh's fault that Leonard Platt was discovered to be a snoop and a Sodomite. It was just…sad. And it left a huge hole in the Cathedral's finance office. After all these years, Hurley didn't want to become a micromanager again, but…

"And you're sure that these church ladies you bring in—for the short term—will be up to the job? I don't have to remind you this is a complex organization."

"They'll be up to the job," said Merribaugh. "I'm sure we'll have someone in place by the end of the month, and the summer is usually quiet. All they'll have to do is handle some data entry and cut a few checks. *I* will take care of the cash."

Hurley smiled at Merribaugh, who sensed the smile was more a display of iron will than agreement and reassurance.

"*We* will take care of the cash, Dennis. *We*."

$ $ $

Despite his position as chief operating officer of the Virginia Cathedral of Love, the Rev. Mr. Dennis Merribaugh's office was significantly less glamorous than that of Dr. Oscar Hurley. Both men were headquartered in a four-story former plantation house, now a warren of offices and conference rooms, known as Cathedral House. It was located a quarter mile up the road from the actual cathedral, but Hurley's 750-square-foot workplace—with its accompanying reception area, wardrobe, full bath, and powder room, not to mention the security office just down the hall—took up a large part of the second floor at the top of a twin set of sweeping staircases framing the entryway.

Merribaugh's workmanlike corner office was tucked up on the fourth floor, with the other administrative offices. A calendar and a dry-erase board—not expensive tapestries—decorated the walls. Heat was provided by a temperamental radiator, not a grand fireplace. The only celebrity photo was a cheaply framed picture of Merribaugh with Victoria Jackson watching over the office from atop a metal filing cabinet. Two threadbare chairs stood in for Hurley's three couches. And there was no seal on the navy blue throw rug he'd purchased for $12.99 at Walmart.

And, of course, he only had a standard-issue desk of indeterminate wood veneer. It was decidedly *not* the Desk of Christ.

Still, it was comfortable and large enough, and the windows overlooked the side of the cathedral where architects had somehow managed to install five-story reinforced stained-glass panels across most of the length, width, and height of the church, breaking the effect only at evenly spaced intervals to allow for load-bearing columns. When the morning and early afternoon sun hit the stained glass, the beauty could take Merribaugh's breath away. He'd even shed a few tears on occasion.

Spreading out from the rear of the cathedral was Dr. Oscar Hurley's latest pet project, an addition that, in Merribaugh's opinion, added nothing to the aesthetics of the cathedral. The new auditorium wasn't ugly, exactly, but it also didn't quite mesh with its surroundings. The squat two-story building—with a seating capacity of three thousand people and twelve concession stands—didn't detract much from the grand cathedral, since half the ground floor burrowed into the hillside, but it also didn't complement it. Although to be fair, at certain times of day the auditorium's skylights picked up reflections of the stained glass, rendering it simply beautiful.

Merribaugh's office also had a view of the church's claim to fame: the Great Cross towering 199 feet above the grounds…although, come to think of it, most other people in this part of Loudoun County had that view. That *was* the point of having a 199-foot cross piercing the sky, after all.

The Rev. Dennis Merribaugh had certainly had his cynical moments over recent years—darkly cynical, more often than not—but when entering his office and looking at his view, he was almost always filled with the power of God. Those massive stained-glass works of art…the Great Cross…no matter what he had just done, he always felt a moment of redemption and joy.

But not on this day.

On this day, he walked into his office and booted up the computer without even glancing out the window. The old Dell slowly came to life, and he clicked on a desktop icon labeled "Project Rectitude," then clicked again and waited—again, interminably—for a spreadsheet to open.

Finally it displayed the names and addresses of fourteen men and two women, the only people who had registered to date for Beyond Sin, the conference he'd scheduled for the beginning of the following month. Just weeks in the future…it might as well be tomorrow.

Hurley had been right: Project Rectitude was Merribaugh's baby. If it failed, Merribaugh would have to face the consequences.

It had seemed like a no-brainer for a mega-church like the Virginia Cathedral of Love to host an ex-gay ministry, so Merribaugh had fought for it, and finally Hurley acquiesced. True, Project Rectitude hadn't cost much money over its first few years—a few dollars here and there for soft drinks and doughnuts, mostly—but now that he'd taken the next step and moved forward with the Beyond Sin conference, tens of thousands of dollars—maybe more; maybe *a lot* more—were on the line.

Not to mention the potentially damaged reputations of Project Rectitude, the Moral Families Coalition, and the Virginia Cathedral of Love. That cost would come without a price tag.

And all Dennis Merribaugh had to show for it were sixteen names.

Sixteen names, when two hundred was the break-even minimum.

Fortunately, Dr. Oscar Hurley had not asked to see the report he'd held in his sweaty hands fifteen minutes earlier…the report that said, more or less, that the parishioners of the Virginia Cathedral of Love thought the gay issue was increasingly a big yawn. Hurley had been only too willing to believe Merribaugh when he told him the issue still trended as a hot topic, which—like his antipathy over Project Rectitude and Beyond Sin—had more to do with Hurley's dislike of the very *thought* of homosexuality than with anything concrete.

The numbers—absent Hurley's prejudices—didn't lie.

Happily, Hurley's prejudices outweighed mere statistics when it came to guiding the ministry.

And at least that bought Dennis Merribaugh a little breathing room. And a little more time to bring in the two hundred people he'd originally promised Hurley for Beyond Sin.

4

"So this is beautiful Northern Virginia," muttered Grant, sitting in the front passenger seat as their car idled at a red light outside the sixth strip mall they'd come across in the past two miles.

"This is it," Farraday confirmed, sitting behind the wheel of the dark blue—almost purple, in the wrong light—Mercury Mystique he'd stolen five hours earlier from a Manhattan side street near the Holland Tunnel. As he waited for the light, he half turned toward Leonard, sitting behind him in the backseat. "This is where we want to be, right?"

"Right. The Cathedral is just a few miles down the road."

Grant drummed his fingers impatiently on the armrest. "Just drive past ten more Walmarts and Home Depots and we should be there."

But he was wrong. When traffic finally broke, the Mercury passed through the end of the commercial sprawl and they were soon traveling a few miles per hour over the speed limit toward the Virginia Cathedral of Love. Minutes later, Leonard leaned forward and pointed through the windshield.

"See the cross?" Grant, Farraday, and Chase looked out to the horizon and saw it towering over green hills pockmarked with signs announcing future development. "That's the cathedral."

Another several minutes passed, and Farraday was cruising down Cathedral Boulevard in Nash Bog, slowing almost imperceptibly as they passed the entrance to the Virginia Cathedral of Love. A signal light had been placed on the boulevard where it intersected with the six-lane road leading into and out of the grounds, indicating cathedral traffic needed some management. As the car rode over a shadow of the cross cast on the asphalt, Chase reflexively blessed himself, a learned habit he'd never quite been able to *un*learn.

"Big church," Chase said, stating the obvious and hoping to distract attention from his lapse into piety.

"Maybe *too* big." Grant eyed a guardhouse set near the entrance. "Farraday, go down the road a bit and pull over. I need to eyeball this from outside the car."

A quarter mile down the road, Farraday gently pulled onto the shoulder and stopped.

"Don't make this too long, Lambert. I got no idea what the cops in Virginia will think seeing this car with New York tags parked on the side of the road."

"I wouldn't worry," Leonard piped up from the backseat. "The Cathedral has an international following. All fifty states and more than thirty foreign nations. Out-of-state visitors are very common. If the police come by, I can tell them I'm giving you a tour of the area."

"I'm not worried about *us*, Leonard. I'm worried about the fact this vehicle is stolen."

"Oh." Leonard slinked back into his seat and reminded himself that he was not dealing with the world as he was used to dealing with it.

Grant was first out of the car and motioned for Leonard and Chase to follow him, which they did. Then, Leonard leading, they walked back down the shoulder in the direction they'd come, stopping a few hundred feet from the main entrance, just out of sight of the guardhouse.

"I don't know if I should be out here," said Leonard, his hands fidgeting in his pants pockets. "If they see me, they'll know something's up."

"Then don't be seen," said Grant. "But I want you with us in case we have questions." He pointed to the grassy slope rising up from the side of the road, a berm forming the separation between church and traffic. "Up here."

The three men scrambled up the slope, stopping at the top and taking in the view of the Virginia Cathedral of Love. The late-morning sun bounced off the massive stained-glass panels lining the front wall of the cathedral, which—along with a few smaller buildings—sat in the center of a basin ringed by green hills.

Grant looked at Chase. "How big, you figure?"

Chase sized up the property. "Farraday could do this better, but I make it to be about twenty city blocks from the road to the far end."

"So a mile."

"Yeah, give or take."

"So that would put the cathedral about a half mile from the road, and that big cross maybe five-eighths of a mile."

"'Bout that."

While most of the land had been paved for parking lots and sidewalks, the acreage of the grounds still allowed for abundant greenery, although not the kind of coverage Grant felt they could use to their best advantage. The only heavy foliage was near the five-eighths of a mile point, where a concentration of trees and shrubbery lined four symmetrical walkways fanning out from the base of the mammoth cross.

Grant didn't like what he saw. There was nowhere to hide out there except near the cross, but since that wasn't where the money was stashed, it wouldn't do them any good.

"The cross is *huge*," whispered Chase, fighting the urge to bless himself again. "Even bigger than it looks from the road." He took in the immense structure, the lower half encased in scaffolding. Because he was more practical than devout, he asked Leonard, "What's the deal with the scaffolding?"

"In a place this size, there's always something that needs fixing." Then Leonard, who was trying to think like a criminal, figured he knew why Chase was asking. "You're thinking of attaching a zip-line to the scaffolding and riding it to Cathedral House, right?"

Chase studied his face to see if he was joking. "No."

"Pretending to be a day laborer on the repair crew to get access to the grounds?"

"Why would we do that? Anyone can walk in." He patted Leonard on the shoulder. "Thanks, but you'd better leave the plotting to us."

Grant carefully studied the nearly treeless landscaping and flat, paved parking lots. "I don't know about this. Everything's right out in the open." He motioned to the old house set away from the cathedral at the far end of the property. "What's that building?"

"Cathedral House," said Leonard. "That's where the administrative offices are located."

"Meaning that's where the money is."

"Uh-huh."

"Looks old," Grant said.

"Almost two hundred years old. It used to be the manor house for a large plantation. Hurley had it completely restored when he built the cathedral."

"And had it wired, I assume."

Leonard looked at him. "You mean for electricity?"

"I mean for alarms."

"Oh!" Leonard was still having trouble thinking like a criminal, but was starting to pick up the rhythm. "You'd better believe it. Alarms and cameras."

Chase said, "And I'm sure they patrol the grounds…"

"Actually," said Leonard, "it's funny. They're not fanatics about that. Not like a lot of the other mega-churches. At night, a security patrol drives through once every couple of hours, but they don't have regular foot patrols."

"Any patrols during the day?" asked Grant.

"Not really. There are so many people around, there wouldn't be much value in it. Just the shack at the entrance, and some guards based inside Cathedral House."

"Exterior cameras? Alarms? Motion detectors? Anything like that?"

"Nothing too elaborate, as far as I know," said Leonard. "There are a few exterior cameras at the back of the property"—he indicated the far side of the campus, back by the old house—"but only because it isn't visible from the road."

Grant wrinkled his brow. "That doesn't make sense, especially with all this cash you tell us they're holding. Not to mention the money they're collecting legitimately. Why not spend a few bucks on security?"

Leonard just shrugged. "I can't tell you their reasoning, but Hurley and Merribaugh have focused almost all the security on the inside of Cathedral House. There are cameras and two security offices…"

Grant frowned. "Two security offices for a four-story building? I'm not crazy about those odds."

"One's in the basement. That office is manned around the clock, but not really staffed up. Usually five or six guards. Mostly, they watch the camera feeds. The other is on the second floor near Hurley's office, but guards are only posted when he's there."

Grant shook his head. "None of this makes sense. You're positive the only exterior cameras are in the back? There's *nothing* trained on the front entrance or the grounds?"

"I'm positive."

The three men were silent for a while until Chase, thinking it through, said, "I have an idea why all the exterior cameras are in the back. Maybe this Dr. Hurley doesn't want his comings and goings captured permanently on tape."

Grant shrugged. "That doesn't make sense, either. If there are cameras inside the offices…"

"Cameras *Hurley* placed. And can probably have turned on and off at will. Is that the way it works, Leonard?"

"I…I really wouldn't know. I was only the bookkeeper."

Chase looked back over the expansive property, and seeing only the paved six-lane road running between the guardhouse at the Cathedral Boulevard entrance to the former plantation house, asked, "I take it this place only has one entrance?"

"This is it," Leonard confirmed. "The other sides of the property are too hilly or swampy to build a road, so the church left it wild. Hills… trees…marshland…an occasional deer hunter during the season…That's about it."

"So if we grab the safe and try to make it out the back way…"

"You'd never make it. It's forever wild."

"There you have it," said Chase, feeling a bit proud of his deduction. "Hurley can control what's taped inside the buildings. A camera on the only entrance means there'd be a record of when he comes and goes…"

"And maybe," added Grant, "what he leaves with."

"Exactly."

Grant thought out loud as he continued to survey the property. "We're gonna need a few people on the inside. This ain't gonna be as easy as driving a truck in, loading the safe, and driving away." He took another look at the cathedral and converted plantation house. "Leonard, I'm gonna need a detailed layout of the administration building."

"No problem."

"Including the locations of the cameras."

Leonard faltered. "I'm not sure I know where they all are. But I'll try."

"Do your best. Whatever you can remember. As long as it's perfect." Grant took another look at the grounds, then abruptly turned and started walking. "I've seen enough for now. Let's get out of here before someone gets suspicious of Farraday parked out by the road."

They carefully walked back down the slope toward Cathedral Boulevard, Leonard leading the way. Chase, a few yards behind, noticed Grant was deep in thought.

"You see a problem?" he asked.

"A few dozen of them," said Grant. "Starting with, how are we gonna get people into the church?"

"It's a church. How hard could it be?"

Grant frowned as they reached the pavement and started walking toward the car. "Another thing: You think we can trust Leonard?"

Chase shrugged noncommittally. "We're gonna have to, I guess."

"I suppose. In which case, we'd better do some shopping."

"For what?"

"Real estate. This job is gonna take us a few weeks, if we're lucky. Probably more like a month. So the first thing we're gonna need is a place to hole up."

When they were all back in the car and buckled in, Grant told Farraday to drive.

"Where?"

"Anywhere. Just keep driving while we talk."

It didn't occur to Farraday to question Grant. Instead, he eased the car onto Cathedral Boulevard and did as he'd been told, driving away from the Virginia Cathedral of Love.

Without looking toward the backseat, Grant asked Leonard, "What kind of cash you have?"

"I don't know...Fifty, sixty bucks?"

"Not in your pocket. In your bank account."

Leonard knitted his brow. "Why?"

"We're looking at a long-term job here. I can tell by looking this isn't one of the jobs we back a truck up and drive away with the loot."

"Security seems pretty lax," said Chase. "Maybe it *could* be that easy."

"It's what we aren't seeing that worries me. I figure we'll need at least two people on the inside, which is gonna take a little time. So we're gonna need a place to live for a while. Close to the cathedral. Walking distance, if we can find it. Meaning we'll need seed money for rent and whatever else we think we'll need. Probably ten thou minimum. Twenty to be safe."

Leonard sputtered and one hand flew to the second button of his shirt. Chase hoped he didn't tug too hard; the button already looked loose. "I don't have twenty thousand dollars!"

"You'll get it back on top of your take."

"But I don't have it!"

"Ten?"

"No!"

"What kind of bookkeeper are you? You never siphoned off a little for yourself?"

Leonard shook his head. "No. And if you're so smart, why don't *you* have twenty thousand dollars in the bank?"

"I don't know what they taught you in bookkeeping school…"

"Business school." The button came off in Leonard's hand.

"Whatever. An occupation like mine doesn't come with vacation days and a 401(k)."

Leonard nodded his understanding and sat back in his seat.

They drove around the area for a while, Farraday following Grant's spontaneous directions to turn right here and left there. After the better part of an hour, those who weren't already familiar with Nash Bog—meaning everyone who wasn't Leonard Platt—had a good feel for the community. It was affluent, professional, orderly, and pretty much the last place they'd fit naturally.

But for seven million dollars, they figured they could try to adapt.

Grant finally turned to Farraday and said, "Enough of Virginia for now. Let's get back to civilization."

"New York?" Farraday asked.

"New York."

As Farraday maneuvered the Mercury Mystique out of Nash Bog, Chase leaned forward from the backseat and said, "I think I know someone who could lend us the money. *And* who can also find us a place to stay while we do the job."

Grant nodded. "I know who you mean."

When they were finally back on the highway, Farraday cast a sidelong look at Grant and asked, "You gonna tell the rest of us who this mystery financier is?"

"Just drive," said Grant, moving the visor to block the sun from his eyes. "We've got five hours ahead of us on the road and plenty of time to talk…"

5

The paperwork signed and in her purse, Lisa Cochrane clasped the heavyset, sixtyish man's hand in both of hers, flashed a smile, and said, "I'm *thrilled* to have this opportunity to sell your home, David. Just *thrilled*!"

For his part, the man whose hand had been clasped and which was now was being squeezed with enthusiasm mustered his own smile. His pink cheeks glowed. "I'll miss this place. But with the publishing industry in the state it's in, I don't think it's advisable to hang on to sentiment."

David R. Carlyle IV often comported himself as an important person in publishing, and many people were willing to believe it. But although his father had co-founded the firm Palmer/Midkiff/Carlyle, David had never quite lived up to the family name.

Yes, he had worked his way into the title of Senior Editor and had been responsible for a number of bestsellers, but the position of Editor-In-Chief had eluded him, let alone his dream title of Publisher…a position that would finally have him living up to his legacy. In addition, his proclivity for a lavish lifestyle and the second home in the Hamptons on the east end of Long Island had never made financial sense, much less in a difficult economy.

Fortunately, Lisa Cochrane had swept into his life at just the right moment. The four or five million dollars she seemed to think she could get for the property would keep him in champagne and Brooks Brothers for years to come, even if it was less than he thought a beach-adjacent home should fetch. But he knew that real estate, like publishing, was a cruel, cruel business.

She'd already been through the house a few times but wanted to take one last walk-through. He was happy to escort her, since someday soon his Hamptons house would be only a vague memory.

"You know," she said as they passed through the living room, "I got top price for Romeo Romero's home in Water Mill a few years ago. I'm sure I can do the same for you." Lisa Cochrane continued to ooze reassurance. Her voice might have sounded like she'd gargled lye, but she knew how to play it like a musical instrument, finding just the right note she needed at just the right moment.

He laughed. "Romeo Romero. Now *there* was a scoundrel." She nodded knowingly. "But he did have a beautiful home." He led her into the formal dining room. "Have you had other celebrity clients?"

"Oh, yes. I showed more than a few homes to Madonna…"

"Really!"

"I could tell you stories, David. So many stories…"

A stroke of inspiration came to him. "Have you ever written?"

David Carlyle was not a short man, but Lisa stood several inches taller, so she leaned closer.

"Me? No, why?"

He took her by the arm and began guiding her toward the kitchen. "Here's my thought. How about if you write the copy for an illustrated book—a coffee-table book—about the homes you've sold and your celebrity clients?"

"Oh, I don't know…"

"We could send photographers out to capture images of the homes and décor, wrap your text around them, and… *Oh*, I can see this selling well during next year's holiday season!"

"David, I'm flattered, but…"

Caught up in his thoughts, he walked her through the kitchen and out the back door without stopping. As his pace quickened, the long white strands of hair carefully arranged over his scalp began to unravel; once outside, they danced in the breeze.

Lisa could hear the Atlantic Ocean surf breaking on the other side of the dunes. Two women—one in her late forties, short, scowling, and modestly dressed; the other taller and younger and wearing a swimsuit that was suggestive but not too revealing—sat in lounge chairs watching them. If David Carlyle noticed them, he was too consumed with his brainstorm to bother with introductions. Lisa—who'd figured him for gay about ten minutes *before* they'd met—couldn't quite figure out why the women were there.

"I even already know what it should be titled: *Celebrity Bedrooms I've Known…and the Walk-In Closets, Too*!"

She scrunched up her nose. "Celebrity Bedrooms I've Known?"

"*And* the Walk-In Closets, *Too*!"

"I don't know, David. Again, I'm flattered, but…"

The older, shorter one spoke. "Don't do it, lady. Carlyle talks a good game, but take it from me: publishing sucks." With that, she lifted a glass to her lips and drank. "It buys decent bourbon, but it still sucks."

That, at least, brought David out of his daydream.

"Ignore her, Lisa. She's just jealous because her sales are down."

"Not my e-book sales."

He said to Lisa, "You might like her when she's speaking for herself and isn't letting the bourbon speak *for* her."

Still not smiling, the short woman rose from her chair. Her voice had the authority of a woman who got what she wanted or went down fighting. "Since Carlyle isn't going to introduce me…"

"Sorry." Chastened, he said, "Lisa Cochrane, this is Margaret Campbell. Lisa will be selling this house. Margaret"—he nodded in the direction of the woman—"probably needs no introduction."

Lisa's face went blank for a moment, then came alive with recognition. "The *novelist* Margaret Campbell?"

"Guilty." Lisa couldn't tell from her expression if she appreciated or loathed the recognition.

"Yes, that's our Margaret," said David. "Palmer/Midkiff/Carlyle's best-selling novelist. 'Grande Dame of the American Mystery.'"

"According to *People*," Margaret said with a snort as she took another sip of bourbon. "Not according to me."

"Nor me," David said, and then wondered why he'd said it out loud. It would only come back to haunt him.

He tried to cover himself by pointing to the younger woman in the swimsuit. "And this is Denise Hanrahan. An old friend of mine."

Denise waved and shifted in her lounge chair, showing a bit of leg that Lisa thought she might have looked at for a second too long, not that anyone seemed to notice. "Pay no attention to the David and Margaret Show. I've known them forever. Deep down, they have quite a bit of affection for each other."

It must be buried way *deep down*, thought Lisa, but what she said was, "Nice to meet you, Denise."

Margaret took a step forward. "Remember what I said. Stay away from publishing."

"Nonsense," said David. "Real estate porn is so hot right now..."

That caught Lisa off guard, especially after hearing his proposed title. "Real estate porn?"

He waved away her concern. "A term to describe the way people look at pictures of property they'll never be able to afford. I really think this could be a profitable collaboration."

That caught her interest. "Profitable? *How* profitable?"

He barely thought about it. "I could probably get you a fifty-thousand-dollar advance. Maybe more. And if sales are strong when your royalties kick in..."

"Lady, just run," said the Grande Dame of the American Mystery, and Denise Hanrahan—more comfortable than Lisa with their back-and-forth—laughed. As she laughed, she stretched, unintentionally showing a tiny, harmless patch of stomach and once again drawing Lisa's eyes.

Mustn't do this, Lisa cautioned herself. *Stay professional.*

That was the fortunate moment a car horn sounded from the front of the house, startling Lisa out of her exercise in self-control. It was just as well. She'd never actually do anything, but it was nice to look every now and then.

"That's my ride," Lisa said, adding her good-byes to the two women. She thought maybe Denise gave her a particularly friendly send-off, but she didn't dwell on it. Because she was a professional. And because there was nothing she could do about it. And because, well...because Mary Beth was waiting out front.

David walked her back through the house to the front door. In the driveway, Mary Beth Reuss—face hidden behind large, dark sunglasses—sat at the wheel of a rented BMW.

"David, once again thank you for the opportunity to list your house."

He held her hand. "It's my pleasure. And please think about the book. I'm sure it will make us both a lot of money."

She smiled noncommittally and walked down three brick steps to the driveway where—after moving a half dozen heavy shopping bags to the backseat, because Mary Beth had clearly been a busy, busy girl while she'd been working—she climbed into the passenger seat next to her girlfriend.

Mary Beth raced the engine, put the car in gear, and drove off.

When David Carlyle turned around, Margaret Campbell was standing behind him.

"Don't you think she's kind of a phony, the way she turns the charm on when she wants something?"

He harrumphed. "I thought she was fine. Even so, who cares? I hired her to sell a house, not invest my trust fund." He looked into the distance. "Not that there's much left since Madoff…"

Margaret wasn't listening. "And what about those looks she was giving Denise. Not to mention the woman who picked her up. That spells lesbian to me."

David looked at her and sighed. "I seem to recall someone calling *you* a lesbian on a Barbara Walters special a few years ago, and you continue to be the Grande *freakin'* Dame of the American *freakin'* Mystery. Now go drink your bourbon and leave me alone."

It was only after Margaret Campbell skulked away that David looked at the dust still settling over the driveway in the wake of the BMW and thought, *No, not Celebrity Bedrooms. Celebrity* Boudoirs*!*

No one could accuse him of not always thinking creatively about the Next Big Book.

$ $ $

As a real estate professional, Lisa Cochrane strongly encouraged her clients to wildly overspend on property, the better to feather her nest in commissions. What point was there in scrimping and saving, she'd ask her clients, if you're not happy? And how can you put a price on your own happiness?

She practiced strict frugality, however, when making her own real estate decisions. She was not about to sacrifice luxury or scrimp on comfort—Lisa wouldn't like that, and Mary Beth wouldn't allow it—but she knew how to find a bargain.

She also wasn't a slave to convention, which made the bargain-hunting much easier. That's how the high-end Realtor ended up being among the first to move into Aquaterra Tower II when it opened several years earlier, days after the luxury high-rise cut the ribbon on its leasing office. That it was in Long Island City—meaning it was in the Borough of Queens and not in the Borough of Manhattan—had no impact on her decision. She'd doubled her square footage, cut her rent, and had a great view, which was more than one could say for most Manhattan properties in her frugal price range.

And she already had one money pit in Mary Beth Reuss. She loved her partner deeply, but it was clear she'd made the right decision when they moved to Queens, since Mary Beth—who paid none of the rent but seemed to dominate most of the space—had put up such a fuss about leaving her dear, and dearly expensive, Manhattan. Mary Beth was used to getting her way, but the move to Long Island City had been one of the occasions when Lisa's eye for a deal and stubbornness had won out.

Mary Beth did grow to love it—or at least *tolerate* it—over time, but there was a lot to love. Expansive views of Manhattan from across the East River, a host of amenities, a terrace, and even the all important in-unit washer and dryer, so hard to come by in Manhattan's older housing stock. There was even the convenience of being only one subway stop from Grand Central Terminal, which few locations in Manhattan could boast, even though Grand Central was *in* Manhattan.

Until Lisa Cochrane was ready to buy a home, Aquaterra Tower II would do quite nicely. And since she had no inclination to buy—despite her profession and healthy bank balance—that wasn't a decision she anticipated making in the near future.

It was just past 7:30 p.m. when Lisa and Mary Beth entered the building and greeted the gray-haired concierge, who in turn nodded toward the lobby.

"Some gentlemen"—he rolled his eyes slightly at the word—"have been waiting to see you." With a glance at his watch, he added, "For quite some time."

Their eyes focused on the lobby, which was every bit as impressive to look at as it was uncomfortable to be in, due to the management company's not-so-subtle efforts to meld pleasant aesthetics with the firm desire to keep tenants in their units.

Mary Beth saw them first. "Oh, Christ."

Then it was Lisa's turn. "What the hell are *you* doing here?"

Grant Lambert and Chase LaMarca sat in the austere lobby, doing absolutely nothing while they waited except waiting.

"We came to see you." Grant looked at Lisa, pointedly ignoring Mary Beth.

"I figured. I don't know what you're peddling, Lambert, but I'm not buying. My dance card is more than full for the next couple of weeks."

"I'm not looking for a dance partner, so that works for me." He glanced around. "Can we talk?"

"I really don't see what…"

He leaned forward and whispered, keeping his voice low so the doorman wouldn't hear. "It's not about you. And it's not about your dancing. It's about your money."

"If it's about my money, that makes it about me, right?" She sighed. It wasn't the first time they'd had this discussion. "Okay, let's go up to the apartment and talk."

They rode the elevator to the twenty-eighth floor in silence, barely acknowledging each other until Lisa unlocked the door to her unit and ushered them out of the hall. She flicked a few switches and brought the track lighting to life, then closed the door and got down to business without bothering with pleasantries.

"You need money. Since I'm pretty sure you're not remodeling or buying a decent wardrobe, I figure you're working a job." She leaned against the cushioned arm of the couch. "What's the caper?"

Uninvited, Grant took a seat in her favorite chair. "I need you to bank me twenty thou for the setup. Figure I'll need the cash for about a month. Maybe six weeks at the outside."

She whistled. "Twenty thousand dollars is a lot of money, Lambert."

"Too much money," Mary Beth added as she stood behind the couch, her arms folded across her chest. "Especially for one of Lambert's dumbass schemes."

Grant nodded, deferential to Lisa and again ignoring Mary Beth. "I know it's a lot of money, but I think you'll like the rate of return. If this works out…"

Mary Beth grunted at the "if."

"*When* this works out, you'll find it worth your while." He thought for a moment. "Also, I'm gonna need your real estate connections."

"House or apartment?" asked Lisa.

"Better make it a house," said Chase, who had been idly looking out a floor-to-ceiling window at the Queensboro Bridge while listening to the conversation. "It's a 'house' kind of community. Plus we'll need the privacy."

"How long?"

"Like Grant said, four to six weeks. Starting as soon as we can get keys."

Lisa sat down on the couch across from Grant, tucking one leg underneath her. "I think you'd better fill me in on the details."

Chase stepped away from the window and looked at Grant, who sighed and finally said, "There's some money in a safe in Virginia. And we plan to get it."

She looked at her nails, although that wasn't really where her attention was.

"I think you can share a bit more information than that. If we can't trust each other after all these years…"

"The safe's in a church."

"Technically, it's not in the church," added Chase. "It's in an administration building, which is near the church."

"I don't know how specific we have to—" Grant began before Lisa cut him off.

"No, I *like* specific. You want twenty grand, and I want every specific detail. That seems like a fair trade." She smiled triumphantly at their silence. "How much money is in that safe?"

Again, Grant and Chase exchanged glances and held their silence.

"Okay," said Lisa, when the standoff passed the thirty-second mark, "if you're not going to tell me how much money's involved, I'm not going to bankroll the job."

The words tumbled out of Grant's mouth. "Seven million dollars."

Lisa's eyebrows did a little dance. "*Now* you've got my attention. Seven million?" Grant and Chase nodded. "If I give you the seed money, my share is one-third."

Grant did the math in his head and didn't like the numbers. Depending on how much cash was actually in the safe, a twenty thou investment could earn her back over two million dollars. Maybe more. That was a ridiculous return for a banker. What he was about to propose was still ridiculous, just slightly less so.

"I'll pay you back an even half million. A twenty-five-to-one return on your investment. That's more than fair."

Lisa pulled a cigarette from her pack, lit it, inhaled, exhaled, tapped ash into a glass ashtray stolen decades earlier from the Russian Tea Room, and otherwise left Grant and Chase hanging until she was confident she had the upper hand. All the while, Mary Beth stood behind her, stone-faced.

Finally, Lisa spoke.

"Fair? Not the way I see it. I have the money, and you *don't* have the money. But you need twenty thou. For all I know, I'm going to be dropping big bills and getting no return. And if something goes wrong, how are you going to pay me back?"

"Why do you think something will go wrong?"

"Lambert!" Lisa's laugh had a hard edge. "I *know* you. I'm willing to loan you what you need, but I have my terms: one-third." She took another drag off her cigarette, giving them a few seconds to think it over. "I have to be firm about that."

Grant leaned forward in the chair. "But—"

"Now, if you have another banker…"

He leaned back again.

"Didn't think so."

Chase, slightly less disapproving of Lisa's cut than Grant, asked, "And you can find us a rental, too?"

"Where in Virginia?"

"Place called Nash Bog. Up near the Maryland border, 'bout an hour outside Washington."

"So it's a DC commuter community. You said a house, right?" Chase nodded. "Yeah, I'm sure I can find you a furnished home. Professionals are always renting out their places when they're sent on long-term assignments. How big?"

"I don't think it needs to be too big," said Chase. "We just need enough room for Grant and me. Oh, and Paul Farraday."

Lisa cocked an eyebrow. "That drunk is in on this job, too?"

"Yeah," Grant confirmed.

"What's *his* take?"

"Less than yours." Grant winced at the knowledge that a third of the loot was gone before he'd even seen or touched it. "But he brought us the job. See, his cousin got fired from the church for being gay, and this is the cousin's way of getting revenge."

Lisa asked, "And how much is this cousin getting?"

"Also less than you."

"Okay, then." Lisa stood, announcing the end of the meeting. "I'll advance you twenty thousand dollars and arrange for a furnished house for a month in Nash Bog. I can probably have my end of the bargain wrapped up by late tomorrow afternoon. And when the job is over…"

"You get one-third," said Grant. "Not bad for a few hours' work."

"Right." She smiled. "And Lambert?"

"Huh?"

"Let's both hope Farraday's cousin is right, and the safe isn't full of old newspapers."

"I hear you."

"Because if it is…"

"I hear you."

"…you're going to be pulling a lot of heists over the next few years to pay me back."

"I hear you."

"Every penny," added Mary Beth. She was Lisa's punctuation mark.

$ $ $

As soon as the door closed behind the departing Grant and Chase, Mary Beth turned to Lisa and said, "I *cannot* believe you're lending those losers twenty thousand dollars."

Lisa latched the door and threw the deadbolt, hoping Grant and Chase were still close enough to hear the finality. Then she walked the few steps back to the living room and said, "For one-third of the haul. I think it was a good deal."

"Don't tell me you bought that bullshit. Seven million dollars in a safe? No way."

"No, *that* I don't believe." Lisa sat, finally reclaiming her favorite chair. "Maybe *they* believe that; I don't. But even Grant Lambert can pull off a job bringing in more than twenty-k, and the first thing he'll have to do is pay me back. Then, for every dollar they steal over twenty, I get another thirty-three cents."

Mary Beth slumped back into the couch, a frown on her face. "Thirty-three cents have never sounded so pathetic."

Lisa offered her a smile that danced on the border between patronizing and indulgent. "Maybe we'll be really lucky and Lambert and Chase will steal twenty thousand and *three* dollars! Then you can have an entire dollar all to yourself!"

A throw pillow glanced off the side of Lisa's head.

$ $ $

A half hour later, Lisa poured a glass of wine and retired to the second bedroom, which she'd converted to a home office. It was a great tax write-off that made the apartment even more affordable, and better yet, was the only room Mary Beth mostly ignored.

She logged onto her computer and typed *Nash Bog VA* into a search engine, intending to get a quick overview of the Nash Bog housing market. But the second search result stopped her cold.

"The Virginia Cathedral of Love?!"

From the living room, Mary Beth called back, "Did you say something?"

Maybe her voice had been a little too loud, but still, this was something Mary Beth should know. "Come here."

Mary Beth, now wrapped in a pink robe and matching—also very expensive—slippers, shuffled into the room and looked over her partner's shoulder. Lisa clicked on a link and the screen filled with the image of a large building, sunlight illuminating huge stained-glass windows. Above it, a cross towered in a cloudless blue sky.

"What's that?" asked Mary Beth. "Lambert's church?"

Lisa stared at the screen. "Not just any church. That's the Virginia Cathedral of Love."

"I think I've heard of it." Mary Beth squinted and moved closer… close enough for Lisa to feel her warm breath, which made her heart race a bit.

Still, she kept her composure. What she was looking at was even more exciting than Mary Beth.

"I think *everyone's* heard of it. Everyone except maybe Chase and Lambert. It's one of the largest churches in the United States." She swiveled in her chair and looked up at Mary Beth. "Have you ever heard of Dr. Oscar Hurley?"

"He's the guy who blamed the California wildfires on God's anger because Ellen and Portia got married, right?" Lisa nodded. "Yeah, I've heard of that whack job."

Lisa looked back at the monitor. "Well, if I'm correct, Lambert and Chase are going to try to steal seven million dollars from him."

Mary Beth scowled and backed away. "That sounds like it's way out of Lambert's league."

"It is. It *definitely* is." Lisa focused on the image of the Great Cross towering over the cathedral. "But it also means that the seven million dollars he was talking about, well… Maybe it's not so far-fetched." She glanced at the digital time displayed at the corner of the monitor. "I wonder if they're home yet."

Lisa picked up the phone and dialed; the call went straight to voicemail. That pattern repeated itself every five minutes for the next half hour while Mary Beth returned to the living room and Lifetime TV until, finally, Chase answered his cell phone.

"Hey, Lisa, what's—?"

She wasn't interested in small talk and—to make sure Chase was aware of that—threw all the hoarseness she could muster into her voice. "Are the two of you out of your fucking minds?"

"And nice talking to you, too."

"Put Lambert on the phone."

"You know he doesn't like to—"

"Yes, I know he doesn't like to talk on the phone. He'll just have to buck it up."

She heard muffled conversation, then Grant Lambert's voice.

"'lo?"

She got right to the point. "Lambert, are you seriously thinking of ripping off the Virginia Cathedral of Love?"

He was silent for a long time—so long she almost thought he'd hung up—until he finally said, "Who told you?"

"No one had to tell me. I'm not an idiot, you know."

Again he was silent.

"Lambert?"

She heard him sigh. "That's the plan."

"You realize it's a big church, right? It's not like robbing Dunkin' Donuts."

"Yeah, I know what's what."

"And you think you can do this by yourself?"

"I've got Chase. And Farraday." He paused. "And Farraday's cousin…"

Lisa had thought it, but wasn't quite sure she was going to say it until the words burst out. "*And* me and Mary Beth."

His answer was more silence.

"Lambert?" she finally growled. "You still there?"

"Yeah," a little voice replied.

"Good." She realized she was feeling a bit nervous and light-headed and swallowed hard to compose herself, but *damn it,* she was getting excited. "I'm not saying I don't trust you, but…I don't trust you." He started to object. "Listen, no offense, but you, Chase, and Farraday…"

"*And* Farraday's cousin," he reminded her.

"And Farraday's cousin. You can't do this job by yourselves. This is the *Virginia Cathedral of Love* we're talking about! Either Mary Beth and I are in on the job, or you can kiss my twenty thousand good-bye."

"But, Lisa…"

"Let me make this a little easier for you." She tried to take some of the edge out of her voice; to be soothing, not confrontational. "There's no decision for you to make. We're on the job. And look, it'll be fun!"

He didn't think he'd heard her correctly. "Fun?"

She remembered that, to him, this was work, not play, and adjusted accordingly. "Not *fun* fun. *Camaraderie* fun."

"Well..."

"Also, I have to insist."

There was another long pause, until he finally said, "I guess I've got no choice."

"No, you really don't." The tough edge was back in her voice, and now she didn't particularly care if she sounded confrontational. It was *her* twenty thou, damn it!

Grant Lambert was a man defeated. "Okay, then. Find us a house in Nash Bog, and we'll talk tomorrow."

Lisa disconnected the line and looked up to see Mary Beth standing in the doorway to the home office, still in pink robe and slippers.

"What's going on? What was that about?"

Lisa swiveled on the chair and smiled. It was the same, blissful, everything-is-peachy-keen smile she was always able to muster no matter how painfully her stomach was cramping. And her stomach was cramping not because she might lose twenty thousand dollars, and not because Grant Lambert might yet cause them all to end up in jail, but because Mary Beth *could* occasionally be game for a scam, but it wasn't in her nature.

So Lisa plastered a benign, loving smile on her face. "We both need a vacation, don't we?"

"Maybe." There was wariness in Mary Beth's voice.

"It'd be nice to get away for a few weeks." That benign, loving smile flared just a bit. "And Virginia would be so peaceful..."

"Oh, no!" Mary Beth brought the palm of her hand to her forehead and Lisa knew she'd seen right through her...as she usually did. "You want to get in on the job, don't you? *Bad idea*, Lisa. *Bad! Bad!*"

Which maybe would have stopped a cocker spaniel, but Lisa could be a pit bull—albeit a pleasant-sounding pit bull with a benign, loving smile—when she really wanted something.

"But...we'd have peace and quiet. *And* we could keep an eye on the twenty thousand."

Mary Beth's hands went to her hips, and the pink robe shook. "That's what you *say*. But I *know* you. You want to be in on the scam. You love that stuff."

Lisa would never acknowledge that to Mary Beth...or anyone else, for that matter. She barely acknowledged it to herself. "No, sweetie, I promise. I just want to make sure Lambert doesn't screw up and cost me twenty thousand dollars."

Hands glued to hips, Mary Beth closed her eyes. "I really don't like anything about this idea."

"It will be fine! Fresh air…dogwood blossoms…suburban living…"

"You're not making me feel better about this."

Lisa raised one finger. "How about this angle, then…"

"I'm waiting."

Benign, loving, smiling Lisa turned into hard-nosed businesswoman Lisa, determined to seal the deal.

"If we pull this off, our share will be over two million dollars. Something like two-point-three million and change, if there's really seven million in the safe. Since we're talking the Virginia Cathedral of Love, I'm willing to give Lambert and Chase the benefit of the doubt." She stood and wrapped her arms around Mary Beth's shoulders, nestling her lips near Mary Beth's ear and finding the exact words she needed to close.

Her voice was almost a whisper. "That kind of money buys a lot of shoes."

Mary Beth squared her shoulders, trying to pull away but backing off no more than an inch. "I…I'll think about it."

But Mary Beth—like Lisa—had already made her decision. More than two million dollars in spending money could do that to a girl.

In her head, she had already spent hundreds of thousands of dollars on Christian Louboutin alone.

And if Grant Lambert fucked the job up, well…each one of those very expensive red heels would have to be medically extracted from his ass.

6

In the kitchen of their apartment in Jackson Heights—only a few miles away from Lisa's place in Long Island City but light-years away in the level of luxury—Grant clicked off the phone and cast a mournful glance at Chase.

"Lisa's decided that she'd rather be an active partner than a passive partner."

Chase looked up from the counter where he was mixing a vodka-cranberry, shaking his head. "I *knew* it. I *knew* she wouldn't be able to resist horning in on the job."

"Yeah, well..." Grant pulled a battered wooden chair out from the table, scraping it over the scuffed linoleum, and sat. "She doesn't think we can do this alone. But I think she really just wants to keep an eye on her money."

"I think it's more than that. I think she likes being in on the jobs."

Grant cocked his head toward his partner. "You think she *likes* pulling jobs? Really?"

Chase stirred his drink for too long a time before answering. "I do. I mean, she complains a lot, but you can see it in her eyes." He stopped stirring and, drink in hand, joined Grant at the table. "Maybe that's a good thing."

"How's that?"

"No matter how we try to cover, it's gonna look strange for a group of men to move into a suburban house in an upscale neighborhood on a short-term rental. You, me, Farraday...Leonard. If a few women are in the mix, we'll have a better chance of not attracting unwanted attention."

“Or attracting more,” Grant observed. “Lisa’s all right, but drama follows Mary Beth around.”

Chase took a sip of his vodka-cranberry. “You just don’t like Mary Beth.”

That much was true. Just *thinking* about Mary Beth brought a dull ache to Grant’s head.

“It’s mutual.”

“True. But you’ve worked well together in the past. And she’s smart—”

“She’s mean.”

“Smart but mean.” Chase took another sip. “Okay, whatever. The fact is that she could be an asset to our team.”

Grant was noncommittal. “Maybe.”

Chase decided to leave that track, since there was no way he’d be able to change Grant’s mind about Mary Beth. Certainly not that night; maybe not ever. So he tried another approach: grim acceptance of the reality of the situation.

“Beyond everything else, we can’t really stop them, can we? Not if we want Lisa to bankroll the job.”

“Okay.” Grant sighed and tried to shake his concern away. “We still have the same game plan, just with two more players.”

“Exactly.” Chase nodded, encouraging Grant down that path of acceptance. “Think of them as backup. Just in case.”

Lost in thought, Grant stared at the battered surface of the kitchen table. “Now what I need to do is figure out who to get on the inside of the church.”

“I just assumed *I’d* be going in,” said Chase.

“You, yeah,” Grant agreed. “But we’ll need someone else. Maybe even two more people. We’re looking at a long-term project, and we need to do it right.”

Chase sipped his drink. “Not you or Farraday.”

Grant scoffed. “Of course not. People look at us and the first thing they think is ‘guilty.’ Even if we ain’t done anything.”

“Lisa?”

Grant thought about that, and then thought better of it. “Nah. She’s got a big mouth.” Another very good reason popped into his head. “Not to mention she’s our banker. If something goes wrong and she gets arrested, we’re screwed.”

“Yeah. The bank’s not much good when the bank’s in jail.”

"Exactly."

Chase tried to think of a name from their loose association of confederates who might prove helpful. "What about Nick Donovan?"

"No. We bring him in, we get that mother of his, too."

"Chrissy Alton?"

"No. She's great at working the department store scam, but she's not right for this kind of thing. If we ever hit Bloomingdale's again, we'll call her."

"Michael May?"

"In jail."

"Really?"

"Seven to ten."

"Hadn't heard that." Chase shrugged. It was an occupational hazard. "Jamie Brock?"

"*Hell* no." Grant shook his head forcefully to emphasize the point. "He's the last person I ever want to work with again."

Chase looked up at the flaking paint on the ceiling. "We've gone through the roster. Except…nah."

"Except nah *who*?"

"Except Mary Beth."

Grant planted his elbows on the table hard enough to make Chase's vodka-cranberry jump and stiffened his jaw. "I take back what I said about Jamie Brock. *Mary Beth* is the last person I ever want to work with again."

Chase was prepared for his reaction. "I know, I know. You don't like her and she doesn't like you. But think about it. She did a great job for us on that job we pulled in the Hamptons a few years ago."

"The job that went down the toilet?"

"That's the one," Chase agreed. "But that wasn't her fault. That was just…*circumstances. Bad* circumstances. And remember, if it hadn't been for Mary Beth, we would have walked away with nothing."

"Why do you keep pushing for her?"

"Because she's already in, whether you like it or not. And she's good…when she wants to be."

Grant thought about it. "But she's…she's…she's *Mary Beth*!"

It was hard for Chase to argue with that. She was indeed Mary Beth. "True, maybe she's not the nicest person we've ever worked with. But when she commits, she commits. Quick on her feet, too. She'd be perfect on the inside."

"I'll think about it," Grant said, even though he doubted that.

It was only hours later, when they were pressed against each other in bed, that a new thought occurred to him.

"I've got it!" Grant flipped the switch to the lamp on his nightstand.

Chase, who'd almost fallen asleep, rolled away from the light. "Got what?"

"Hand me your cell."

Chase took the phone off the charger on his own nightstand and started to pass it across the bed before he faltered. He looked at Grant as if he'd just asked for a colonoscopy.

"You want my *phone*?"

"Yeah."

Chase wondered if maybe he was dreaming. That would make more sense than this. "But you *never* use the phone."

Grant took the unit from his wavering hand. "This is the exception that proves the rule."

He punched a number into the keypad from memory.

7

The last time Grant Lambert had crossed paths with Constance Price, she was working a scam out of a down-market real estate office on the up-market Upper East Side of Manhattan. Besides picking up a regular paycheck, she also passed the keys to vacant units to her girlfriend, and occasionally, the girlfriend's brothers, who'd then strip them of small—and sometimes not-so-small—appliances and fixtures. It wasn't going to make anyone rich, but it was a nice supplement to an honest living. Not to mention it kept them in practice, and there was nothing worse in that occupation than getting rusty. In a way, it was sort of like baseball, except instead of getting sent to the minors if you were off your game, you got sent to Riker's Island.

Eventually, though, the boss started to figure out that his apartments were being ransacked at an alarming rate, and she'd put an end to the scam before he traced it back to her. A few weeks after that, she realized that merely working for a living was boring without the extracurricular fringe benefits, so she gave her notice.

Some people were made for honest nine-to-five wages; Constance Price wasn't.

In any event, the scam had dried up. There were only so many microwaves a person could fence or sell on eBay. It was time for something new.

Over the next year or so she'd pulled a few jobs—nothing elaborate, just enough to keep food on the table—but was starting to feel the need for a more substantial income. Those good old days of cheap Harlem rents were a thing of the past. She'd even considered going back into the real estate business. But then Grant Lambert had called around midnight, mumbling something cryptic about a job she might be interested in and saying he had to see her right away, and she put that consideration right out of her head.

After all, if Lambert was on a phone, it had to be big. Everyone in their business knew Grant Lambert hated the phone.

"So why me?" she asked a few hours later, after he outlined his plans as they sat in the living room of her small one-bedroom on West 133rd Street in Harlem. "Sounds like you've already put together a big enough gang."

"Maybe too big," he acknowledged. "But I'm missing one key element. I need someone who'll be a natural on the inside."

"Again, why me? What about your boyfriend?"

"He'll be going in. But this job is gonna take time, and the only way it goes down the right way is if we have the right people on the inside. Chase is good, but he won't be able to do it alone." He cleared his throat. He always had a tough time complimenting another crook's work, which was what he was about to do. "And you're the best inside-scam artist I know."

She nodded, but said nothing. He was *right*, after all.

She'd worked jobs from Al Sharpton headliners to Rockefeller Foundation fund-raisers, and no one had looked twice. They probably didn't even figure it out after their coats went missing from the coat-check, meaning they couldn't give their car-checks to the valet because the car-checks were in their coats. Not that it mattered, because their cars had left the lot hours earlier, along with their keys and wallets, if they were among the usual minority who checked those with their coats.

And God help 'em if Constance got their wallets and keys, because their wallets and keys meant their home addresses and access, which in turn meant she'd have their television, DVD player, jewelry, and whatever else she could grab before they were done arguing with the coat-check attendant about their missing claim ticket.

She *was* that good, and she knew it. But it was nice of Grant Lambert to acknowledge it.

"So the real estate office scam you were pulling," said Grant, when it was clear Constance had accepted the compliment. "Did you keep the books?"

She nodded. "I know how to keep books, Grant Lambert. I knew how to do that long before the real estate job. A girl's got to have skills to fall back on, after all. But I still want to know…"

"Why you?"

"Why me."

He swallowed hard and looked at his shoes. "Because this is a Southern church we're gonna rob. In Virginia. You don't have a problem robbing a church, do you?"

Her voice was soft, almost hurt. "It's like you don't know me at all. So where in Virginia? It's a big state."

"Less than an hour outside Washington."

Her eyes widened. "You're talkin' Northern Virginia? Why, Northern Virginia's about as Southern as Long Island. So, again, *why me*?"

"Most of the members are real Southerners. Like 'Deep South' Southern, so…"

Constance threw back her head and laughed. "I'm just giving you a hard time, Lambert. You want me on this job because I'm black, right?"

He snapped his head up so quickly they both heard a crack that maybe they shouldn't have heard.

"Damn, you're getting old, Grant."

Nothing hurt, so he ignored it. "I told you, I want you because you're the best."

"*And*…I'm black."

His eyes returned to his shoes. "That probably helps."

She laughed again. "You're an idiot. I thought we were friends, Lambert. It's okay to notice I'm black. You look damn white to *me*." He started to say something, but she stopped him. "And I get what you're thinking. I *am* good, but a bunch of dumb crackers aren't gonna think some pious black woman's a threat. Am I right?"

"Yeah."

"Okay, then. Piece of cake. You meet my price and I'm in." She started to stand, figuring they'd negotiate her fee on the walk to the door.

He cleared his throat. "There's one other thing you should know. The church is a place called the Virginia Cathedral of Love."

All thoughts of a quick negotiation stopped, and Constance dropped back onto the couch. "You shitting me?"

"You heard of it, I take it. Seems like everyone has but me."

"That's because you're an idiot. That's Oscar Hurley's church. The guy who blamed the wildfires on Ellen and Portia." Constance stared at nothing as she contemplated whether or not this fools' errand was worth it, until she knew how to determine the answer. "So instead of telling me you want to rob a mega-church, give me some details."

He shrugged. "Big church. Big congregation. I've gotten through better security before…"

She wagged a finger in front of his face. "Not that. How much money we talking about, and where are they hiding it?"

"Oh, that." He didn't want to lowball, because then she wouldn't think it was worth her while. If he told her the truth, her cut might bleed him, but it'd be better to negotiate in good faith. He could always try to shortchange her later, if he had to. "We think maybe seven million."

She didn't spend a lot of time thinking it over. "In that case, my fee is five hundred."

The numbers ran through his head: roughly two-three to Lisa; one-five to Leonard; a hundred grand to Farraday; and now five hundred Gs to Constance. It was, perhaps, the only time in his life a possible two million dollar-plus payday left him feeling poor.

But Constance Price was the woman he needed on the inside. No doubt about it.

"Okay. I'll meet your price."

Now she stood again and took Grant's hand as he also stood. "Good. It's been a long time, and I'm really looking forward to working with you again, Grant Lambert."

"You won't even have to get your hands dirty," he said. "Just work your way into the good graces of Hurley, get into the office, and leave a door open on the night we come to collect it. In fact, you'll probably even show up the day after we crack the safe like nothing is wrong. Because for all they'll know, you're just an earnest volunteer." He paused for a moment, then asked, "How are you on your Bible?"

"I could use some brushing up," she admitted. "But that isn't going to be a problem. It doesn't matter what I know. It only matters I know the talking points."

"Whaddaya mean?"

She took his elbow and began leading him to the door. "These people don't know—or care, really—about what's in the Bible. They pick and choose. That's how they can justify hating the gays but loving the shellfish."

"Shellfish?"

"Hell, yeah. The same part of the Bible that tells you not to be gay also tells you not to eat shellfish. Now, how many of these Bible Belt types do you see passing up a shrimp cocktail?" When he didn't answer, she added, "See, here's the thing: the guys that wrote the Bible made up most of those stories to fit whatever was going on at the time. People getting sick from shellfish? Just tell 'em that God says not to eat it."

"Huh," said Grant. "The things you learn…"

Constance opened the door but stopped him at the threshold. “You wait here and I’ll get you a car.”

“Beg your pardon?”

“Trust me, white boy. Four a.m. in this neighborhood, you want me to get you a car.” She smiled. “See? I notice skin color. Nothing wrong with that. So get over your white self and let me find you a ride.”

$ $ $

It took ninety minutes for him to get home. Chase was waiting expectantly when Grant finally walked through the front door of their apartment in Jackson Heights.

Chase tried to read his poker face. “Do we have a gang?”

Grant slumped onto the couch without answering. “How come whenever I try to put together a gang, they take all our money?”

“Uh…so we *don’t* have a gang?”

“No, we’ve got a gang.”

Chase started to let out a whoop, but Grant stopped him. “She wants a half million.”

“Leaving us with…” Chase tried to calculate.

Grant already had the number. “Two million plus. We might end up making less than Lisa.”

“But,” Chase reminded him, “you pulled it all together. And two million ain’t exactly nothing.”

“I guess not. But no more people.”

Chase agreed. “Everything is in place. Now it’s time to go to the Virginia Cathedral of Love and make some *real* money.”

Grant grunted and slumped back onto the couch.

8

Lisa Cochrane worked fast, especially when she had more than two million dollars on the line. Which was why just two days later, on another swelteringly hot morning, Paul Farraday was driving a stolen '98 Cadillac with Connecticut plates down Old Stone Fence Post Road in Nash Bog, Virginia, looking for the house numbered 455.

The owner—a corporate lawyer—had been sent to Hong Kong for three months to negotiate some sort of deal none of them would ever be able to understand. All that mattered was that Lisa had rented it for the duration, reasoning that Grant's track record wasn't always perfect on the first attempt.

Or the second or third, for that matter. Meaning it might take them a little bit of time, but the payoff would be worth it. In any event, any extra money out of pocket would come back on top of her twenty thousand dollar investment, so she didn't care.

As Farraday followed the winding road, Grant looked out from the passenger seat at a succession of houses, each one remarkably, if not exactly, like the others. There were slight variations in exteriors and landscaping, but it was apparent the homebuilder of this subdivision gave buyers only a handful of options, all virtually identical to the naked eye.

From the backseat, Chase said, "McMansions."

"What's that?" asked Grant.

"Big houses. Small lots. All kinda the same. McMansions."

"If you say so."

"Like burgers at McDonald's. One in New York's the same as one in San Diego."

"Yeah, I figured that's where you were going. Now…"

"Actually," said Farraday, "the New York McDonald's ain't that good. You want good fast food, go to Jersey."

"Really?" said Chase. "There's that big a difference?"

Farraday nodded knowingly. "Oh, yeah. If you take Route 46 off the George Washington Bridge…"

Grant interrupted. "I'd like you both to shut up now."

Chase leaned forward, straining against his seat belt. "See, if these houses looked a bit different and had bigger lots, you'd consider them regular mansions. Or at least, uh, big houses. But they're built close to each other, which makes them—"

"McMansions," Grant said. "I got that."

"Exactly."

"And now *I've* said the word, so we can *all* stop saying the word."

"Why?" asked Chase.

"I dunno. The word just annoys me, and I don't wanna hear it anymore."

"And all *I* know," said Farraday, behind the wheel, "is it's good I'm driving, 'cause no one else could find this place in the daylight, let alone after dark. Not unless they live here already."

"I thought you could drive anywhere," said Grant.

"*Drive* anywhere, yeah. Asphalt, I know. But there ain't any landmarks around here. All these McMansions look the same."

"Don't say that word."

A squirrel darted across the road and Farraday muttered an expletive. "I'm worried about pulling into the wrong driveway and having someone take a shot at me."

"I wouldn't worry about that," said Chase. "This subdivision is full of doctors and lawyers, not gun-slingers."

"This neighborhood," Farraday reminded him, "is in *Virginia*. Need I say more?"

To which Chase said, "Don't worry, Farraday. The doctors and lawyers of Virginia are probably more afraid of crooks from Brooklyn than you are of them."

"Guess we'll find out soon enough." Farraday maneuvered the car around yet another curve in the road. Before them, another two dozen almost-identical McMansions lined both sides of Old Stone Fence Post Road, bricked front façades and pale yellow siding and rear façades almost blending together.

Grant pointed at a mailbox just ahead of them.

"Four-fifty-five."

"So it is." Farraday slowed the car and turned into the driveway.

When the engine was off, they sat in the car for a moment, staring at the house.

"Nice place," Grant finally said.

"McMansion," said Chase.

"Shuddup."

They took their bags from the trunk and followed a slate walkway to the small concrete porch. Grant fished a key from his pocket and unlocked the front door. Their entrance was greeted by a loud chirp; Grant found the security alarm panel on the wall behind the door and punched in the code Lisa had given him. A mechanical voice of indeterminate gender cheerfully announced, one evenly spaced syllable at a time, "A. Larm. Off. Wel. Come. Home."

Grant picked up at the point the alarm's voice left off as they stepped into the foyer. "Welcome to our living quarters for the next several weeks, gentlemen." He flipped a light switch and a chandelier glowed, barely noticeable in the sunlight already flooding the atrium stretching two stories above them.

They eyed the foyer warily, as if afraid the legitimate owner would show up and call the cops. To the right, a wide curved stairway ascended to the second floor; to the left and straight ahead, arched openings led to the house's interior; left-center, a carpeted stairway led downstairs.

"I don't know if I can handle this many ways in and out and up and down," said Grant.

"Think of 'em as escape routes," said Chase.

"I guess if we have to hole up, this is as good as it's gonna get." Farraday selected the opening under the center archway to start his exploration of the house, then made a sharp left.

Chase followed. "Yeah, you only wish you could live in a place like this."

Grant followed Chase. "I know *I* do."

Farraday said, "Might as well get familiar with the place, since it's gonna be home for the next—Holy crap!" He stopped so abruptly that Grant and Chase walked into him.

"What's this?" asked Chase, trying to make out the dark room.

Farraday said, "I think it's a kitchen. A *real* kitchen, not a New York kitchen."

Grant found the light switch. It was indeed the kitchen. "Did this lawyer guy run a restaurant out of the joint or something?" He gawked at the room, mentally tallying the number of cupboards, stoves, and pantries, instinctively working out how much they could hide and how well they could hide it. "The kitchen's bigger than our apartment. It's almost a shame we're gonna mostly use it for takeout pizza."

Farraday rubbed his hands along the wide island in the center of the room. Chase noticed his thick body was pressed tightly against the granite countertop and his eyes were closed.

"You okay, Farraday?"

A smile—small, but since this was Farraday, it counted as a smile—worked its way to the driver's lips. "Better than okay. This is heaven."

Grant wasn't buying Farraday's happiness. Farraday was *never* happy. "What do you know about kitchens? Except they can be used to store booze."

The big man's hand continued to stroke the granite. "I'm a chef."

To which Grant said, "Get the hell outta here." When Farraday didn't answer, he added, "Really?"

Farraday finally opened his eyes. "Really." He looked at his companions; doubt was painted on their faces. "There's a lot of things you don't know about me, Lambert." He stroked the granite one more time. "You think all I can do is drive? We're gonna do some good eating on this job."

That was another thing Grant wasn't buying. "Weren't you the guy who was just telling us the Quarter-Pounders are better in Jersey?"

"Actually," said Farraday, "I'm more of a Big Mac man. Especially from the McDonald's out 46 near Teterboro. But that don't mean I can't handle a kitchen."

"Okay, if you say so." The skepticism was pronounced in Grant's voice. "Now let's check out the rest of the place. And it might be a good idea to memorize all the exits, 'cause I got a feeling a grease fire is in our future."

And so they did, and nothing disappointed them, not that their standards were especially high. They were used to grimy walls, peeling paint, and vermin. Anything else could pass for the Waldorf.

But this place topped the Waldorf, or at least what they imagined the Waldorf was like, since the doormen would've never let them through the front door and the Teamsters kept chasing them away from the loading dock. From the living room with the 72-inch high definition television mounted on the wall to the pool table and bar in the finished basement to the six large bedrooms on the second floor, every inch of every room was fully furnished and designed for comfort. They shared an unspoken belief that it'd almost be a shame to have to leave it to pull the job.

"Maybe we should forget the Cathedral and just steal the house," joked—or maybe *half* joked—Chase as they stood on the second floor landing, fifteen feet above the flagstone floor of the foyer on one side, the carpeted living room on the other.

"Tempting," Grant agreed. "Too bad Lisa rented the place under her own name, so it's out of consideration unless we screw her over. Although…" He stepped to the other side of the landing and looked down into the living room. "That TV *would* look nice in our apartment."

"The only way that TV gets into our apartment," noted Chase, "is if we knock out most of our walls, and a few of our neighbors'."

The three men began their descent down the stairs to the first floor. Grant stopped them as they passed an oversized window framing the front door and pointed.

"Get a load of that."

Above the tree line, and above the roof of the McMansion across the street, rose the cross marking the location of the Virginia Cathedral of Love.

"Lisa promised us close," said Chase. "She got us close."

Farraday sized it up, as only Farraday could. "That's about three-eighths of a mile away." He squinted. "Make that three-sevenths. Less than a ten-minute walk if there's a direct route, but the way these streets twist, I doubt it's walkable."

"Since our cars tend to be of the borrowed-without-permission variety," Grant said, "we'll have to work something out when Lisa gets here."

"We'll figure it out," said Chase. "Anyway, walking is good exercise."

Grant and Farraday stared at Chase. They didn't believe in exercise, and they weren't sure they believed too much in good, either.

$ $ $

Their bags were not yet unpacked. They'd tossed them in the first bedrooms they'd come across until the rest of the gang—the female contingent—arrived.

In the meantime, Farraday hid the Caddy in the garage, since they all agreed a stolen car should not be sitting in their driveway where any passing busybody cop might see it. But besides exploring the house and playing six games of pool in the basement, that was all they'd done.

The three men stood in the kitchen trying to think of what they should do next, figuring maybe another game of pool sounded like a good idea.

That's when they heard a "yoo-hoo" coming from outside the front door and hoped it was meant for someone else, because they were far more inclined to play another game of pool than answer a *yoo-hoo*.

"Yoo-hoo!" the woman's voice sang out once again, which answered the question of what they'd do next.

They looked at each other and no one said or did anything until Grant slumped his shoulders. "I'll see who it is."

It wasn't a visitor; it was visitor*s*. As in two people. As in the *yoo-hoo*ing woman—blond and toothy with excessively taut, excessively tan skin—and a man who could have been her blond, toothy, taut, tan twin.

Grant opened the door and eyed them warily. "Can I help you?"

The woman looked very briefly and quizzically at the man, and then focused a ferocious smile back at Grant.

"Welcome to the neighborhood!" she said, a bit too loudly. "I'm Tish Fielding, and this is my husband Malcolm."

"Malcolm," said Malcolm, feeling the need to *also* introduce himself. He stuck out his hand and Grant shook it. It felt impossibly soft and cool to the touch, like he soaked it in moisturizer whenever he wasn't using it to do absolutely nothing.

"We live at 462." She tossed her too-blond mane—a color that looked as if Chase's highlights had taken control of her entire head—in the general direction of the opposite side of the street. "And we're thrilled to have you as our neighbor!"

"Yes," Malcolm added, causing Grant to wonder how he spoke without moving his jaw.

He nodded politely—or at least in an approximation of politely—and started to close the door. "Nice meeting you…"

"Just one thing," said Tish, broadening her smile as she reached out and stopped the door from closing. Grant couldn't help but notice the red of her nails as her fingers clamped onto the door.

"But an important thing." Malcolm raised one index finger as he also pretended to reach for the door, but didn't quite make contact. The tenseness in his eyes showed that he hoped his soft hands wouldn't have to touch anything solid. Not this door; maybe nothing. Ever.

"Go ahead," Grant said, holding the door in the half-closed position as Tish's red nails balanced it from the other side. In his experience "just one thing" usually wasn't good...especially when it was also "important."

Tish said, "It's the condition of your yard."

Grant looked out over the yard. He lived in urban New York City and therefore didn't have much experience with trees and grass and leaves and bushes and other green things, but it looked fine to him. "What about it?"

Lock-jawed Malcolm said, "The lawn needs to be mowed."

"Oh." Grant looked again, and again it seemed fine to him. It was green, wasn't it? "You sure?"

"And," Trish added, talking right over Grant's doubt, "the hedges need to be trimmed. It probably wouldn't hurt to weed the flower beds, either."

"Oh."

Malcolm rubbed his palms together. "We were going to complain to the HOA. But when we saw you move in, Tish and I felt it would be the neighborly thing to knock on the door and take care of things in a neighborly way." He oh-so-neighborly strained to give Grant a neighborly smile, which made a vein in his neck quiver.

"Yes," his wife agreed. "No sense in dragging the HOA in for such easily remedied violations."

Grant was confused. "HOA?" He tried pronouncing it out. "What's a hoa?"

Which in turn confused Tish. "Hoa? I have no idea what..."

"I think," sniffed Malcolm, "our new neighbor was trying to pronounce H-O-A."

Tish and Malcolm narrowed their eyes. Their smiles dimmed slightly and they exchanged glances that Grant read as *the new neighbor doesn't understand what we're talking about.*

So Grant asked, "Whatcha talking about?"

The Fieldings exchanged another glance, as if to decide who had the duty to explain The Way Things Worked Around Here to the imbecile in front of them. Grant picked up on that, too.

With a noncommittal shrug from Malcolm, the explanation fell to Tish. "The Home Owners' Association, of course. HOA: Home Owners' Association."

"Oh." Grant thought about that. "But I'm not a homeowner. I'm just renting."

Tish thought that was one of the funniest things she'd ever heard and emitted a high-pitched laugh for a full twenty seconds until she realized that Grant wasn't joking. When that reality hit her, the laughter stopped abruptly, although she mostly managed to hold the strained smile on her face that sort of passed as friendly.

"Seriously, Mr....?"

"Williams." It was a last name he often used when he wanted to blend in. "Mr. Williams."

"Mr. Williams." Her eyes narrowed again. "Do you have a first name?"

"Doesn't everyone?"

She tried again. "Do you have a first name you'd be willing to share?"

He shrugged. "Grant."

"*Grant*. Grant, I know you're new to this, but Old Stone Fence Post Estates has a certain reputation, and our immaculate lawns are part of that reputation." Her arm swept across the vista of McMansions. "Weeds are pulled, grass is cut, hedges are trimmed and tidy. Our neighbors with children keep their yards free of debris—"

"She means toys," said Malcolm.

"Yes, toys. Cars are parked neatly and *never* on the lawns." She whispered, "That's trashy. Don't you agree?"

Grant nodded, not that he cared.

"Barbecue grills are kept in the backyard. Hoses are coiled in the garages. Trash and recycling bins always stay in the garage until the morning of collection day. Do you understand what I'm trying to say?"

Grant thought, *Yeah, lady, you're trying to say you and your neighbors are tight-asses*, but what came out of his mouth was, "We'll keep everything neat as a pin. Neater."

Tish flashed her teeth, which was all the smile she was able to muster at that point. "I have no doubt you will, Mr. Williams."

Grant finally freed himself from Tish and Malcolm Fielding and returned to the kitchen.

"So what's the story?" asked Chase.

"The story," said Grant, "is that Old Stone Fence Post Estates is no place for a New Yorker. And to prove that, get ready to do some yard work."

"Yard work?" sputtered Farraday. "You mean, like, outside?" Unlike Grant and Chase, he'd never even spent the younger years of his life outside New York City's five boroughs. Paul Farraday was born-and-bred Brooklyn, and not in one of those neighborhoods where a tree might grow.

Grant nodded a confirmation. "You'll love it. And you need to get outside more."

"That is not a true statement, Lambert."

$ $ $

Across the street at 462 Old Stone Fence Post Road, Malcolm Fielding opened a bottle of Pinot Grigio while Tish retrieved the wineglasses. They were quite proud of their visit with Grant Williams and the way they had pleasantly but firmly laid out their rules for the neighborhood.

Williams had potential to be the perfect neighbor. It was clear he didn't want any trouble with the residents of Old Stone Fence Post Estates, and he seemed agreeable enough. True, he appeared to be more than a little déclassé for the subdivision, but he wasn't belligerent, like those Herrens and Fords on Black Oak Manor Terrace, with the kiddie pools in their front yards and the unfortunate habit of leaving their bins out at the curb all day on recycling day, exposing the entire neighborhood to empty liquor bottles.

It was outrageous that the HOA kept letting that type of incivility slide without so much as a warning. That was why there were HOA Rules—and there were better, more exacting Fielding Rules.

Which reminded Tish…

"Can you believe that blank look he gave me when I mentioned the HOA?" She laughed, shaking her blond mane, and took a sip from her wineglass.

"He's certainly crude." Malcolm's jaw moved ever so slightly, an indication of what might have been excitement. "But I can live with that. As long as he keeps the property up, I can live with a *soupçon* of crudeness."

"Agreed." Tish clinked her glass gently against her husband's, then laughed again, and in a broad imitation of Grant, said, "But I'm not a homeowner. I'm just renting.'"

The Fieldings sank to the kitchen floor in peals of laughter, Tish sinking so quickly she almost chipped the red polish off a nail as she tried to steady herself.

They were, they knew, the perfect couple. And perfect together.

And if they ruled Old Stone Fence Post Estates with an iron fist, it was in pursuit of continued perfection. College sweethearts, they'd been together for twenty-five years and married for twenty-one without so much as a single fight. They were just that much in sync.

Oh, perhaps they had both started to drink a bit too much, and too early in the day, but it was a harmless diversion. If Malcolm was spending later and later hours in DC at his job as a telecommunications lobbyist, and Tish was increasingly frustrated by her inability to become one of *The Real Housewives of Washington, DC*, and if his secretary was just a bit too good-looking for her tastes, and if her tennis instructor called her at inappropriately late hours, and if they each kept a tiny secret or two from the other every now and then, well…

That was okay. Just…perfect.

They knew these were the types of things that would never come between them, which was precisely why they never talked about them. Because they were perfect, and lived in a perfect house in a perfect subdivision with perfect rules.

Which was pretty much perfect, they thought, as Malcolm opened another bottle of wine. A *perfect* bottle of wine.

$ $ $

They found what they needed in the garage.

"Think you can handle the lawnmower?" Grant asked Farraday.

"Rider?"

"Yeah."

"I can drive anything."

"Okay, you take the grass and I'll take the hedges." He turned to Chase. "You're on flower duty, lover boy."

"I don't know anything about flowers. All my knowledge comes from the Korean deli, and even then only on Valentine's Day and your birthday."

"The deli does it, so how hard can it be? Fake it."

Farraday backed the lawnmower out of the garage, Grant grabbed the hedge trimmers, and Chase picked up a spade and a pair of shears.

The lawn never stood a chance.

9

It was early evening when Lisa Cochrane finally guided her rental car into the driveway in front of 455 Old Stone Fence Post Road.

"Good Lord, would you look at this place?" Mary Beth's mouth was agape as she looked out the windshield. "What the hell?!"

From the backseat, Constance said, "What's the problem? This place looks perfect."

"Not the house, the lawn!" Mary Beth gestured at it. "Who takes care of it? The Three Stooges?"

The rental car was non-smoking, which didn't stop Lisa from flicking the dying stub of her cigarette out the window. It landed in the ragged edging between the driveway and the lawn, which could have been described as freshly mown, although a more accurate term would have been freshly scalped.

"We're talking about Lambert, Chase, and Farraday. That's about as close to Moe, Curley, and Larry as *we're* ever going to get."

"I always thought of Lambert as more of a Shemp," said Constance, which made Lisa laugh. Constance hadn't met them until that morning, but she'd had an instant rapport with Lisa. Mary Beth, on the other hand…well, she still held out hope. It might take time, but she held out hope.

"This isn't funny, you know," said Mary Beth, which underscored the differences between the three women. "The lawn looks like crap."

"Mmm-hmm," muttered Constance.

Lisa caught her accompanying wink in the rearview mirror but kept her control. Instead of laughing, she turned off the ignition and popped the trunk, and soon they stood—wheeled luggage behind them—on the front porch. Chase opened the door moments after Lisa rang the bell.

"Hi, honeys, you're home!"

With the greeting, he gave them a welcoming smile, which was answered when Mary Beth forced her hand into his chest and shoved him out of the way.

"You guys better not have taken all the good bedrooms. If you did, I'll set your crap on fire and throw it out the fuckin' window."

Chase knew she wasn't joking.

"Nice seeing you, too, Mary Beth," he said as she passed him, walked into the foyer, and kept going.

"Sorry." Lisa stood behind on the porch with Constance, taking in Mary Beth's wake with a pained smile. She wiggled her shoulders. "We had a *long* drive."

"Long," Constance agreed, and she and Lisa began giggling again.

"I've made the drive a few times over the past couple of days, so I know what you mean. But at least there won't be any more long-distance hauls in our immediate future."

Constance shook her head. "Long as Mary Beth's around, don't bet that your long hauls are in the past."

They found Mary Beth in the kitchen, where Farraday was rummaging through a cupboard.

"Better put the car in the garage," he said, offering his own abrupt greeting. "Don't leave it outside."

It took Lisa a moment to realize what he meant. "It's not stolen."

"It's not?"

"No. Grant told me to rent a car. Told me I'd be reimbursed."

"Oh." He thought about that. "Uh, if you don't mind me asking… how much is he reimbursing you?"

Lisa stared him down. "Don't worry about it, Farraday." She held the stare as one hand dug through her purse, hunting for her cigarettes. "I'm bankrolling the job, so I think I'm allowed to spend some of the money. Unless you want me to pull out, that is."

"Oh, no, no!"

She smiled. "I figured as much."

"So anyway…" Farraday smiled crookedly, his version of pouring on the charm. "If the car is clean, how 'bout if I borrow it for a half hour."

"Why?"

"I need to go to the supermarket." He nodded in the general direction of the garage. "And I'd just as soon not…"

"Gotcha, Farraday."

Mary Beth leaned against a wall, still tense and still holding her suitcase as if she weren't sure she'd be staying. "He doesn't mean the supermarket. He means the liquor store."

Farraday didn't bothering arguing. "Well, *yeah*, that, too. But first I have to go to the supermarket and pick up things for dinner. I'm making a leg of lamb and homemade mint jelly. Long as I can find all the ingredients, that is."

Mary Beth looked at Farraday as if he'd just levitated. "Did you just say what I think you said? You can make a leg of lamb? And you make your own mint jelly?"

Farraday looked at *her* as if she'd asked if he could breathe. "Of course! I'm a chef. How come no one believes this?"

"Farraday's a chef," Chase said confidently as he stepped between them, even though he only had Farraday's word to take for that and wasn't sure it was quite enough.

"Long as I can find good lamb, that is. And marjoram to make the jelly. It ain't the same without the marjoram."

Lisa finally found her cigarettes at the bottom of the purse and pulled out the pack. "First, before anyone does anything, I want to smoke…"

"You just had one." It was another thing Mary Beth wasn't happy about. She tolerated it at home because Lisa paid the rent; on the road, though, she felt less restricted.

"And now…I'm going to have another."

Still standing in the doorway, Constance stifled a laugh.

Farraday shrugged as Lisa dangled the cigarette between her index and middle fingers. "Long as it's not in the kitchen, I don't care where you smoke. See, part of the charm of homemade mint jelly is the aroma."

"Thank you, Paul." Lisa tossed a self-satisfied smile in Mary Beth's direction, then returned her attention to Farraday. "Since you're being such a gentleman about my bad habit, I'll keep it away from your kitchen. *And* your minty aroma. Is there a basement?"

"You better believe it," said Chase. "A big one. With a pool table…a bar…"

"Nothing says 'place to smoke' like a room with a pool table and bar, so lead the way." They took a few steps toward the basement stairs when she thought to ask, "Hey, where's Lambert?"

Chase nodded toward the kitchen ceiling. "Upstairs washing up. He sorta had a bad reaction to nature."

They took a few more steps toward the stairs when Farraday interrupted. “Uh, Lisa?”

“Yeah?”

“Keys?”

Lisa shrugged and tossed the car keys on the kitchen table.

$ $ $

Farraday was gone and Lisa had returned to the kitchen by the time Grant Lambert finally descended from the upper floor, scratching his head distractedly. He barely acknowledged the new arrivals.

“I think I’m allergic to the bushes,” he said to no one in particular. “I’m all itchy. My eyes are watering. And I *almost* sneezed.”

Constance waited until he’d finished scratching his shoulder before asking, “What the hell were you doing in the bushes? *You* don’t know anything about gardening.”

“The neighbor lady said they had to be trimmed, so I trimmed them.”

Mary Beth shook her head. “*You* massacred those hedges? I thought we were just joking about the Three Stooges.” She turned to Lisa and Constance, looking for support, but the looks on their faces told her there was never any joke. “I shoulda known. You can’t even trim a hedge right, but we’re supposed to follow your plans to rob one of the biggest churches in the world. We’re gonna end up in Attica.”

“Not Attica,” said Constance. “That’s New York. In Virginia I think they send you to Wallens Ridge.”

“You’re not helping,” said Lisa, who then turned to Grant. “Why did the neighbor tell you to trim the hedges? Doesn’t the owner have a lawn service?”

“What’s a lawn service?”

“A service. A service that services lawns.” He gave her a blank look. She sighed. “You’ve got to get out of Jackson Heights more often.”

Grant shrugged. “I dunno. They looked okay to me. But she said if we didn’t cut the grass and fix the bushes, the IHOP would be on our asses.”

“The IHOP?”

“The homeowners’ mob.”

Lisa thought about that for a moment then managed to translate. “Ah. You mean the H-O-A.”

"Yeah, that."

She shook her head. "Sorry about that, Lambert. I didn't think to ask."

He scratched his forearm. "Well, hopefully we won't have to do it again."

"Once they see the yard," said Mary Beth, "I think they'll *insist* you don't do it again."

Grant sat at the kitchen table. "It doesn't look *too* bad."

"It looks like it's been attacked by a herd of stampeding bison. *Drunk* stampeding bison. Wielding chainsaws. *Rusty* chainsaws..."

Lisa stopped her. "That's enough, Mary Beth. Okay, our new neighbors seem to have control issues. Welcome to the suburbs."

"Whatever. We're not here to do yard work. We're here to rob a church." Grant looked at Lisa, then at Constance. He made a point not to look at Mary Beth. "You see the cross on your way through Nash Bog?"

Lisa nodded. "Can't miss it."

"You can even see it from our front window. Farraday eyeballed it and thinks it's about three-eighths—"

"Three-sevenths."

"Three-*sevenths* of a mile, although the way these streets weave around, there's no direct route. Which means Chase and Constance and whoever else has to get inside the church will probably have to drive."

Lisa's frown—which had been playing at the corner of her lips since Mary Beth's brief tirade—deepened with the realization that Grant had played her.

"And by that, you mean they'll drive my rental, instead of the stolen car I'm *sure* you have stashed in the garage." Grant shrugged an agreement. "Which is why you wanted me to rent a car instead of riding down with you."

Grant scratched his nose. "Correct on all counts. You're a very smart woman, which is why I like you."

She squinted. "You like me because I have money."

"That, too." He turned to Mary Beth. "So, Mary Beth, on the ride down we sorta decided to use you on the job. Long as you're here already."

"And who decided that?"

"Me and Chase." He glanced at his boyfriend, who looked away. "Mostly Chase, if you're looking for someone to blame. Anyway, you, Chase, and Constance will become members of the church..."

She stopped him. "And how are we gonna explain that? The three of us just show up one day out of the blue?"

"Something like that," said Grant. "It's a church. They like it when people show up out of the blue and join. That's sort of the point of being a church."

"What's the cover story?"

"Let's not worry too much about a cover story," he said. "We don't need to overcomplicate things."

Mary Beth was about to make the point that Grant Lambert *always* overcomplicated things, but stopped at the sound of Chase's voice.

"Hold on!" Usually calm and soft-spoken, Chase was unexpectedly animated, which startled the other criminals in the kitchen. "What if Mary Beth and I pretend to be husband and wife?"

Mary Beth didn't give that idea a chance to make an impression in her brain. "Are you fucking kidding me?"

The room fell silent, and every head turned to Grant, who sat in his chair at the table and tried very hard not to meet any of their stares.

Finally, he raised his head and said, "You know what? That'll work."

"No way!" Mary Beth crossed her arms across her chest and fell into a pout. "You cooked that up with Chase. That's not fair!"

Grant ignored her. "It's a conservative church, so who better to join as new parishioners than a happily married couple?"

"Lambert…" There was ice in Mary Beth's voice.

But Lisa was now as enthusiastic as Grant. *She* got it, at least. "I think that's a great idea."

"Lisa!" Now Mary Beth's attitude was edging past annoyance.

Chase looked at Mary Beth and leered, adding an exaggerated wink for good measure. "I like this plan, too, honey bunch."

Mary Beth was having none of it. "I will kill all of you and bury your body parts in the backyard."

And she might have, had the doorbell not opportunely rung. They looked around the kitchen at each other, no one volunteering, until the bell rang a second time.

Finally Lisa stood. Unhappiness was in her voice as she said, "I'll get it."

The woman at the front door was somewhere in her forties, no matter how hard she tried to hide it with Clairol and Botox, and exhaled a vague, stale aroma of white wine. Lisa received a perky smile.

"Mrs. Williams?"

Lisa cocked her head. "Pardon me?"

"Aren't you Mrs. Williams?"

Lisa began to back into the foyer. "I'm afraid you have the wrong house."

The woman put her hand on the door, neutralizing Lisa, although Lisa was unsure if that was to steady herself or to prevent it from being closed. And she now had an annoying singsong inflection in her voice.

"But I met *Mr.* Williams earlier, and I know it was *this* house." When Lisa didn't react, the Clairol blonde scrunched her face. "Mr. Williams? Mr. *Grant* Williams?"

Lisa's face betrayed no reaction, but her thoughts were altogether different: *Okay, Lambert, if you're going to use a fake name, that's something you should share with everyone else. It would make life* much *easier.*

Lisa moved her head from the door and gave the woman a thin smile. "I'm sorry for the confusion. What threw me off is…is…" Her mouth took charge when her mind went blank. "I'm not Mrs. Williams."

The blonde's smile flickered, although the flesh around her mouth barely moved. "Then if you don't mind me asking…"

"I'm Lisa, Mr. Williams's, uh…" She blanked again for a moment until she realized a non-answer wouldn't work. "I'm Mr. Williams's *sister-in-law*." She offered her hand and the blonde took it. "Mrs. Williams died in a tragic accident last year, so…" Lisa laughed nervously, which she realized probably seemed inappropriate. Still, she lifted her hands, palms stretched outward. "So…no more Mrs. Williams!"

"Oh, dear!" The woman clutched at her throat. If there had been pearls, or a necklace, or anything around her neck to grab except drum-tight flesh, the gesture might have worked. Instead, it looked practiced. "I'm *so* sorry to hear that." She waited expectantly for Lisa to continue, but when it became clear that the story was over she finally introduced herself. "I'm Tish Fielding. From across the street. I asked Mr. Williams to tend to the yard earlier today, and well…" She looked around the lawn, shaking a nervous hand at the carnage, and quickly returned her gaze to Lisa. "Would it be possible for me to have a word with him?"

"I'll get him." Lisa smiled at the opportunity to close the door in Tish's face, which she did, even as Tish tried to stop it, chipping one red nail in the process. As she walked back to the kitchen, she called out, "It's for you, Williams."

Grant, now nursing a beer at the kitchen table, looked up. "Oh… right. Sorry I forgot to clue you in."

"The next time you give a neighbor a fake name, it'd be a good idea to share the information with your housemates." She nudged a shoulder in the direction of the door. "You'd better talk to her and make her go away. Then we're gonna figure out how we're all supposed to be related to each other."

Grant did as he was told. Tish was still waiting on the front porch, looking more than a little agitated.

"I'm sorry about the loss of your wife," she said when he finally worked up the nerve to poke his head out the front door.

A quizzical expression played on the edge of his mouth, but he managed to stammer out, "Thank you."

"If there's anything you need..."

"Well, it was a long time ago, but thank you. I'm fine."

Tish reached out to stroke his shoulder, a gesture she hoped would be comforting, but then remembered it was *him* and pulled her hand back before she actually made physical contact.

"A year may seem like a long time, but it's still recent. Those memories will keep coming back. If that happens, let me or Malcolm know. Dr. Bradean on August Morning Lane is a grief counselor, and I'm sure she can help."

"Uh...thanks."

"Anyway," Tish squared her shoulders and continued, forcing chipperness into her voice, "the reason I'm here is because of the lawn."

He showed a tiny bit of teeth between his lips. Grant Lambert wasn't used to smiling, so he hoped it looked friendly. It didn't.

"You wanted it neatened up, and we did it."

"You did...well, *something*." She took another look at the mutilated greenery. "Something I hope can be fixed."

Grant surveyed his work. "Maybe the hedges could be a bit more even."

"And the grass."

"Maybe."

"And I have no idea *what* happened to your flower beds, but...Well, what *did* happen to your flower beds?" She looked at petals littering the slate walkway that used to be attached to stems, destruction Chase had left behind earlier that afternoon.

He shrugged. "I don't think the guy who owns this joint took good care of them."

"Joint?"

"I mean, house."

"You mean Mr. Yee? But Mr. Yee is an amateur horticulturist!"

"He'll never be a professional if he keeps killing his flowers." He looked up to see Farraday pulling the rental car into the driveway and knew it was time to wrap up their conversation. "Listen, I appreciate your concern about wanting the neighborhood to look nice. I'm afraid we're just a bunch of city people who don't have lawns, so maybe we're a bit out of our league. But we'll try harder. Maybe we'll even get one of those service lawns."

She stared at him. "Do you mean a lawn service?"

"Uh…yeah. That."

"Thank you," she said, but her attention was now on Farraday as he unloaded grocery bags from the trunk. She turned back to Grant. "My, there are certainly a lot of people living in this house."

"Yeah. That's Farraday. He's our driver." The moment those words spontaneously came out of his mouth, he wished he could stuff them back in, and hoped she wouldn't notice.

But she did, and her eyes widened. Grant noticed that, for once, she seemed impressed. Her skin even moved.

"You have a chauffeur?"

"I mean…uh…" He stood stupidly in the doorway for a few seconds, then decided to go with it. She *had* been impressed, after all.

So he said, "Doesn't everyone?"

Tish leaned close to him, as if they were now confidantes. "Can I ask you a personal question? I mean, now that we're neighbors…"

He thought about that. "Maybe."

"What do you do?"

He thought some more. "I guess you could say I'm sorta in the financial sector."

"Hedge funds?"

Grant shivered a bit at the word "hedge" and scratched at his rib cage.

"This and that," he said.

Tish winked. "Hedge funds, right?"

He scratched an elbow. "Sure. Why not?"

$ $ $

Grant was back in the kitchen, seated, and the rest of his gang hovered around him.

There were other rooms in the house—many larger, even though the kitchen was pretty damn large—but they still all naturally congregated in the kitchen. Plus, Farraday had been right: the aroma of homemade mint jelly was part of its charm. Good thing he'd found the marjoram.

"I wasn't counting on nosy neighbors," Grant said to no one in particular.

"Whether you counted on 'em or not, we got 'em," said Lisa.

"I just figured we'd do what we do, and that would be that. I didn't think anyone would question it."

"I just wanna know why *I've* gotta be the hired help?" Farraday, who'd learned of his new cover as he toted grocery bags into the house, clearly wasn't happy about it.

"It's only for a few weeks. You'll live with it. Just like I'm gonna pretend to be a hedge fund guy named Williams and live with it."

"Yeah, but you get to be the finance guy, and Lisa gets to be your sister-in-law. It ain't fair that I'm the menial laborer. The chauffeur and chef. I mean, what kind of bullshit is that?"

Grant leaned forward. "But you *are* the driver and cook."

"*Chauffeur* and *chef.*" Farraday smacked a spatula against a pan on the stovetop. "But whatever you say, *Mr.* Williams."

Grant tried to ignore him.

"After we steal seven million dollars from the Virginia Cathedral of Love, you can bet the people we stole it from are gonna be looking for us. I don't want to make it any easier for them than it has to be. And there are a lot of Williamses in the world." He turned to Lisa. "You give Tish Fielding your name?"

"Just my first name."

"First names are okay." He had a philosophy when he was pulling jobs: whenever possible, his crew should use their real first names. It was too easy to slip up and forget an alias, a lesson he'd learned the hard way.

And first names were hard to trace. Last names were a different story, which is why he tried to use a common one—like Williams—when he was working. Calling Farraday "Farraday" was a mistake he was still kicking himself over, although he doubted Tish Fielding would present a problem.

Mary Beth looked annoyed, which wasn't surprising since that was the way she usually looked. "We'd better get the cover story together before there are any more screw-ups. Like identities sprung by surprise. Or dead wives."

"Right," said Grant. "So Farraday is our chauffeur, and Lisa is my sister-in-law. Lisa, you're gonna need a last name. Something common, and something you can remember."

Lisa didn't even take time to think. "Hudson."

"Hudson?" asked Grant.

"As in Kate."

Mary Beth covered her eyes. "I should've seen that coming. You had to go and steal my Kate Hudson thing, didn't you?"

"You don't want something more common? Like maybe Smith? Brown?" Lisa shook her head. "Okay, then, as long as you can remember and keep it straight."

"Oh, I can remember," Lisa said, with a hoarse laugh. "Hudson, Hudson, Hudson." That made Constance laugh, too, which in turn made Mary Beth glower.

"Hudson it is, then," Grant said, and Mary Beth thumped her head against the wall a few times. "Now, Chase and Mary Beth, you're pretending to be a married couple, so you'll be…"

"I'll be Lisa's nephew: Chase Hudson!" Those were two bones he threw to Mary Beth. She'd get to use the Hudson name, too, and they knew Lisa would hate pretending to be his aunt. She'd hated the role in a past job they'd pulled together, after all.

Lisa didn't disappoint, snapping out of her triumph over adopting the name of Mary Beth's crush as quickly as she'd taken it on. "How come I always have to be the aunt?"

"Because you don't like being the aunt," Chase teased. "Discomfort keeps us on our game."

"But I'm only a few years older than you. I could never pass for your aunt."

Mary Beth snorted. "Twelve years are considered a *few* now?"

Lisa flicked her middle finger at Chase. She would have done the same to Mary Beth, but she wasn't afraid of Chase. "That's it! I'm keeping the Hudson name for myself."

"No way." Mary Beth had warmed to Chase's suggestion and was digging in her Prada heels. "Chase will be Chase Hudson, and I'll be Mary Beth Hudson, and you will be his aunt. We're now the Hudson family, and *that* is the end of the discussion."

"She read *you*," Constance said to Lisa.

Lisa's voice was barely audible as she glumly leaned back in her chair. "If that's the end of the discussion, that's the end of the discussion,

I suppose." As she said those words, she thought of other last names Chase and Mary Beth could assume. *Asshole* had a nice ring to it…

Grant didn't like having all these Hudsons in the house—what the hell was wrong with Jones or Wilson or Carter?—but knew a lost battle when he saw one. He did, however, have to insist on one change.

"Chase, you're not Chase anymore."

Chase sighed loudly. "Charles again?"

"Charles again. Chase is too uncommon."

It *was* his given name, and Chase understood Grant's logic. Still, if he'd wanted to be known as Charles, he'd be known as Charles. The fact that he didn't and wasn't was beside the point in the middle of a seven-million-dollar job, though, so he accepted Grant's dictate without argument.

Constance tossed a little wave into the air. "Excuse me, all you Williamses and Hudsons, but there's one more person in the house you'll have to explain. It's gonna be pretty obvious to the neighbors that I'm not related to you."

Grant sized her up. "Oh, yeah. Sorry, Constance, I wasn't thinking."

"Don't get me wrong, Grant Lambert. I'm thrilled that you've gone color-blind. Dr. King would be *so* proud. But the rest of society—especially in *this* neighborhood—is definitely gonna notice the difference in pigmentation."

Standing at the granite island in the center of the kitchen, chopping an onion, Farraday said, "International moneyman Grant Williams has got a chauffeur. Maybe he should have a maid, too."

Constance put her hands on her hips. "Seriously, Farraday? You want me to be the maid? That's the only way you think we can pass off a black woman in this house?" She swiveled to face Grant. "I gotta put up with this, Lambert?"

Grant sat in silence for a long time, carefully weighing his words before speaking. But finally he had to say something, and that something was, "Actually, Constance, maybe Farraday's onto something…"

"What?"

"Would being called a housekeeper make you feel better?"

The answer—courtesy of a hurled toaster—was no.

It was an expensive toaster. Lisa would be adding the cost of the damages to their expenses. And Grant and Chase's share of the loot shrank by another eighty-nine dollars and ninety-nine cents.

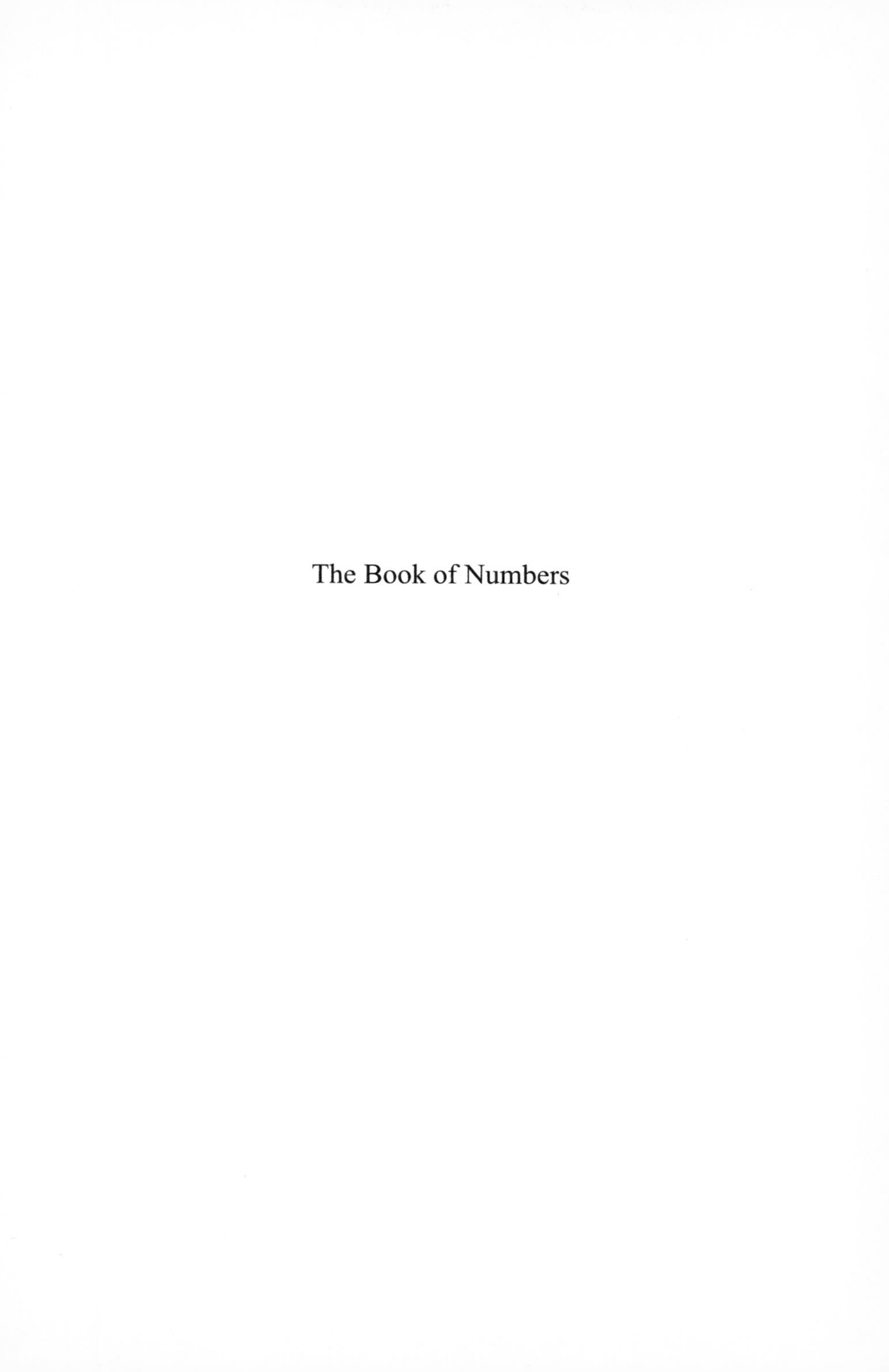

The Book of Numbers

10

If not for the economic recession and oil crisis of the late 1970s, the world might never have heard of Oscar Hurley. Except, that is, for people looking for new and pre-owned Chevrolets in the general vicinity of Roanoke, Virginia, many of whom had grown familiar with the slogan, "If Oscar says it's good, it's *great*!" over a decade of late-night television.

But Oscar Hurley Chevrolet—never a big moneymaker in the best of times—was devastated by the financial double-whammy. Some men would have toughed it out; others would have walked away; and still others would have curled up in a ball and cried.

But those men were not Oscar Hurley.

Oscar Hurley had a vision.

Moses had a vision of the Burning Bush. Saul had a vision of Christ on the road to Damascus. Hurley's vision was every bit as vivid, and every bit as life-changing.

The vision had come to him in his sleep and remained throughout the next day. When it was *still* in his head days later, he sat Francine, his wife of four years, rail-thin and pale, down on the living room couch and made his announcement. His voice was crisp and confident.

"I'm going to start a ministry and preach the word of God."

Francine looked into his clear, gray eyes and quietly said, "Are you out of your friggin' mind?"

"No, no! Listen to me!" He gestured around their modest living room, an assortment of secondhand furniture and garage-sale tchochkes. "See this? Do you see this room?" She nodded disapprovingly. "Why do we live like this?"

"We live like this," she said coolly, "because you don't sell enough Chevys."

"Well, yes, there's that, too. But that's not what I meant. We live like this because we are not allowing God to provide for us. The other night, I had a vision…"

"Oh, Oscar," she said, with a sad shake of her head. She was so thin, so pale, he was afraid she'd faint.

"No, it was a *good* vision! It was a vision of us—Oscar and Francine Hurley—living in a mansion, surrounded by luxury."

She stared hard into his face. "Have you been drinking again?"

"Francine, this was a divine vision! God told me what I had to do!"

She started to struggle to her feet. "Because if you're drinking again…"

"God told me to preach His word, and He would provide."

And then, because his wife was now fully convinced he'd been drinking again, he gently forced her back to the couch and explained in more detail.

Oscar Hurley the Chevy dealer would become *Dr.* Oscar Hurley—there were plenty of theological diploma mills in their neck of southern Virginia; that part would be easy enough—and he'd use the same oratorical skills he'd been wasting selling new and pre-owned automobiles to sell the word of God. In time, he'd have followers, and followers always had money they were willing to part with if it helped their favorite preacher reach more people. Better yet, those followers not only wouldn't begrudge him if he lived high on the hog off their offerings, they pretty much thought it validated the importance and righteousness of their favorite preacher.

It took several hours and a few shots of bourbon, but Francine Hurley finally saw merit in her husband's vision. Especially when it became clear his newfound religious fanaticism was really nothing more than a redirection of his career from selling Chevrolets to selling God. Undoubtedly, God would prove to be much more popular. God hadn't produced the Vega, after all.

Time passed quickly. Within the first year of his new calling, Dr. Oscar Hurley was making a name for himself and collecting increasingly enthusiastic audiences in the small border towns of southern Virginia, West Virginia, and North Carolina. Through his traveling salvation show, he met some religious broadcasters and soon had a weekly regional radio show, which in short time evolved into a weekly regional television show.

And still his ministry grew. New, larger crowds necessitated a permanent structure instead of rented halls and borrowed pulpits, so supporters dug deep into their pockets and built the first Virginia Cathedral of Love on an acre of land a few miles outside Roanoke. Another few years later, as his early cable TV presence grew and attracted more worshippers, the congregation was over capacity. The building was razed and a second, larger cathedral was built.

By the mid-1980s, Dr. Hurley commanded a small army of congregants, and politicians began paying calls. After personally noting the size of the congregation and experiencing Dr. Oscar Hurley's charisma, those politicians began taking orders. They'd never admit to that, of course—they'd insist they were representing the views of their constituents—but it amounted to the same thing. A prayer breakfast was arranged in Richmond one year; the next year, the North Carolinians wanted one, so he went to Raleigh. Then to Charleston…to Annapolis… to Harrisburg…

He even went into the belly of the beast: *Albany*.

President Reagan brought him to the White House late in his second term. So did the first President Bush, President Clinton, and the second President Bush. He testified before Congress. He led a prayer breakfast for conservative Christians in Congress. He led a vigil against liberals in Congress and on the Supreme Court.

And with every notch up in his visibility—every mention in a newspaper, every pat on the back from a devout elected official, every condemnation by a secular liberal talking head on television—more money gushed into his coffers. Every day the mail brought more checks; every day the congregants offered up more cash.

It wasn't easy, though. It was certainly not as easy as he'd supposed when he told Francine of his vision that preaching would bring him fame and, more importantly, fortune. In fact, there was a lot of hard work involved.

Because Oscar Hurley hadn't planned on *strategy* when he began his ministry, and it soon became apparent that continued relevancy had everything to do with strategy. As the years and decades rolled past, he'd learned that his message had to mirror the times. What sold in 1978 was not necessarily what would sell in 2011. The word of God may have been timeless and eternal, but the interest of the flock had an expiration date.

So he had learned how to stay relevant; to stay in sync with the people he led. He was nothing if not adaptable.

That was where politics came into play. The definition of sin might be flexible—even *he* had given up railing against cohabitation before marriage by the late '90s, realizing that was a lost cause—but politics would always be relevant. Politics was a high-profile affair, and politicians—even the liberals—constantly sought to define themselves as righteous and God-fearing. There was a reason there were almost no self-avowed atheists or agnostics in public office, especially in Washington, DC.

With an overflowing bank account and his popularity still on the rise, Dr. Oscar Hurley began planning another expansion of the Cathedral of Love. This time, though, Roanoke would not be its home. Instead, he would take his mission a couple hundred miles up the road, to the outskirts of the nation's capital.

Access, after all, was *access*.

Soon he was symbolically scooping the first shovelful of dirt at the site of the new Virginia Cathedral of Love in Nash Bog. It would be, he thought, their last and permanent home.

The town offered quick access to the District of Columbia and Dulles Airport, and its leaders agreed to some zoning concessions. Better yet, they promised to build him the access road that would become Cathedral Boulevard.

In exchange, Hurley had promised nothing but a constant parade of the faithful who would shop, dine, and perhaps buy property in Nash Bog. Millions of people each year. That was a lot of commerce.

Everyone involved agreed it was a good deal.

The cathedral was built quickly, and Oscar and Francine Hurley abandoned Roanoke without so much as a glance in the rearview mirror, their limousine leading a convoy of moving trucks—one devoted exclusively to the Desk of Christ, which he'd had hand-crafted by a North Carolina furniture maker some years earlier—two hundred miles north along I-81 to Nash Bog. As he suspected, his old congregation didn't begrudge this step up in his status. They reveled in it, and many members even moved to Loudoun County to be closer to him.

The sheep had followed their shepherd. He'd counted on that. Once again, his long-ago, Carter Administration–era vision had proven to be on target. It may have taken longer than he'd originally thought, but it had happened. God—and entrepreneurship—had provided. Everything had grown so big. Even Francine, once rail-thin, had trebled her weight.

Hurley not-so-subtly let the town leaders know that their concessions to his cathedral had brought all those new residents to Nash Bog. *And* that they voted. From that point forward, church and state coexisted amicably. Even the Buddhist councilmember attended services several times each year.

The *new* Virginia Cathedral of Love was a worthy anchor for the moral authority of Dr. Oscar Hurley. But…

Within a few days, he realized there was something missing.

A cross.

Of course there *was* a cross. It soared some fifty feet into the air above the church building. It was fine enough for a normal church, but it was thin and relatively unimposing, not the sort of symbol he thought should represent the Cathedral. Massive as it was, the Cathedral of Love demanded a cross that would soar into the heavens, with a heft and girth that would announce to the world that Christ resided here with Dr. Oscar Hurley.

By the end of the following week he had personally drafted a blueprint for an appropriate cross, 280 feet tall and 120 feet in circumference at the base. That cross would have been a beacon for Christians throughout the world had the meddlesome Federal Aviation Administration not informed him that he'd have to attach a blinking red light to the top to warn away aircraft.

Since the cross on which Jesus Christ was crucified did *not* have a blinking red light at the top—the fact that Jesus was also not crucified on a 280-foot-tall cross had never really been a consideration—and since no amount of persuasion could convince Congress to strip the agency of funding until the FAA saw things *his* way, Hurley was forced to rescale his plans. So he took a four-by-four sheet of reinforced cardboard, retooled the dimensions, and personally drew a new cross.

At 199 feet, the new cross would fall twelve inches short of the FAA's restrictions, and so, a few years after the Virginia Cathedral of Love opened its doors, construction finally began. Even though every time Hurley now looked at the Great Cross he regretted paring 81 feet, it was still an amazing structure, visible from large swaths of Loudoun County.

Dennis Merribaugh had overseen construction of the cross. It was his first official assignment since leaving his small church in Delaware to join the staff of the Cathedral as its chief operating officer. Merribaugh had taken one look at the blueprint for the solid cement structure, grabbed a pen, and made some sound recommendations on ways the Great Cross could be constructed cheaply and efficiently and without, he said, sacrificing the overall aesthetics or quality. Plus he figured out how to make it functional. Hurley was sold on the spot and construction began as soon as Merribaugh was able to find the encampments of day laborers who serviced those good people of Loudoun County that didn't want to get their hands dirty.

But all of that was then, and this was now.

$ $ $

Now the structures and grounds of the Virginia Cathedral of Love were starting to show their age, most notably the Great Cross.

A visible crack had appeared late the previous winter, and as spring became summer it deepened. Work began, and soon scaffolding covered the lower half of the cross while day laborers were shuttled in and out—never the same ones from one day to the next—under Merribaugh's watchful supervision.

It wasn't the crack that bothered Hurley so much—these things happened—but the fact that it was taking so long to repair. That, and an overall shabbiness that was starting to overtake the entire complex.

Dennis Merribaugh may have been the right man for the job at one point, Hurley thought, but now perhaps he was overextended. Routine maintenance was slipping, and some bad personnel decisions—including the hiring and firing of Leonard Platt—were causing administrative confusion. None of this was good, and all of it fell under Merribaugh's responsibility as chief operating officer.

Hurley was sure he knew what the problem was: Merribaugh's obsession with his ex-gay ministry, Project Rectitude. As far as Hurley was concerned, the deviants should be sent to their own island. Even the ones who claimed they'd been cured of homosexuality were probably fooling themselves.

In any event, they creeped him out.

But Merribaugh was hell-bent on saving those sinners through conversion therapy. Hurley had indulged him—it made for good public relations, if nothing else—but if the price of his indulgence was a Cathedral that was literally falling apart, he would have to reconsider sooner rather than later.

He stood out in the morning sun, looking again at the scaffolding encircling the Great Cross, his face pinched with annoyance. God had created the world in six days, but Merribaugh couldn't even get a decent concrete patch finished in six weeks.

Hurley turned and followed the tree-lined walkway leading away from the Great Cross toward Cathedral House, visually inspecting the foliage as he passed. What had been small shrubberies when first planted had grown tall and full, but also untrimmed and tangled. He would have to remind Merribaugh that they were supposed to be a tasteful landscaping touch, not a forest.

That was not supposed to be *his* job. Merribaugh was supposed to address problems before they came to his attention.

If the unpatched cross and the untamed shrubs hadn't done enough damage to Dr. Oscar Hurley's mood, he approached Cathedral House and a light breeze carried with it the sounds of music and song from the auditorium. He scowled. That was *another* thing he didn't like, although this couldn't be blamed on Dennis Merribaugh. At least there was a reason for *this* outrage.

The Cathedral had spent five million dollars to build the auditorium, extending out of the side of the cathedral but sharing none of the stained-glass glory. Live performances, he believed, would help keep the congregation entertained *and* help neutralize the revenue loss.

Under ordinary circumstances, he might be delighted to hear music coming from the new building, but the new music director—one of Merribaugh's effeminate "ex-gays" by the name of Walter Pomeroy, who had once done something or other on Broadway and had been in decline ever since—had insisted that the inaugural performance would be *The Sound of Music*, a show Hurley loathed with all his heart.

He'd attempted to discourage Walter Pomeroy by insisting on rewrites—since the main characters were Roman Catholic, and Catholicism was considered a cult by the Cathedral, he'd demanded that Maria and the von Trapp family become devout Protestants—but to his dismay, the music director had happily agreed, adding his own born-again, "ex-gay" flourishes to the denominational alteration. The result was, perhaps, more in keeping with the Cathedral's teachings, but did nothing to make the musical more palatable.

Which was why he now had "The Lonely Goatherd" stuck in his head. It didn't make the scaffolding seem the least bit less annoying.

$ $ $

"The first thing you need to know," said Leonard, pacing the kitchen and twiddling with a shirt button, "is that these people are very sincere about their beliefs. Very prim and proper. So remember to act as if you believe everything. One true God, heaven and hell, a literal interpretation of the Bible, the whole thing. And whatever you do, don't let any obscenities slip out. *Especially* blasphemy."

Constance leaned against a granite counter and nodded with boredom. This was nothing she hadn't heard before. "Sounds like spending Easter with my family. And stop telling me not to swear. Do you think you have to do that because I'm black?"

Leonard gulped uncomfortably. "No, of course not."

"Then stop fuckin' saying it."

Grant sat at the table, taking it all in. "You sure you're up to this? Could be pretty intense."

"Don't insult me, Lambert. I *invented* this game."

Leonard had been summoned to brief her on pretty much everything she'd need to know before she had to improvise. His admonition not to swear or blaspheme had been his first and most repeated instruction.

"So what do you think?" Grant looked at Leonard. "Have you told her everything? Is she ready?"

He shrugged. "If you're sure she's one of the best…"

That annoyed her. "Listen, Cousin Leonard, I'm not *one* of the best. I *am* the best."

"She is," Grant agreed.

Leonard swallowed again. He'd already been nervous around Grant, and Constance was just a darker female version of the graying ringleader. When the two of them were together, he felt hopelessly overwhelmed.

"In that case, I guess she's ready." He thought for a second before returning his attention to Constance. "First, you'll want to find Merribaugh. Tell him…"

She swatted his words from the air as if they were pesky insects. "That I was an office manager in New York. Yeah, you've already told me that four or five times. I've been listening, and I know what I have to do. I'd know what to do if I'd never met you, so don't be so nervous."

"Nervous? I'm not nervous." He paused again, then said, "And the safe…"

"Is in the closet in the finance office. Yes, you *told* me."

"Oh. Uh…okay then. I guess that's, uh…everything…"

Grant looked him over. Leonard's lack of confidence wasn't especially reassuring. "Let me ask you a question. Why Merribaugh? Why not Hurley? He's the big guy there, right?"

Leonard allowed himself an indulgent scoff, as if to indicate their education was far from complete and therefore his jitters were justified. "Dr. Hurley is *far* too important to worry about the bookkeeping. He doesn't deal with day-to-day business. That's Merribaugh's job."

"You think maybe Merribaugh's a softer touch than Hurley?"

Leonard shook his head. "Hurley is more dangerous, but don't start thinking Merribaugh is a fool or can be trusted. True, Hurley makes him look like Mother Teresa, but Merribaugh makes almost everyone else look like Mother Teresa. Understand?"

"Gotcha."

Constance stood. "Guess I'll go upstairs and brush up on my Bible a bit. Unless…" She turned to face Grant. "Unless, that is, you want me to mop the floor or dust."

"Keep it up, I will."

She said something unpleasant they pretended not to hear and walked away.

When she was gone, Leonard asked, "What was that about?"

Grant rubbed his eyes. "My housekeeper aims to please."

Leonard leaned anxiously against the center island. "It's not that I don't trust your judgment, but…"

For a moment, Grant thought maybe he should be reassuring. Leonard was new to this, after all.

Until he thought again and realized Leonard *was* questioning his judgment.

"We're gonna be fine," he said. "And you're never gonna speak to me like that again."

$ $ $

Later that evening, after Leonard left and Constance had returned to her Bible studies, Grant went down to the finished basement where Chase and Lisa were engaged in a spirited pool match while Mary Beth sat at the far end of the room thumbing through a fashion magazine.

"You," he said, and pointed to Chase.

"Me?"

"You. Something's been bugging me, and I just figured it out."

Chase looked hurt. "Something about *me* has been bugging you?"

Grant nodded. "It's your hair."

That hurt more. "My hair? I've got *great* hair!"

"He does," Lisa agreed.

"Right." Grant studied Chase's highlights under the light hanging over the pool table. "But not great hair for the Virginia Cathedral of Love." Chase started to object. "This isn't negotiable. Cut it or dye it."

Lisa set her stick against the table and looked at Chase's head thoughtfully. "You know, Grant might have a point. Your hair is very… metrosexual." Which wasn't the *first* word that came to mind, but she was trying to be diplomatic.

Chase wasn't going to accept their judgment without a fight. "I paid a lot of money for this hair! You know how much those salons on Madison Avenue charge?"

"This is why you should just go to that barber on Queens Boulevard, like I do."

"You're just jealous," sniffed Chase.

"I'm just making sure everything is right for the job," said Grant. "And that hair isn't. So should I get my clippers?"

Chase covered his head. "*God* no!"

Lisa gave Chase a look of sympathy and stepped away from the pool table. "There's a drugstore just down the road. I'll be back in a few minutes." She took another glance at his head. "Dark brown should work for you. Or maybe chestnut."

"Just jealous," Chase muttered as Lisa went upstairs to get her car keys.

$ $ $

Grant woke, rolled to his right, and opened his eyes. And then he almost jumped out of bed until he remembered it was Chase under the dark brown head of hair.

"What the hell, Grant," Chase muttered, his eyes still closed. "Can't you get out of bed quietly, like a normal person?"

Grant pulled away the sheet and slapped his partner on his naked ass, gamely pretending he hadn't been startled when he thought he was waking up next to a stranger for the first time in close to two decades. "Time for you to get up. Remember, you're going to church this morning."

Chase's eyes were still closed. "It's only Thursday. I don't understand why we can't wait until Sunday…"

"We've been through this. On Sunday the place will be packed. On Thursday, it'll be less packed. And if you're gonna get face time with this Merribaugh, we want less packed."

Chase groaned and rolled away from him.

"If you're not downstairs in five minutes," said Grant, as he stood and started to pull on a pair of pants, "I'm sending Mary Beth up to get you."

In the kitchen, Farraday was about to serve eggs Benedict.

"Where's Chase?" he asked as Grant walked into the room. "He's gonna miss breakfast."

Grant sat at the table across from Lisa and Mary Beth. "He'll be here."

"I just don't want him to miss breakfast. It's the most important meal of the day, you know."

"He's used to coffee and maybe a Pop-Tart. I don't think breakfast is as important to him as it is to you."

Farraday set breakfast in front of Lisa and Mary Beth and returned to the stove as Chase stumbled into the kitchen.

"I made breakfast for you," said Farraday.

"Just coffee," said Chase. "And maybe a Pop-Tart, if we have 'em."

"Toldja," said Grant.

Farraday ignored them both, but their plates of eggs Benedict were plunked a bit too heavily in front of them.

Grant picked up his fork and turned to Mary Beth. "Ready to hit the cathedral?"

She looked at him through heavy lids. "Fuck off, Lambert."

"Not a lot of morning people," he said, taking in a mouthful of Farraday's eggs Benedict.

"And here's another one who's not a morning person," said Constance as she shuffled in and took the last chair at the table. "The things I'll do to my body for a lot of money."

At last someone had said something they could all agree on.

$ $ $

Tish Fielding wasn't snooping, really. She just happened to be staring out the window at the house across the street when Mr. Williams's chauffeur led three people who were neither he nor his sister-in-law out the front door and to the car: a dark-haired man, a compact woman who projected attitude even at a distance, and a black woman.

That was strange.

She made a mental note to check the HOA rules about unrelated people sharing a home. And if those guidelines didn't meet her standards, she'd issue her own.

$ $ $

There had been no question Mary Beth would ride in the front seat—she hadn't even bothered to ask—so Chase and Constance sat in the back of the rental car as Farraday wheeled it through the winding residential streets toward the Virginia Cathedral of Love.

Chase said, "So we're agreed we go our own way when we get to the church, right? Me and Mary Beth will pretend we don't know Constance, and Constance will pretend she doesn't know us."

Mary Beth nodded. So did Constance, but she couldn't resist tweaking Chase.

"You don't want people to think you're helping your maid find the Lord?" she asked.

"You're never gonna let this drop, are you?"

"Should I? I mean, you get a two-fer with me. You can be saving a domestic worker *and* a Negro at the very same time. That's very 1950s. If I know my Bible-bangers, they'll love it."

Chase slumped back and tried to ignore her. Fortunately it was a short ride—even without a direct route, as Farraday noted more than a few times—and soon they were deposited in front of the cathedral, immediately walking a short distance in opposite directions when they were out of the car.

It was the first time they'd seen it up close. From a distance, everything looked huge; up close, it was mammoth. They turned, looked at each other, and nodded.

It was show time.

$ $ $

As they would later tell the story, things went predictably at the cathedral.

Chase and Mary Beth, posing as Charlie and Mary Beth Hudson, went off in one direction. The people they tended to encounter were parishioners, although they stumbled across an associate pastor or two. Charlie Hudson discussed his deep faith; his wife tended to stand unapproachably to the side with her arms folded across her chest.

The problem was, Mary Beth Reuss was used to getting her own way. She didn't understand Mary Beth Hudson.

She was also, pretty much everyone they encountered would agree, opinionated. There was a place for that, but that place wasn't in the middle of a discussion about abortion.

"Honey," said Chase, gently trying to pull her away before the heated words combusted. "Maybe we should save it for another day."

"I'm not gonna let some man tell me what I can do with my body!"

Chase smiled apologetically at the associate pastor and circle of very nice, very conservative women surrounding him. "She's been a little tired lately."

"Bless you, Mr. and Mrs. Hudson," said the associate pastor, who genuinely felt sorry for that poor husband. It had to be difficult to be married to a communist.

Constance fared better…

$ $ $

It was a point of pride in the administrative offices of the Virginia Cathedral of Love that they had never been late on a payment. Not sixty days, not thirty days, not even fifteen days. Invoices were promptly processed and payment was made.

But since Leonard Platt had been fired, even that simple task had fallen apart. How Dr. Hurley had found out, Merribaugh didn't know. But he had.

The bookkeeping situation was going to have to be resolved sooner rather than later. If Merribaugh hadn't already known that, Hurley's tongue-lashing reprioritized it.

He stood in the cavernous sanctuary, trying to gather his wits, when he heard a woman ask, "Excuse me, but are you the Rev. Mr. Merribaugh?"

"I am," he said with a sigh, and turned to face a fortyish black woman in a modest dark blue dress with a bit of white lace at the collar.

She extended her hand. "It's so nice to meet you. I'm Constance Brown, a new member of the Cathedral."

He smiled. "Welcome, Constance. I hope you'll feel very much at home here."

"I'm sure I will." She looked around the sanctuary. "Quite a place. How many worshippers do you get here?"

"We usually have eight thousand people in attendance for a normal Sunday service, but we've been able to accommodate as many as fourteen thousand."

"Praise the Lord!" she said. "It must be almost impossible running a place like this."

"Some days," he agreed.

"Well, if you ever need a volunteer…"

"That's very kind, but…"

"…I have twenty years of office management experience, and I would love to dedicate my time to helping the Cathedral."

Merribaugh raised an eyebrow. "Twenty years of real experience?"

"Oh, yeah," she said. "I've been an office manager. HR director. Handled corporate payroll. You name it, I've had hands-on experience with it."

"Really," he said. "Maybe we can use your skills." He leaned close to her, as if they were now confidants. "You see, we're a bit overwhelmed right now. Our bookkeeper unfortunately, uh, had to leave our employ."

"I know bookkeeping," she said.

Merribaugh smiled. "Ms. Brown, I would love to talk about this at greater length."

$ $ $

Lisa hung up the phone, then turned to Grant and said, "I got us a lawn service, Captain Nature. Now please stop scratching yourself. Especially…*there*."

Grant stopped scratching there. "I'll never understand the suburbs."

"And I doubt they'll ever understand you." She would have said more but she was interrupted.

"Yoo-hoo!"

Grant frowned. "It's that Tish lady. And what's with the yoo-hoos? Doesn't she know how to work a doorbell?"

"I'll get rid of her," said Lisa, who obviously failed because seconds later Tish Fielding was marching into the kitchen, with Lisa tailing.

"Good news, Mr. Williams," she said. "I talked to Dr. Bradean and she's willing to drop her rates for you."

He cocked his head. "Huh?"

"Mrs. Bradean," she said again. "The grief counselor from August Morning Drive."

"Oh. Right. Maybe I'll give her a call if I ever have a chance."

Tish smiled sympathetically. "You'll get through this, Mr. Williams. Just stay strong."

"I'm trying."

"Good!" She looked around the kitchen with a bit of envy. Even though every house in the subdivision had a similar layout, this room felt bigger than hers. She'd have to check the blueprints later. "Also, I wanted to make sure you knew about the neighborhood barbecue on Saturday."

"Barbecue?"

"Oh." She frowned. "I'm sorry; I assumed you'd heard." Tish turned that frown upside down. "It's good I stopped by! The entire neighborhood will be there. You and Mrs.…Mrs.…" She looked at Lisa.

"Hudson."

"You and Mrs. Hudson *must* join us!"

"I don't know," said Grant. "We're not really very social. We sorta keep to ourselves."

Tish's smile didn't fade exactly, but it was clear she wasn't about to take no for an answer. "Everyone wants to meet the new neighbors. I have to insist…"

"We'll try to be there," said Lisa, in an effort to shut up Tish and get her out of the house.

"Oh, good!" She looked over Lisa's shoulder into the living room. Was that a 72-inch high-definition television mounted on the wall? She and Malcolm only had a 60-inch TV…

"So thanks for the invite," said Grant, which refocused Tish's attention. "Now…"

She stopped him by holding a finger in the air. "Oh, I just remembered one last thing."

"Of course you did."

"How many people are living here?"

Grant and Lisa exchanged glances. "Why?" he finally asked.

"The HOA rules say that no more than two unrelated people can share a home."

Grant and Lisa exchanged another glance, and Lisa asked, "Does that include the help?"

Tish thought about that. "I'm not sure."

"Because if you don't include the live-in help, we're all related."

It wasn't the answer Tish wanted, but until she could clarify the rules about domestic employees, she'd have to live with it. It could always wait a day or two, after all. Maybe not another week, but certainly a day or two.

Grant began to rise and said, "Thanks for coming by," but Tish remembered yet another "one last thing," so he sat back in the chair.

"There's the matter of your lawn…"

"Don't worry about it, Tish," said Lisa. "I just hired a service."

Grant felt defensive. "We would've gotten better."

"I'm not so sure about that," said Lisa, and Tish was happy *she* didn't have to say it.

Instead she smiled graciously. "Thank you for doing your part to help keep Old Stone Fence Post Estates one of the world's best residential communities." To Lisa, that sounded suspiciously like a real estate pitch line, but Tish began walking toward the foyer, so she decided not to call her on it. Any further conversation would delay her exit.

But then the front door opened and that exit was ruined by the entrance of Chase and Mary Beth, with Constance and Farraday bringing up the rear.

"Oh, hello!" said Tish, recognizing the group she'd seen through her window that morning when she wasn't really snooping.

Lisa tried unsuccessfully not to roll her eyes and failed, but she covered it by making introductions before anyone could do or say the wrong thing. "This is my…my nephew, Chase. And his wife, Mary Beth. This is Tish, our neighbor from across the street."

They exchanged unenthusiastic hellos.

"And you've met Farraday," she said.

Since he was the help, Tish nodded in his direction but didn't engage him. "Yes, of course." Her eyes fell upon Constance. "And you are…?"

Constance's hands went to her hips. "I'm the maid."

"I prefer to think of her as the housekeeper, not the maid," said Grant. "'Maid' seems like sort of a demeaning word." He smiled at her. "Constance is so much more than that. We think of her as almost part of the family."

"You got that right," Constance muttered.

"A chauffeur and a housekeeper? Oh my!" Tish was impressed, even if she didn't want to admit it. "You're certainly fancy, Mr. Williams."

Grant scratched at his stomach and said, "That's what I keep tellin' myself."

Farraday put himself into the conversation. "Y'know, I'm not just his chauffeur. I'm his chauffeur *and* his chef."

Tish eyeballed him. "You cook?"

"Why does everyone keep questioning that? Yeah, I cook. Like I said, I'm a chef." He held up the grocery bag in his hand. "Tonight I'm even making *daeji galbi*."

"Huh?" asked pretty much everyone.

"Korean barbecued pork ribs. Lucky I found a place I could get *kochujang*. Otherwise, it ain't the same."

"So…" Tish shook her head. "So a chauffeur and a chef!"

"I'm whatcha call multitalented."

"How…nice for you." Tish smiled and broke eye contact, despite the fascination now mixed in with her revulsion. Still, one really shouldn't stare at the servants. "Now, Mr. Williams, Ms. Hudson…the neighborhood barbecue…"

She was interrupted by a loud rumble from the driveway, which attracted their attention until it died off in a series of coughs of exhaust, followed eventually by silence.

"Sounds like someone needs a muffler," said Farraday, and—as if that were his entrance cue—Leonard walked through the front door.

Grant ignored him and turned back to Farraday. "Go fix Leonard's muffler. Can't have him driving around disturbing the peace."

"I was going to take my car in next week," said Leonard.

"Let me explain something, Leonard." Grant chose his words carefully, since Tish was standing just inches away. "See, when you drive a car with a bad muffler, you're not just disturbing the nice people of neighborhoods like this one. You're also breaking the law, and the cops might pull you over. And you wouldn't want the cops to pull you over, would you?"

Leonard got it. "No. No, of course not."

"Good. Farraday, fix his muffler."

Farraday wasn't happy, but couldn't do anything about it. "Yes, Mr.…Williams."

After Farraday dropped the groceries in the kitchen and stalked out, Tish looked at Leonard and said, "And this is…?"

"My accountant," Grant told her, nodding at Leonard with a look that told him to play along. "You'll probably be seeing a lot of him."

"I'm impressed, Mr. Williams."

"Call me Grant." He said it not because he wanted to be friendly, but because he'd always react more spontaneously to being called by his actual name, and no matter how hard he tried there was always going to be a split second when he wouldn't react to Mr. Williams.

"I'm impressed, Grant. Sometimes Malcolm and I can barely get our accountant on the phone, and you get house calls!"

"Yeah, well, we need to be very close."

Eventually what they thought might never happen happened, and Tish Fielding went home. When they were sure she was gone, and not about to reappear like some killer from a slasher movie, Grant asked Chase, Mary Beth, and Constance how it went.

"It was all right," said Chase.

"I hated every second," said Mary Beth. "Close-minded idiots. They hate gays, women…even the *women* hate women."

Chase cleared his throat. "Some of us maybe had a tougher time adapting than others. But…" He turned and smiled at Constance. "Some are naturals."

Grant saw a smile playing around the edge of Constance's face. "Sounds like you had a good day. What happened?"

Her smile broadened. "I met the Rev. Mr. Dennis Merribaugh himself. I really poured it on, and he ate it up."

"And?"

"Give me a week and I'll be running the place," said Constance. "I got it from Merribaugh himself that the office is in shambles. Since he fired Leonard, he's been trying to run the place with a bunch of blue-haired volunteers. Things keep going from bad to worse, and Hurley is riding his ass about it."

Grant smiled, which made everyone take a second look since it was one of those rare sights, like seeing a double rainbow.

"So you're in."

"Like Flynn, Lambert." She motioned around the kitchen. "Better not get used to this place, 'cause I don't think we're staying long."

11

"Congressman Skinner!"

Hurley saw the congressman before the congressman saw Hurley, which gave him an important advantage. Representative Donald Skinner had been hoping to avoid him by slipping out the side entrance of the hotel after his breakfast meeting with the In-Ground Pool Manufacturers Association, never expecting Hurley to use it as a shortcut to the Moral Families Coalition rally in the ballroom.

Skinner had guessed wrong.

Turning to face him, the congressman forced a smile and tried his best to rally. "Dr. Hurley! As always, it's a pleasure!"

Hurley's white teeth flashed, and he put a hand on Skinner's shoulder. "Your words of praise embarrass me, Congressman." He dropped his voice and his eyes dashed side to side. "Are you going somewhere?"

"Uh…I'm afraid I have a full schedule back at my office, Dr. Hurley."

Hurley sized him up. "Is there a place we could talk privately for a few minutes?"

There was a small empty room off the hallway into which Skinner led Hurley, and Merribaugh hurried to catch up, reaching them just before the door closed. When the three men were alone, Hurley shot his cuffs and got down to business.

"First, I want to thank you again for your, uh, *insight* into the Federal Bureau of Investigation and Internal Revenue Service. These are difficult, dangerous days to preach the word of God. It's good to know that we have a friend in our government who is watching out for us."

Skinner smiled weakly. He hoped this would be brief. "You're welcome. But you didn't hear it from me."

"Of course not. Although I'm deeply troubled that you won't be with us at the Moral Families Coalition meeting this morning." Hurley paused for just a moment, heightening the tension, before asking, "We don't have a problem, do we?"

Skinner cleared his throat. "Not really, but..."

"But?"

"You've been asking for some heavy lifts lately." Nervousness was apparent in his whispered voice.

Hurley looked at Skinner, shaking his head slightly but not enough to make his silver pompadour move. "I'm asking for no more than the Lord asks, Congressman. To His word be true, and let your faith guide you. *Not* Oscar Hurley. *Not* the Moral Families Coalition. *Not* your constituents. Your *faith*!"

Skinner tried to puff out his chest, to no great effect. "Look, I have a tough re-election campaign coming up, and the anti-gay rhetoric isn't playing well in my district. Not like it used to. But that seems to be all you and the Moral Families Coalition are talking about these days."

Hurley pretended to think about that for a few beats, and moved past the pretense.

"Leaders don't follow polls or trends, Mr. Skinner. Leaders *lead.* But if it helps any, the gay issue polls at...what were those numbers, Mr. Merribaugh?"

"Ninety to ninety-four percent."

"Ninety to ninety-four percent. That should be one hundred percent, but, in any event, the numbers don't lie."

Skinner stared at the floor. "Yes, well, that's food for thought, but I don't know that the numbers are the same in my district as they are at the Virginia Cathedral of Love."

Hurley clapped Skinner on the back. His hand stayed there, threatening to become a permanent appendage.

"Congressman, let me tell you a little story. It's about a man who came to Washington a few years back with nothing but a single cheap, rumpled suit and an old car, eating at McDonald's because that's all he could afford...and because it was the only cuisine his palate was familiar with. Now he's wearing...what is that, Burberry?" He opened Skinner's jacket and looked at the label. "Oh, *Calvin Klein*! Nice! Anyway, this man is now well-dressed, driving a big Cadillac, and eating at five-star restaurants." Hurley dropped the fabric of the suit coat and his hand patted Skinner's stomach. "Got a taste for fois gras, too, I see. And all because he has been rewarded by the Lord for doing His work on the Hill."

"Yes, well—"

"Would you like to see that go away, Congressman?"

Skinner was sweating. "Of course not, Dr. Hurley. It's just that…"

Hurley talked over him. "You have been rewarded—by God; through me, His servant—because although we reject material appearances, often we have to adopt an attractive façade to reach the masses. That's why God invented cashmere." He chuckled; Skinner didn't, and he noticed.

"When you came to Washington, Congressman…oh, you were a sad sight. *That* Donald Skinner, the man in a wrinkled seersucker suit, well…maybe that works in northern New Hampshire. But that Donald Skinner was not going to be seen on CNN. Or even Fox, no matter how sincere and God-like your political positions were. But God told *me* to make you presentable, and now you're on Fox, CNN, and I even hear rumors that you might be under consideration as a vice-presidential candidate. God's will has certainly worked out for you, Congressman Skinner. Has it not?"

"Well…yes, but…"

"'But'? I'm going to pretend I did not hear that. But if I *did* hear that…" Hurley let the pause linger in the air, which seemed to Skinner almost more threatening than whatever words might follow. "Have you practiced for your next career?"

Skinner swallowed hard. "Next career?"

"Have you practiced asking, 'Would you like fries with that?'"

Congressman Donald Skinner's face turned red. This, he thought, was over the line, although he doubted he had the courage to say that to Hurley. Still… "Are you threatening me, Dr. Hurley? Are you blackmailing me?"

He tried to sound like the CNN and Fox regular he was. He tried to sound vice-presidential.

He failed on both counts, and Hurley's unworried smile was the evidence.

"No, sir. I would never threaten you. Nor would I blackmail you. But…" He took the lapel of Skinner's Calvin Klein suit and ran it through his fingers. "The Lord giveth…and the Lord taketh away. If necessary."

"Dr. Hurley…"

"Let me put this in earthier, less God-like vernacular." Hurley leaned close to the congressman's ear, so close even Merribaugh couldn't hear him.

"Don't fuck with me, Don."

$ $ $

A half hour later, fifty-seven members of the United States Congress—senators and representatives; men and women; Republicans and Democrats; even one or two Jews with re-election constantly on their minds and a hope of maybe becoming president one day—sat in the audience as Dr. Oscar Hurley commanded the stage above them. And fifty-seven heads turned to follow as he paced the floorboards, the conclusion of his speech reaching a crescendo.

"You *cannot* claim to represent people of faith if you *do not* vote consistent with Biblical teachings. And when I use the word 'consistent,' I do not mean 'mostly.' It's like that old joke about being pregnant. You can't be just a little bit pregnant, and you can't be just a little bit Biblical. You either *are* Biblical, or you are not."

A murmur of assent rose from the assembled officials. A freshman congressman from Colorado even added an "Amen!" into the mix.

Hurley continued to roar. "Item number one—the most important thing you can do as our elected representatives—is to stop the pernicious spread of homosexuality in this society and protect our nation's moral fiber. *No* homosexual marriage! *No* homosexuals in the military! *No* special rights and protections for homosexuals!"

A four-term congresswoman from Minnesota jumped to her feet and led the applause. Hurley paused for a moment, affecting thoughtfulness, before continuing.

His voice was reassuring now; almost gentle. "If you love your children, you set rules. If those rules are violated, your children are punished. This is how we teach children right from wrong. Well, we need to apply those same rules to our society. If you love homosexuals, teach them the same way you would teach your children. Help them come out of homosexuality, don't make it easier! Don't strive for acceptance. Strive to enforce societal and Biblical standards of decency and holiness."

Another round of applause. Hurley used it as an opportunity to check his watch, and saw that he was almost out of time.

"One final thing," he said, feet now firmly planted dead center on the stage. "I know that many of you are already planning to visit us next week for the first Beyond Sin conference right here in Washington, DC. This is the first conference sponsored by Project Rectitude and the Moral

Families Coalition, and we expect to use this opportunity to bring over two hundred people *out* of homosexuality! For those of you who have already offered to take part in this event, I thank you. For the rest of you…I expect to see you there!"

And he knew they would be there. They didn't have a choice in the matter. To confirm, he found the face of Congressman Donald Skinner in the crowd, and saw Skinner nodding. Yes, he *would* be there. He belonged to Hurley, not New Hampshire.

"Thank you, God bless you, and God bless America!"

He stepped off the stage, offering only the most perfunctory of greetings to the elected officials as he made a beeline to the spot where Merribaugh stood at the side of the room. Merribaugh didn't even warrant a perfunctory greeting.

"So how'd I do?" Hurley asked.

"It was great," Merribaugh said. "They ate it up."

Hurley sighed. "That was really a rhetorical question, Dennis. *Of course* it was great, and *of course* they ate it up. I could read the phone book and they'd eat it up. They'd have to." He glanced around the room. "Skinner stayed, meaning he must have at least half a brain. But I didn't see that other problem child, Gordon Cobey. Did you?"

"No, Oscar. He definitely wasn't here."

Hurley frowned. "We should pay him a visit. I think the good senator needs some encouragement…"

$ $ $

They reached the suite assigned to Senator Gordon Cobey, Republican of Ohio, and let themselves in, not pausing long enough to give their names to the senator's assistant as they walked through the anteroom and let themselves into Cobey's private office.

The senator looked up and smiled when he saw them. He didn't seem surprised.

"I love the way you make an entrance, Dr. Hurley," Cobey said, rising in shirtsleeves from his chair and offering his hand, which Hurley took for only the briefest of moments before dropping it.

"We missed you at the breakfast this morning, Senator," said Hurley, taking a seat without being invited.

Cobey smoothed his tie. "Sorry I had to miss it. Unfortunately, I was overbooked."

"Hmm." Hurley's eyes darted around the office, taking in the array of Ohio memorabilia. "Many of your constituents are members of the Moral Families Coalition." The senator nodded. "It would be a shame if you were voted out of the senate and had to live full-time in Toledo again. Where you'd have no need for all this memorabilia, since you'd already be surrounded by, well, *Ohio*."

Cobey—a bit too aware of his smile, since he'd had his teeth bleached the week before—nevertheless offered him one. It wasn't returned.

"Now, Dr. Hurley. You know I'm with you and the Moral Families Coalition on ninety percent of your issues."

"Just ninety?"

"Isn't ninety percent considered pretty friendly?"

Hurley laughed, but it was for himself, not Cobey. "Senator, I have neighbors who are liberals. I think they're going to hell, but I'm certainly friendly with them." Cobey's smile vanished. "Before I start sounding too cryptic, let me spell things out for you. I've been getting reports back from our affiliates in Ohio that you've… Well, people tell me you've been buying into the radical gay agenda lately."

"Oh, that."

"That."

Cobey twisted his wedding ring and looked down at his desk. "I guess you could say I've been reevaluating the issue, Dr. Hurley."

Hurley looked to Merribaugh and knew they were thinking the same thing. If this conversation progressed down the path it was heading… well, it would be inexcusable.

"Senator Cobey," said Merribaugh, leaning forward slightly. "Are you trying to, uh…tell us something?"

Cobey looked up, the quizzical expression on his face quickly replaced by laughter when he realized the implication behind Merribaugh's question.

"Not me! *I'm* not gay!"

"That's a relief, because—"

"But my press secretary…well, *he* is."

This was better, but still Hurley arched an eyebrow. "Really, Senator? A homosexual is working in the office of a God-fearing Republican?"

Cobey tried his smile again. "There's a lot of that up on Capitol Hill, Dr. Hurley."

"But not everyone is Senator Gordon Cobey."

The senator shrugged, as if that were meaningless. "I've known the kid for more than a decade. He worked his way up. He's a moral man. Just, well…a moral *gay* man. And to be perfectly honest, the more I get to know about his life, the more I'm rethinking the gay issue."

Hurley took his time answering, using that time to stare down the senator. "You mean 'homosexual.' There is nothing 'gay' about homosexuality."

"Well…"

"Senator Cobey, you're either with the Moral Families Coalition or *against* the Moral Families Coalition. There is no room for a pro-gay ninety-percenter."

Merribaugh jumped in, trying to play his usual role as the diplomat to Hurley's autocrat. Their good cleric/bad cleric routine usually worked, but there were times when Hurley went too far. This was shaping up to be one of those times.

"Senator, we know you've done a lot for people of faith over the years, and we appreciate that. It'd be a shame to have this become a…a *black mark* on an otherwise admirable record." He paused, then continued in an effort to seal the deal. "Perhaps your press secretary should attend our Beyond Sin conference next week. Over two hundred men and women struggling to overcome the sin of homosexuality through Project Rectitude. If you can convince him to join us, I can guarantee we'll straighten out his life." Merribaugh chuckled. "Pardon the pun."

Cobey didn't join in appreciation for the pun, intended or not. "This gay conversion thing…It troubles me."

Merribaugh folded his hands in his lap and smiled confidently. "This program works, Senator. It will change your aide's life. If you really care about him, you should help deliver him to righteousness."

"Think about it very seriously," added Hurley, with no smile at all. Merribaugh took an envelope from his breast pocket and set it on Cobey's desk as Hurley continued. "Dennis has given you an opportunity—a final, one-time opportunity—to save a soul…and very possibly yourself."

Cobey looked at the envelope. "What's this?"

"Do the right thing, Senator," said Hurley as he rose from the chair.

When they were gone, Cobey looked at the unopened envelope for several long minutes. Then he picked up his phone and dialed a few digits. "Dan, please step into my office for a moment."

Less than a minute later, Dan Rowell—his press secretary—was standing in front of him. Before he had a chance to speak, Cobey said, "I'm afraid I have to ask you to do something very difficult. For me. And for America."

$ $ $

An hour later, Hurley sat with Merribaugh in the backseat of a Lincoln Town Car as it sped down the George Washington Memorial Parkway along the Potomac River, en route to Nash Bog.

"Do you think Cobey and Skinner are with us?" asked Merribaugh.

"Cobey, I'm not so sure of. We might require the Ohio affiliates to turn up the heat. Maybe Indiana and Michigan, too. I don't see that Skinner has a choice but to play ball, though. For one thing, I think it's considered bad form for a sitting congressman to discuss ongoing FBI and IRS investigations he's come across in the course of official business."

"Especially with the subjects of the investigation."

Hurley nodded his head toward the driver. Both men fell into several minutes of silence, looking out the window as they raced along the road hugging the Potomac.

Finally, though, Hurley leaned back and stretched. "It might not be a bad idea to make sure some things are taken care of, though. Just in case. If Don Skinner knows what he's talking about—and he's *certainly* in the position to know—we should be prepared."

"Agreed," said Merribaugh. "I'm on top of it."

That was the wrong thing to say. Oscar Hurley had been biding his time waiting for Dennis Merribaugh to get his act together, but perhaps it was time to have a little talk, because that act was *not* coming together no matter how much Merribaugh claimed to be on top of things.

So Hurley swiveled in his seat and said, "Speaking of taking care of things and being on top of things and the rest of the drivel that's been coming out of your mouth lately, let me ask you a few questions."

Merribaugh knew he was in trouble, but there was no way to escape the Town Car so he also knew he had no choice but to mumble his agreement.

"Is the repair work to the Great Cross *ever* going to be finished?"

"Two weeks. Maybe three, at the outside."

Hurley shook his head. "This is taking longer than it took to build it in the first place. Get it done. And speaking of maintenance, what the hell has been going on with the groundskeepers? I was out inspecting the work on the cross the other day and noticed that the landscaping is overgrown. It looks shabby, and that's not the image we want to give our congregation."

"I'll have that taken care of."

Hurley leaned back in his seat and stretched again. "I just don't understand why *I* need to be the person who sees these things. They should be taken care of *before* I see them. When the repair work is finished—when*ever* that might be—those walkways are supposed to be beautiful paths offering visitors an opportunity to contemplate and reflect as they approach the Great Cross. Right now it looks like...like... *nature*! Nature untamed by man!"

Merribaugh was sweating. "I promise I'll take care of it the minute we're back at the cathedral. I'll trim them myself if I have to."

He needn't have bothered. His words didn't register with Hurley, who was on to his next topic.

"Now, about that bookkeeping position..."

Finally Merribaugh had an opportunity to stop sweating. "I have very good news on that front, Oscar. We have a new member of the church who was an office manager in New York, and wants to help us in any way she can. I think she'd be perfect to take care of the books while we search for a permanent replacement for Leonard Platt."

Hurley rolled his eyes. "No offense, Dennis—or maybe just a little offense—but I think I should meet this woman before you hand over the keys to the office."

Merribaugh took *more* than a little offense but knew who was boss. "Of course, Oscar. I'll arrange that as soon as possible."

"Do that."

Dennis Merribaugh felt himself relax. He had managed to end the interrogation on a high note. Or so he thought, until Hurley finally added, "Now let's talk about Beyond Sin."

Merribaugh tensed up. "Things are going, well...They're coming along."

Hurley sighed. "Coming along? What does that mean?"

"The program is booked and confirmed, and—"

"How many homosexuals and former homosexuals have registered? Because it's fine and dandy that you've booked your speakers and printed your programs, but unless you have a decent turnout of homosexuals—and those homosexuals are convinced to become *ex*-homosexuals—it's all worthless."

"Applications continue to—"

Hurley stopped him. His voice was clipped and controlled. "How many people have enrolled, Dennis?"

That number was now twenty-two, so Merribaugh said, "Forty-four." It still wasn't a good number, but it was twice as good as twenty-two.

"Forty-four?" Hurley closed his eyes. "Meaning this is shaping up to be a public relations debacle *and* a financial debacle."

"But people always take their time registering for a life-changing…"

Hurley was having none of that. "*Jesus fucking Christ*, Dennis! Your little ex-homosexual experiment is shaping up to be a huge black mark on my ministry!"

Since there was nothing to say, Merribaugh wisely said nothing. Minutes later—minutes during which Dr. Oscar Hurley kept his eyes closed, deep in thought—Hurley finally opened his eyes and broke the icy quiet in the backseat of the Town Car.

"All right, it looks like—*once again*—I'll have to fix one of your fuck-ups. I'll pump up the publicity for Beyond Sin from the pulpit, and talk about it on this week's TV and radio broadcasts. Maybe we can keep this from becoming a complete train wreck."

"Thank you, Oscar." It was, really, the only thing Merribaugh could say.

Hurley looked out the window in the opposite direction of Merribaugh. "But after this is over, I think we'll be pulling the plug on Project Rectitude." He shook his head. "You and your homos…"

12

The Town Car deposited Dennis Merribaugh at the cathedral before continuing the quarter mile to Cathedral House with Dr. Oscar Hurley as its lone passenger. Once again breathing fresh air—and away from his boss's criticisms—Merribaugh's head felt a bit clearer.

In fact, Hurley wasn't wrong. Things had been getting shoddy. There was too much on Dennis Merribaugh's plate these days, and everything was suffering as a result.

But now, standing in a gentle breeze outside the cathedral, he could see things with a bit more perspective and optimism. Soon the conference would be behind him. Soon the Great Cross would be repaired. Soon he'd hire a new bookkeeper.

Soon things would be back to normal.

Because he was standing in front of it, he walked up the handicapped ramp and into the cathedral's entry hall, a grand atrium stretching the width of the building. His heels sounded on the marble floor until they were cushioned by one of the three large royal blue carpets placed strategically in the hall. At one end of the hall, the carpet depicted the story of Adam and Eve. The center carpet, a bit larger than the others, depicted the Crucifixion. The third carpet, at the other end of the hall, set out the Ten Commandments.

Merribaugh respectfully walked around the image of Christ's suffering as he crossed the center carpet and entered the sanctuary. An associate pastor was delivering a sermon to a few hundred parishioners, and Merribaugh shook his head when he saw he was using the projection screen. That was a waste of resources for a weekday service—at least for a weekday service when Dr. Hurley wasn't preaching—and he'd have to remember to admonish the associate pastor later for his lack of humility.

He passed unseen through the rear of the vast room and exited through a side door into an institutional hallway that shared a wall with the new auditorium. From the other side of that wall, he heard voices rehearsing a number from *The Sound of Music.*

Merribaugh continued through the building until he finally reached the rear doors and let himself out to the loading dock, where he found the groundskeepers and a few day laborers hard at work.

Unfortunately, they were hard at work playing cards, not landscaping or repairing the Great Cross.

"Ahem," he said, and repeated it in a louder voice until he attracted their attention.

The head groundskeeper folded his cards on the table and nervously said, "We're on a break, sir."

"Break's over," said Merribaugh, his arms folded sternly in front of him. "Back to work or consider your break to be permanent."

When they were gone from the loading dock, he continued his walk for a short distance until he reached the base of the Great Cross. He looked up to the top of the scaffolding, hoping to note progress. He was not satisfied with what he saw.

"Mr. Merribaugh!"

He turned and saw that new member of the congregation, Constance Brown, approach down one of the walkways leading to the cross.

"Sister Constance," he said in return, trying to muster enthusiasm. "It's so nice to see you back at the cathedral again."

"Yes, well…I don't want to waste any time."

He hiked an eyebrow. "Waste time…*how*?"

"In getting to know the Lord better, of course."

Merribaugh chuckled. "Oh, yes. Of course."

Her eyes traveled up the scaffolding. "Looks like you got yourself a big project there."

"Bigger than it should be." He smiled sadly at her. "Come walk with me."

"If you don't mind me saying so," Constance said as they walked, "you look troubled."

He felt himself about to sigh, but held it back. "God gives us no burden too big to handle, Sister Constance."

Her agreement came through in a "Praise the Lord."

They circled through a parking lot and around the auditorium, heading in the general direction of the front steps of the cathedral. Now the voices and music were louder, streaming through the open skylight, and the air was filled with a slightly off-key version of "Climb Every Mountain."

"What's with *The Sound of Music*?" she asked.

He stopped and gestured at the auditorium. "This building was recently completed as part of a recent five-million-dollar expansion, and *The Sound of Music* will be the inaugural performance. Only two weeks from now." A particularly sharp note pierced the air. "Two *long* weeks from now." He turned to her. "I don't suppose you sing..."

"I'm afraid not."

"That's a pity. We desperately need sopranos. And a new Rolf wouldn't hurt, either." He shook the thoughts away; there was no sense dwelling on the negatives. "But I'm sure this show—and the shows to follow—will be a welcome addition to our ministry. By giving the public a version of *The Sound of Music* with a new Christian orientation, we'll be much better able to meet the spiritual needs of our flock."

She thought about that. "I thought *The Sound of Music was* Christian. Aren't there a bunch of nuns in it?"

Merribaugh rolled his eyes. "The characters were Roman Catholic, if that's what you mean."

"But—"

"Here at the Virginia Cathedral of Love, we respect our Catholic friends. But Catholicism isn't *real* Christianity."

"It's not?"

He shook his head, as if wondering why he had to explain this. "Catholicism is a sect that split off from Christianity. With its Pope, and worship of Mary...it's not real Christianity."

Constance nodded, as if every word out of his mouth was, well, *gospel*.

"That's why we had to rewrite *The Sound of Music*. In our version, Maria and the von Trapps are Baptists."

"And the nuns?"

"Not nuns. Good Christian women, but not nuns."

"And the Nazis...?"

"Still Nazis."

Merribaugh began walking again. She moved quickly to catch up and said, "I didn't know you were allowed to do things like change around the plot of a well-known musical."

He thought about that. "I don't know the rules. But our musical director—*there's* a character—our musical director once had some success doing something similar on Broadway, so I suppose it's all right."

"You got someone from Broadway to come to Virginia for this?"

Merribaugh smiled. "He was a fallen man. The Virginia Cathedral of Love and its affiliates have brought him redemption." Noting the blank look on her face, he decided to explain. It wasn't as if they had any secrets. "Walter Pomeroy is his name. A few years ago he turned *Annie*, the beloved family musical, into a piece of homosexual propaganda filth called *Andy*, and inexplicably won a Tony Award."

"I've heard of that." She didn't bother adding that she'd not only heard of *Andy*, but she and her girlfriend had seen it three times.

Merribaugh continued walking; Constance kept pace.

"But Walter Pomeroy wasn't a happy man. He had a degree of success, but no happiness. His life wasn't fulfilling…until the day he happened upon Dr. Hurley's television show. One thing led to another, and soon, through Project Rectitude…"

"What's that?"

"Ah!" He stopped again and smiled with pride. "Project Rectitude is the Cathedral's ministry dedicated to bringing people out of the homosexual lifestyle. Walter Pomeroy is one of that ministry's most prominent graduates!"

She could now hear "My Favorite Things" coming from the auditorium, which seemed to be particularly inappropriate background music to Merribaugh's chatter about his ex-gay programming.

"In fact," the clergyman continued, "Project Rectitude will be hosting a conference soon: Beyond Sin. I expect it will be a defining moment for the ministry." He turned and looked at her. "Tell me, Sister Constance…"

"Yes?"

"Do you know any homosexuals?"

In her head, to the tune of "My Favorite Things," a voice sang, *Lambert and Lisa, and me and my girlfriend…*damn song.

"I don't think so," she said, trying to think over the earworm. "But I'll keep my eyes open."

Merribaugh smiled benevolently. "I'd appreciate that. Every soul we save is a step forward for Project Rectitude." He leaned a bit closer. "And I don't forget who my friends are, Sister Constance."

She smiled back. "I'll bet you don't, Mr. Merribaugh. I'll bet you don't."

$ $ $

After Farraday had collected her and returned home, they gathered around the kitchen table for the daily debriefing.

"So tell me how it went," said Grant.

"Lambert, you need to get yourself a gay."

Grant smiled. "That's a strange thing to say in a house full of gays…"

"Hey!"

"And Farraday."

"Nah, none of *us*," she said. "Anyway, half of us have already been to the church. But if I could bring them someone they could try to make straight, I'd be golden with Merribaugh!"

Grant didn't like the idea. Every extra person meant a bigger payroll, as well as the potential for some loose links in the chain. Bad enough he was paying for seven people, a house, a rental car, a lawn service, and a toaster. "I don't know. There's gotta be someone we can recruit. Maybe someone in DC…"

"I may know some people," said Leonard.

"That's not a good idea," said Chase, as diplomatically as possible. "How would we know we could trust a stranger?"

"Well, *I'd* know them," said Leonard.

"But we wouldn't," said Grant. "And we outnumber you six to one. So that's a no." He looked to Chase. "Do we even *know* anyone we can trust?"

"What about Marika Christian?"

"No. Great on the phone scam, not so much on the inside job. Plus, it'd only complicate things having a straight girl play lesbian."

"That Green guy we worked with that one time?"

"Who?"

"You remember. Green. That one that was into horror movies."

"Oh, him. No."

"Jamie Brock?"

Grant sighed. "Do we really have to go through this again?"

"So Jamie is a no?"

Grant answered with a very unpleasant glare, and Chase took a step back.

They sat for a while, clicking through their mental Rolodexes, but every time someone had a thought, someone else had a second thought. That was the tough thing about trying to find an honest criminal.

It was Chase who finally broke the silence.

"What about Jared Parsells?"

Grant dismissed the suggestion. "We're looking for someone to play *ex*-gay, not *extra*-gay."

That got Constance's attention. "The gayer the better with this crowd. They do *not* do subtle."

Chase picked up on that. "In that case, we *should* bring in Jared. He's sort of the opposite of subtle."

Grant was unhappy. "We don't need him. We'll figure something else out."

Chase offered him a half smile. "Still jealous?"

"I'm not jealous." Which might have been more convincing if he hadn't said it a bit too quickly. "Just because you're into men with the brains and body of a nine-year-old girl, why would I be jealous?"

"Lambert, you sound jealous," said Constance.

"He doesn't like him because Jared has a little thing for me," said Chase.

"I'd say it was mutual," said Grant. "Inexplicable, but mutual."

"Also," Chase continued, "Jared is afraid of Grant."

"On that, we agree. In fact, that's Jared's only redeeming feature."

"I don't know," said Constance. "You know him; I don't. But from what Chase is saying, this Jared character sounds perfect. If I can bring them a stereotype, I'll have Merribaugh in my pocket. And then I'll be in that office, keys and all."

Grant fixed his eyes on Chase. "Okay, fine. You think Jared can do it, call him. But he's not getting more than ten grand. And it comes out of your share."

"Fine," said Chase as he pulled his phone out of a pocket and dialed.

$ $ $

Jared Parsells looked at himself in the bathroom mirror and smiled. Then he tried out a different smile, one showing slightly more teeth. He didn't like the second version; his dimples looked better in the first.

The third smile—head bowed slightly down, eyes looking slightly up—also showed off his dimples to great effect, though, so maybe *that* was the best one. Although the third smile might be too seductive, while the first was more playful.

It was hard to make a decision, but he supposed he could always use whichever he needed at the time. Although maybe a fourth variation would do the trick…

So engrossed was he in watching himself smile that he almost didn't hear Lady Gaga start singing in the living room, but the ringtone eventually attracted his attention and he managed to answer before Chase's call went to voicemail.

"Hey," he said, having already seen Chase's name appear in Caller ID. "Are you in the neighborhood?"

"Hardly," said Chase. "I'm in Virginia."

"Virginia?" Jared dropped his slender frame onto the couch. "What are you doing there?"

"I'm on a job. Which is why I'm calling…"

Jared flashed Smile Number Three, even though Chase couldn't see it. It was all about the attitude. "I thought maybe you were calling because you missed me."

"That, too. But if you're interested in making a few bucks, I'll see you soon enough."

"Where's the job?"

"Here in Virginia."

That didn't even warrant Smile Number Two. "Sorry, but I don't go anywhere with 'virgin' in the name."

That statement caught Chase off guard. Mainly because he was shocked Jared knew how to spell Virginia. "Not even for ten thousand dollars?"

"Oh." He thought that might be worth a smile, but wasn't sure. "What would I have to do?"

At least Chase wouldn't have to lie. "Just be yourself."

Jared thought of all the things ten grand could buy. Maybe he'd even use some of it to pay off a little back rent on his studio. But probably not, because his wardrobe was looking very 2010.

And it wasn't as if he had anything better to do. Plus, Chase was there, although if Chase was there, that probably meant…

"Is your boyfriend there, too?"

Chase paused, hoping it wouldn't be a deal-breaker. "Yes, he is."

"I don't know…"

"Ten thousand dollars, Jared."

The young man sighed and rubbed a hand over his flat stomach. It was a lot of money, but…

"Jared?" Chase dropped his voice, his verbal equivalent of

Smile Number Three. "It'd be good to see you again. Down here. In Virginia…"

The voice did the trick. Jared had Smile Number Three on his face as he said, "Okay, I'll go. When?"

Just for good measure, Chase continued in that low purr. "Can you come down tomorrow?" When Jared said he could, Chase gave him all the information he'd need to get to Union Station in DC, hopefully without getting lost.

$ $ $

Chase clicked off the phone and smiled. Across the kitchen table, Grant scowled at him.

"What was with the Barry White routine?" he asked.

He shrugged. "It worked, didn't it?"

"Remember, that ten thou comes out of your share."

The front door opened and Lisa and Mary Beth, each carrying four or five shopping bags although every bag was Mary Beth's, walked into the house.

Grant glanced at his watch. "You've been gone long enough."

Lisa shook her head in the direction of her partner. "It took us a while to find a store with a name that didn't end in 'mart.'"

"You're lucky I finally found a Macy's," said Mary Beth, dropping her bags in the middle of the kitchen. "Now can we *please* finish this job and get the hell back to New York? I miss Barneys and Bloomingdale's."

"Almost," said Chase. "We just added one more person to the team. He'll be here tomorrow."

Mary Beth snorted. "Typical. Once again, you people have overmanned a job."

"Yeah, what was I thinking?" said Grant. "You're man enough for all of us."

That didn't faze her. "Maybe when your testicles drop you'll be able to handle it, too."

"Bitch."

"What?!"

"You heard me."

And then Chase was between them. "Okay, fun's over. Everyone keep cool so we can work together, which is the only way we'll walk away with seven million dollars."

The reminder of a bigger objective quieted them down.

"Okay," Mary Beth said cautiously. "So this new person…Anyone I know?"

"Oooooh yeah," said Grant.

Mary Beth didn't like the look in his eyes. It told her he was about to get great enjoyment at her expense. "Who?"

"Jared Parsells."

"*That* fuckin' twink? Why?!"

"We need gay," Chase explained. "And no one's gayer than Jared."

"I am *not* happy with this."

Grant said, "That makes this the *second* best part of this plan…"

She scowled. "I am *always* intrigued to hear what you consider the best part of one of your plans."

"The best part is that Jared really isn't part of it. He just has to be the gay bait."

Mary Beth considered that. "Yeah, that's not a stretch for him. That's just Jared being Jared. Even *he* can do that."

13

The next morning—after making huevos rancheros for breakfast and a few dozen deviled eggs for the barbecue—Farraday borrowed Lisa's keys and set off for Union Station to retrieve Jared, leaving the rest of the gang a few hours to figure out how to avoid the neighborhood get-together.

Mary Beth had already figured it out.

"I'm not going," she announced flatly, to no one's surprise. "I hate this place, and I hate these people."

Grant tried to stare her down, but his heart wasn't in it. "I sorta wish there was a way out of this. But it sounds like we'll stand out if we don't go."

"I'm fine with that."

"You would be." With a sigh, he added, "Anyway, if we don't go, we gotta eat all those deviled eggs ourselves."

So promptly at noon, the crew—minus Mary Beth—exited 455 Old Stone Fence Post Road with faces that looked like they were going to the electric chair, not a barbecue. Across the street at 462, a small group had already gathered around a grill in Tish and Malcolm's driveway.

"Grant!" Tish called, spotting them. "Lisa! Come meet the neighbors!"

She introduced them. Each neighbor was a variation on low-key, with only Tish and—to a lesser extent—Malcolm serving as the life of the party. Which, to Grant and his confederates, only underscored how much they didn't belong there.

But they *were* there, and determined to make the best of it…until their earliest opportunity to get out.

Lisa hoisted the platter in her arms at Tish. "Deviled egg?"

Tish wrinkled her nose. "Uh…"

"Try one. They're delicious."

"Uh…"

"Farraday made them."

Ms. Jarvis from 488 reached for the plate. "May I?" Before Lisa could answer she had a deviled egg in her mouth. She chewed. She swallowed. And then she said, "Oh my God, these are so *good*!"

With Ms. Jarvis's seal of approval, other neighbors gathered around the platter. Tish stood unhappily to the side.

"You should have a deviled egg," said Constance, approaching her. "They're really good."

"I'll take that under advisement." Tish had been dismissive, but then eyed Constance with more interest. "And shouldn't *you* be the one serving them?"

"Me?"

"Well, yes! You *are* the housekeeper, after all."

Oh, you did not just go there. It took all of Constance's willpower to keep those words in her head and off her tongue.

Malcolm, who was wearing plastic baggies under over mitts as he worked the grill, announced, "The Black Angus steakburgers are ready. Who wants one?"

"That like a regular burger?" asked Grant. Malcolm nodded. "In that case, I'll take one. All of Farraday's recipes from Mongolia or wherever ain't been sitting right in my stomach the last couple'a days."

But no one else paid attention to Malcolm. They were still devouring the deviled eggs.

"These are divine," said Mr. Scribner, from 420. "How did you make them?"

Lisa shrugged. "I can't take credit. Our chauff—I mean, our *chef* made them."

Ms. Jarvis raised an eyebrow. "You have a chef?"

Lisa did her best to keep a straight face. "Doesn't everyone?"

Loud male voices rose from the yard between the Fieldings' and the neighboring house, attracting the attention of most of the neighbors in the driveway. Tish frowned. She thought she knew those voices.

Sure enough, those black sheep of the subdivision—Mr. Ford and Mr. Herren, who left clutter on their lawns and liquor bottles in the recycling bins, no matter how many times she'd admonished them—soon emerged between the houses. Tish didn't know which violation of community standards was the worst: that they had cut through private property; that they were carrying beer bottles while they did so; or that she'd made a point of not inviting them in the first place.

"Hey, great! They've got deviled eggs," said Mr. Ford, grabbing for the platter.

As discreetly as possible, Tish said, "I wasn't expecting you."

"Herren and I figured we'd pop over. It's always fun times with you and Malc." He waved at her husband. "Hey, Fielding! How're they hanging?"

Malcolm smiled weakly and waved his oven mitt.

Grant watched as Farraday pulled the rental car into the driveway across the street. He turned to Chase and said, "Just what this party needs. Farraday and Jared."

"Could be worse," said Chase. "Mary Beth could be here."

"What the hell is Jared wearing?"

Chase focused. "That shirt is kind of sheer."

"So are the shorts. He looks almost naked. Get over there and tell him to change his clothes."

Chase didn't respond, so Grant shook his shoulder.

"Stop looking at *him* and start listening to *me*. Tell him to put on something respectable. This ain't Chelsea or Hell's Kitchen."

"Okay," Chase said. He was about to leave when Grant stopped him.

"One other thing. You know how we're calling you Charlie?" Chase nodded unhappily. "I want you to tell Jared he's gonna go by his real name while he's working this job."

"He's not gonna like that."

"I don't care."

Grant had more than a few reasons not to particularly like Jared Parsells—including his crush on Chase, and Chase's crush on him—but one of his pet peeves was Jared Parsells's name, since it was really Jerry Stanley. He hadn't changed it for a scam; he'd changed it because he thought it sounded sexier. That bugged Grant a lot.

Farraday and Jared walked into the house, and Chase darted across the street to catch up.

"Did I just see what I thought I saw?" Constance asked Grant. "Did a naked boy just get out of the car and go into our house?"

Grant sighed. "Meet your new partner."

On the other side of the driveway, Malcolm was reluctantly serving up Black Angus steakburgers to Mr. Ford and Mr. Herren. He knew Tish wouldn't approve of feeding crashers, but he was trying to be polite. Not to mention that no one was eating from the grill because they were gorging themselves on deviled eggs.

Mr. Herren waved his beer bottle in Malcolm's face. "Want a brewski, Fielding?"

Malcolm wouldn't meet his eyes. "No thank you. I'll have some wine. Later."

Mr. Ford grabbed the ketchup bottle and shook. A dollop of redness landed on the burger, and another dollop landed on the driveway.

"Oh! My! God!"

There was immediate silence.

"Oh my God!" Tish said again, although this time in a slightly less ear-piercing tone.

Lisa looked at her. "What's wrong?"

Tish's voice was strained. "He...he...he..." She pointed at Mr. Ford. "This *beast* just poured ketchup on our driveway!"

Mr. Ford looked at the red blotch on the black asphalt. "This?"

"Malcolm, get the hose! And you two"—now her finger moved between Mr. Ford and Mr. Herren—"I want you out of here!"

"Hey, Tish, it was just ketchup..."

"That's exactly the kind of attitude we don't want in Old Stone Fence Post Estates!"

"That is one high-strung lady," Constance said quietly to Lisa. "I'm getting over to the cathedral before she goes postal on the entire neighborhood."

$ $ $

"...then add a pinch and a half of paprika and you're done," Farraday told the neighbors gathered around him. He took a sip from the large tumbler of scotch in his hand. "But remember: a pinch *and a half*. It's all about that last half pinch. Other than that, it's really easy."

"And *so* good," Ms. Jarvis said again.

A few yards away from Farraday's impromptu cooking class, Jared, now in non-see-through clothing, stood brooding.

"You'll get used to it," said Grant. "It *is* your real name, after all."

"*Was* my real name. If I wanted it to still be my name...it'd still be my name."

Tish, now somewhat calmer than she'd been during the ketchup incident, approached and gave Jared the once-over. "And who do we have here?"

"This is Jerry," Grant said, before Jared had a chance to screw things up.

Tish was ever-mindful of the HOA's rules. "And how is Jerry related?"

Grant was ever-mindful that Tish was ever-mindful. "He's my, uh…"

"Son," said Jared, a small bit of triumph in his voice. Grant curled his lip.

"Son?" She studied their faces, looking for a resemblance and finding none.

"Jerry was adopted," said Grant. "From an orphanage. Where he was placed because no one wanted him."

Jared looked stricken and put a hand to his chest. "I was? How come you and Mom never told me?"

Tish backed away, and then quickly disappeared into the thinning crowd.

"Don't ever do that to me again," said Grant. "On top of everything else, I'm too young to be your father."

"Actually," Jared said, "you're older than my father."

"Shuddup." They watched as Farraday passed, leading a half dozen neighbors—including Ms. Jarvis and Mr. Scribner—in the direction of 455. "Where are you going?"

"They want me to show 'em how I braise my short ribs."

Grant shook his head. These suburbs were going to kill him yet.

$ $ $

The day he abruptly left his pulpit in Newark, Delaware, could have ended the religious calling of Dennis Merribaugh—some might say it *should* have ended that calling—but Merribaugh and the church deacons had a gentlemen's agreement that the past was the past, and as long as he went away it would stay buried. It was, perhaps, the best solution to a very awkward situation.

That he had ended up with a better position at the Virginia Cathedral of Love was indeed proof of God's benevolence. It made Merribaugh believe all the more in the power of redemption, and he was determined to spread that word. In a sense, that was what Project Rectitude was all about.

It was also what drew him to Sister Constance. Although tight-lipped about her past, he could sense her presence at the Cathedral was an effort to atone for sins. He would help her find redemption, and he knew just how to do that.

He summoned her to his fourth-floor office in Cathedral House, sat her down, and said, "Sister Constance, I continue to be impressed by your commitment to the Virginia Cathedral of Love."

"I feel I've found a home, Rev. Merribaugh. Praise the Lord!"

He thought maybe he should tell her that not every sentence had to end with "praise the Lord," but if it made her happy…

"And I have news, Mr. Merribaugh!" She didn't wait for his reaction. "I've found a sinner for your ex-gay ministry!"

He dropped his elbows to the desk and leaned forward. "You have?"

"I have indeed."

Merribaugh smiled. With Hurley's extended push, the number of registrations for Beyond Sin had topped one hundred twenty. Sister Constance had just helped him climb a bit closer to the goal, which was especially timely given the imminence of the conference.

"Delightful!" He was genuinely happy. "Just delightful! And what's this person's name?"

She looked at him, her sly smile covering for the fact that she couldn't remember.

"This is an extra-special offering to the church," she said finally. "I'll bring him around tomorrow, so you can meet him personally."

He gave her a broad wink. "You know how to tease a man. All right, I can be patient. But I can't wait to meet your extra-special homosexual!"

"I can't wait for you to meet him, either!"

Flush with the good news, Merribaugh almost forgot why he'd summoned her. A glance at his datebook refreshed his memory.

"I wondered if you had the next half hour free."

"Yes, I do. Why?"

Merribaugh smiled. "There's someone I want you to meet."

Minutes later she was following him to the elevator, which descended two floors. And then they were standing on the landing outside Dr. Oscar Hurley's office. Merribaugh rapped on the door, and Hurley's distinctive voice said, "Come in."

Merribaugh, ever the gentleman, held the door open, allowing her to enter first. She clutched both hands to her chest as she walked inside.

"It's like I died and went to heaven," she said. "You are Dr. Oscar Hurley himself!"

He smiled at her from his side of the Desk of Christ. It was a common reaction from congregants when they crossed the threshold for the first time.

"I am indeed. Please have a seat." Behind them, Merribaugh closed the door.

"Praise the Lord," said Constance, sitting on one of those plush couches as her eyes scanned the décor and her head affixed price tags to various items. "Praise the Lord indeed!"

Hurley gave Merribaugh a look that asked, *What's with all the Lord-praising?* to which Merribaugh could only shrug, *I don't know*.

"This is a thrill for me," she said. "I only hope my mama and papa are looking down from heaven and watching." Her real mother and father were retired and living in Atlanta, but this version sounded so much better.

Because he had good news and because he wanted to stop her babbling, Merribaugh leaned forward. "Sister Constance has also brought us a homosexual who wants to be delivered from sin."

"Really." Hurley smiled at Constance. "That's wonderful work, Sister Constance."

"*Oh!* You know my name! Praise the Lord!"

Hurley's smile vanished and he rubbed a temple that had started to throb. "Yes. Praise the Lord. Anyway, Mr. Merribaugh tells me you have office management experience."

"Yes, sir. I ran offices for over twenty years when I lived in New York. Did the books, managed inventory, all that."

"We might have a position for you here at the Cathedral." She put her hands to her mouth and gasped. "Now, I can't promise this will be permanent…"

"Praise—!"

He held out a hand and stopped her. "Yes, yes, we know."

"Perhaps I should take Sister Constance to the finance office," said Merribaugh.

Hurley drummed his fingers on the Desk of Christ. "Yes, that's an excellent idea, Mr. Merribaugh."

Constance tried to force a tear, but that wasn't one of her better skills. So she was dry-eyed when she said, "Dr. Hurley, thank you so much for this opportunity to serve the Virginia Cathedral of Love. You've made my dream come true."

Merribaugh and Constance took the elevator back up to the fourth floor, where he unlocked the door and gestured for her to precede him into the finance office. It was surprisingly small and stuffy, and cluttered with the detritus of a dozen years of use. She spotted the security camera right away. It was exactly where Leonard said it would be.

"Please make yourself at home," he said as he fished through a pocket, finally extracting a key on a small fob. "After all, this is now your office."

"Mind if I open a window?"

"Not at all."

With some effort Constance lifted the lower pane, and fresh air began to fill the room. In the distance, she could hear the chorus rehearsing "Do Re Mi" in the auditorium.

The view—who could see in was more important than what one saw looking out—could work to their advantage. The finance office didn't face the front of Cathedral House, which would have exposed it to the cathedral and most of the campus. Like Hurley's office, the view faced the rolling hills to the rear of the complex.

Next she looked below the window, hoping to see a fire escape, but there was only a twenty-foot drop to a terrace. Given the layout of the building, she figured the terrace led to Hurley's office, meaning it probably wouldn't be the route they'd want to use if they had to steal the safe.

When Constance turned around, Merribaugh was unlocking the closet door with that key on the fob. The door opened and she saw the closet was empty except for the safe.

"What's that?" she asked.

"Just a safe we use to temporarily safeguard donations to the church. Nothing you'll need to be concerned about." With that, he bent down and opened the safe. Mindful of the camera, she tried to subtly look over his shoulder, and caught a glimpse of cash. Merribaugh stuffed some in a pocket before he closed the safe, and then closed the closet door and locked it.

Minutes later he departed, with his own "Praise the Lord" followed by an invitation to e-mail if she needed supplies.

Constance smiled. She'd gotten inside and Leonard's information was proving one hundred percent accurate, neither of which had seemed a sure thing just a few days ago. This job was well ahead of schedule.

If there was a downside, it was that she now had "Do Re Mi" stuck in her head. She closed the window and sat behind her new desk…a desk she wouldn't be spending more than a day or two at, the way things were shaping up.

"Praise the Lord, indeed," she said and laughed quietly to herself.

14

I'm the gay bait? Is that what you said?"

Jared wasn't sure how he felt about that. Yes, he'd been warned in advance that his only role in the job was to be himself, and he'd be paid handsomely to be himself. But when Mary Beth had said he'd be the "gay bait," it almost felt as if he was being insulted.

"Don't listen to her," said Chase. "We wanted you on the job because we needed someone young and attractive and thought, who better than Jared?"

That mostly mollified Jared, so Chase turned to Mary Beth. "We really don't need dissension in the ranks, so can we try to work as a team?"

She shrugged. "I speak the truth. Just because you have a problem with that..."

Jared picked up on that. "Oh yeah? Well, your boobs are too big. How do you like *that* for truth-telling?"

Mary Beth looked at him with distaste. "You don't really have a firm grasp on how insults work, do you?"

They had been sitting at the bar in the corner of the finished basement, on the opposite side from the pool table, and looked up when they heard heavy footsteps descend the stairs.

"What's all the racket down here?" asked Grant, who perched on a step. They could only see him below the waist.

"Nothing," they replied in unison.

"Well, keep it down." With that, the lower part of his body disappeared back up the stairs.

"I'm still not sure I follow," said Jared to Chase, in a decidedly quieter tone of voice. "If you need someone gay and good-looking, why didn't *you* do it?"

"Oh, brother," said Mary Beth, tossing her magazine aside and following Grant's pant legs upstairs.

Chase smiled and rumpled Jared's hair. The product made his hand sticky. "Thanks. But I'm needed on the inside. It's gonna be an easy job, though, Jared. And you'll be perfect for it."

"So tell me again what I have to do?"

"Tomorrow Constance will take you to church and introduce you around. All you have to do is pretend you don't want to be gay anymore." Jared made a face. "Just for a few days. Next weekend, you'll have to go to a hotel in Washington, DC, for a few more days, then you'll collect your ten grand and go back to New York. It'll almost be a vacation!"

Jared still had doubts. "Except I'll have to pretend I hate being gay."

"Well, yeah, there's that…"

He sighed. "Tell me what the deal is with Washington? Why am I going there?"

It was Chase's turn to sigh. Depending on Jared's attitude, this could be easy or very difficult. "It's an ex-gay conference. A whole bunch of gay men and maybe some lesbians who don't wanna be gay."

Jared shook his head. "That sounds ridiculous." He thought about the concept. "They must be ugly or something."

"It *is* ridiculous." Chase shrugged. "But that's what you're gonna be doing. At least you'll have a nice hotel room."

Jared put a hand on Chase's forearm. "Will you be at the hotel, too?"

"Uh…" He moved the hand away. "No. I'll have to be here."

Jared folded his arms and pushed out his lower lip. "I don't want to go to the conference."

But Chase knew the right words to convince him it was a great idea. And those words were not even "ten thousand dollars."

$ $ $

Later, over dinner, Jared was enthusiastic about the conference, although maybe for the wrong reason. "Chase says an ex-gay conference is the perfect place to find sex! And if the guys aren't hot, they won't be telling people and ruining my reputation."

Grant shook his head at Chase before turning his attention back to Jared. "You *worry* about your reputation? Go figure."

Constance ran her fork through a spear of broccoli. "Farraday, this hollandaise sauce is fantastic."

He frowned. "You don't think it's too lemony?"

"It's perfect."

He shrugged. "I think it's too lemony."

Through a mouth full of broccoli, she said, "Nuh-uh." Then she swallowed. "I wouldn't worry about it, Jared. The way things are going, you probably won't even have to go to that ex-gay thing. If we can figure out how to get around those cameras in the next couple of days, we can clear out of Nash Bog. No more cathedrals, no more meltdowns over ketchup on the driveway... We can get ourselves back to New York, where life is normal."

Grant pointed out, "Getting around the cameras is the tough part."

Leonard, who had joined them for dinner but had to stand at the center island when they ran out of chairs, nodded. "I'm sure there's a way. I just don't know how."

"That's the problem." Grant looked over at Jared. "Elbows off the table."

Chase weighed in. "Leonard, do you know if there's an above-ground cable we could cut? Something like that might do the trick."

"I have no idea. It never occurred to me to look. I'm not a crook..."

"You *weren't* a crook," said Grant.

"Technically," said Leonard, "I'm still not a crook. You people might be crooks, but not me."

Grant shook his head. "Another one who thinks if he doesn't get his hands dirty, he hasn't crossed the line. Let me put it this way, Leonard: If you bring a potential crime to the table, then sit with real criminals to plot it out, that makes you a crook, too."

"But..."

"Of course, if you don't want to be a crook, then I've got no problem *not* thinking of you as a crook."

Leonard cocked his head. "Really?"

"Sure." Grant fixed him with a glare. "You walk away from your share of the loot, and I promise you no one in this room will ever accuse you of being a crook. Fair?"

Leonard sighed. "Okay, forget I said anything."

"It's already forgotten. So tell me what you may or may not know about when that camera is on."

Leonard began playing with a shirt cuff button. "Like I said, I don't know much. Sometimes it's on, sometimes it's not."

"Is it ever on when Merribaugh's in the finance office?"

"Not that I noticed. But I doubt it. I mean, cash contributions were always taken directly to the office as soon as they came in, and I'm sure he went to great lengths to make sure there's no record of that."

Chase said, "Maybe Merribaugh can override the camera. Turn it off when he's making a deposit or withdrawal, then turn it back on when he's done."

Grant thought about that. "It'd make sense. But we'd need access to Merribaugh's office. Constance?"

She wasn't in love with that idea. "If I come on too strong, Merribaugh's gonna know something's up. Then say good-bye to my job in the Cathedral...and our access to the safe."

$ $ $

The next morning, Constance led Jared by the hand, like a mother dragging her child, around the campus for a while until she spotted Merribaugh in the cathedral entry hall. His attention—or lack thereof—was somewhere far, far away.

"You ready?" she asked Jared.

"Ready."

"Mr. Merribaugh!" Her shout made his head snap in their direction. "I have some wonderful news. Praise the Lord!"

Merribaugh closed his eyes for a moment. All her Lord-praising was starting to eat at him. But then he remembered to feign politeness, and more importantly, noticed she was holding the hand of a very attractive young man, leading him through the entry hall like an offering to the church.

Or maybe a lamb to slaughter. Whichever. It wasn't one of those days he felt the need to get his metaphors straight.

"Sister Constance!" Merribaugh feigned enthusiasm as well as he feigned politeness. He took a deep breath and sucked in his stomach. "Praise the Lord indeed. And who have we here?"

"You told me Dr. Hurley wants to save homosexuals, didn't you?"

"I did."

"Then I am bringing you a homosexual to save." She took a step back, leaving Jared directly in Merribaugh's line of vision. "This is Jerry Stanley. He's my hairdresser."

The young man cocked a hip, smiled, and tossed him a tiny wave. "Hi."

Praise the Looooooorrrrrd, thought Merribaugh, although what he said was, "Do you want to be saved, Jerry?"

"I guess so."

"Do you want to feel the tender love of God?"

Jared thought about that. "Tender love is good. Most of the time, at least. Although sometimes it's sort of vanilla and boring."

Merribaugh coughed, trying to fight the dryness suddenly tickling his throat. "I mean…I *meant*…I…I…Oh, never mind."

Constance took her own moment to recover, using that time to remind herself that Grant and Chase—*especially* Chase—thought Jared would be perfect for this assignment, and who was she to judge them? Then she thought again and judged them harshly. But she had to work with the tool on hand, and Jared was that tool.

"Oh…*ha*!" She laughed, the sort of instinctive sudden recovery that had made her a success in her chosen, illegitimate line of work. "I get it! Jerry was making a joke."

"But it's true," Jared said, not understanding what was supposed to be a joke. "There's nothing worse than boring—"

Constance talked loudly and quickly, drowning out his voice. "Jerry wants to be saved from sin. Do you think you can help?"

Merribaugh sized up Jared. "If *anyone* can…" He caught himself. "I mean, we *certainly* can!" He grasped the young man firmly on one bony shoulder with a touch that was slightly too familiar. "Project Rectitude can save you, my son. Project Rectitude *will* save you."

Jared giggled. "It sounds like you're saying Erectitude." He giggled again. "Like erection."

Merribaugh blushed and stammered. "Son, if Project Erection—I mean, Erectitude…I mean *Rectitude*—can cure you, there is *no one* it can't cure." He looked heavenward, then returned his eyes to the humans. "We will teach you to reclaim your manhood, Jerry. In fact, I'm going to take the liberty of enrolling you in Beyond Sin, our upcoming ministry to change fallen men like yourself. We'll even waive your fee for the week."

"Week?" Jared looked at Constance uneasily. He hadn't followed much Merribaugh had said after that bit about boring tender love, but an entire week…something like five or six days? That sounded like more than he had bargained for.

"But you must!" said Merribaugh.

Behind his back, Constance nodded. She wanted him to say yes. After all, he was going one way or the other, and it'd be better if it was on Merribaugh's dime.

"Okay." There was a trace of wavering doubt in Jared's voice. "I'll do it."

Tears came to Merribaugh's eyes and he looked up. "Praise Jesus! You will be cured of the sin of homosexuality, my son!"

"Uh…okay?"

Merribaugh dropped to his knees on the royal blue carpet featuring images depicting the Ten Commandments, landing squarely in the center of Thou Shalt Not Steal. "Let us pray right now. Let us pray for your salvation!"

Again, Jared glanced at Constance, but she had already dropped to her own knees on the fringe of Steal. Jared—used to dropping to his knees for much less than ten thousand dollars—needed no further encouragement to follow suit, and landed on Thou Shalt Not Bear False Witness for the block.

$ $ $

"So how'd things go?" Grant asked when they finally walked through the front door after another half hour of Merribaugh-led prayer.

"All good," said Jared, bounding past Grant and down the staircase to the basement.

"Hey!" Grant hollered after him. "No running in the house!"

When he was out of sight, Constance stared down Grant. "You sure about him, Lambert? He's kind of…"

"Flighty."

"I was gonna say he's a moron, but flighty works, too."

"I know, I know." They heard the crack of pool balls from the basement. "Trust me, I know. But he's not as completely stupid as he comes across. Mostly, but not completely."

"I'll try to take your word for it."

$ $ $

Hurley heard Merribaugh's knock and considered not answering. But when he knocked a second time, he ran a hand through the silver pompadour, sighed, and boredom heavy in his voice, said, "Come in."

"Good news," said Merribaugh, taking a seat exactly in the middle of the center couch. "Project Rectitude is about to convert the gayest person I've ever met!"

Hurley blinked. "It is?"

A smug smile crossed Merribaugh's lips. "It is. I was going to surprise you at the service tomorrow, but now's as good a time as any to share the news. Sister Constance Brown brought us her hairdresser, a young homosexual named Jerry who really wants to change! And he is *so* gay…well, I can assure you he'll become the next poster boy for the ex-gay movement!"

"You're sure about this?"

"Positive, Oscar! They don't come gayer than Jerry Stanley."

Hurley looked at the half-written sermon on his desk. "Very well, then. Make sure he's prepared to meet the congregation tomorrow."

Merribaugh stood and turned toward the door when he heard Hurley call to him in a voice that could almost be described as "singsong," if that was ever a term that could be ascribed to him.

"Oh, and Dennis? If you embarrass me…"

"Never, Oscar. This one is the real deal."

$ $ $

Like the rest of the gang, Constance used an untraceable cell phone bought on the streets of New York. They firmly believed it was important to leave as few tracks as possible, just in case someone wanted to find them who they didn't want to be found by.

That was the phone number she'd given Merribaugh earlier at the cathedral, but still she hadn't expected him to call. Yet it was his voice on the line.

When she hung up, she looked at Lambert and shook her head. "They want to feature Jared at the service tomorrow as the new face of Project Rectitude."

"Huh," said Grant. "Sounds like Jerry Stanley finally impressed someone."

15

"What the hell is Old Stone Fence Post Estates Day?"

Grant stared at a fluorescent yellow sheet of paper that had been neatly folded and tucked into the front door handle.

Chase read over his shoulder. "Looks like another barbecue."

Grant looked up. "Didn't we just have one?"

"If there's an upside to having to go to church," said Chase, as he walked to the living room, "it's missing these neighborhood get-togethers."

Grant followed, still clutching the fluorescent yellow paper, and his expression soured. "I might ask you to take me to church with you."

He handed the paper to Lisa, who looked up and said, "Don't these people have jobs? Every time I turn around, they're planning another neighborhood event."

"It's like Stepford," said Chase, taking a seat next to her on the leather couch. "I've never seen such a group of tight-asses manage to ruin a picnic. You'd think dropping ketchup on the driveway was a hanging offense. What's Tish gonna do when someone drops an entire hot dog?"

"Oh, I don't know." Lisa folded the yellow invitation and handed it back to Grant. "I sort of feel bad for the neighbors. The Fieldings have them terrorized. Most of them seemed okay."

"They loved my deviled eggs," said Farraday, walking in from the kitchen and still wearing an apron. "Ms. Jarvis said she'd make them for her book club and report back to me." He looked wistfully out the window into the backyard. "Y'know, I think she kinda likes me."

Grant, Chase, and Lisa stared at him. And after about thirty seconds of silence he realized that.

"What? What's wrong?"

Lisa said, "Don't get me wrong, Farraday, but you're acting very un-Farraday-ish right now."

"Hey, you got Mary Beth." He motioned to Grant and Chase. "These two have each other. What's wrong with wanting a little companionship?"

He didn't wait for a response before turning and walking back to the kitchen, muttering something about preparing a pupu platter for Old Stone Fence Post Estates Day.

"So…that was strange," said Chase, and Grant and Lisa murmured their agreement. They might have even gossiped about it, except the wistfulness Farraday had left in his wake was broken by the noise Jared made as he clomped down the stairs from his bedroom.

"I'm ready to go!" he announced.

"The hell you are," said Grant. The black biker boots were bad enough. The see-through gauze shirt was worse. And he didn't know how Jared had managed to get into jeans with what appeared to be a twenty-four-inch waist, but those were *not* the kind of bulges anyone needed to see in this living room, let alone the Virginia Cathedral of Love.

"You are not leaving this house dressed like that, young man. Get upstairs and change."

Jared stood defiantly. "You're not *really* my father, you know."

"Shoulda left you in the orphanage," Grant growled, and the growl was enough to wear down the younger man's defiance.

"Okay, fine."

He clomped back upstairs, passing Constance at the landing. Then they heard his bedroom door slam.

"Kids," said Constance.

Ten minutes later, Jared returned. This time he was wearing khakis, a button-down shirt, loafers, and a lot less attitude.

"Better?" he asked.

"Better," Grant agreed.

With that, Jared walked to the door. "Time to get to church." He smiled mischievously. "It's my coming-out party."

"I think you mean 'going in,'" said Constance, following.

Chase sighed and lifted himself off the couch, where he'd grown far too comfortable. "Okay, I'm off to church. And I can't wait until this job is over and I have my Sundays back."

Farraday, still wearing his apron, brought up the rear. "If Ms. Jarvis calls…"

"We'll tell her you'll be right back," said Lisa.

When the door was closed, Grant looked at her.

"Maybe it's the lawn chemicals that are doing this to us. We'll have to look into that."

$ $ $

Dr. Oscar Hurley stepped back onto the stage and smiled a hundred-watt smile, visible not only to the two thousand people who'd arrived early enough to fill the best, closest seats, but also the other six thousand toward the back—including Chase and Constance—watching on the huge projection screen positioned to Hurley's left.

"Ladies and gentlemen," he said. "Children and servants of God…" His voice died off to a whisper before roaring back to life. "People sometimes ask why we do what we do. They call us zealots for preaching the word of the Lord. They ask us to compromise…to not make waves."

His voice dropped to a purr. Now he wasn't preaching; he was your next-door neighbor.

"They ask us to ignore sin. They ask us to condemn ourselves to eternal damnation because they don't want to feel uncomfortable." He had been strolling across the stage but stopped, and his volume rose again. "They want to enjoy their lustful, sinful lives without being called on the carpet."

His voice began to boom again and he held tight to the microphone.

"I say *NO*, brothers and sisters! *NO* to compromising on sin! *NO* to compromising on eternal salvation! *NO! NO! NOOOO!!!"*

A congregation of thousands, caught up in Hurley's oration, joined him for the final "*NO!!!*" then fell silent except for a smattering of "Amens!" and a "Hallelujah!" or two.

Hurley paced wordlessly in front of the altar for more than a minute—seemingly contemplating his next words, looking a bit angry, but really building anticipation in the audience—before continuing.

He looked up and bit his lower lip. His tone was neighborly again.

"I want to introduce you to a young man who also says *no* to lust and sin." He paused and looked off into the wings. "Jerry, could you join me on the stage?"

Jared Parsells took a few tentative steps from the wings. Dr. Oscar Hurley walked to him and wrapped an arm over his shoulder, guiding him to stage center.

"In just a few days, Jerry will be joining over two hundred other men and women in our nation's capitol for an intensive conference we call Beyond Sin, sponsored by Project Rectitude and the Moral Families Coalition. Through testimony, education, and of course prayer, by the end of that week their lives will have changed. By the end of that week, Jerry will no longer be a homosexual!"

The cathedral resounded with a roar and a torrent of *"Amens!"* Jared, always comfortable as the center of attention, even when he didn't fully understand why, smiled and took a little bow.

In the congregation, Chase's eyes found Constance. They gave each other the slightest of smiles.

Hurley continued. "This is why we spread the word of God, brothers and sisters. To save souls. *Not* to compromise. *Not* to play footsie with Satan. But to save people like Jerry, the future face of ex-homosexuals, and a young man who will lead thousands of others away from sin and into righteousness!"

If televisions in any of the dozens of gay neighborhoods around the world where Jared Parsells was well-known had been tuned into *Live from the Virginia Cathedral of Love* that morning, a collective *"What the fuck?"* would have been heard. But, of course, that didn't happen, because Dr. Oscar Hurley and Jared Parsells had quite different demographics.

$ $ $

After the service, safely hidden away in his spacious office in Cathedral House, Hurley looked at Merribaugh from across the Desk of Christ.

"Sister Constance seems to be a true asset to our mission. I know I'm hard on you sometimes, Dennis, but you did a good job bringing her into the fold. Not only is she doing a fantastic job with the books, but bringing us young Jerry Stanley was a stroke of brilliance. He's perfect…*exactly* what we need."

"He *is* perfect," Merribaugh agreed, and his mind drifted for a moment before focusing again on Hurley. "And when he becomes a spokesman for the cause…"

"Let's not get too far ahead of ourselves, Dennis. First, he has to change."

"He will, Oscar." Merribaugh smiled. "Oh, he will…"

$ $ $

Jared was gushing. "And then Hurley said I was going to be the new poster boy for the ex-gay movement!"

Grant thought maybe he needed his hearing checked. He looked over to Constance, and Chase, but they met his eyes with affirming nods.

"You're certainly gonna present him with, uh, a *unique* challenge," said Grant. "That's for sure."

"So, Jared," said Mary Beth from across the kitchen table, "when you become straight what are you gonna do with your manscara and guyliner?"

Under the table, Lisa gently kicked her, a signal to knock it off.

Besides, she'd stolen Lisa's line.

16

At the end of the week the neighborhood was abuzz. Literally. From every direction came the sound of lawnmowers and weed-whackers and hedge trimmers. Because everyone had received a fluorescent yellow invitation to Old Stone Fence Post Estates Day, and no one wanted to incur the wrath of Tish Fielding.

Grant and Chase stood on the small front porch in front of their house and watched the employees from their lawn service do their work for them.

"We would have gotten better at it," said Grant.

"I know," Chase agreed. "But isn't it better watching other people do it?"

"Yeah. Less itchy, too."

Jared joined them, conservatively dressed in brown cargo shorts and a pink polo shirt. Between Grant's firm parental skills and almost a week with the congregation at the Virginia Cathedral of Love, he was starting to fit in.

He spotted Malcolm Fielding across the street watering his lawn and waved. Malcolm returned the wave, then refocused his attention on the grass.

"C*lllll*oset case," Jared drawled.

"Who?" Grant looked back across the street. "Fielding?"

Jared nodded. "I can spot one a mile away."

Grant looked at Malcolm again and shook his head in disagreement. "Nah. Henpecked, maybe, but not a closet case. I figure him for one of those guys that puts up with his wife's crap at home because he's having an affair at work."

Jared licked his lips but his eyes never left Malcolm. "Want me to prove it?"

"No. I want you to behave yourself. And I want you to remember that you're about to go to ex-gay camp."

Jared sighed. The nearer the date of the conference, the more he dreaded it. "Do I have to?"

"Yeah," Grant said. "I thought you were looking forward to a lot of sex there."

Jared licked his lips again. "Why, when I can get it right in the neighborhood?"

That was when Grant and Chase both decided three was a crowd on the tiny porch.

"Think we can convince 'em to start ex-gay camp this afternoon?" Grant asked when they were back in the kitchen.

"Technically," Chase said, expanding on a point Grant had no interest in, "it's not really a camp. More like a heavily supervised week in a hotel."

"I'll pay for the extra night. Two, if I have to. Couldn't cost more than the damn toaster, could it?"

Chase laughed. "Maybe a little bit more. It's a nice hotel. Expensive. It might even be the one where Eliot Spitzer met that hooker."

Grant took a glance out the window. "Speaking of hookers…"

"What?"

"It's our fault. We never should've left Jared alone. Now he's across the street talking to Fielding."

With that, Chase was at Grant's side to see for himself. "I'd better break that up."

Grant stared at him. "Are you jealous?"

"Of course not. It's just not acceptable behavior."

"I think you're jealous."

Chase pulled himself away. "Don't be ridiculous."

"Okay. Just asking." Grant took another look out the window. "Now what…? Why are Jared's shirt and shorts wet? Looks like he must've accidentally gotten sprayed by the hose."

"What?"

"*Annnnd*…now the shirt comes off!"

"I don't believe you."

"Hmm. Maybe Jared was onto something. Fielding ain't exactly looking away."

Grant continued to watch the scene unfold. First Chase rushed across the street, then tried to pretend he wasn't rushing, and then half dragged Jared back home.

"I'm not jealous," said Chase, when he was back in the kitchen. "But I've been watching the clock, and it's almost time for Jared to get to the cathedral."

"Mmm-hmm," said Grant, with a tiny smile on his lips.

$ $ $

A short time later, Jared—now in dry clothes—and Constance waited for Farraday, who was on his way back down the block from where he'd been repotting Ms. Jarvis's pansies. Grant waited, too, along with Chase, who was still definitely, absolutely, unquestionably not jealous.

They'd decided that Chase would be going to church that day. Not to ensure Jared didn't fall into the baptismal font and be forced to strip off his wet clothes, but to case the finance office with Constance and figure out if there was a way to get around the cameras.

Because they'd now been in Nash Bog for a few weeks, and that was a few weeks too long.

No sooner did Farraday walk through the front door than Grant handed him the car keys and made him turn right around. Constance and Chase followed, with Jared trailing and tossing a wave to Malcolm Fielding as they approached the car.

In Jared's wake, the front door remained wide open.

Grant yelled across the lawn. "I'm not paying to air-condition the entire neighborhood, y'know!"

In the living room, Lisa looked up from her book. "We really have to find out what's in those lawn chemicals."

$ $ $

"Afternoon, Miss Brown," said the elderly security guard sitting at his post in the lobby of Cathedral House.

Constance offered him a friendly smile and said, "Good afternoon. Are Dr. Hurley or Mr. Merribaugh in today?"

"Not today. I think I heard they were going to Washington." The guard took a look at the man accompanying her. "Who's this?"

"Oh, this is Mr. Hudson. He's offered to assist me in getting the books in shape."

The security guard waved them on.

It was hot in the finance office, so Chase opened a window. "Nice view," he said. "Private."

"You're probably gonna want to close that window," said Constance.

"I just want to get some air circulating. It's stuffy in here. Why not keep it open?"

"Be quiet and listen. You'll figure it out soon enough."

It took a while, but soon he heard music from the seemingly endless rehearsal taking place in the auditorium. Roughly three minutes after that, "The Lonely Goatherd" had wormed its way into his ear.

He closed the window and said, "Let's get down to business. Where's the camera?"

"It's mounted on the wall opposite the closet door." He picked up some papers from her desk and pretended to look at them while checking the camera out of the corner of his eye. From the way it was angled, he figured it captured most of the office.

"Is there anything we can use to block the camera for few minutes?" he asked. "Something that won't be obvious?"

Their eyes glanced around the room, until Constance spotted a large foam core panel half-tucked behind a cabinet. She pulled it out and said, "How about this?"

The image on the panel was a rendering of the Great Cross, with a note on the bottom indicating it predated construction. It might have been a cathedral artifact except someone over the years had defaced it, drawing spirals through the vertical section that blossomed into the horizontal section. Chase hated people who defaced property; it was the only type of crime short of physical harm he'd never participate in.

But for now, the defaced drawing would do. He held it up and stood behind it. "Think this will provide enough cover?"

"Maybe," said Constance. "Of course, people are gonna wonder why you're standing in the middle of the office holding that dusty old thing."

"Then you hold it."

"Uh-uh." She pulled over a metal chair and motioned for Chase to use it as a prop, but the board slid off. "There's gotta be something around here…"

"Just hold it. This isn't gonna take that long."

But she saw what she needed so didn't bother answering him. In a corner of the office, next to an unused coat rack, stood a folded easel.

Constance retrieved it, opened the legs, and helped Chase guide the foam core board into place.

"I feel like MacGyver," she said, when the obstruction was between them and the security camera.

Chase took another glance to make sure he wasn't being watched, then inspected the closet door.

"I don't think we'll have a problem getting in the closet. The safe is another thing." He looked at her. "You didn't happen to notice what kind it was, did you?"

"Sorry. Safes aren't my thing."

Chase shook his head. "I'm gonna assume the safe is nothing special. Still, we'll need a pro to get into it. And if we can't do that, we're going to have to steal it." He licked his lips. "I'll bet Grant could get in with no problem."

"*Our* Grant?" She thought about that. "I knew he had his talents, but I didn't know they included safe-cracking."

Chase shrugged. "Oh, yeah. He's great on safes. All kinds of locks. That's how we met." She stared at him, not saying anything, and he took that as a sign to continue. "It had to be…well, we've been together for seventeen years, so seventeen years ago. I was pissed off at my dead-end job at Groc-O-Rama…"

"The one you still have?"

"Well…yeah. *Anyway*, I decided to rob the safe. Turns out, Grant was planning to rob the safe the very same night."

"Hmm…"

"Right? But it worked out, and the rest is history."

She shook her head. "Burglary…breaking and entering…safe-cracking…That might be one of the most romantic love-at-first-sight stories I've ever heard."

He blushed and looked away. "Yeah." Then he remembered their job at hand and returned his attention to the locked closet door. "We just have to get Grant into Cathedral House. After that, we're golden."

Constance was by nature an optimist, but she was also a realist. "Long as nothing goes wrong."

Chase shook his head. "I've been on capers where things have gone wrong, but this one? You got a job here and they love you. Jared will be the perfect gay bait. Everything on this job is going right."

Which was the moment a knock on the door threatened to change that.

Without making a sound, Chase grabbed the foam core panel and tucked it back behind the cabinet, while Constance folded the easel and set it aside. Then she smoothed her skirt, put a pleasant smile on her face, and answered the knock.

"Sister Constance!" said Merribaugh, greeting her. "Working on a Saturday?" He turned and saw Chase, and a quizzical expression crossed his face. "And…Mr. Hudson?"

"Charlie offered to help me get organized," she said. "The books are a mess." Then she thought to add, "Praise the Lord."

Merribaugh cringed at that, but accepted the rest of her words at face value. He knew what a mess the books had become since Leonard Platt was discharged. "Mr. Hudson, I didn't realize you knew finance."

"A little," he said. "Just a little. But I wanted to help out the Cathedral, so…"

"Well, thank you! I'll make sure Dr. Hurley knows what a wonderful volunteer you've been."

Merribaugh fully entered the room, and for the first time they realized he was wheeling a small suitcase.

"The guard downstairs said you were in Washington, DC, today."

"Not yet." He parked the suitcase next to her desk. "Dr. Hurley and I are leaving in an hour. But first I wanted to get something out of the…" He didn't want to say too much in front of Charlie Hudson, so, to Constance, he motioned his head toward the closet door. "Now if you'll be kind enough to excuse me for a moment, I need a little privacy."

Chase and Constance walked into the hallway, and Merribaugh closed the door behind them. They heard locks click on the other side of the door, and the sound of the suitcase being unzipped and zipped again. Minutes later, the door reopened and Merribaugh emerged, rolling the suitcase behind him.

"That's everything," he said. "Now I'm off to the Beyond Sin conference where, among other things, we'll be curing Sister Constance's hairdresser!"

"Praise the Lord," she said, with no enthusiasm whatsoever, as she and Chase returned to the office.

Chase listened to the wheels of the suitcase roll down the hall and felt a slight flutter in his stomach. When he heard the elevator doors close, he looked out into the hall, then back to Constance.

"Remember how I said everything is going right?"

"Yeah."

"Maybe everything *was* going right."

"You mean that suitcase?"

"That suitcase is either full of clothes for his week at the hotel, or… Nah, never mind. It has to be clothes, right?"

She shook her head. "That suitcase isn't big enough to hold seven million dollars. At the outside he could maybe get twenty-five, thirty thousand in it. So if it wasn't clothes, it was just a little walking-around money for him and Hurley to spread around in DC. Not seven million dollars."

The hesitation in Chase's voice let on he was troubled. "I suppose…"

"Merribaugh's a fool," she said reassuringly, "But even *he's* not a big enough fool to be wheeling seven million dollars in cash around the District of Columbia. Plus, that suitcase…no way it holds that much money."

"Right," Chase said, more to himself than Constance. "Right."

$ $ $

"Good news," Constance announced when they returned home several hours later.

Grant looked up from his newspaper. "Oh, yeah?"

"Yeah." Chase stared. He'd never seen Grant read a newspaper before. "Uh…anyway, it looks like a simple safe-cracking job."

"And we figured out how to block the camera," she added.

Grant set the newspaper on the floor. "Nice. But you think we can get a crew in and out without problems?"

"Piece of cake," said Chase. "The security guards all know Constance. She can tell them she's called some repairmen for something, the repairmen show up…"

Grant finished his sentence. "And the repairmen walk away with seven million dollars."

"Exactly."

"So when do you think we can pull it off?"

Chase and Constance exchanged glances.

"How does tomorrow sound?"

"Pretty close to perfect," said Grant, and he smiled.

17

After breakfast the next morning, Chase found Jared in his bedroom. Even though he'd been there for nearly an hour, only half the suitcase was full.

"Can't make up your mind?" asked Chase. "Or are you putting this off as long as possible?"

The younger man held up a skintight see-through shirt—one of his favorites—and inspected it. "Maybe a little of both." He looked at Chase with pain in his eyes. "Do I really have to go through with this?"

Chase nodded. "That's pretty much the only reason you're here. You want the ten grand, right?"

"Oh, yeah." He started to pack the shirt, but Chase pulled it back out of the suitcase and draped it over a chair.

"I don't think this will cut it for an ex-gay conference."

Jared took the shirt from the chair and started to pack it again. "But it's my *favorite*. I *rock* this shirt."

Chase started to take it back out, Jared grabbed at it, and for a brief moment they were locked in a tug-of-war until, finally, Jared gave in and tossed the shirt angrily to the floor.

"Fine! I'll dress like a straight guy."

Chase looked into the suitcase. "Is that your cell phone?"

"Yeah, why?"

"The rules say no phones."

Lines appeared on Jared's forehead. If he'd known that, he would have been troubled, because to Jared, only old guys had lines on their foreheads. "But…but…No phones?"

"No phones." Chase reached down and retrieved it from the bag. "If they find this, they might kick you out."

"But my music is on it. And what if I want to text someone!"

"No phones."

Jared's forehead wrinkled a bit more and he jutted out his lower lip. "This is gonna suck so much! Straight guy clothes and no phone."

"I like your spirit." Chase glanced at his watch. "But not so much that I'm going to let you miss the conference. Finish packing and Farraday will give you a ride to the city."

"You're not my mother."

"Do you want me to send Grant up here?"

"Okay, okay, I'll pack!" Jared began filling the suitcase. It was only when Chase turned to leave the room he added, "I wish you were going with me."

Chase allowed himself a slight smile. After all, Grant wasn't too far off-base about the lightly flirtatious relationship he had with Jared. That nothing would ever come of it was understood; that Chase encouraged it and enjoyed it was his private indulgence.

"I'm sure you'll be fine on your own," he said, meeting Jared's gaze. "And it'll only be for a few days. You'll be back here with me—I mean, *us*—before you know it. And ten thousand dollars richer for the effort."

"I guess so…" Jared turned to finish packing, and Chase used to opportunity to adjust himself and make an exit.

A short while later, Jared—suitcase in hand, frown on face—appeared in the foyer.

"Ready to go, kid?" asked Farraday.

"Ready." His voice said it, not his expression.

When they were finally on the road, Farraday turned the radio down. "Don't seem like you're looking forward to this."

Jared stared out the window. "It'll be all right, I guess. I just wish I wasn't going alone."

"You'll be fine." Farraday thought about turning the radio back up before deciding against it. "It'll be a new experience."

Jared took his time before answering. "I'm sort of nervous about being around all those ex-gays. What if I catch it?"

"Catch what?"

"Some ex-gay thing! I mean, I don't know how to *do* anything else!"

Farraday laughed. "You ain't gonna catch an ex-gay thing. For that matter, probably no one else will, either." He glanced to his right and saw Jared still staring absently at the countryside. "Listen, if it makes you feel any better about the next few days, I've been *non*-gay my entire life. It ain't so bad. You can get through this conference."

Jared didn't respond—he just kept staring—so Farraday continued. "There's nothing all that horrible about *not* being gay, y'know. Well, not usually. 'Course, I don't really date anymore, but I got around when I was younger. Yeah…" He smiled for a moment, but only a moment, as he remembered a dating chronology that ran straight from "getting around" to "getting married" to…

"Nah, it ain't so bad. Well, 'cept for when your fuckin' wife screws you over and leaves you without a dime, and you have to make a living boosting cars and pulling jobs on the side just so's she can't get her hands on your wallet…"

Jared finally broke eye contact with the scenery and turned to face Farraday.

"Is this supposed to make me feel better?" he asked.

Farraday stared out the windshield and sighed. "Started out that way."

$ $ $

At his U Street Northwest apartment in the District of Columbia, Dan Rowell—press secretary to United States Senator Gordon Cobey, Republican of Ohio—was every bit as unhappy about his imminent attendance at Beyond Sin as Jared Parsells.

But like Jared, he knew he didn't really have a choice in the matter. He was going, and that was that.

Dan also knew that, in politics, sometimes unpleasant things needed to be done that were hard to square with a clear conscience. Elected officials had to take tough votes that didn't jibe with their personal convictions because the leadership—or their constituents—demanded it; unsavory people sought assistance, and one was honor-bound to try to help; campaign rhetoric was geared toward painting one's opponent as virtually satanic…

Those were unfortunate aspects of politics, but Dan Rowell had learned to live with them. He'd been on Cobey's staff for years, and if there was a heaven, he'd have a lot to atone for. But he also knew that most times, those actions that seemed unjustifiable on the surface were part of a whole that served a greater purpose. The morality was in the big picture, not in the tiny details rife with hypocrisy and compromise.

But even after several long talks with Cobey—talks in which the senator repeatedly stressed the greater good—Dan Rowell was resentful that he was being sent to what essentially was an ex-gay camp, albeit an ex-gay camp held in a swanky hotel one block from the White House. For the next week, he'd be subjected to brainwashing and behavior modification programs, and—perhaps worst of all—trapped in a hotel with dozens of people who *wanted* to be there.

He threw some clothes—clothes much different, much more preppy, than those Jared had packed, and far less revealing than those Jared had wanted to pack—into his suitcase and tried to swallow his resentment. Cobey had been surprisingly good to him when he'd fearfully come out several years earlier, and for a conservative Republican, he was beginning to put together a decent voting record on gay rights legislation, so Dan supposed he owed his boss this much.

But *only* this much. No more.

18

Farraday's pupu platter was a hit, which was about the best any of them could say about Old Stone Fence Post Estates Day.

At its heart, it was a warmed-over version of the earlier neighborhood barbecue. Once again, Tish and Malcolm Fielding held court in the driveway as cowed neighbors stood round and tried not to spill condiments on the driveway. Once again, Farraday's appetizers were popular, while Malcolm manned a lonely grill. Once again, Tish circled the crowd with a ferocious smile, forcing small talk when she wasn't hunting for infringements of whatever new neighborhood rule she'd invented.

Only two things kept them sane. There would be no appearance by Jared, since this was about the time he'd be checking into his hotel room; and by the end of the day they intended to be seven million dollars richer.

Constance and Chase were the lucky ones. They got to go to church and get called sinners for a few hours. With Farraday and Jared on the road, and Mary Beth boycotting, it was left to Grant and Lisa to represent 455.

For his part, Grant had been doing his representing from the end of the driveway next to the mailbox.

Lisa took a break from passing the pupu platter and joined Grant, lighting a cigarette.

"I know this is a stupid question, but…"

"Yeah, I'm over the suburbs. I'm really looking forward to going home to gridlock, honking horns, pigeons, the subway, and rude people who are at least up front about their rudeness. And no HOA rules. That's a good thing, too."

Ms. Jarvis wandered over. "Where's Farraday?"

"Taking Jerry to DC."

"Jerry?"

He sighed. "My adopted son, I guess."

He needn't have bothered. She wasn't paying attention. "When you see Farraday, tell him the pupu platter is *amazing*."

"I'll do that. But I'm sure he knows it already."

Ms. Jarvis leaned a bit closer. "You know, the neighborhood has been so much more fun since you moved in." She glanced back to make sure Tish couldn't hear. "Mrs. Fielding can be a bit much."

Mr. Scribner had overheard. "She's intolerable. And getting worse every day."

Mrs. Huffine, who'd walked over from Black Diamond Circle, joined them. "Tish forced me to seal my driveway last weekend. She said she'd call the HOA if I didn't." Her chin quivered. "My husband was out of town and I had to do the work myself."

"No!" gasped Mr. Scribner.

Ms. Jarvis giggled. "You know what makes these get-togethers more tolerable?" She held up her red plastic cup. "Rum and fruit punch! Farraday taught me that trick. Isn't it wild?"

Mr. Scribner's eyes darted. "You'd better be quiet. Tish wouldn't like that."

Then, attracted by the growing knot of people, Tish Fielding was among them. The conversation immediately died.

"What am I missing?" she asked, in her annoying singsong tone. "No secrets allowed in Old Stone Fence Post Estates!"

"Oh, there aren't really any secrets," said Lisa, who took a drag from her cigarette and exhaled into the air. "Everyone thinks the same thing."

Tish waved her hands in front of her face and said, "Oh. No. *No no no no no*!"

"Huh?"

"Smoking is *not* allowed."

Lisa shrugged. "But I'm standing outside. Away from the house. By the street."

"*And* blowing carcinogens all over the neighborhood." Tish dropped the pretense of a smile. "You could be killing us all right now."

Under his breath, Grant said, "Not the worst idea."

"What if I was to become pregnant? You could be harming my baby!"

"Pregnant?" asked Lisa with a derisive chuckle. "At your age?"

Ms. Jarvis giggled.

Blame the rum, Grant thought.

Tish spun on her. "You think that's funny?"

"Sort of."

They waited for Tish to respond, but instead she simmered for an entire minute before walking to the middle of the driveway, where she raised her hands and waved.

"Excuse me, everyone! Can I have your attention?!"

The neighbors turned to look at her.

"I'm afraid the party's over. I don't feel well. The cigarette smoke has given me a migraine." That she said this while standing in the smoke from Malcolm's grill was not commented upon.

Grant looked at his watch. The big neighborhood event had lasted less than ninety minutes.

"That was one of the least painless parties she's ever thrown," Ms. Jarvis said. Mr. Scribner and Ms. Huffine agreed.

Grant watched Lisa as she ground the cigarette under her heel on Tish's driveway. "I knew that bad habit of yours would prove useful someday."

$ $ $

Farraday arrived home a few hours later in a blue pickup. He'd bought some reflective peel-off letters, which he handed to Grant upon arrival.

"Your pupu platter was the highlight of the party," Lisa told him.

"That, and the way you're turning Ms. Jarvis into a drunk," added Grant.

Farraday smiled. "She's a very special woman."

$ $ $

The blue pickup with reflective letters spelling out DAVIS PLUMMING on the cap over its bed came to a stop next to the guard shack in front of the Virginia Cathedral of Love. The driver's window rolled down and Farraday, a gray cap pulled low over his eyes, leaned out.

"Gotta call to fix the toilet," he said. "Some place called Cathedral House?"

The security guard gave a bored once-over to Farraday, then to the truck. "Take the road all the way to the end. You can't miss it."

"Thanks." Farraday's foot was still on the brake as he started to crank up the window.

"Hey, buddy?" The guard's hand was now outside the booth, motioning the window back down. Farraday didn't like the looks of that, but complied.

"What?"

"You're spelled wrong."

"I'm spelled wrong?"

"You're spelled wrong." The guard pointed to the back of the pickup. "'Plumbing' has a 'B' in it."

"Not where I come from." With that, Farraday took his foot off the brake and started on his way to Cathedral House. As he did, he turned to Grant, who sat in the passenger seat, also wearing a gray cap. "Told you there was a 'B.'"

"I guess I stand corrected."

Farraday couldn't help but smile that he'd been right for a change.

"There's something very strange about this place," said Grant as the pickup rolled onto the grounds. "It's too easy. Almost like they're asking to be robbed."

"That, or they're so sure they won't be robbed that they don't care about appearances."

"Maybe."

"Even in New York we got places like this, right? Tons of cash layin' around and no real security. They just figure no one's gonna take it. Usually they're right. Until they're wrong."

Grant eyed the cathedral as the truck passed it and continued another quarter mile down the road toward Cathedral House. "Yeah, I guess you're right. If joints in New York don't sweat it, we shouldn't be surprised that some church in Virginia doesn't think about it. Doesn't mean it's not strange, though. You sure Cousin Leonard knows what he's talking about?"

Farraday pulled to a stop in front of Cathedral House, which was helpfully marked with a sign reading CATHEDRAL HOUSE, although he'd already known exactly where he was going.

"I'll let him out of the pickup bed and you can ask for yourself."

Leonard hadn't wanted to go along on the job, but Grant and Farraday had made it clear that he was going whether he liked it or not. The bumpy ten-minute ride on the hard, bare metal bed of the pickup with a rattling toolbox had convinced Leonard he should have made more of a case for himself, but he was smart enough not to complain when Farraday unlocked the tailgate and he could finally scramble out.

Grant looked over Leonard's fake mustache and sideburns—as well as his gray cap—to make sure everything was still in place, then sent a text message to Chase to tell him they were outside. A few minutes later, Chase was standing at the top of the front steps.

"You the plumbers?" he asked, playing his role.

"Yeah," said Grant.

Chase looked at the truck. "You're spelled wrong."

Grant muttered something inaudible and hoisted the toolbox. "Let's go look at your toilet."

No one spoke while they took the small elevator to the fourth floor, then followed Chase down the hall to the finance office.

Constance was waiting inside. When the office door was closed, she barely moved her lips. "Don't look, but the camera is mounted on the wall to your left."

Grant turned his back to the direction of the camera. "You sure there's no audio, Leonard?"

"There's no audio."

"You'd better be right. 'Cause if you're wrong, we're already busted."

"I'm not wrong."

"Okay, then." Grant turned around. "Let's remove the seven million clogs and get out of here."

Farraday bent over and reached for random pieces of metal in the toolbox, most of which were the kinds of tools you'd use to fix a toilet, and some of which were tools you'd use to crack a safe.

"What the hell, Farraday!" Constance averted her eyes. "This is supposed to be about *safe*-cracking, not *plumber's*-cracking."

Farraday stood and pulled his pants up an inch or so before bending over again. "Gotta look the part." To Grant, he said, "Want the drill?"

"Not unless I need it. First I wanna take care of the camera." He looked at Chase. "Ready?"

"Ready."

Grant, in an exaggerated pantomime that would have made Mack Sennett proud, gestured a few times for the benefit of whoever might be watching them while Chase moved the easel from against the wall and propped it in the middle of the office directly in front of the security camera. He then set the foam core panel with the rendering of the Great Cross on the easel, back to the camera.

They stepped back to better appraise their work, acting as if they were actually interested in looking at the drawing. Chase stood at the edge, still partially in camera range to reassure anyone viewing them from the security office that everything was on the up-and-up on the fourth floor.

Grant looked at the picture of the cross. "What's with the squiggles?"

"What squiggles?" asked Chase

"The ones someone drew on the cross."

"Those look more like spirals to me."

"No, those are definitely squiggles."

"Whatever. They were there when we found it."

"Some people," said Grant, "have no respect for other people's property." His eyes lined up the foam core panel with the camera. "Move the easel up a little closer." Chase slid it forward a few feet until Grant was about as satisfied as he was going to get. "That doesn't give us a lot of room to hide, but I'll make it work."

Constance returned to her desk, directly in view of the camera, and pretended as if everything happening in the office was completely normal. In the meantime, Grant had the closet door open and was studying the safe.

"You want the drill now?" asked Farraday.

Grant shook his head. "Drilling is the last option. That's the option we run with if there's no other way in, because once we drill they're gonna know we were in the safe as soon as they look at it. I can't speak for everyone here, but I'd like a bit more of a head start."

As it turned out, the drill stayed in the toolbox.

Crouched on the other side of the easel and out of camera view, Grant went to work on the tumblers. It took a few minutes, but the safe opened easily.

At the final click—the satisfying sound of a combination lock beaten—Grant said, "Now let's see what we've got here."

He pulled the latch.

Even Constance walked out of camera-range and joined them as they gathered around the cracked safe. They watched the heavy door slowly open, and then they looked inside at neat stacks of United States currency.

Their faces dropped.

It was Farraday who spoke first. "Unless those bills are all thousands, no way is that seven million dollars."

Grant reached in and thumbed through a few bound packets, then did a quick calculation in his head.

"Ninety thou, give or take." His announcement was met by a chorus of groans.

"That ain't even my fee," said Farraday.

"Shut up," Grant ordered, and they all obeyed. He looked at Leonard. "So where's the rest? You promised us seven mil. We wouldn't have gone through all this for a measly ninety thou job."

Leonard's eyes darted around the room, suddenly fearful he was being set up, but not sure why or by whom. "I…I…I don't know. There should definitely be more money in there."

Grant snarled. "But there isn't. So where is it? Where'd it go?"

"I don't have any idea," he said. "All I know is that Merribaugh has been putting money in that safe for years."

"Yeah, but does he ever take it out?"

"Sure," said Leonard. "But not often. And not nearly as much as he's put in there."

"What about at night?" asked Constance. "Maybe after you went home he'd come in…"

Leonard thought about that possibility. "I suppose that could have happened, but…that doesn't make sense. Why would he tell Hurley that they were sitting on seven million dollars if they were only sitting on ninety thousand dollars?"

They looked at each other for several long, tense moments…

Until Chase finally swallowed audibly, at which time they all looked at *him*.

"Merribaugh's suitcase," he said.

"Oh, damn!" said Constance. "That has to be it."

Grant's eyes traveled from Chase and Constance and back a few times. "You wanna explain for the rest of us?"

So Chase did. "Yesterday, Merribaugh came in with a suitcase, and told us to wait outside…"

"You don't think this is something we should have known about before now?"

Chase shrugged helplessly, mostly because he knew Grant was right. "It was just a small roller suitcase. One of those ones on wheels. It just seemed so…*small*! Too small to fill it with seven mil."

"Unbelievable." Grant's head was starting to pound. "Here we are committing a burglary and we didn't have to be here at all."

"But Chase is telling the truth," said Constance. "Remember, I was there, too. It was just a tiny suitcase. If he took money from the safe, it couldn't have been more than, well…" She pointed at the safe. "Had to be less than *that*, at least. A lot less."

"We figured thirty thousand dollars max," Chase added.

Grant squeezed his eyes closed and wished the headache away. The fire was out of his voice when he finally spoke.

"So where's this money now?"

"I can't say for sure," said Chase. "But we know where Merribaugh is."

Constance nodded. "The Project Rectitude conference. In DC."

"The one Jared's at?" They nodded.

"So Jared is now our *only* link to seven million dollars?" They nodded again.

Grant sat down on the floor and put his head in his hands. When he finally was able to speak again, it was with a voice drained of all trace of hope.

"I hate Washington, DC."

$ $ $

At one far end of the basement, tucked away from the busyness of Cathedral House, was the security supply room.

The room had two purposes. It was primarily, and logically, the space where the Virginia Cathedral of Love security team kept its supplies. But a corner had also been turned into a hidden sleeping nook for Captain Joseph Enright, Chief of Security, complete with cot, nightstand, alarm clock, and pornographic magazines hidden inside the covers of old editions of *Newsweek* and *Highlights for Children*.

Most officers under his command knew of Captain Enright's hideaway, if not the magazines, but he knew they would never talk. Because if they did, they'd be looking for new jobs, and why would they want to do *that*?

Cathedral security officers generally made it a point to avoid waking Enright—they could handle the occasional religious zealot or fender-bender without supervision, and he did *not* appreciate being woken from his naps—but on rare occasions, something extraordinary would happen that begged for his attention. Which is why the most junior officer was sent to rouse him not long after the blue pickup truck with Davis Plumming lettered on its side drove off.

Grumpily wiping sleep from his eyes, Enright began reviewing the security tape. Ten minutes and a few fast-forwards later, he picked up a phone and dialed Merribaugh's cell phone. The call went to voicemail so he looked up another number and dialed again.

"The Rev. Dennis Merribaugh's room, please," he said when the phone was answered, then waited while the call was transferred and answered again.

"Merribaugh."

"Enright here," he told Merribaugh. "This may be nothing, but some plumbers came by about a half hour ago. Told the guard out front they were called to fix a toilet in Cathedral House."

This did not interest Merribaugh at all, and his response let Enright know the level of that disinterest: a sigh and a "So?"

"Thing is, Camera 7 on the fourth floor hallway shows 'em going to the finance office, but not coming back down the hall to the bathroom."

Now Merribaugh had *minor* interest…but only minor. "Hmm."

Enright continued, determined to make the most of that minor interest. "On top of that, the cameras in the finance office didn't pick up anything. Something was blocking the view."

"What?"

"We don't know yet. I sent a guard up to take a look a few minutes ago, but he said everything looked normal."

"Nothing's missing?"

"Not that we could tell."

Merribaugh mulled that over. "Who was up there with the plumbers?"

"That black woman who's been working there. Also a Caucasian male. Fortyish, dark hair…"

"Sounds like Charlie Hudson," said Merribaugh, which meant nothing to Enright.

"Those two are on most of the surveillance tape. It's only the plumbers we never saw. We have video of them entering the building, walking into the office, disappearing behind the obstruction, and leaving the premises. The black woman and Caucasian man left maybe ten minutes later, but we saw nothing else."

"This doesn't concern me. Maybe they found a leak in a pipe or something, and had to get into the wall."

"Just thought you'd like to know."

"And now I do." With that, he hung up.

Merribaugh clicked on the remote and the television blinked to life.

Enright's call had almost vanished from his mind when a sudden thought came to him. He found his cell phone and dialed.

"Yessir," answered Enright, recognizing the number.

"This obstruction," said Merribaugh. "Did it block the camera's view of the closet?"

"It did."

He didn't like that. "Send your officer back and make sure he checks the closet door. There's a safe there I use to store some personal effects. Make sure that door is locked and the hinges haven't been tampered with, and call me back."

Enright looked at the disconnected phone, then looked at his officers, trying to figure out who he could trust to make sure the job was done properly.

"Cason!"

Officer Cason looked up from his comic book. "Huh?"

He decided he'd better do it himself.

A few minutes later, Captain Joseph Enright let himself into the finance office. Everything looked secure, and the closet door was locked firmly. He called Merribaugh back.

"Sorry, sir. False alarm. All is secure."

19

"Yoo-hoo!"

Farraday had been frying bacon in the kitchen when he heard Tish at the front door. He was going to ignore her but figured her next move would be the doorbell, so it'd be better to take care of her right away.

He caught her moments before her red-nailed finger pressed the bell. "What?!"

His abruptness caught her off guard. "Is Mr. Williams home?"

"He's in bed."

"How about any of the Hudsons?"

"They're in bed, too. Look, lady, it's seven o'clock on a Sunday morning. *Everyone's* in bed."

She didn't like his tone, and made that clear. "I will not let you talk to me that way. I'm not sure, but that could be against HOA rules. And if it isn't, it *will* be by the end of the day."

He closed the door in her face.

Thirty seconds later—time Tish Fielding used for some deep breathing to calm herself—the doorbell rang. Thirty seconds later it rang again.

Grant voice hollered from upstairs. "What the hell! Get the door, Farraday."

"No," he said. "It's for you, so *you* get it."

The doorbell rang twice more—each ring bringing more shouts from above—until Grant, in bare feet, wrinkled khakis, and an untucked shirt, stormed down the stairs and flung open the front door.

"What?"

"Mr. Williams, you really need to have a talk with your chauffeur. He was just very rude to me."

Grant struggled to open his eyes. “He’ll get a talkin’ to. You can be sure of it. But why are *you* ringing the bell at seven in the morning?”

She shifted gears and smiled. “It’s Old Stone Fence Post Estates Clean-Up Day!”

“Huh?”

“The day we clean up from the party!”

He poked his head outside and looked up and down the street. “What are you talking about? There’s no mess. You were practically followin’ people with a vacuum cleaner yesterday. Nobody had a chance to make a mess.”

“Mr. Williams,” she said, and her hands went to her hips, “the worst messes are the ones that aren’t obvious. Like…like…” She pointed to the flower bed at the front door. “There’s one of Mrs. Hudson’s cigarette butts. God only knows how many more are strewn throughout this neighborhood.”

He forced open his eyes. “You’re kiddin’ me, right?”

“Certainly not.”

Grant sighed. “Look, we had a late night, and…”

“Cleanup starts at eight o’clock,” she announced and spun on her heels.

When the door was locked behind him, Grant said to no one in particular, “I really hate her.”

$ $ $

Over bacon and French toast sprinkled with cinnamon, Grant informed his crew they’d soon be policing the neighborhood, rooting out cigarette butts, gum wrappers, and—knowing Tish Fielding—dust mites, too.

“You can do it,” said Mary Beth as she sipped coffee and refused to look at him. “I’m done with this crap. We pull a job that brings in less than two percent of what you said it would…”

“*Who* pulled a job?” Grant asked.

“*We* did. Hey, I went to church, too. For one day. Anyway, all we’ve got to show for the work is ninety thousand dollars in a Wegmans bag hidden under the sink. Big freakin’ haul, Lambert. So there’s no way I’m gonna go outside and pull weeds just to keep the bitch across the street happy. No way!”

“Okay, sit here and watch television. I don’t care. But the rest of us are gonna fit in with the neighborhood." He looked at the others, who wouldn't meet his eyes. "Right?"

Chase cracked first. He was still feeling guilty about not reporting Merribaugh and his suitcase, so anything he could do to mitigate Grant's aggravation was a step in the right direction. "All right. I'll help."

Grant looked at Mary Beth. "But don't get too comfortable in front of the TV, because we're taking a little drive after we finish cleaning up the neighborhood."

"Who is?"

"You, me, and Farraday. We're going to DC."

She snorted. "For what?"

"Because," he said, "that's where the money is. You don't expect *Jared* to grab it, do you? He doesn't even know it's there."

"And we can't call him," added Chase. "They don't allow phones."

"Why does she get to go?" Lisa demanded.

Mary Beth agreed. "Yeah, why me?"

"Because I might need a woman, and since Lisa's the banker she has to stay here in Nash Bog. Just in case something goes wrong."

Mary Beth flapped her arms. "Oh, so I'm expendable…"

She was, Grant thought, but what he said was, "Nothing's gonna go wrong. But if there's a hiccup, you want Lisa to be able to bail you out, right?"

"This isn't fair, Lambert," said Lisa, and Grant finally realized that Chase was right. She really *did* want to be in on the job. "You're discriminating against me because I have money."

"Look, Chase is gonna stay behind, too. This is nothing personal."

But Mary Beth had figured out a way to avoid getting enmeshed in another one of Grant Lambert's schemes.

"I can't go," she said. "They've met me."

He dismissed that. "You lasted one day. Hopefully you weren't as memorable as we all know you can be. If so, we'll just have to deal with that."

$ $ $

There were a lot of people prowling the bushes, flower beds, and gutters of Old Stone Fence Post Road that morning. Too many for eight o'clock on a Sunday.

Grant, carrying a plastic bag, was studying the ground beneath a rose bush a few houses down the block when he heard a hushed "Psst." He looked up and saw Mr. Scribner, half-hidden in shrubbery.

"What's up, Scribs?" asked Grant.

Mr. Scribner laughed. "I love that! Say it again."

Grant was confused. "What?"

"Call me 'Scribs.'"

That was strange, but if that's what he wanted… "Okay…Scribs."

He laughed again, but at least this time he tried to explain. "That's what we're missing in this neighborhood, Williams. No one has fun. No one has nicknames. The minute something like that happens, the Fieldings tamp it down."

Grant scratched his head. "You realize they're just homeowners, right? No different than you and…well, okay, maybe different from me. Still, they're not king and queen of the subdivision."

"Yes, but they're so forceful."

Grant wouldn't let him get away with that. "You know everyone in the neighborhood hates them, so stop putting up with it. Go meet with those Jarvis and Huffine dames and do something. Rise up!"

"That sounds…very radical!"

Grant decided he was done with the cleanup, and probably done with the conversation, too. But not without a parting shot.

"Then unleash your inner radical. Leave a hose on the lawn. Go a week without cutting your grass. Let your freak flag fly high, Scribs!"

Back at the house, he tossed the plastic bag in the garbage and said, "This is one screwed-up neighborhood."

"You're just noticing?" asked Mary Beth.

"How would you know about the neighborhood? You haven't been off that couch in weeks." He turned to Constance and Grant. "And you two better clear out and get to the cathedral, in case anyone notices that someone paid a visit last night. It'd be too obvious if neither of you went back."

Instructions given, he was ready to relax. But not before he took a quick glance out the window…and saw Scribs standing in the street, deep in conversation with Ms. Jarvis.

Maybe their freak flags would fly after all.

$ $ $

Jack Hightower was not a happy man. And that, he thought, was the burden of being a heterosexual male working in the hospitality industry.

On an average Sunday, he'd be home relaxing. Or if he was called in to work, he'd be doing what assistant managers of elegant, upscale hotels do: hiding in his office until the occasionally unruly guest became too unruly to be handled by the front office staff. That once-every-two-day occurrence was survivable.

Then came the booking of Project Rectitude's Beyond Sin conference, and suddenly every gay man who worked at the hotel—and not a few of the women of every sexuality—couldn't work that weekend. The employees claimed dying grandparents and emergency surgeries and contagious diseases, but Jack Hightower knew better. He knew they weren't at work because they objected so deeply to the very presence of the conference in their workplace.

He agreed in principle, but *someone* had to work the desk. So now he stood in the lobby, checking in guests and fielding all those annoying complaints and inquiries he thought he'd left forever in the past with his promotion to assistant manager. He could only hope some of the other employees would soon need money more than a clean conscience, because he couldn't work the front desk alone for an entire week.

He looked across the lobby and finally spotted someone on whom he could focus his anger. The trim, silver-haired Dr. Oscar Hurley made his way through the room, smiling politely at guests lounging on chairs and couches. He was accompanied by his roundish, middle-aged aide de camp and a tall woman Hightower thought might be a Member of Congress. They paraded past without looking at him and walked into a waiting elevator.

"The next time," he said aloud to himself, as well as to a tourist from Milwaukee who'd been waiting to check in for seventeen minutes, "I hope they go to the Mayflower."

The tourist from Milwaukee, still waiting, wondered if the Mayflower might have any vacancies.

$ $ $

Dr. Oscar Hurley had a lovely suite on the top floor of the hotel. It came with a large four-poster bed that would have been big enough to accommodate Francine, had he bothered to bring her. It had a terrace with a partial view of the White House. And it had a parlor, which provided the perfect meeting space to discuss things better discussed in private with the congresswoman from Minnesota.

As they talked, he looked her over. In another term or two, she might prove even more useful than she already had as one of his principal House warriors against all things gay. But one day he'd have to make her over, as he'd made over Congressman Donald Skinner. Her helmet hair, drab clothes, and poor eye contact were off-putting to many people.

He'd polish her, though. In time, he'd polish her.

Their discussion came to an end, and Dennis Merribaugh appeared at Hurley's side. He held an envelope.

"This," said Hurley, "is for you."

The congresswoman began to reach for the envelope, but her hand stopped in midair.

"What is it?" she asked.

Hurley smiled. "Let's just call it contribution to your reelection campaign."

"If I'm not mistaken, the Moral Families Coalition has already maxed out on contributions to my campaign for this cycle."

"Which is why this is cash."

"Oh." She sat back. "I don't know…"

"Congresswoman, I am a man of the cloth," said Hurley. "No harm will come to you. This is not a bribe. Think of it as a tithe."

She ran a hand along the edge of her helmet-hair and looked at the envelope. "Are you sure it's okay?"

Hurley's smile was gentle. "You cannot do the Lord's work on Capitol Hill if you don't get reelected, can you?"

Recognizing his logic, the gentle-lady from Minnesota took the envelope.

When she was gone, Hurley said to Merribaugh, "It makes me nervous keeping that suitcase in a hotel room. Especially since we know the FBI and IRS are watching."

"What do you want me to do with it?" asked Merribaugh.

"Put it in the hotel safe." He thought for a moment. "And I doubt this will happen, but let's be prepared. Just in case the federal government decides to set up a showy raid to try to reassure the American public they're doing their jobs."

"What do you want me to do?"

"In case of emergency," said Hurley, "be prepared to swallow the claim ticket."

Dennis Merribaugh really hoped there was no raid. Especially when, after waiting twenty minutes in a long line at the front desk to check the suitcase, the clerk handed him a hard plastic claim ticket the thickness of a credit card.

"Thank you," he said to the clerk, who nodded unpleasantly in return.

How rude, thought Merribaugh. *Next year I should take this conference to the Mayflower.*

$ $ $

Chase and Constance inspected the finance office one last time. Everything looked good; just the way it had looked the first time Constance walked through the door.

The safe had been locked, and the closet door had also been locked. The defaced foam core rendition of the Great Cross was back behind the cabinet, and the easel had been returned to the corner.

Everything was perfect.

Right up until the moment the door burst open and a half dozen men rushed in.

With their weapons drawn.

And one of them yelled, "FBI! Don't move!"

$ $ $

In the security supply room in the basement, Officer Chris Cason shook Captain Joseph Enright awake.

"What?" he grumbled.

"Sir, we have a problem."

"Go away."

"No, I mean a *problem*. A *biiiig* problem!"

$ $ $

Sitting in the back of one of several black armored trucks parked outside Cathedral House, Special Agent Oliver Tolan of the Federal Bureau of Investigation looked Constance in the eye and said, "So where's the money?"

She rolled her eyes. "I told you before, I'm gonna tell you again. I have no idea what you're talking about."

He held his stare without blinking. "So you're saying you know nothing about the contents of the safe?"

"I didn't even know there *was* a safe," she said. "I just started a few days ago. I came down from New York after seeing Dr. Hurley on television, and they asked me to help out in the office."

He made it clear he didn't believe her. "You mean they just gave a newcomer a set of keys and turned her loose? Is that what you're saying?"

Well, yes, that *was* what she was saying. She wondered how many times she'd have to repeat the story before it sank in, but—in this case—a knock on the door gave her a break.

"Come in," said Tolan, and one of the other agents poked his head inside.

"I got a name on the other one," he said. "Charles LaMarca. Lives in Jackson Heights, Queens." The other agent looked at Constance. "Does that name ring a bell, Ms. Brown?"

She didn't answer.

Tolan asked, "Did this LaMarca tell you why he's going by the name Hudson?"

"Said he was trying to start a new life in Virginia, and a new name was part of that."

"Where'd he get Hudson from?"

"Kate."

"Oh." Tolan thought about that, and realized there wasn't much to think about. "You believe him?"

The other agent held a neutral expression. "He's probably on the level. Look, all these folks are guilty of is being in an office where no cash was found."

"Maybe." Tolan turned his attention back to Constance. "So is Constance Brown your *real* name?"

"No," she confessed, seeing a great deal of hope in the casual way they regarded Chase, and thinking maybe this situation would turn out all right after all. "It's Price. Constance Price."

"So why were you using a fake name?"

"Same reason as Mr. LaMarca," she said. "Same reason a lot of people who attend Cathedral of Love use fake names. Dr. Hurley tells us it's a way to give rebirth to our souls."

Tolan had never heard that one before. "Really?"

"Really." And she thought, *Damn, I'm good.*

Tolan asked for her real name, real address, and real social security number. Then he said, "Agent Waverly will run this information to confirm your identity."

"Right," said Waverly, who was the other agent. "And if your criminal record comes back as clean as LaMarca's, you'll both be free to go."

Wait a minute? Criminal record?

And it was too late to again insist her last name was Brown. Damn.

$ $ $

The first thing Chase did when he was released—and out of sight of any FBI agents—was dial Grant's cell and give him the news.

"So where did they take her?" asked Grant. Acid was churning in his stomach.

Chase covered his free ear to block out noise from the passing traffic. "No clue. All I know is once they found out she had a criminal record, they decided to hold her for further questioning."

"Keep me posted." Grant disconnected and filled in Farraday and Mary Beth.

Farraday, sitting behind the wheel as they inched through a construction-related traffic jam, asked, "Do you think she might have scammed us? I mean, she was alone in that office all week, then we busted in and there was no money. It's a little fishy…"

"Constance is good people," said Grant. "I've pulled a lot of jobs with her over the years, and she's never been less than honest. For a thief, at least."

Mary Beth asked, "Should we get her a lawyer?"

Grant shook his head. "This is not something Constance is unfamiliar with. Let's ride that out for a while and trust her to keep her own counsel. It's not like the feds are gonna lock her up with no evidence."

His stomach said otherwise.

$ $ $

Minutes after ending his brief conversation with Captain Enright, Merribaugh rapped lightly on Dr. Oscar Hurley's hotel room door. When the knock was answered, Merribaugh got straight to the point.

"Enright just called. The FBI raided Cathedral House about an hour ago."

Color drained from Hurley's face and he gestured for Merribaugh to come into the room. It was only when Hurley had a moment to think things over—realizing that if the FBI had found what they were looking for, he'd likely have been arrested before they knew about the raid—that he managed to find his voice again.

"Why did it take Enright an hour to call?"

"They were questioning him." Merribaugh shook his head. "At least they let Enright go. Charlie Hudson, too."

"Who?"

"Charlie Hudson. He's a new member of the congregation who's been helping out in the office." Hurley's face betrayed no hint of recognition, so he continued. "But the FBI is still holding Constance."

"Constance?" Hurley shook his head sadly. "This is why we plan ahead, Dennis. Has she been arrested?"

"Not yet. The problem is…Constance apparently has a criminal record."

Hurley took a step back. He'd thought himself a better judge of character than that. "For?"

"Enright is looking into that. But one thing we *do* know is the woman we've been calling Constance Brown is really Constance Price. At least that's what she told the FBI."

"Interesting."

"One other thing you should know…" Merribaugh swallowed hard. "The FBI broke into the safe." He swallowed harder. "It was empty."

For the first time since Merribaugh had entered the room, Hurley's face expressed genuine surprise, instead of puzzled confusion. "So Constance *is* a thief! She *was* casing Cathedral House!"

Merribaugh didn't want to admit that, because he knew Hurley would again blame him for a bad hiring decision. But facts were facts. She'd been with the plumbers, hadn't she? Not that that was something Hurley had to know. "It looks like that was the case."

"How much did she get?" he asked.

"I'm not sure. Maybe one hundred thousand dollars."

Hurley frowned. "I suppose it's a drop in the bucket, all things considered. Still, Dennis, I do *not* like to have that kind of money just sitting around. You've got to move it out of the office faster than you do. I mean, can you imagine if the FBI had found more than one hundred thousand dollars in the safe? Let alone seven million. How would we explain that?"

Merribaugh had an answer for that. He'd had an answer for that for most of the time they'd worked together.

"In the case of a hundred thousand dollars, I'd tell the FBI the money was offerings we had not yet had the time to deposit in the bank. That part is easy."

"And how would we explain *seven million dollars*, Dennis?"

Merribaugh felt a cool sweat break out on his brow. Hurley very seldom mentioned that amount. The fact that he had mentioned it twice underscored his concern.

"They'll never find it," he said, hoping he sounded convincingly reassuring.

"I suppose…But from this point forward, I don't want cash in the safe for more than one day. It's not as if you have to go far to take care of it."

"Fair enough," said Merribaugh. "It won't happen again."

Hurley sat on the edge of his bed. "Well, this has been an interesting morning. Very interesting, indeed. But if the FBI had to pay us a call, I suppose they picked the right day to do it. And they managed to catch the woman who stole from us in the process."

"That's one way to look at it," Merribaugh agreed.

"I realize she did us an inadvertent favor, but I want you to find out how Sister Constance got into that safe and got our money. Then I want you to get it back. Understood?"

"Understood."

"Good. And now we should pray for Sister Constance."

And then Hurley laughed. It was the laugh of a man who was willing to lose one hundred thousand dollars in order to cover his own ass.

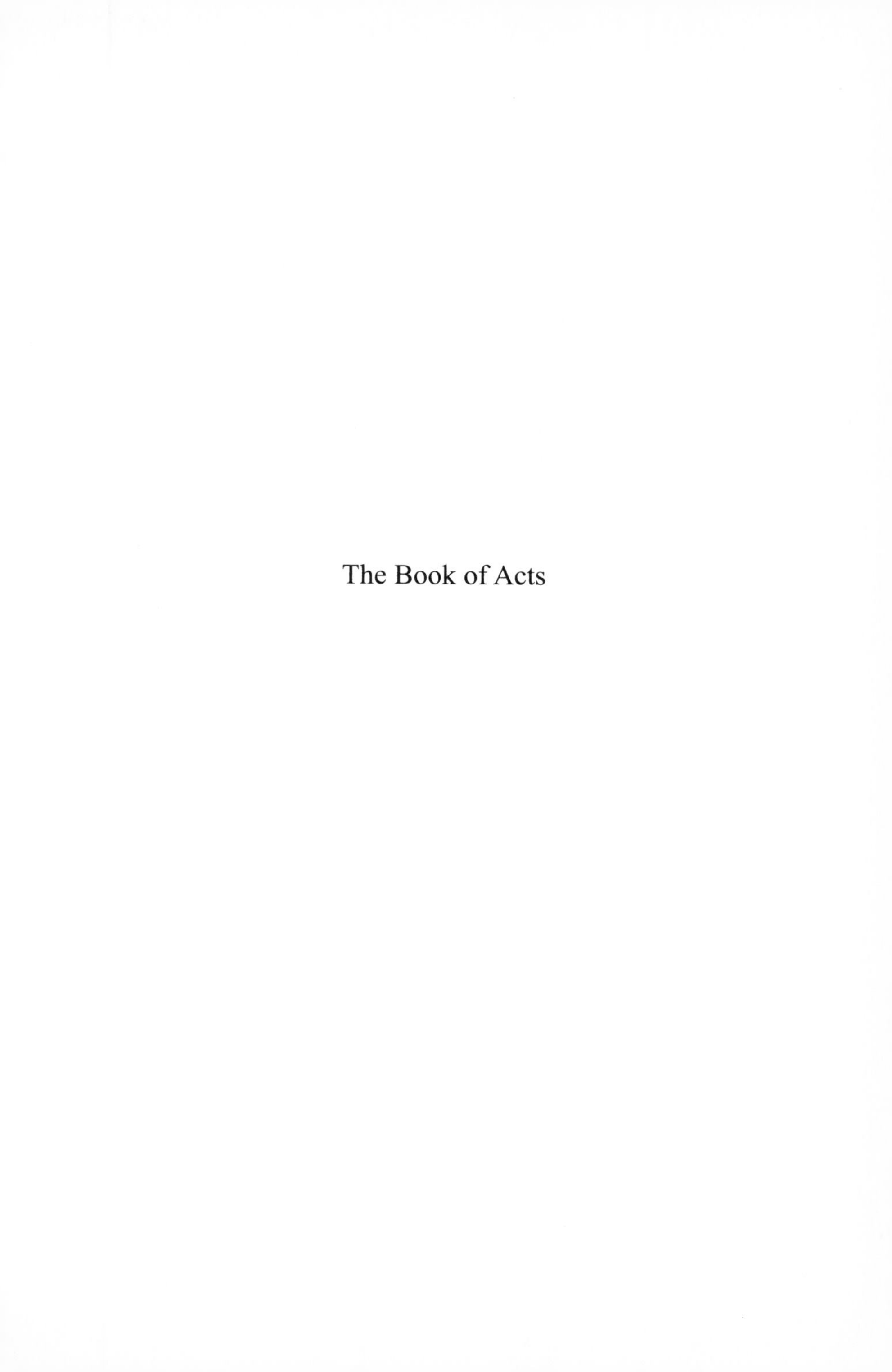

The Book of Acts

20

Jared sat on the bed and idly clicked a button on the remote, flipping through television channels. Golf…gardening…history…golf again…home makeovers…politics…golf yet again…religion…politics…more golf…

Who knew things would become so boring? They had started out so promising.

When he arrived the previous night, he'd checked in, unpacked, and immediately hit the hotel gym. He had no intention of working out, but he was sure there'd be another conference participant or two attempting to sweat the gay out, or if not, some random man who'd be ripe for seduction. So sure, in fact, he didn't bother wearing underwear.

He hadn't necessarily liked what he found in the gym, but his instincts had been right. And anyway, that ex-gay wouldn't talk about what happened in the men's room off the gym, so Jared's reputation wouldn't suffer.

Same thing with the guy he met at the business center when he wandered in an hour later, still wearing cute gym shorts, cuter sneakers, and a tight tee, a slightly used towel slung over his shoulders. And still *not* wearing underwear.

He almost felt sorry for his business center conquest, who began crying and praying to God for forgiveness and reciting The Lord's Prayer the minute *his* part of the encounter was over, but…no. Jared couldn't feel bad for someone who'd taken care of his own needs without worrying about Jared's, so he left him on his knees in front of the HP printer and, whistling, went off to explore the rest of the hotel.

The conference didn't start until the following day, but already it was teeming with gay men who desperately didn't want to be gay. He rode the elevator floor to floor, getting off only to walk the halls as if walking a runway, and got more than his share of double takes. On the seventh floor he passed Business Center Guy as he hurried to his room, still reciting The Lord's Prayer under his breath, but their eyes didn't meet. On the eighth, Gym Guy also brushed past without acknowledging him.

He felt a sense of power over these gay men who didn't want to be, but who still couldn't resist a hot piece of ass like…well, like *Jared Parsells*. So he took a position in an extremely uncomfortable high-back chair just outside the tenth-floor elevator, threw one leg over the arm so one cute leg—and one cute sneaker—dangled in midair, and waited for the next encounter.

It didn't take long until a man—fortyish in body, late-fiftyish in face—got off the elevator, gave him that now-familiar double take, and kept looking back as he walked two doors down. He inserted his keycard in the slot, walked into the room, and the door closed…

Almost all the way. But not quite. And even Jared knew that a door ajar was an invitation.

Tenth-Floor Guy, to his credit, didn't cry when he got back down on his knees…this time to pray.

Jared was still satisfied that no one would talk; he just wasn't… *satisfied*. So for the next few hours he investigated the rest of the hotel until—at some point after 4:00 a.m.—he decided the night had dried out. It hadn't been the most exciting night he'd ever prowled through—not even the most promiscuous; not even in the Top Fifty, for that matter—but it had given him some insight into the people he was dealing with.

They were gay. They would *always* be gay.

Oh, they didn't *want* to be gay. But as much as they tried to pray and cry the gay away, they were gay. Given the right temptation—Jared Parsells, for example; maybe the *best* example—they couldn't resist nature.

They were also selfish. He was fine being objectified—he *lived* to be objectified—but these men were missing the whole "us" aspect to their sexual encounters. It was all about them until they got off, then it was over.

No wonder their heads were so screwed up, he thought as he turned off the TV a few minutes before the sun would peek over the horizon and prepared to sleep alone.

$ $ $

Golf...gardening...history...golf again...home makeovers... politics...golf yet again...religion...politics...more golf...

Bored, he powered off the television and reached for his cell phone on the nightstand. As if to rub it in his face, his hand landed on a Bible instead of a cell.

He knocked the Bible to the floor and remembered the phone was back in Nash Bog, because cell phones weren't allowed at Beyond Sin. Nothing was allowed at Beyond Sin. Especially this morning, when the attendees in the hotel were no longer limited to the early arrivals.

Today it was going to get real.

Hurley and Merribaugh would be there. Members of Congress would be there. The prayers would begin today; the brainwashing would kick into high gear tomorrow.

Which meant no more hanging out on random floors, naked under sheer gym shorts as he dangled his cute leg and super-cute sneakers and picking up random guys getting off of the elevators.

Or did it? There could potentially be some prime hunting during this conference. Not that the night before had been so great, but it *could* get better. Maybe Gym Guy, Business Center Guy, and Tenth-Floor Guy were the exceptions, not the rule.

He didn't add Off-Duty Room Service Waiter to the mix. That one really didn't really count, after all.

He ran through the rules for the conference one more time.

No cell phones. Well, his was gone, and sadly missed.

No outside phone calls. The phones had been programmed to go directly to the front desk; not even room-to-room calls were allowed.

No illicit fraternization. Jared assumed that meant he shouldn't have any more sex with the ex-gays and wannabe ex-gays, but—after the previous night—that rule seemed sort of flexible.

No alcohol, drugs, or pornography. He would miss the occasional drink—and porn, of course; did he even have to go there?—but he could survive.

Participants should reflect, pray, and read the Bible during downtime. Whatever. Jared was going to watch *The Golden Girls* as soon as he was free of the conference and he could find a cable channel that wasn't politics or golf.

But there was no requirement that participants stay in their rooms, and while "illicit fraternization"—whatever that meant besides sex with ex-gays, although maybe that was all it meant—was discouraged, no one said you couldn't make friends.

In fact, wasn't one of the purposes of this conference to help build ex-gay support networks? Jared couldn't quite remember, but it seemed to make sense. So if he stayed out of the gym…and the business center…and the elevators…and…well, if he *behaved* himself—*and* wore underwear—there was no reason to stay cooped up in his room.

He chose the tightest clothes he could find. Chase had a sharp eye, but not sharper than Jared's when it came to packing a suitcase. Soon he was wearing jeans so tight they almost showed a blemish on his lower leg and a shirt that, if he yawned, would expose a stomach that—if not exactly a six-pack, because that would require actual gym time with weights, not just the steam room—was so taut you could bounce a quarter off it and get back two dimes and a nickel.

And then it was time to check out the check-ins.

$ $ $

First, Oscar Hurley had to walk a gauntlet of Merribaugh's limp-wristed ex-gays on his way through the lobby. The way they practically leered at him—no doubt imagining him naked, despite their avowed if probably futile hope to change their sexualities—was bad enough.

Worse was the realization that more than a few of them bore a passing resemblance to his wife. Not the rail-thin Francine he'd married; the three hundred pound Francine to whom he was *still* married.

Worse yet was the realization that their makeup was better than Francine's.

And worse still, Merribaugh was now standing in the open doorway of his hotel room. And he had one of them *with* him! That was just too much.

"Can I help you, Mr. Merribaugh?" Hurley tried not to look at the young man standing at Dennis Merribaugh's side. "As you know, I have a lot on my mind today."

Merribaugh understood. "I know, but this will only take a moment, Dr. Hurley. Can we come in?"

"No." To emphasize the point, he motioned to the robe he was wearing. "I'm not dressed."

"Oh, uh…" Merribaugh recovered from his momentary fluster. "But I thought you'd like to meet Daniel Rowell."

Hurley didn't try to hide his contempt. "Why?"

"Oh, uh…Because Daniel here was referred by one of our friends."

Hurley began to close the door. "I don't have time..."

"Our friend Senator Cobey!"

Hurley held the door in the half-closed position and finally took a look at the young man standing in the hall. He was presentable, he finally decided. Not a flaming queen like that Jerry Stanley. Dressed in khakis and a blue button-down shirt, with a conservative haircut, he could almost pass as normal. In short, he was one of those *dangerous* gays: the type who moved among respectable people without giving off warning signals, infiltrating society from within.

Hurley would have to keep an eye on him.

"Welcome to Project Rectitude, Daniel," he said, holding his gaze as long as possible, which wasn't very long. "I assume you're the young man Senator Cobey mentioned the other day."

"Yes, sir." Dan nodded respectfully. "He wants me to...to...get well."

Hurley clutched his robe tightly. "I heard hesitation in your voice. Do *you* want to get well?"

Again there was the briefest of pauses, almost imperceptible. "I do, sir. I want to be normal."

Merribaugh, standing in the hall behind Dan, clapped his hands. "I am so pleased that Senator Cobey is helping you get your life back on track, Daniel! Isn't this good news, Dr. Hurley?"

Both Hurley and Dan grunted an affirmation.

"If that's all..." said Hurley, who began closing the door without waiting for a response.

"I have one question," Dan said quickly, and Hurley again held the door, although not without a slight eye-roll. "Will there be electro-shocks?"

Hurley neither knew nor cared, so Merribaugh answered. "Oh, no! No one uses electro-shocks anymore!"

It was probably Hurley's imagination—it *had* to be Hurley's imagination—but the kid seemed almost disappointed. Again, he started to close the door.

"Will I have to sleep with a woman?"

Hurley held onto the door handle and it stopped its swing. "What kind of question is that?" he asked sourly, as Merribaugh stuttered.

"I was just wondering what you'll be doing to make me normal."

Finally composed, Merribaugh said, "Nothing like that, Daniel. In fact, we frown upon sex outside of wedlock. You will learn to get beyond this sin through reflection, prayer, and the testimony of those who have already learned to leave homosexuality behind and love normally. No electro-shock treatment, no sex with…" He blushed, unable to finish the sentence. "Trust me though, son. When this conference is over, you will only want to have personal relationships with women!"

"And only in a marriage sanctified by the Lord," Hurley added, tightening his grip on the robe.

"Oh, yes. Of course."

"Okay," said Dan. "Thank you. I was just curious."

But by then, Hurley had finally closed the door and thrown the lock.

$ $ $

Jared sat in an overstuffed chair in the lobby, watching the slow trickle of guests check in. His gaydar told him that at least half the people who'd passed by the registration desk were there for the conference, but few were even passably his type, his type being "pretty" and/or "rich." Pretty was obvious, rich less so, but there seemed to be little of either in the hotel that afternoon.

There was, however, a lot of "sad," "angry," and "self-conscious"; usually in the same package. He could see it in their faces, in their walks, in the way their shoulders slumped and their eyes darted warily.

He'd been sitting for the better part of an hour—time in which he hadn't even pretended to do something other than watch the passing crowd—when a middle-aged man swept in with such a sense of self-importance that Jared had to take notice. He was trim, tall, fair, and square-jawed, with red hair trimmed short and the hint of a bristly five o'clock shadow. His expensive clothes had obviously been tailored to show off his body.

Jared thought, *Hmmm…*

He exchanged seats for one a bit closer to the registration desk in time to hear the clerk say, "Here's your room key, Mr. Lombardo. Enjoy your stay."

Jared's eyes followed Mr. Lombardo as he strutted through the lobby to the elevator bank and watched his ass under the perfectly tailored fabric as he waited. Finally, the doors opened; Mr. Lombardo made a half turn toward Jared, smiled, and stepped inside. He held the door open for a few seconds—maybe waiting for Jared to join him?—but finally it closed.

He might have followed him if not for the appearance of another hottie, this one considerably younger than Mr. Lombardo. The sad, angry, self-conscious ex-gays seemed to have made way for eye candy—albeit eye candy of indeterminate sexuality—and that was fine with Jared. This was why he'd come to the lobby, after all.

The hottie wore a blue shirt and khakis that hung loosely on his frame, offering more than Mr. Lombardo to the imagination. It was a preppy look, reinforced by a conservative haircut. Not a bad effect, overall; not Jared's look, but who *else* could carry off Jared's look? *Although...* He glanced down at the boring clothes Chase had forced him to bring to the conference and sighed.

Jared watched the hottie cross the lobby until he reached the chair Jared had vacated to get closer to Mr. Lombardo, then looked around the room, his eyes passing right over Jared. He picked up a newspaper from the granite-topped table positioned next to the chair, shook it open, and began reading.

Did he really just look right past me? thought Jared. That was not acceptable behavior, no matter how ex-gay he wanted to be.

$ $ $

Hidden behind the newspaper, Dan Rowell was deconstructing his first meeting with the infamous Dr. Oscar Hurley.

It was clear he didn't like Dan—except for, perhaps, the curiosity appeal of his job with Gordon Cobey—but that wasn't worth taking personally. Hurley clearly didn't like *any* gay people.

Hurley had, in fact, made it clear from what he had *not* done that Project Rectitude and this ridiculous Beyond Sin conference were Merribaugh's brainchildren. Merribaugh had been welcoming and maybe a little bit too familiar; Hurley was a cold fish. That knowledge only made Dan resent his attendance all the more.

Equally unsettling were the stares he kept getting in the halls. He'd expected to be the subject of interest, because what kind of hopeful ex-gay or recent convert wasn't curious about the other men who'd show up for a conference like this? But these were the sorts of stares he'd expect in a bathhouse, not in a hotel full of men who resented their own homosexuality and wanted to change.

He should have dressed to repel. And a bad haircut wouldn't have hurt, either. But it was too late now. He'd have to tough it out with a decent wardrobe and great hair.

Dan was three paragraphs into an article about the latest turmoil in the Middle East when he sensed the presence of someone on the other side of his newspaper. He lowered it a few inches until his eyes could see over the top, and there stood the kid with the blond, blond, *blond* hair he'd noticed when he'd walked into the lobby minutes earlier.

He stared over the top of the newspaper. The kid stared back.

"Can I help you?"

"I'm Jared."

Dan sighed and folded the paper into his lap. "Nice to meet you, Jar—"

"Are you here for the conference?"

Dan had no doubt this Jared was gay—there were gray areas to almost everything in life, but not that—but he was unsure how to answer. Jared seemed like the last person whose psyche was burdened by the curse of homosexuality.

"Which conference?" he finally asked.

Jared put a finger to his lower lip. "Oh, wait. I always get this wrong. Project…not Project Erection." He thought a moment. "Project *Erectitude*?"

Dan laughed, despite himself. "You mean Project Rectitude?"

"That's it!"

"Why do you ask?" Dan still wasn't sure how he should answer. Something felt off.

Jared leaned forward until one knee brushed Dan's. "That's why *I'm* here. I was just curious."

Dan raised an eyebrow. "*You* want to give up homosexuality?"

"Oh, sure. Whatever. And you?"

"I'm here because…" He stopped himself and considered how much he wanted to say. "I guess I'm here for the same reason. My boss wanted me to come."

"Your boss wanted you to…?" Jared looked perplexed, and then got it. "Oh, you mean your boss wants you to *be ex-gay*! Gotcha. That's sort of why I'm here, too."

Dan set the paper aside. "It's kind of rough when we have to come to a thing like this for the job, right?"

"Right. The last job I had like this, all I really had to do was crash a pool party."

"A pool…?" Sometimes when Dan was having a hard time keeping up, he blamed his own distraction, but this time he was quite sure Jared was the cause.

It didn't matter. Jared's stream of consciousness continued. "So here's the good thing about Project Erectitude…"

"Rectitude."

"Right. The good thing is that I get to be the new poster boy!"

"You...*what*?"

"Hurley and Merribaugh are going to make me the new face of ex-gay! That's pretty cool, right?"

"*Ex*-gay?" Dan stared at Jared. "Are you sure you aren't confusing this with 'before' in the before-and-after shots?"

"No!" Jared's expression turned serious. "Do you think they'll have me make a commercial? Or pose for billboards?"

Dan shook his head. "I'm having a hard time with this. No offense, but you..." He took a deep breath. "Well, let's just say I'm having a hard time with this."

Jared was put out. This "poster boy" concept was the only thing that made him slightly enthusiastic about the conference. If this guy wasn't buying it...

He spotted Merribaugh across the lobby and waved him over.

Before Merribaugh had even had a chance to greet him, Jared asked, "Isn't it true that I'm going to be the poster boy?"

"Yes. Yes, it is." It was only then he realized Dan was in the chair below him. "I see you two have met."

"Not really," said Jared. "All I know is he's here for work. I don't even know his name."

"Dan Rowell." Dan extended his hand. "And I'm *not* here for work. I'm here because my boss thought it would be a good idea." He looked up at Merribaugh and remembered to add, "And so do I, of course."

"I'm *thrilled* you're both here," said Merribaugh. "Dan will be living proof of our success on Capitol Hill, and Jerry, well..." He looked affectionately at the younger man. "Jerry will be a wonderful spokesman for the cause."

After Merribaugh left, Dan asked, "Why did he call you Jerry? Is that, like, a nickname?"

"It's a stupid name," said Jared. "I prefer Jared. Except here, where they want people to call me Jerry."

Dan blinked. "They? They *who*?"

"Never mind." He realized Dan looked a lot like a guy back in Manhattan he'd had a huge crush on, and wondered if he was built the same way under those loose clothes. For that reason, and since he had nothing better to do, he asked, "Want to hang out?"

Dan exhaled a "What?" before he'd had a chance to think.

"You seem cool. I just thought we could hang out." Dan felt Jared's hand brush his thigh and was pretty sure it wasn't accidental.

Dan thought about that and realized he, too, had nothing better to do. However, there were rules. "We're sort of restricted, aren't we? The bar is out of the question, and the lobby is getting boring."

"Let's go up to my room."

"I don't think that's a good idea."

"It's *my* idea! Who cares if it's good or not?"

$ $ $

"I know I sound like a broken record," said Farraday, "but I *really* hate driving in this city. My instincts keep failing me."

In fact, his instincts had been failing him for almost twenty minutes, and the car circled block after block but never seemed to get any closer to the hotel.

Grant looked impatiently at his watch. "Just drop me off up at that bus stop and I'll walk. I've got to get to Jared."

Farraday pulled to the curb. Behind them, a Metrobus driver laid on his horn.

"What do you want me to do while you're at the hotel?" asked Farraday, ignoring the horn.

Grant shrugged. "Just keep circling. You're getting good at it."

$ $ $

"Here's the thing I don't understand." Special Agent Patrick Waverly sat casually on the edge of a table, looking down at Constance. "The Virginia Cathedral of Love has hundreds of millions of dollars in assets—maybe more—but they've entrusted financial management to you. An ex-con using a fake name who's just arrived in town. That doesn't make sense to me."

Constance shook her head. "I didn't make any decisions. I just did what Dr. Hurley asked."

He smiled. "The question, Ms. Price, is whether you're a collaborator or a dupe. Or perhaps you just decided to take your life of crime on the road, and figured a mega-church was a tempting target."

"Excuse me? Who'd be foolish enough to try to rip off a mega-church?" She looked almost disappointed in him. "Get real, Waverly."

A few minutes later Waverly stood outside the holding room with Special Agent Oliver Tolan, who'd been watching their session on a monitor.

"You've got to get meaner with her, Patrick. Break her."

"Yeah," said Waverly. "Maybe we could waterboard her."

Tolan smiled. "Now, you're talking. Good times, my friend, good times." He looked back at the monitor. "She's a tough one, though. One of those name, rank, and serial number types. I don't know how much information you're gonna get out of her."

"She claims she doesn't even remember her address," said Waverly. "Which makes me think…"

Tolan interrupted. "She shares an address with Charles LaMarca?"

Waverly nodded. "That's what I'm thinking."

Tolan nodded. "Only one way to find out." He pushed a button next to the monitor, and moments later, a laser printer deposited a photo of Constance in the tray. "Why don't you take this up to Old Stone Fence Post Estates and find out."

$ $ $

"So tell me, Dan," said Jared, after he'd made sure the door to his room was locked, "what makes you tick?"

"Huh?"

"What do you like to do?"

"I like…well, I like work."

Jared smiled. "That's not what I meant. What do you *liiiike*?" He drew out the word, making every effort to let the thought behind it come to the surface, and knew he'd made himself loud and clear when he saw a thickening in Dan's khakis.

But on the surface, at least, Dan played it straight. "I like sailing. And softball."

Jared leered. "And hardball?"

He isn't very subtle, thought Dan. "Politics *is* hardball."

Jared had been moving in for the kill, but now stepped back. "You're in politics?"

Dan shrugged. "We're in Washington, DC. It's a company town. So…yeah."

"I don't understand politics." Jared sat on the bed, a little too close to Dan. "Maybe you could teach me."

Dan laughed. "I could teach you all night and only scratch the surface…"

Jared took his hand. "I like that 'all night' part…"

At that, Dan's hand was back in his lap. "Look, I think…I think we're doing this ex-gay thing the wrong way. I don't think flirting in a locked hotel room and holding hands is the way to…uh…cure our same-sex desires."

For a brief moment, Jared was going to object. Until he remembered the job was bigger than seducing Dan just because he was sure he could.

Merribaugh obviously felt Dan was important—not as important as Jared, of course, but still…—which made the situation delicate. If he played it wrong—or if, God forbid, Dan became remorseful—his fraud could be quickly discovered, which would in turn bring the house of cards down. He had to play it cool.

But of course, because he was Jared Parsells, what came out of his mouth was, "I won't tell if *you* don't tell."

That almost worked. But then there was a knock at the door.

"Room service."

Jared stared at the locked door. "I didn't order…"

"Compliments of Dr. Hurley."

Jared smiled at Dan, and in a near whisper said, "There are advantages to being the ex-gay poster boy! I hope he sent champagne and strawberries."

Dan raised an eyebrow. "Uh…I don't think they send those to people at an ex-gay conference. Even to the poster boys."

"I guess we'll find out!" Jared bounced off the bed and was halfway to the door before Dan caught him by the back of his belt and he came to an abrupt stop. "What?"

So low Jared could barely hear him, Dan hissed, "What if it's Merribaugh? Or even Hurley?"

"But it's *room service*!" Jared twisted away from him and reached the door before Dan could again reach for the belt.

The door was opened. A frowning man with salt-and-pepper hair stood on the other side of it.

"Oh." Jared looked around him and into the hall. "Where did the guy from room service go?"

Grant Lambert shook his head. "That was me, you nitwit." He looked past Jared to Dan. "Who's that?"

"Another ex-gay."

Under his breath, Grant muttered, "Not for long, if I know you."

Dan walked up behind Jared, taking care not to make any physical contact that could look questionable. "Can we help you with something?"

"It's okay," said Jared, turning to face him. "It's not room service. It's…it's…" He glanced at Grant, then returned his attention to Dan. "It's my father."

Grant's frown deepened, and Dan offered one to match. Because if Jared's father was here, it meant he was complicit in sending him to this ex-gay conference. Certainly someone like Jared wouldn't be here on his own. Which meant Jared's father was one of *those* types of parents.

Not unlike his own.

Still, the politician in him sought to make peace. There would be time to rescue Jared later.

"I can see the resemblance," said Dan.

"Shut up," was the mumbled response, and Dan involuntarily took a step back.

Jared's head bounced back and forth between Grant and Dan several times while he tried to decide what to do or say, but finally he remembered that if Grant was standing in front of him it probably meant seven million dollars was at stake. And he could—no, he *would*—catch up with Dan later.

"Can you excuse us, Dan? Pops and I need to talk."

When they were alone and the door was secure, Grant handed Jared his cell phone.

"I'm not supposed to have a phone," he said. "The rules…"

"Forget the rules. We have our own rules now."

Jared looked lovingly at his phone. "Hey, I missed seventeen texts!"

Grant took the phone out of his hand. "Forget those until you're back in New York. What I'm about to have you do will require all your concentration. Can you do that for me?"

"Uh…sure?"

Grant sighed. He hated to play this card, but… "Can you do that for Chase?"

"Sure!"

Grant wanted to say something about how inappropriate it was for Jared to lust after his boyfriend right in front of him, but let it go. There'd be time for that later.

"Okay, then, listen closely. It's time to put you to work…"

"Oh, I've been working. Three blow jobs already. These ex-gays are *sex-crazed*!"

"That's far too much information." He backed Jared deeper into the room. "I need you to get something from Merribaugh, and I'm not too particular how you do it, if you know what I mean."

Jared mulled over Grant's words. "You want me to sleep with him?"

"I don't care. Whatever works. From what I've heard, I figure you stand a chance with him."

Jared didn't think much of that idea. "But Merribaugh wears polyester suits!"

"Merribaugh might be wheeling around a suitcase with seven million dollars inside."

Jared's distaste vanished. "Now that I think about it, he's sort of hot. In a 'daddy' kind of way."

Grant shook those words out of his head. "Just find out where the suitcase is. However you do it is fine with me, as long as we get the money."

Jared was confused again. "I thought the money was in the safe."

"So did we. But it wasn't." He tried to be patient but failed. "Which is why I'm here telling you to find the suitcase."

"And steal it?"

"No. I don't wanna put you in a dangerous spot." He also didn't want Jared to screw it up. "When you find it, text me the location and I'll take it from there. I've already programmed my number into your phone."

"Okay," said Jared, but then he stopped. "How did you program your number into my phone? You don't know the password."

"The password," said Grant, "was JARED. It really wasn't that difficult to figure out."

$ $ $

Off the lobby was a registration table for Beyond Sin, making it logically the first place Jared went to look for Merribaugh. He was surprised that he wasn't there.

A former lesbian who was overcompensating with Sephora said, "I think he went up to Dr. Hurley's suite, but he should be back soon."

Jared sat down to wait, and he was still waiting an hour later. He spent his time checking out the ex-gays as they tentatively made their way to the registration table and wasn't particularly impressed. Although it was nice to know he'd be the prettiest one.

Mr. Lombardo, with his swagger, seemed to be the only person who wasn't fazed as he approached the table. Sephora Girl greeted him warmly.

"There's our poster boy!" said Merribaugh, approaching from the lobby, and Jared started to rise until he realized he was talking to Lombardo. The men embraced.

"Ahem," said Jared.

"Ah! Jerry!" He turned to Lombardo. "Louis Lombardo, I'd like you to meet Jerry Stanley. Jerry, Louis."

"*I'm* the poster boy," said Jared, finally standing to shake hands.

"Yes," said Merribaugh. "And Louis was *last* year's poster boy. This year he's going to conduct a workshop on redirecting deviant energy into positive results."

"That's right," said Lombardo. "The time and effort homosexuals waste on finding and having sex is time and effort that can be better used to improve oneself."

"Depends on how you're finding and having sex," said Jared.

"Huh?"

"Uh…Just joking. *Anyway…*" He took Merribaugh's elbow and gave Louis Lombardo a dismissive sneer. "Is there somewhere we can speak in private?"

Merribaugh was concerned. "Is there a problem?"

"Sort of."

"Well…" He looked past the registration desk, where a large ballroom was mostly empty. "Let's go over there and…"

"No," said Jared. "Someone might see us talk."

"Well, uh…"

"How about my room?"

"Your…" Merribaugh gulped. "Hotel room?"

Jared smiled. "I need to be in my comfort zone."

$ $ $

Mary Beth's first reaction to Grant's plan was not favorable.

"Your wife? I have to pretend to like you?"

"Of course not," he said. "Keep hating me, and we'll be just like every other heterosexual married couple."

They were leaning against the car, which Farraday had finally managed to park around the corner from the hotel. He figured for the ride home he'd grab something from the line of cars waiting for the valet, which would be much more convenient.

Grant continued. "It helps that Jared's on the inside, but that's not enough. We need to be in there, too. Especially because, well, we're talkin' Jared."

That part she understood. The rest, though…

"Don't get me wrong, Lambert, but I'd just as soon not share a hotel room with you."

"You think I'm crazy about the idea? But if we check in together as husband and wife, it'll look natural. And, unlike me, you can be charming. When you want to. Charm isn't one of my strong points."

"That's true," said Farraday.

"Shuddup."

Mary Beth said, "And how do we explain not having any luggage?"

Grant nodded to a pile of trash set out at curbside across the street. "There's a suitcase."

"You have *got* to be kidding me."

He waited for traffic to clear and crossed. Reluctantly, she followed, more out of curiosity than anything else.

The suitcase was definitely trash-worthy, covered with scuffs, dents, and dirt. But the zipper worked, which was all Grant cared about.

"Here," said holding out the handle to her.

"I'm not touching that."

Grant shook his head and muttered, "Gotta do everything myself," then grabbed the handle with one hand and opened the suitcase with the other. It was empty, which was good, because he'd imagined the worst.

He scanned the trash pile until his eyes settled on some bundled magazines. He set down the suitcase to unbundle them.

"What are you doing?" she asked.

"Making an empty suitcase not empty."

Mary Beth looked over his shoulder as he started filling the suitcase with magazines. "Wait! I haven't read that issue of *Vogue*!"

$ $ $

When they reached Jared's room, the young man got straight to the point. "I don't feel special."

Merribaugh hadn't known what to expect, but this would have been last on his list. "But you are special, Jerry. You're a special creature of God."

"That's not what I mean. I mean, no one is making a fuss over me. I'm stuck in this hotel room and I'm bored."

"You'll make friends. You'll find things to do. Maybe if you went to the gym…"

"I've been to the gym." Which was at least the truth. "That didn't do it. I thought I was going to be treated special, and that's not happening." Merribaugh started to say something, but Jared stopped him. "And now I discover there's another ex-gay poster boy in the house. That's like adding injury to insult."

"You mean insult to…Never mind. Louis Lombardo was last year's attraction. That has nothing to do with you."

Jared slumped face-down on the bed and sobbed. "I'm having self-esteem issues."

Which would have been the second-last thing on Merribaugh's list. He leaned forward and gently stroked the boy's hair. "Jerry, you'll be fine."

Still face-down, Jared's muffled voice said, "I think I know the problem."

"What? Tell me."

"My clothes are gay."

"Your clothes are…what?"

Jared rolled over. "All the clothes I brought with me—everything I own—are things I bought when I was gay. And I bought them because they reinforced my, uh, *gayness*. I need non-gay clothes." Jared thought about that. "*Pretty* non-gay clothes."

"Huh?"

"I mean, if I'm going to be the star attraction at Project Erection…"

"Project *Rectitude*."

"That's what I said," Jared said with a nod. "Anyway, if I'm going to be the star, I need to stand out, right?"

"Well, uh…"

"I need…" Jared stopped. "How much cash do you have on you?"

"Why do you ask?" Merribaugh had been taken by hustlers at similar conferences before, with their innocent faces and treacherous hearts, and he wasn't about to let it happen again. One even had to be careful around someone as seemingly, well, *dumb* as Jerry Stanley. Appearances could be very deceiving.

"Because the cute shirt I saw at Brooks Brothers costs two-forty, and I don't have that kind of cash on me."

"That's a lot for a shirt."

"I know!" shrieked Jared, in part because he couldn't imagine himself wearing Brooks Brothers. "But it is *so* cute! And so non-gay! I mean, it's *Brooks Brothers*! That's about as non-gay as you can get."

"Well…"

"No, you don't understand. I *need* it." Jared fixed his jaw. He was not unfamiliar with playing the spoiled brat. "If I don't get that shirt from Brooks Brothers, I don't go on. And then you'll have to recycle that tired old queen Louis Lombardo if you want a poster boy."

Merribaugh looked the young man over. "What's wrong with the shirt you're wearing now?"

"It's gay."

"I think it looks quite nice," said Merribaugh, and Jared found the opening he'd been waiting for.

"In that case," he said, as the buttons were unbuttoned, "*you* wear it."

And then Jared's shirt was off and he stood in front of Merribaugh, naked from the waist up. The older man's eyes traveled up and down the slender torso.

"Oh, dear," Merribaugh mumbled and finally forced himself to look away. "Is it hot in here, or…"

Jared's voice was soft. "Oh, yeah…it's *hot*. It's *soooo* hot…"

Merribaugh took off his sport coat and dropped it on the bed. This was all too sudden. He hadn't had time to prepare himself.

But Jerry Stanley's moods seem to change faster than the temperature in the room, because he crossed his thin arms in front of him and began pouting again.

"I really want that shirt, Mr. Merribaugh."

And Merribaugh surrendered. If Jerry thought he needed that shirt, maybe he needed that shirt.

"Very well," he said. "I'll run over to Brooks Brothers."

He excused himself to use the bathroom, which made Jared's life much easier because he hadn't been able to think of a way to separate the preacher from his sport coat, short of asking to try it on. And while he would have done that, it would have been *icky*.

When the bathroom door was closed—but not, Jared noted, locked—he removed Merribaugh's wallet from the sport coat and shoved it deep between the mattress and box spring. He perched on top of it and practiced his smiles in the mirror until he finally heard a flush, followed by water running in the sink. And then Merribaugh was back.

"Okay, Brooks Brothers." He grabbed the sport coat and began putting it on.

Jared nodded. "Just down the street from the hotel."

Merribaugh patted his breast pocket and concern showed on his face. "Where's my wallet?"

Jared sat on the bed and shrugged his naked shoulders. "No clue."

"I could have sworn I had it when I came in."

"I don't remember seeing it." He picked up a pillow from the bed and looked underneath. "Not there."

Merribaugh dropped to his hands and knees and looked under the bed. "This is very strange."

"Maybe you left it in your room."

"I suppose that's possible." Merribaugh sounded thoroughly unconvinced that he could have done something that irresponsible.

They searched the room for a few more minutes without finding the wallet, which was not surprising since it was under the mattress…and Jared, sitting on top of the bed, was not about to move.

Finally, the older man raised his hands. "I must have forgotten it in my room. There's really no other explanation."

Jared offered Merribaugh his most open, wide-eyed, innocent expression, the one that always seemed to work when he wanted to look particularly angelic. "Nope. None at all."

Merribaugh struggled to his feet. "Well, I'll just pick up a new key from the front desk and check my room. It was probably right in front of me when I left."

Jared opened his eyes just a bit wider. He could only imagine how innocent and angelic he looked. "It happens to me all the time. But while you're gone I'll keep looking. Just in case."

"Good, good." Merribaugh was almost out the door when Jared called him back.

"Don't you want to know my size?"

"Your size?"

"For the shirt."

"Ah, oh…" Merribaugh looked perplexed. "I thought it would be best to find my wallet now, and do the shopping later."

A pout appeared on Jared's face. "But what if they sell out? I'd… I'd have nothing to wear. Nothing except these homo clothes that remind me of the old days when I was gay. And promiscuous. Like yesterday."

He forced a single tear to one eye. It wasn't his best performance, but he was sure it would work. "And then I couldn't go to the conference. Because I'd still be gay."

Merribaugh watched the tear roll slowly down the young man's cheek, and knew he would do whatever it took to make Jerry Stanley happy. After all, he could always expense the cost of the shirt.

"I suppose I can get the shirt first, and find my wallet later."

His words brought Jared's smile back. "Oh, thank you! I promise to be the best ex-gay ever!"

Jared wrote down his size, as well as a description of the imaginary shirt, and Merribaugh left. Thirty seconds later he peeked out the door and watched the elevator doors close, and then dashed down the hall to Dan Rowell's room.

"What's going on?" Dan asked, when he answered the knock.

"I can't really explain, so you'll just have to trust me for now. I need you to follow Reverend Merribaugh."

Dan furrowed his brow. "Follow him where?"

"Brooks Brothers."

Dan stood in the doorway, carefully weighing the request and hoping for details. When none were forthcoming, he narrowed his eyes. "I get no explanation?"

Jared shrugged, as if telling a virtual stranger to tail someone to Brooks Brothers was an everyday occurrence. "Sorry. I'll tell you everything later, but he's already on the way to the store, so you have to get moving."

"I don't know…" He paused as a thought came to him. "Does this have anything to do with that visit from your father?"

"My father? Why would…? I mean, *yes*! Yes, it does."

"Is Merribaugh on his way to meet him?"

Jared's face registered Thoughtful Expression Number Two. It wasn't perfected, but he seldom had the need to appear thoughtful.

"That's what I want you to find out."

Less than a minute later, Dan was fully dressed and in the hall. "This is really crazy, Jared—"

For a moment, Jared—jumpy as he was—was on his game. "Please call me *Jerry*!"

"And that's another thing I don't understand. How come you go by Jared with me, but," Jared began pushing him toward the elevator, "Jerry with everyone else?"

"I'll tell you *later*!" As he rushed Dan down the hall, he added,

"Oh, and text me when Merribaugh's on his way back to the hotel. That's very important."

Dan stopped. "You know I can't do that, Jared."

"Jerry."

"*Jerry*. You know we're not allowed to have cell phones, so how am I supposed to text you?"

Jared's hand found a bulge in Dan's pocket that was *not* happy to see him. "On your iPhone, of course."

"How did you know…?"

"I can spot an iPhone bulge from twenty yards. That's how. And," he added, once again pulling Dan toward the elevator, "I have a phone, too. So I'll keep your secret if you keep mine. Now get on the elevator. He's got, like, five minutes on you!"

"Fair enough." Dan was no less confused than he'd been when Jared had first pounded on his door. More, really. He was every bit as curious as Jared to find out what this conference was all about, but for Dan, that might have included smuggling in a cell phone but didn't include tailing the Rev. Dennis Merribaugh. "Number?"

As they waited for the elevator, he programmed Jared's number into his phone—entered only as "J"—and then the elevator doors opened. Jared gave him a shove, Dan stumbled inside, and the doors closed.

Back in his room twenty-four seconds later, Jared liberated Merribaugh's wallet from under the mattress. The American Express card was tempting, but too dangerous. Maybe later. There was another plastic card tucked behind the AmEx bearing the name of the hotel. He left that, too.

He grabbed the keycard and set off for Merribaugh's hotel room, congratulating himself on a cleverly executed plan.

$ $ $

When the doorbell rang at 455 Old Stone Fence Post Road, Chase told Lisa, "I'll get it." Then he glanced out the kitchen window and changed his mind.

"It's the FBI."

Lisa had been agitated. It wasn't that she was worried; the rest of the gang could all take care of themselves. It was that she felt cut out of the action. At least *this* would be something.

"Then I'll get it," she said, and had the front door open before he could object.

The attractive man on the porch smiled, dimpling his cheek, and said, “Mrs. LaMarca?”

She smiled back, although without dimples. “No, Mrs. Hudson. Can I help you?”

He showed her his badge. “Special Agent Patrick Waverly, Federal Bureau of Investigation. May I come in?”

In the kitchen, he opened a manila folder. Constance’s defiant face looked back at her.

“Do you know this woman, Mrs. Hudson?”

Lisa stared at the photograph. “I, uh…”

“Yoo-hoo!”

Lisa looked up. “Oh, for Chrissakes!” She turned to Agent Waverly. “Would you excuse me for a minute?”

“Take all the time you need.”

Tish Fielding, of course, was at the front door. And Lisa was *not* in the mood.

“What is it, Fielding?”

She motioned to the black SUV blocking the driveway of 455. “It’s against HOA rules to park in front a driveway. That could present a very dangerous situation.”

“You want danger, Tish?” Lisa might have said more, or she might have just punched without saying more, but suddenly Agent Waverly was standing behind her.

“Are you one of the neighbors?” he asked over Lisa’s shoulder.

Tish nodded, and he held up the photo.

“Do you know this woman?”

“Of course,” she said. “That’s their housekeeper.”

“You mean she’s Mrs. Hudson’s housekeeper?”

“Yes, she works for Mrs. Hudson, and Mrs. Williams, and Mr. Hudson, and the other Mrs. Hudson. Oh, and Mr. Williams’s son.”

“But not Mr. LaMarca?”

Tish wrinkled her brow. Lisa hadn’t thought the Botox would allow her to do that.

“You mean Farraday?” she asked.

Waverly stared at her. “Who’s Farraday?”

“Their chauffeur.”

He looked at Lisa and smiled. “You have a housekeeper and a chauffeur? Living large, aren’t you?”

She sighed and said, “We try.”

"So who's this LaMarca?" Tish asked, but Waverly merely thanked her and closed the door in her face.

Back in the kitchen he said, "Hudson?"

"Okay." She sat. "My name is Lisa Cochrane, and I'm a real estate agent from New York City. Better?"

"So if you don't mind me asking…what's going on?"

"Am I under arrest?"

He smiled and shook his head. "No one's under arrest, Ms. Cochrane. Not even Ms. Price. I'm just trying to figure out what you're up to. If you tell me nothing, then it's nothing."

"Nothing's going on. Nothing at all."

When Waverly was gone, Chase came out of hiding.

"We are *so* screwed," she said. "They know about you, they know about Constance, and now they know about me."

Chase thought the circumstances over. They weren't great, but they weren't *that* bad. Not yet, at least.

"Unless they catch us with the Cathedral's cash, then we're just a bunch of eccentrics who use fake names. They can't throw you in jail for that."

Lisa's eyes traveled to the cupboard under the sink, where a plastic Wegmans bag hid roughly ninety-five thousand dollars. "You'd better be right. Because I'm not going to jail for a few thousand dollars."

$ $ $

Jared was groping deep beneath Merribaugh's mattress when his phone buzzed. It was a text from Dan telling him the preacher was leaving Brooks Brothers.

Just as well, thought Jared. After twenty minutes of searching, it was clear there was no suitcase full of cash in the room. Hell, there wasn't even a *suitcase*.

He took the elevator back to his room and texted Grant to report that he hadn't found the suitcase. Moments later—before Grant had a chance to respond—came the anticipated knock. Jared was about to answer when, in the corner of his eye, he spied Merribaugh's wallet on the nightstand. He tucked it back under the mattress.

Another knock sounded. This time before he answered he remembered his contraband cell phone on top of the comforter and hid it next to the wallet.

Another knock, this one more urgent. He hollered, "I'm coming," but since items had been in plain sight that weren't supposed to be, he made a final visual inspection of the room before opening the door.

Merribaugh greeted Jared with a hangdog expression. It was, Jared thought, sort of touching.

"I looked all over Brooks Brothers," he explained. "But I couldn't find the shirt. I even asked the sales associates, but…" He turned his palms up in defeat. "No luck. Are you sure it was Brooks Brothers?"

"Positive." Jared folded his arms across his chest, trying to create the illusion of pectoral muscles but mostly creating the illusion of a twelve-year-old boy trying to create the illusion of pectoral muscles. "You probably could have looked harder for it."

"You seem… Can I come in?" Merribaugh entered without permission. "You seem a bit put out. I understand you're under a lot of stress, Jerry, but there's really no reason to be upset."

Jared could play the spoiled brat much better than the angelic innocent—it was more of a natural fit, after all—so he kept his arms crossed and defiantly stared down Merribaugh.

"I wanted that shirt."

"But…but…"

"How am I supposed to be the star ex-gay if I look like a boring heterosexual?"

"But…I thought the problem was that your clothes were, uh… *gay*."

"Oh yeah." Jared thought for a moment. "But they're still boring."

Merribaugh finally found his footing. "But that's what an ex-gay is *supposed* to look like! I don't understand the problem here."

Jared rolled his eyes. "The *problem* is that I'm the star, but I'm not getting treated any better than anyone else."

After years of running Project Rectitude, Merribaugh was not unfamiliar with Gay Diva Syndrome. Jerry Stanley's outburst was extreme even by that standard, but not uncontrollable.

Still, he was the star attraction. That much was true. Maybe there was some other way to accommodate him…

"Maybe I could upgrade you to a suite. Would that make you happy?"

Jared peered at him through half-closed lids. "Does anyone else at the conference have a suite?"

"Only Dr. Hurley."

Jared mulled that over. "Maybe…"

"And Louis Lombardo."

Jared sneered. "I *definitely* deserve a suite."

"I'll try to arrange it." Merribaugh gazed into young Jerry's eyes, which once again projected innocence. A demanding innocence, yes, but innocence not unlike that of a three-year-old child with tantrum issues.

"Okay."

Merribaugh took a few steps toward him and smiled reassuringly. "But first…what can I do to help relieve the stress you're feeling?"

"Uh…" Jared had seen enough bad porn to know what was coming next, and sure enough, Merribaugh didn't disappoint him.

"I think you need a massage."

Jared's first impulse was to do something—*anything*—to get the old man out of his room. But that impulse was tempered by the knowledge he was on a job, and—since the suitcase wasn't in Merribaugh's hotel room—he'd have to play along until he could figure out where it was.

Because his share of ten thousand dollars out of that seven million dollars was a lot more important than any revulsion he might feel at the thought of Merribaugh's pudgy fingers kneading his back. As long as those fingers stayed on his back, that was.

So Jared took a deep breath and said, "A massage sounds like it could be nice."

"I thought it would." And he might have been mistaken, but he thought Merribaugh punctuated his sentence with a wink, although one so slight he could deny it if Jared called him on it.

"So…what should I do?" asked Jared, as he backed slowly into the room until he felt the back of his thighs touch the bed.

"First, strip to your underwear."

Jared's jaw dropped. That didn't sound right. "My underwear?"

Merribaugh nodded. "Yes, your underwear."

"Maybe if I just took my shirt off…"

"No, strip to your underwear. It's better that way. You see, when I give you a Jesus Rub…"

"A *what*?"

If the exchange fazed Merribaugh, he wasn't letting on. "A Jesus Rub. It's a holy stress management ritual dating back to the time of Christ. In fact, it's almost a certainty that the apostles gave each other Jesus Rubs to relieve their tension and anxiety. And there are pressure points in your, uh, lower region that can throw your entire body out of whack, which is why you have to strip to your underwear."

Jared stared at Merribaugh and tried to envision a stack of money standing in front of him—the ten thousand dollars he'd get as his share, in this case—instead of the man. He wasn't sure how big a stack that would be, but at least the mind trick worked well enough to get his shirt off.

"Now your pants," coaxed Merribaugh.

That took a mental image of the entire seven million dollars, but finally Jared was laying face-down on the bed, wearing nothing but a pair of white Calvins. He felt Merribaugh's hands on his upper back and mostly didn't mind…until those hands left his flesh, followed moments later by the sound of a zipper being unzipped.

"Uh…" said Jared, not quite sure what else to say and afraid to look back. "Are you, uh…?"

"In my underwear, too? Yes." Those were exactly the words Jared didn't want to hear. "Relax, Jerry. This is all part of the ritual."

"And you're sure Jesus was chill with the Jesus Rub?"

"Chill?"

"Cool."

"Oh. Yes, yes, Jesus was *very* chill." Merribaugh's hands again began rubbing his back, and Jared closed his eyes and pictured piles and piles of money. And then a few more piles for good measure.

And then more. And a few more…

Maybe the seven million was an underestimation. Maybe the haul would be *twenty* million. A man could justify a lot for twenty million…

Merribaugh's voice interrupted his self-justification. "You know, Jerry, if you want to be authentically Christ-like, you should take off your underwear."

Jared's eyes popped open. "What?"

"Christ and the apostles didn't wear underwear."

Hell no, he thought. *There was no amount of money…*

"But…but I'm supposed to be ex-gay!"

"If it would make you feel more comfortable, I'll take my underwear off, too."

If the fire alarm hadn't gone off at that moment, Jared might have spontaneously combusted.

21

Inappropriate as he may have been at times like the one just ended, the Rev. Mr. Dennis Merribaugh did have a sense of propriety. When the alarm started blaring, he knew it would not do to bolt from the hotel room—in his underwear—with a twenty-something ex-gay—also in his underwear—so he'd quickly dressed and rushed from the room before Jared had a chance to struggle back into his pants.

When he was alone, Jared checked his messages. Grant had sent an earlier text—HURLEY'S ROOM?—but nothing else.

Jared hoped he wouldn't have to also try to seduce Dr. Oscar Hurley. Not that he had anything against seduction, but men like Hurley and Merribaugh were an underutilization of his talents.

$ $ $

"Sorry," Jack Hightower said, barely looking at Mary Beth as the deafening alarm rang. "No room at the inn."

"But I'm sure we had a reservation!"

Hightower ignored her. "All rooms are booked. Now would you *please* evacuate the building? Because until you evacuate, *I* can't evacuate."

She wheeled the trashed suitcase away from the front desk and plowed through the evacuees until she found Grant outside.

"No go," said Mary Beth. "I even tried to be charming."

He motioned for her to follow him down the block, and she did. When they turned the corner, Farraday was waiting.

"Thanks for helping with this piece-of-crap bag," she muttered.

"You're welcome. Okay, we need a new plan."

"And a drink," said Farraday.

Grant ignored him. "If we can't get a room, we'll have to hang out in the area. Maybe sleep in shifts in the car."

That didn't sit well with Mary Beth. "Are you kidding me? We're gonna spend all night outside?"

"That, and maybe a little time on the inside. Stairwells, the loading dock…"

She kicked the suitcase and it toppled to the sidewalk. "You sure know how to treat a girl, Grant Lambert."

Farraday spotted a neon liquor store sign down the block. "This might be workable."

$ $ $

Finally dressed, Jared casually walked down four flights of stairs to the lobby and out the front door. He didn't see Merribaugh, but did quickly spot Dan. Or maybe Dan spotted him.

They walked away from the crowd until they stood out of earshot.

"Don't be mad at me," Dan said, "but I pulled the alarm."

"You did?"

He nodded. "I needed to talk to you."

Jared thought about that. "Aren't there easier ways to do that?"

Dan looked at the sidewalk. "And…And I also wanted to get Merribaugh out of your room. I sort of listened at the door and didn't like what I was hearing."

He wasn't sure if Jared would be angry or not, although he couldn't imagine Jared had welcomed Merribaugh's massage.

"Thanks for *that*," said Jared, and Dan finally looked up again.

Now feeling as if he was on more solid ground, Dan pressed on. "Can I ask you why you're flirting with him? Is that some sort of ex-gay poster-boy requirement?"

Jared put a finger to Dan's lips. "I'll explain everything. Just as soon as I can." His eyes scanned the crowd and he quickly dropped his finger. "Merribaugh at two o'clock."

They saw him before he saw them, which gave them an opportunity to separate. Merribaugh walked past Dan without seeming to notice as he made his way to Jared.

"It was a false alarm," he said. "Nothing to be concerned about. Now, shall we continue that massage?"

Jared yawned and stretched. "That would be nice, but I'm *sooooo* tired."

"But your stress..."

"I think I just need a good night of sleep. In the morning, I'll be in top shape."

"I really think..."

Jared winked and even gave Merribaugh Smile Number Three, much as he hated to waste it. "You know what? As a man about to give up the homosexual lifestyle, I really shouldn't put myself—or anyone else—in that position."

Deflated, Merribaugh heaved a sigh and looked out into the night. "Well, then...In that case, sleep tight, Jerry."

A tiny piece of Jared Parsells felt sorry for Merribaugh as he sadly walked away. Until he remembered Merribaugh was a pervert who wore polyester suits. Then he was pretty much okay with everything again.

He took a few more steps away from the crowd, then slipped around a corner where no one would see him on his cell before sending Grant a short text: *where r u?*

"Right next to you."

Jared started to type a response.

"No, seriously. I'm standing right next to you."

He stopped and looked up, and there stood Grant, as Mary Beth and Farraday leaned against a car a few yards away. The phone disappeared into his pocket.

"You search Hurley's room yet?" asked Grant.

"That one could be tough."

"We've got to find that suitcase. No suitcase means no cash, which means we're wasting our time. And I don't like to waste time."

Jared was about to agree when a thought occurred to him. "There's a card in Merribaugh's wallet—about the size of a credit card—with the name of the hotel on it. Do you think it means anything?"

Grant rubbed his jaw. "Could be a claim-check for the hotel safe."

"That's what I was thinking!" said Jared, even though it hadn't been.

Mary Beth leaned forward, liking what she heard. "So Jared gives us the card, we claim the bag and get the hell back to New York. Perfect plan! Let's move."

Grant held up a hard. "Not yet."

"Not yet? Why?"

"Two reasons. First, because we're gonna want to swap out luggage and claim-checks, and make sure we get the wrong one in Merribaugh's hands. That way we'll get a head start before he realizes anything's wrong. The other reason we're gonna sit tight for a while is 'cause the front desk clerk just saw you, so we'll wait until he won't remember you or until there's a shift change."

"Are you trying to tell me…?"

"Yeah," he told her. "Whether you like it or not, we're spending the night out here."

She folded her arms. "I hate you, Lambert."

Jared smiled and began to walk away. "If you'll excuse me, I'm going back inside the hotel. To my warm, comfortable bed. And fluffy pillows."

"And I hate *you* more."

$ $ $

Constance heard a knock, then Special Agent Patrick Waverly opened the door.

"Good news. You're free to go."

She looked at him, not quite believing what she was hearing. So Waverly repeated himself.

"What's the angle?" Constance eyed him up and down, sensing a scam.

"No angle," Patrick said. "You checked out, so you're free to go. With apologies from the Bureau for the inconvenience."

"Hmm."

Waverly shrugged. "What do you want from me, Ms. Price? You're free to go."

Constance, now beginning to believe him, found her inner feistiness. "Yeah, you'd better be sorry for the inconvenience. Dragging me out of my church like I was some common criminal. Holding me almost all day…"

Waverly smiled at her indulgently and brushed a forelock of hair out of his eyes. "Do you really want to go down this road, Ms. Price? Because you were brought in as part of an active investigation, and we can continue to hold you if we want."

She looked down, chastened. "No."

When she was gone and Waverly had returned from the holding room, Special Agent Oliver Tolan looked up from the monitor and said to him, "You can't possibly trust her."

"Of course not. But one thing I'm sure of is she isn't working on the inside with Hurley and Merribaugh. She's got *something* up her sleeve, but not that. Here's the thing, though, Ollie: I think they might be able to lead us to the money. She and LaMarca are more valuable to us out there than in here."

"If you say so."

"Oh, and I need you to run a name for me. Lisa Cochrane, a real estate agent from New York."

"Another one of them?"

"There's an entire household of them over in Nash Bog. My gut says they're not involved with Hurley. They just stumbled into this at the same time we did. But let's keep an eye on them."

Tolan wasn't convinced. "You feel good about this hunch?"

"Do you have something better?"

He grunted. "Let's see where this goes, then."

"I love your flexibility, Ollie."

"You should know about flexibility, gay boy."

Waverly leaned against the wall and smiled. "Someday, Ollie, when I'm ready to retire, I'll remember this moment when you called me a gay boy. You've created a very hostile work environment. That should be worth ten or twenty million bucks in a settlement from the Bureau, which will really help stretch my Social Security."

Tolan nodded his agreement. "As long as I get half."

"That can probably be arranged."

"In that case," said Tolan, "I'll do whatever I can to help, you fuckin' faggot."

They exchanged a fist-bump.

$ $ $

It was completely normal for Jared Parsells to wake up in a strange hotel room wrapped tightly against a slumbering male body, but it usually took him a few minutes to put together the events leading up to the hotel room and the naked stranger as he forced sleep out of his head.

This time it took a bit longer than normal, but he finally remembered that he was in a hotel room in Washington, DC. At an ex-gay conference. With an ex-gay in his bed.

An ex-gay who was not doing a very good job at being ex-gay. Whatever. He was just thrilled someone had stayed the night and that there had been no praying and crying involved.

Jared smiled at his memories of the previous night and gently nipped Dan Rowell's ear.

When Dan finally stirred after another nip, Jared said, "Good morning."

Dan smacked his lips a few times before returning the smile. "Morning. What time is it?"

Jared glanced at the clock. "Almost seven. Want water or something?"

"No." He felt Dan's hand grasp his ass and pull him forward. "But I'll take some more of this."

Jared leaned into Dan and they found each other's mouths. It was pure bliss…

For fifteen seconds or so, until a loud knock sounded at the door. Their heads both turned in its direction.

"Fuck," muttered Dan.

"Yes, please," said Jared, whose tongue was back at Dan's lips.

Dan pushed him away. "Stop it. I'm not supposed to be here. Remember where we are."

"Oh, yeah." Jared sat up in the bed as Dan scrambled from beneath the sheets. "Should I answer it?"

"It's probably Merribaugh. You'd better get it. But he can't see me."

"The closet," Jared suggested.

Dan hiked an eyebrow. "Isn't that sort of a cliché?"

Jared shrugged. "I don't know. What's a cliché?"

Another knock sounded, this time accompanied by Merribaugh's voice. "Jerry! Time to wake up, son."

"One moment!" Without a word, and despite it being one of those cliché things or whatever, Jared led Dan to the closet and closed him in. Then he kicked Dan's clothes under the bed, wrapped the sheet around himself, and, a length of cotton trailing along the carpet in his wake, finally answered the door.

Merribaugh stood in the hallway, smiling at the sight of Jared wrapped in the sheet.

"Sorry," Jared said. "I'm running a little behind. Let me just shower and…"

"Today is your big day!" Merribaugh clapped his hands together, as if encouraging excitement in a toddler. "Today you officially become the new face of the ex-homosexual movement! Are you excited?"

Jared pulled the sheet tightly around his body. "Uh…yes?"

"I'm sure you are. Please allow me to step in for a moment." Jared, seeing no option, took a few steps back and Merribaugh entered the room, closing the door behind him. "Speaking on behalf of everyone at Project Rectitude and the Moral Families Coalition, let me just say we're *thrilled* to have you on the side of righteousness."

"Uh…you're welcome."

Merribaugh took a few more steps forward, forcing Jared back until he stepped on the sheet and almost tumbled over. To balance himself, his hand dropped the sheet, exposing flesh and a nipple. He caught it before it slid too far down his torso, but not before he caught Merribaugh staring.

Still, Merribaugh stayed professional, not even acknowledging the bead of drool that had formed at the corner of his mouth. "Above all, it's very important that you be relaxed at the conference, Jerry."

"Oh, I'm relaxed." He watched as Merribaugh took a small vial from his pocket. "What's that?"

"Massage oil. Made with traces of gold, frankincense, and myrrh: the gifts the Wise Men brought to the Christ Child."

Jared was no longer relaxed but still said, "Seriously, I'm relaxed."

Merribaugh held the vial toward Jared. "When you are massaged with this oil, you will feel reborn."

"Is this like the Jesus Rub? Because I'm already relaxed."

"It's even better with the oil."

"Very, *very* relaxed. Maybe *too* relaxed."

Jared's words were waved away. "I'm afraid I have to insist, Jerry. A Jesus Rub is the only way we can get those last vestigial traces of homosexuality out of your system before putting you on the public stage."

"Do I have to?"

"Jerry, please!" Merribaugh almost looked as if his feelings were hurt. "This is a very common relaxation technique in the ex-homosexual community. Now, if you'll just take off the sheet and lie face-up on the bed, we can get underway."

Jared's mind raced as he tried to think of a way to avoid another Jesus Rub, but he knew he was trapped. If he rejected Merribaugh's therapy, there was a chance he'd expose himself as a fake ex-gay. Better to get it over with.

Maybe it wouldn't be so bad. He'd sort of survived the first, non-oily Jesus Rub, hadn't he? And maybe Merribaugh wouldn't actually try to molest him, although he thought the odds weren't on his side.

He started to slip out of the sheet. Merribaugh's eyes focused like lasers when he fully exposed his slim, smooth torso, and Jared lost even the slight hope that there would be no molestation.

There was another knock, and Merribaugh's eyes shifted from Jared's hairless chest to the door. When he looked back at the young man, they were open wide in fear, not lust. So much fear that Merribaugh no longer seemed to notice Jared's pert, hairless nipples.

"I can't be seen here," he hissed.

"Why? What's the big deal? You're only here to give me a Jesus Rub."

Merribaugh didn't answer, unless making a beeline for the closet could be considered an answer. Jared tripped over the sheet, still wrapped around his waist but now pulled low enough to expose a hipbone, rushing to stop him before he reached the closet door.

"Not there. It's a clay-chi."

Merribaugh stopped at looked at him. "A what?"

"Cla-chay?"

"Do you mean cliché?" Merribaugh whispered.

Jared just shrugged as another knock sounded. "Hide in the bathroom."

When Merribaugh and his vial of gold, frankincense, and myrrh were finally hidden away, Jared answered the knocks.

"Where are your clothes?" asked Mary Beth, trying not to look at the mostly naked Jared.

He held a finger to his lips and led them into the hall.

"What she said," said Grant, when the door was almost closed, but still a half inch ajar so Jared could get back inside. "Where are your clothes?"

"It's complicated." A man squeezed past them in the hall, smiling as he eyed Jared and tossing him a sly wave. Jared waved back and called out, "See you at the conference."

"You're making friends?" asked Grant.

"A few." Jared shrugged, and the sheet slipped a few inches on his hip. Mary Beth cringed. "Anyway, what do you want?"

"We need your keycard to check our suitcase into the safe," said Mary Beth, still trying not to look at the flesh Jared was exposing.

"I'll get it." As Jared turned to reenter the room, a pair of men walked down the hall, greeting him with leers and nervous smiles. He smiled back, then went inside the room, emerging seconds later with the keycard. Again he closed the door behind him so that his guests—one invited, one not—wouldn't hear.

"Thanks," said Grant. "We'll get it back to you later. And stay sharp, because we've got a lot of work coming your way."

"I'll be sharp." Jared watched them until they were out of sight. Only then did he realize he'd locked himself out of Room 513.

Several ex-gays stopped to offer assistance to the young man partially draped in a sheet who'd locked himself out of his room, and under other circumstances Jared would have happily taken more than assistance opening the door from at least a few of them. But Merribaugh finally answered his knocks and let him in.

"Who was at the door?" he asked when Jared was safely inside.

"Just some random lesbian. I mean, *ex*-lesbian."

$ $ $

At one point during the night, Jack Hightower had been able to grab four hours of sleep in his office. It wasn't the most satisfying sleep he'd ever had, but even four hours of bad sleep were better than four hours of no sleep.

"Excuse me! *Hellooooo!*"

His sleep-deprived brain snapped back to the reality in which he had to be civil to the guests, so he smiled at the compact, pretty woman standing in front of him as if there'd been nothing odd at all about his behavior. "Can I help you, ma'am?"

She hoisted a bag onto the counter. "I need to check this."

Of course you do. He eyed the small scuffed-up suitcase. *I am sure it's just full of irreplaceable valuables, because everyone carries their freakin' million-dollar jewelry in a bag that looks like—*

"Are you all right?"

He smiled weakly. "Sorry. I was distracted. Can I see your room key?" She produced it, and he checked it into the system before looking back at her quizzically. "Room 513?"

"Yeah, that's right."

"And, uh…what is your relationship to the guest?"

"I'm his girlfriend."

Jack Hightower lifted a questioning eyebrow. "But, uh…I don't mean to be nosy, but it says here that 513 is one of the rooms rented for the Project Rectitude conference."

"Hey, what can I say? It works!"

"It works fast, I see."

"*Goddamn* fast. Now check the bag."

$ $ $

The drop-in from Grant and Mary Beth, unfortunately, had done nothing to discourage Merribaugh's determination to give Jared a Jesus Rub.

It had only put off the inevitable for a few minutes, and now Jared lay face-down on the bed, the sheet still just barely wrapped round his ass, as Dennis Merribaugh dripped massage oil from the vial onto his back. It was cold when it first came in contact with his flesh, and his body reacted to the chill by clenching everything that could be clenched. That was, it turned out, the wrong reaction.

"You have very muscular buttocks, I see," said Merribaugh, as his hands began working the oil into Jared's flesh.

Jared forced his eyes closed. He reminded himself this wasn't the worst situation he'd ever been in. It was close, but that time in Vegas with the guy that looked a lot like Donald Trump was definitely worse.

Merribaugh continued speaking as he rubbed Jared's back. "Do you feel yourself relaxing?"

His voice was unenthusiastic. "I guess so."

The massage stopped, and for a brief moment Jared hoped he'd been given a reprieve. But, no.

"I don't want to get the oil on my suit," he heard Merribaugh say. And then he heard the unmistakable sound of a zipper unzipping.

Now it was the worst situation Jared had ever found himself in.

"You know," Jared said, keeping his eyes tightly shut, because there were some things even Jared Parsells wasn't curious about. "I'm really feeling very relaxed. Maybe we should put off the massage until later. I'll probably be stressed after the conference. And then…"

"Nonsense." He heard items of clothing drop to the floor. "This will feel *so* good. It will be a divine exp—"

The chirp of a cell phone interrupted Merribaugh. Jared knew it wasn't *his* ringtone and hoped it wasn't Dan's.

It was Merribaugh's phone. The amateur masseur cursed in a non-blasphemic way and started hunting for his phone on the floor. It slipped twice out of his oily hands before he finally answered.

"Merribaugh here…Yes, Dr. Hurley…Yes…Yes, I'll be there in a few minutes."

And then there was the sound of Merribaugh putting his clothes back on, punctuated by a zipper zipping. Only then did Jared dare open his eyes, still managing to catch an unfortunate glimpse of Merribaugh's sagging chest as he buttoned his shirt.

The pastor smiled awkwardly. "I'm afraid I lost track of time. I'll have to relax you later."

Jared nodded, silently determined that there would be no later.

When Merribaugh was gone, Dan emerged from the closet. They stared at each other for a while until Dan broke the silence.

"So, *that* was weird."

"That was gross," said Jared. "Could you hear everything?"

Dan nodded. "You want a towel to clean the oil off your back?"

"I'll just use the sheet for now." He sat, and the last of the sheet fell away from him.

"Okay." Dan sat down next to Jared on the edge of the bed, their naked thighs pressed together. He furrowed his brow. "Just out of curiosity, uh…"

"What?"

"You wouldn't have done anything with him, would you?"

Jared laughed out loud. "Oh, *God* no!" Then he remembered to add, "Also, I'm not gay anymore."

Dan cocked an eye in his direction. "You're not? I seem to remember…"

"I'm not *desperately* gay anymore. Better?"

"Yeah," Dan agreed. "Better." He cast his eyes to the floor, and his tone grew serious. "Listen, I have something to tell…"

With a click, the door opened. And there stood Grant and Mary Beth. They took one look at the unclothed men sitting on the bed and averted their eyes.

"Lesbian blindness!" said Mary Beth.

"That's what we get for not knocking," said Grant.

Dan turned to Jared. "Who's the woman with your father?"

"My, uh…my *sister*?"

Still looking away, Mary Beth motioned in the direction of Jared. "We need to speak to you in private, brother dear. Please join us in the hall."

"Now? But I have company!"

"Now!" And she added, "Don't make me come over there, or you and your friend will both have four less inches to play with. And neither of you can spare it."

Jared looked to Dan, said, "I'll be right back," and bounced off the bed to join them in the hall.

Grant was trying not to look, but there was something he couldn't ignore. "It's cold in the hall. You might wanna cover yourself."

"Oh. Right." Jared wrapped the sheet around himself once again and padded out to the hall, closing the door behind him.

Mary Beth handed him his keycard and a claim ticket.

"Here's what you need to do," said Grant. "And we kept it simple, so you should be able to handle it. I need you to swap this claim-check for Merribaugh's, then get his bag from the front desk and bring it to me. Think you can handle that?"

"Uh…"

"You've got to do this quickly, though. I'm getting nervous. If they get that suitcase before we do, we get nothing. Remember there's seven million dollars riding on this, and ten thousand is yours. No switch means no money for any of us, especially you. Get it?"

"Then *definitely* yes!"

"You'd better get moving. And make sure that failed ex-gay you've got naked in your room gets lost before you blow this." He thought about his word choice, then thought better of correcting himself. If he did, he'd only draw attention to "blow this," and after a night without sleep he wasn't in the mood to hear Jared giggle.

Again, Jared watched them until they were out of sight. And again he realized he'd locked himself out of the room. It was only when Dan responded to his knocks and let Jared inside that he remembered he'd been holding the keycard in one hand.

Whatever.

Back in the room, Jared said "I guess we should get ready to get our ex-gay on. It's almost time for the conference."

Dan smiled. "We're not doing a very good job giving up homosexuality, are we?"

"No, not really."

"Maybe that's because we don't want to."

Jared had certainly given Dan ample reason to think that. And it was the truth, after all. But he also realized it was time to get serious if this scheme was going to have a payoff.

"I think I want to give up sin." He looked at Dan cautiously. "Don't you?"

"I think…" Dan trailed off, not sure what he could or should say and deciding less was best. "I guess we'll find out. In the meantime, you need to get in the shower."

"Yeah…" Jared smiled. "Care to join me?"

Dan did, so Jared told him they could give up sin after their shower.

$ $ $

After Dan returned to his room, Jared dug Merribaugh's wallet out from between the mattress and box spring. It was almost too easy. One claim check out, another one in. All he'd have to do was let himself back into Merribaugh's room, drop the wallet, claim Merribaugh's suitcase, and run.

But a few minutes later, he realized his plan had a flaw, because when Merribaugh had reported his original keycard—the one Jared now held in his hand—missing, the hotel had issued him a new one…and reset the lock.

So Jared, ever resourceful, figured out another way to return Merribaugh's wallet, and began sliding the contents under the door. Then he took the empty wallet to a service closet and dropped it down a laundry chute.

22

Jack Hightower looked at the clock behind the registration desk, calculating both the time he'd been at work and the time he had left as well as how big his next paycheck would be. Although by now he would gladly give up his *entire* paycheck just to get out of his uniform and into bed. Then he had an even more mortifying thought.

They couldn't make me work another *shift, could they?*

He would quit, he decided. Not even give notice. Just strip off his uniform and walk through the lobby in his underwear, a final defiant good-bye to his employment in the hospitality industry. Let the suits in corporate work double and triple shifts! See how *they* liked it! That would show 'em! They'd be—

"I need to get this bag out of the safe." Jared Parsells stood on the other side of the desk with a claim ticket in his hand.

"Of course you do," muttered Hightower, because there was nothing he'd rather do with a line of thirteen people waiting to register than retrieve something from the safe. Still, he did what he had to do, and several minutes later handed over Merribaugh's suitcase.

"Thanks," said Jared, who of course didn't tip.

In the lobby, Jared pushed down the handle and slid the suitcase most of the way under a chair, which he then sat upon. Seven million dollars was hidden under his hot little ass and he felt the warm happiness of success.

He sent Grant a text: *done. in lobby now.*

He wondered why, whenever he was on a job, no one seemed to think he could handle himself. Hadn't he always come through? Other things got bobbled, but never *his* part. His ran smoothly. So smoothly that he was starting to think he might be worth more than ten thousand dollars.

Maybe…Twenty? He deserved *that* much respect. He'd talk to Grant—no, he'd talk to *Chase*—about that later.

He saw Grant and Mary Beth approach from a service door, and leaned forward to pull the suitcase from under the chair.

"Jerry!" Jared looked up at the sound of Merribaugh's voice. He was approaching quickly. Grant and Mary Beth saw him, too, and veered away. "There you are! I've been looking for you."

"Who, me?" asked Jared innocently, and with a kick from his heel the suitcase was wedged a few inches deeper under the chair.

"Yes, you!" Merribaugh fussed with Jared's collar before setting one hand on his shoulder. It was a gesture that would have been almost paternal, if Papa was a perv. "Come on, now! Dr. Hurley is opening the conference in just a few minutes, and you *have* to be there."

Jared tried to subtly break away from Merribaugh's fingers. "I *have* to?"

"You have to."

As Merribaugh tugged him through the lobby, Jared's eyes found Grant and he shrugged helplessly.

$ $ $

Sephora Girl was manning the door as Merribaugh rushed Jared past her and into the ballroom, where two hundred chairs faced the other end of the room. They walked down the center aisle until they reached the front row, and Merribaugh directed Jared to sit in the second seat.

Merribaugh leaned close to his young charge. "As you can see, it would not have looked good if we were late. Dr. Hurley would have definitely noticed." His voiced verged on giddiness. "You're about to become a *star*, Jerry!"

Jared craned his neck and looked over the crowd. The room was fairly full and more people were entering. It was going to be difficult to get back to the lobby. He could only hope that Grant had figured out where the suitcase was hidden.

Then he noticed Merribaugh next to him, beaming.

So Jared put his head back in the game. "Yeah. A star."

$ $ $

"I'm sorry, sir." Sephora Girl held up her hands helplessly and tried to hide her increasing frustration with Christ-like calm. "But unless you're wearing a lanyard, I can't let you in."

"But I'm telling you," said Grant. "I lost it. Probably in the chapel." He wondered if the hotel even had a chapel, but didn't dwell on it. "And I really need to get in there."

Her smile was patronizing. "I understand, sir, but the rules are the rules. And by restricting this to registered conference attendees, we're helping protect you. Otherwise, radical homosexual activists could infiltrate and disrupt what should be a meaningful, life-changing event."

"Trust me, lady, at this point I need all the life-changing I can get." He thought about Jared. "And I'm also as anti-gay as anyone."

She threw up her hands as Grant walked away. "Again, I'm sorry. But God bless you!"

He was going to find a side door—maybe he could pose as a waiter or something—when a much better idea walked in.

"You," said Grant, grabbing the freshly re-showered Dan Rowell firmly by the elbow and leading him a few yards away before he could react.

"Don't hit me," said Dan when he registered who'd grabbed him.

Grant was puzzled. "Why would I hit you?"

"Because of Jared. I mean, *Jerry*! And you're his father, so…"

It took a moment, but Grant picked up. "Oh, that. Don't worry about it. But I need you to get a message to him."

"Where is he?"

"Merribaugh just dragged him inside, but they won't let me in without one of them neck things."

Dan looked at his own. "You mean a lanyard?"

"Yeah, that. Anyway, I need you to find him. Tell him I need to talk to him right away. I'll be in the lobby."

Dan nodded, understanding the orders but thoroughly confused, and went off to find Jared.

$ $ $

Mary Beth sat in the lobby. She was just eleven feet from seven million dollars, but she had no way of knowing that.

She did know, though, that the tenor of the lobby had changed over the past few minutes. First, a half dozen men marched through the lobby and up to the clerk at the front desk. He'd given them a sour look and the people waiting in line had started to complain, but the men said something and suddenly everyone seemed very deferential.

And then the men, one holding a couple of keycards the clerk handed over, walked to the elevators. They were still waiting when Grant returned.

"What's with those guys?" she asked

He took one short glance and ducked his head. "FBI."

"You sure?"

He didn't bother to take another look. "Oh, yeah."

The men moved the other guests aside while they boarded the elevator, and the doors closed. No one complained about the delay; as a matter of fact, they'd seemed sort of impressed. This definitely wasn't New York City, where ninety-seven-year-old ladies would have fought their way onto that elevator.

When they were gone, Mary Beth asked, "You don't think they're looking for us, do you?"

"I don't think so. I mean, they let Constance go…"

She frowned. "Yeah, but maybe that was just a ruse to get the rest of us."

He looked at the floor, but unfortunately not eighteen inches far enough or he'd have seen the suitcase. "We're small potatoes to them. I think."

"If you say so." She sank back in the chair. "I take it you couldn't get to Jared."

"They wouldn't let me in. But I ran into his boyfriend du jour and asked him to pass on the message." He sighed. "No telling how well that's gonna work."

$ $ $

Almost two hundred men and women—most growing giddy with anticipation, some anxious with dread—waited for Dr. Oscar Hurley in the ballroom. He was fifteen minutes late for his keynote address, but he was Dr. Oscar Hurley, so the audience forgave a lot.

"Hey, poster boy," said a voice behind Jared, which made him smile until he turned in his seat and came face to face with cocky, red-haired Louis Lombardo.

"Oh. You."

And the voice of the man sitting next to Lombardo said, "God forgive me," as the man behind the voice tried to hide his face with one hand.

Jared squinted. He *knew* that face, or at least what he could see through the hand. "Business Center Guy? Is that you?"

Merribaugh turned at the commotion, and when Business Center Guy saw him he said, "God forgive me," again, a bit louder, and this time hid his face with *both* hands.

"What's wrong, Max?" Lombardo asked Business Center Guy.

"You know Business Center Guy?" Jared asked.

"I…uh…" Louis Lombardo looked away. "No. No, I don't."

Business Center Guy moaned. "Lead us not into temptation, but deliver us from evil!" It came out more loudly than he'd intended, given the low profile he'd been trying to keep, and when he realized that he put his hand on Lombardo's leg.

"Yes, you do!" Jared shouted. "You *do* know Business Center Guy!"

Merribaugh turned and, out of the corner of his mouth, said, "Jerry, this is not approp—"

Business Center Guy moaned once again at the sight of Merribaugh. "Lead us not into temptation, but deliver us from evil!" It was *much* louder this time.

"Pipe down, Max," said Merribaugh. Heads were turning in their direction, and not just from the closer rows.

Jared's head swiveled in Merribaugh's direction. "You know him, too?"

Merribaugh's back stiffened and he faced the podium. "Of course not."

"But you called him Max!"

His jaw was the only part of his head that moved. "Well, I just… try to learn names."

"Lead us not into temptation!"

Jared shook his head and said, more to himself than anyone else, "Everyone's been tapping that ass. I do *not* feel special anymore."

$ $ $

Dr. Oscar Hurley knew he was quite late, and he really didn't care. He was good enough to grace the homos with his presence, so let them wait.

But now...*Now* it was time for his entrance.

After thousands of public appearances, he had it down to a science. He would walk from the rear of the room to the front alone; that conveyed humility, and it was important for people to know he was a humble man of God.

At first, only a few people would even notice him, but their smattering of applause would attract the attention of others, and theirs would attract others, and so on, until the hall was full of applause.

Then someone would stand, and that would also have a ripple effect across the audience. And they'd remain standing until he signaled they should be seated. His record was ten minutes, thirty-nine seconds.

It was extraordinarily predictable, and quite gratifying.

Sephora Girl almost swooned as he entered and proceeded to the center aisle. And then he began his entrance...

He stopped after two steps. Was someone screaming The Lord's Prayer in the front of the room?

Then he realized no one—absolutely *no one*—was paying attention to him. They were all straining to see the commotion up front.

The Lord's Prayer...someone hollering that he wasn't gay anymore...someone else hollering that he didn't feel special...

What the *hell* was going on?

$ $ $

Special Agent Patrick Waverly clicked off his phone. "They searched both their rooms, but there was no money."

"None?" asked Special Agent Oliver Tolan.

"None. But they found a claim check for the hotel safe. It looked suspicious, though. Someone stuck it under Merribaugh's door with what appeared to be the contents of his wallet." That was odd, but Waverly had seen odder. It was part of the job. "He'll call me back."

Tolan leaned against a wall and said, "Y'ever stop to think maybe we're on a wild goose chase?"

Waverly nodded. "Always. Every case."

Tolan folded his arms, feeling the satisfying dig of the holster against his chest and the gun against his armpit. "Well, I gotta figure someone knows something. Between the IRS and the Bureau, they've put enough man-hours into it. I doubt they'd be doing that just to watch us chase our tails."

"You'd think that," said Waverly. "But we're talking about Washington."

"Oh, yeah," said Tolan. "Gotta remember that." He sighed. "I guess all we can do is hope your hunch is right and Price and LaMarca lead us to the cash."

Waverly winked. "Trust me on this one, Ollie."

Tolan looked at him. "Did you just wink at me?"

Waverly winked again.

"That's sexual harassment, Patrick. Haven't you ever heard that no means no? I could sue the Bureau for this…"

"Fifty-fifty?"

"Of course."

$ $ $

Grant and Mary Beth tensed up as the elevator disgorged the half dozen FBI agents, who made another beeline to the front desk.

"They didn't look around the lobby," Grant said out of the corner of his mouth. No one more than a few feet away would have known he'd said a word. "That works in our favor."

They watched while pretending not to watch until…

"Oh, shit," Mary Beth said a half minute later, looking back at the copy of *The Washington Post* in her lap and pretending to care. "The clerk just handed them my bag."

Grant finally took a breath and relaxed. "That's a good thing."

She mimicked him, talking out of the corner of her mouth. "How do you figure?"

"That means they're looking for Merribaugh. Maybe Hurley, too. But not us."

"Oh yeah," she said, and looked back at *The Post* as six agents from the Federal Bureau of Investigation, kneeling on the floor, ripped open Mary Beth's suitcase and began rifling through back issues of *Cosmopolitan* and *Vogue*.

$ $ $

"I figured I'd find you here," said Dan Rowell, pulling Jared away from the uproar at the front of the room that had now been joined by at least two dozen allegedly ex- and hopefully-soon-to-be-ex-gay men.

"Hey!" Jared batted his eyes, flashed Smile Number Three, and felt just a little bit special again. Ignoring the chaos, he asked, "What's going on?"

"I'm gonna get you out of here." Dan took him by the hand. "Your father wants to see you."

"My father?" *Why would my father...?* "Oh, right."

While Jared had been the catalyst for the fight, which was growing out of control with every new recrimination, he'd been happy to retreat into the background as Louis Lombardo increasingly became the focal point. For a reformed sinner, Lombardo seemed to get around quite a bit.

Dan led Jared up the side aisle, past row after row of eyes staring at the growing turmoil.

"Ooooh!" shouted the crowd, and they turned back to see Max, the Business Center Guy, slug Lombardo in the nose.

"They should sell popcorn at these things," said Jared as they rushed out past Sephora Girl, who stood horrified in the doorway.

$ $ $

Still in the back of the room, still unnoticed, Oscar Hurley wasn't quite sure what to do. He supposed a man of God should try to break things up, but, well...they were homosexuals. Maybe it was better to let them sort things out among themselves.

Then he saw Dennis Merribaugh in the middle of things. That seemed strange...

And then he saw their poster boy run out, holding hands with Senator Cobey's aide, which was when he realized things were out of control.

It was one thing to have a debacle in the privacy of a hotel ballroom among a bunch of perverts who'd already paid their registration fees. It was quite another to have a public debacle—with its centerpieces a congressional aide and the man he'd introduced in front of the entire congregation of the Virginia Cathedral of Love—that would give a black eye to the Moral Families Coalition and his ministry.

"Dennis!" he screamed, and plunged into the fray.

$ $ $

Six FBI agents marched out of the lobby, and thirty seconds later two gay men ran in.

"What took you so long?" asked Grant.

"You should have seen it," said Jared. "There was this big shouting match, and it was turning into a fistfight when we left."

Grant rolled his eyes. "Okay, that's great. So where's the suitcase?"

"Oh, right!" Jared looked under the chairs, finally spotting it and pulling it out.

"Damn," said Mary Beth. "I was practically sitting on it. I could've just…" She sensed Grant staring her down. "*We* could've just grabbed it and run."

Grant took the suitcase from Jared's hands and snapped the handle into position. "Mary Beth, go find Farraday. He's circling the block. Flag him down and tell him to wait out front."

She left.

"Jared, say good-bye to your friend."

Jared looked at Grant and said, "Maybe I could stay for a few days. That'd be okay, right?"

"Absolutely not."

"It's okay." Dan gently stroked Jared's arm. "We have each other's phone numbers, right?"

"Oh, right."

"And I shouldn't be in the way of your father and sister. They're your family, and you should be with…" Dan stopped and dropped his head.

And then Jared was at his side, an arm wrapped around Dan's shoulder. "Baby, don't cry. It'll be all right."

But when Dan looked up, his eyes were clear and his jaw was firm. "I'm not crying, Jared. I'm angry." He pointed at Grant. "Angry about what *he* is doing to you!"

Grant pointed to himself. "Me?"

"Yes, you! You may not be able to accept Jared's sexuality, but that's *your* problem. Not his."

"Kid, lower your voice. People are staring."

"Let them stare." If people wanted to stare, he'd give them something to stare at. He turned to face the rest of the lobby and his voice boomed. "Attention, everyone!" Heads turned; attention was paid. "My name is Daniel Rowell, and I am a gay man! And I work for a Republican United States Senator!"

"Okay," said Grant. "Now you're *really* embarrassing me."

"And this is Jared...uh...This is Jared! He's a gay man, too! And he'll always be gay, no matter how hard his father"—he pointed to Grant—"tries to change him."

And then everyone in the lobby went back to their own business.

Dan looked slightly dejected. "I sort of thought a few people would applaud."

"They never applaud the good lines," said Grant, which caught Dan by surprise. "Nice try, though."

Grant wheeled the suitcase a few feet and added, "For what it's worth, you've got a few misconceptions. Which is good, because that's what we wanted. In a few weeks when the smoke clears, maybe Jared will fill you in on an edited version of reality."

That should have been the bittersweet, slightly ambiguous moment that ended the morning. Would Jared and Dan ever see each other again? Would Grant prove to be not quite as big of a homophobic asshole as Dan had thought?

And it would have been. Except that was also the moment Dr. Oscar Hurley and the Rev. Mr. Dennis Merribaugh burst into the lobby.

"There they are!" said Hurley.

Grant, having been in this sort of situation before, ducked his head behind a shoulder and found the nearest exit.

"That's my suitcase!" screamed Merribaugh, whose shirt was ripped and flapped open, fortunately exposing nothing more than a T-shirt.

Hurley turned to him. "Your *suitcase*? You mean...you mean..." He swallowed. "You mean *the* suitcase?!"

Merribaugh almost fell to his knees and rasped a *"Yesssssssss"* that sounded like a deflating balloon.

$ $ $

The exchange between Hurley and Merribaugh had taken less than ten seconds, but that's all the time Grant and Jared needed to cross the lobby and exit through a service door to the hotel loading dock. It had been one of Grant's hiding spots during the long night before, so he knew it pretty well.

He counted on Jared to keep up and never looked back, passing a few trucks backed to the dock until he said, "I know this model. Get in."

Grant tossed the suitcase through the door, climbed into the cab behind it, and was looking for a tool to break some plastic so he could rig the ignition when he noticed the keys dangling.

"That makes life easier." He started the engine and threw the truck into gear.

"Did you just steal this truck?" asked a voice that wasn't Jared's in a tone that was a little bit too judgmental, as another voice outside the truck that also wasn't Jared's screamed and threw something that bounced off the frame. Grant figured the second voice belonged to the actual truck driver; he wasn't quite sure about the first voice but he didn't bother to look until he was out of the loading dock and onto the street.

Then he looked. It was the guy who gave gay-affirmation speeches in the lobbies of DC hotels.

He faced forward. "What are *you* doing here? Where's Jared?"

"I'm here." *That* was Jared's voice, coming from the other side of the speechmaker.

"So who's this guy?"

"Dan. Dan Rowell." Dan was very polite and extended his hand.

Grant saw the hand out of the corner of his eye. "Yeah, and you work for a Republican senator. I got it. I don't shake hands while I'm driving. Just tell me why you're here."

Dan puffed out his chest. "Because, Mr.…Mr.…" He looked to Jared, who—since he was unsure what to call himself in front of Grant at this stage of the job, as they pushed their way through stop-and-go traffic in a stolen truck—meekly shrugged.

Dan charged on. "Because, Jared's Father, I don't think you realize that gay relationships are every bit as normal as heterosexual relationships."

"Shuddup, kid," said Grant. "You're boring me."

Traffic stopped again. After twenty seconds of sitting in place, Grant got edgy.

"Get out," he told them.

They did, leaving the truck abandoned in the middle of F Street, which meant when traffic *could* start moving again, it wouldn't. Grant was okay with that.

Wheeling the suitcase with one hand and texting Mary Beth with the other, he led Jared and Dan around a corner and to the end of the block. Seconds later, Farraday pulled a Chrysler with congressional plates to the curb.

"You stole a congressman's car?" Grant asked when Farraday powered down his window.

"Personally saw him get out of it and walk into the hotel, and grabbed it before the valet could. I figure we've got a good hour before he knows it's missing. We can change out the plates in Virginia and be back in Nash Bog without raising a sweat."

"If you say so."

"And this damn city," Farraday muttered, pressing a button to pop the trunk as he got out of the car. "I hate driving in this city."

Grant tossed the suitcase in the trunk and was about to agree about the city's lack of merit when he spotted Hurley and Merribaugh down the block, standing at the corner but not yet looking in their direction.

"In the trunk," he told Jared and Dan, who both stared at him. So he gave the order again, this time grabbing each of them by the collar and dragging them off the sidewalk.

"What gives?" asked Jared.

"Hurley and Merribaugh are about a hundred feet behind you on the sidewalk. And their heads are starting to turn toward us."

Jared and Dan wasted no time diving into the trunk, which, thank God, was spacious enough to accommodate both them and the suitcase. But not Grant, too, he realized, as he prepared to join them.

So he closed the trunk and decided to take his chances.

"You sure about this?" asked Farraday as Grant climbed into the backseat. Mary Beth faced forward in the front seat and ignored them.

"I don't think they had time to make me before we left the hotel." He took a quick glance out the rear window and saw Hurley and Merribaugh a half block away. "Hope not, at least. But if you drive instead of talk, we won't have to worry about it."

Farraday put the car in drive and pulled away from the curb.

He was almost to the green light at Pennsylvania Avenue when a motorcycle cop pulled into the middle of the intersection, blocking their car.

"This ain't good," said Farraday.

From the backseat, Grant said, "You mean it ain't good to get stopped by the cops in a congressman's stolen car with two escapees from an ex-gay conference and seven million dollars locked in the trunk while the guys you stole it from are standing next to you?"

"When you put it that way…"

Farraday, Mary Beth, and Grant sank down in their seats.

$ $ $

After Hurley and Merribaugh passed them with no more than a cursory glance at the Chrysler and turned the corner onto Pennsylvania Avenue, they could finally breathe.

"Told you they wouldn't recognize me," said Grant, with much more confidence than he felt.

"You're the luckiest man in the world," said Mary Beth.

To which Farraday added, "If you don't factor in this motorcycle cop who's still standing in front of us."

They sank back in their seats again.

But the cop wasn't paying them any attention, and thirty seconds later they understood why, as the vice president's motorcade passed.

"All this for the vice president?" said Mary Beth. "We couldn't go through this for someone important?"

After another minute the intersection was clear, and as soon as they had a green light, they were zigzagging their way in the opposite direction of the motorcade through the DC streets on their way back to Nash Bog, Virginia.

23

Everything—money, suitcase, and Jared—stayed in the trunk until they arrived back in Nash Bog, after a brief detour in Alexandria. First they freed Dan at a Metro station, where he'd been sworn to secrecy with not-so-subtle threats of physical violence. Then they exchanged license plates with a Subaru in a mall parking lot. The owners would no doubt be shocked the next time they looked and realized they'd been elected to the U.S. House of Representatives.

Mindful of nosy neighbors, Farraday tucked the car in the garage before opening the trunk. Grant reached over Jared and grabbed the suitcase, then closed the trunk.

"You forgot about the kid," said Farraday.

"No, I didn't."

He opened the door into the house and wheeled the bag into the kitchen, where Chase, Lisa, Constance, and Leonard were waiting.

They eyed the suitcase.

Lisa said, "That doesn't look very big, Lambert."

"Told you," said Chase.

The eight of them stood in a circle around the bag, hoping their perception was wrong. Maybe seven million dollars *could* fit inside that suitcase. It didn't seem likely, but *maybe*.

There was only one way to find out, and staring wasn't going to do it.

Grant broke the TSA-approved lock and unzipped it.

$ $ $

"Twenty-five thousand, six hundred dollars," said Chase, carefully setting the last twenty on top of the pile. "Which, I'd like to point out, is in the range Constance and I estimated when Merribaugh wheeled it out."

She nodded.

"Which, *I* gotta point out once again, still ain't seven million." Farraday wasn't happy. Not that any of them were. "Between this and the money from the safe, we've cleared maybe one-fifteen."

"Correction," said Lisa. "We've cleared around ninety-five thou, because the first twenty—plus my expenses—comes back to me." She thought for a moment. "Make it ninety, because my out-of-pocket expenses are running around five thousand. Not including the lawn service."

"Meaning," said Constance, "you just pulled the hotel job to recoup Lisa's expenses."

Sensing a looming mutiny, Grant tried to put the best spin possible on their relatively paltry take. "Better than nothing."

"But not better than seven million," said Chase, causing Grant to wonder whose side he was on.

For a long time they looked wordlessly at the cash stacked on the kitchen table as if it were pocket change. It was Leonard who finally broke the silence.

"I really don't understand," he said. "I was sure it was in the safe."

"But it wasn't," noted Grant. "And then it wasn't in the suitcase."

Leonard played with a shirt button. "Could they have hidden it in one of their hotel rooms?"

Grant thought for a moment, but realized that wouldn't have been possible. "The FBI raided their rooms while we were there, and they would've found it. Also, this suitcase was pretty full. Even if Hurley and Merribaugh had managed to stash a few thousand here and there, at least three-quarters of their money was still inside the suitcase by the time we got our hands on it."

Everyone stared at the cash again.

"I have one more thought," said Leonard. "If the money isn't in the safe, and Merribaugh wasn't carrying it…" He stopped.

"What?!" demanded Constance. "You got an idea, you'd better keep talking."

Leonard tapped one finger nervously on the table, organizing his thoughts. He finally looked around the table and said, "The Desk of Christ."

Grant scowled. "The *what* of *what*?"

Leonard explained. "The Desk of Christ is an iconic part of the cathedral. It's a symbol of Dr. Hurley's ministry."

"Wait a minute," said Constance. "Are you talking about that ugly old thing in Hurley's office?"

"That's it! That's the Desk of Christ!"

"But it's so *ugly*!"

"Yes," Leonard agreed. "But it's also *huge*!"

Constance considered that and finally nodded an agreement.

Grant asked, "Huge enough to hide seven million dollars?"

Leonard wasn't sure. "I don't really know how much room you'd need to hide seven million dollars. But it's much bigger than the safe. Much bigger than *four* safes!" The more he thought over the idea, the more he liked it. "And the only people with access to Hurley's office are Hurley and Merribaugh."

Grant looked at the stack of currency again. It seemed so…small. He really didn't want to break into Cathedral House again—returning to the scene of the crime was never a good idea—but if the money was still there…

He looked around the table at the other members of his team.

"Whaddya think? Cash out at less than a hundred grand? Or take one more chance on seven million dollars?"

"I'm out," said Mary Beth. "This is ridiculous."

Her girlfriend, though, had a different opinion, and felt an excited shiver run up her spine. "Let's do it."

"Lisa!"

"Oh, Mary Beth! Get a grip. We've got one last chance to multiply our haul by a factor of seventy."

Grant acknowledged Lisa's support with the smallest of smiles. "Anyone else in?"

Chase, leaning against the island, said, "Of course."

Leonard and Farraday nodded. They were in. So was Constance. Jared started to agree, but Grant cut him off.

"Not you. Hurley and Farraday are already hunting for you, so you'll lay low. Mary Beth can be your babysitter."

"What?!!"

He ignored her. "So when do you think we should rob this Desk of Christ?"

"Tomorrow night," said Constance firmly.

"Are you that impatient?"

She smiled. "As a matter of fact, I am. But tomorrow's the night

The Sound of Music opens at the auditorium, meaning there'll be a lot of people and traffic. Buses. Delivery trucks. In other words, a lot of distractions."

Grant was sold and as anxious to get out of Virginia as the rest of them.

"Okay, then. Tomorrow we rob the Desk of Christ."

24

The panel truck had been easy to steal; so had the coveralls and the rope. It took a little longer to find several dozen folding chairs, but fortunately someone had left the rear door open at St. Agnes's Orphanage, so they could check that off their list, too.

The play started at eight o'clock. At seven o'clock they dropped Constance and Chase a few hundred yards down Cathedral Boulevard from the main entrance.

"See you inside," said Grant, and Farraday put his foot on the gas. Less than a minute later they slowed and drove up to the guard shack. Leonard ducked his head as the truck came to a stop. Just in case.

"Got a chair delivery," said Farraday through the open window.

The guard barely looked and directed him to the loading dock on the other side of the cathedral.

$ $ $

"You still think they're not in with Hurley?" asked Agent Tolan as their black SUV passed Constance and Chase at a normal rate of speed as they walked down Cathedral Boulevard.

In the passenger seat, Agent Waverly grunted. "I think they're after the same thing *we're* after. But that doesn't mean they're working with Hurley and Merribaugh." He thought about that. "Actually, it probably means quite the opposite. Price and her gang obviously think the money is still here at the cathedral."

The SUV passed the entrance to the Virginia Cathedral of Love and kept moving.

"They could be wrong, Patrick. These people are small-timers."

"Small-timers who are smart and hungry. And persistent. Trust me,

Ollie: if we keep our eyes on them, they'll eventually lead us to the cash."

"Hope I live that long."

$ $ $

The elderly guard in the Cathedral House lobby widened his eyes in surprise as Constance walked through the front door. Chase, carrying a black bag, was a few steps behind her.

"Uh, Ms. Brown, I thought…" He looked from her to Chase and back again. "I thought…"

"You thought what?" she asked innocently.

"Well, didn't the FBI…"

She offered him a reassuring smile. "Oh, that? That was just a misunderstanding."

He'd never experienced a misunderstanding quite like that, so had nothing to compare it to. No matter how unlikely it seemed.

"We're going up to the finance office to get a little work done," she told him, leading Chase past the guard station to the elevator.

$ $ $

As eight o'clock approached, security officer Chris Cason watched traffic pour off Cathedral Boulevard, directed it toward the almost-full parking lots, and marveled at the long, circuitous journey that had led him to the Virginia Cathedral of Love.

For the first several decades of his life, he had considered himself a liberal thinker. Chris Cason was an aspiring author, toiling away at a Barnes and Noble in Tacoma when he wasn't working on the novel he was sure would propel him to fame and fortune. Circumstance rerouted him to Los Angeles and a job as a production assistant for an entertainment conglomerate, but that was good, too. It took no more work to write a screenplay than a novel, after all.

Or it wouldn't have, if any doors had been open for him. But they weren't. In that sense, LA was just like Tacoma. Chris Cason was the low man on the totem pole, the bottom rung of the ladder, the last kid picked for the dodgeball team.

And it finally got to him. His self-esteem bottomed out.

Worst of all, this crippling emotional crisis had made him doubt his gift. One night, despondent, he had almost ended it all, only snapping out of it as he stood at the edge of a cliff. He'd come so close to throwing his unfinished manuscript and unfinished screenplay into the Pacific Ocean that the thought *still* scared him.

But something had touched him at that moment. Something had given him a renewed sense of purpose.

He knew instinctively it was the hand of God.

And that was the moment Chris Cason decided that he'd no longer let the world consider him a delusional, talentless loser. He would embrace God just as God's hand had embraced him at the top of that cliff, saving his manuscript and screenplay from certain doom.

Oh, and so much for the secular liberalism, too. Because those who tended to speak the loudest on God's behalf didn't abide all that touchy-feely do-gooderism. Chris Cason would follow their lead.

He would give up a lot. Not the writing, though. In fact, it was more apparent than ever that God *wanted* him to write. Now, though, his 832-page novel—and 347-page screenplay—would take a new direction. *Ant!* had been a horror/erotica hybrid with a neo-Marxist point of view about a race of mutant Ant-Women and the scientist who is their creator, oppressor, and lover. It would be easy, he knew, to substitute traditional Christian values for neo-Marxism without losing the heart of the story. In fact, the story would gain the solid moral footing that had been eluding him.

Soon he moved east and became a congregant of the Virginia Cathedral of Love. When the position opened in the security department, he was the first applicant. And now, his life back on track, he could finally complete work on *Ant!* and prove to God that His faith had not been misplaced.

No one would ever—*ever*—think of Chris Cason as a delusional, talentless loser again.

With his flashlight, he waved another car into the parking lot, and tried to imagine what sort of vehicle an Ant-Woman would drive.

$ $ $

Lisa Cochrane pulled into a parking space down the row where she'd been directed by the security officer, neatly positioning the Chrysler that had once had congressional tags evenly between the lines. She grabbed a large handbag from the backseat, checked her makeup in the mirror, and departed for the auditorium, not caring that the keys were still in the ignition.

$ $ $

The Town Car raced down Cathedral Boulevard. In the backseat, Merribaugh tried once again, for perhaps the thirtieth time since they'd left the District, to reason with the other passenger.

"Everything will probably be all right, Oscar."

And for the thirtieth time, Dr. Oscar Hurley wasn't buying what his second-in-command was trying to sell. "It will *not* be all right, Dennis. The FBI tossed our rooms, someone stole our money, and *your* ex-gay conference turned into a melee. Not to mention our two most prominent gays went AWOL. This has been a debacle."

"As far as the conference goes, that's survivable."

"Damn right it is," snapped Hurley. "Because as of this moment I am canceling and disavowing Project Rectitude. As far as I'm concerned, those homos can just die. The hell with trying to save them!"

"I know you're angry, but…"

"Hell *yes*, I'm angry! I listened to you and *tried* to do something nice for them by saving them from eternal damnation in the fire pits of hell, and what did I get in return? A room full of hair-pulling, screeching queens! Well, the hell with all of them. My next sermon is going to be a demand that homosexuality immediately be criminalized. It's time to forget salvation and return to damnation."

The car slowed and turned onto the campus of the Virginia Cathedral of Love.

"Okay," said Merribaugh. "I won't fight you on that."

"You'd better not. And if the FBI…" Merribaugh gently touched his arm and motioned toward their driver. Hurley shook him off. "After today, I don't give a damn. If the FBI gets their hands on that money…"

"But they won't." On this topic, Merribaugh was calm. "They'll never find it. Which means they can raid Cathedral House or our hotel rooms all they want, but we're in the clear."

"We'd better be, Dennis." Hurley fixed him with a hard stare. "Because I am *not* going down alone."

The Town Car stopped in front of the steps leading to the cathedral. The backseat passengers took a moment to compose themselves, then exited the car.

"These problems will sort themselves out. Walter Pomeroy's

version of *The Sound of Music* is just the sort of diversion you need to perk yourself up."

Hurley looked up to the heavens. "I truly wish God would strike me dead right now."

$ $ $

The wide metal offering bowl was passed parishioner to parishioner as it made its way down row after row. At the end of end of each circuit, Lisa emptied it into the oversized handbag, then handed it back for another circuit.

If anyone noticed the offering bowl had five cut-outs, each approximately the diameter of a cigarette, and each with a bit of tar residue, they didn't say anything.

The bowl came back down the row and she emptied it into her bag, smiling as she handed it to a matronly woman sitting in an aisle seat one row back.

"Give generously to support the arts!"

$ $ $

Fifteen minutes before the curtain was to go up, a sandwich board was placed at the main entrance informing latecomers the lots were full and directing them to park along Cathedral Boulevard. That effectively ended Officer Chris Cason's duty as a parking lot attendant, so he decided to take a stroll and make sure everything was secure.

He bypassed most of the crowd walking into the auditorium. Those would be the good Christians thrilled to see a musical about Southern Baptists in Austria fighting the Nazis, and therefore unlikely to cause any trouble. His first inspection would be the loading dock behind the buildings, because who knew what kind of ruffians were there smoking and drinking and daydreaming about fornication?

The white panel truck stood out. It was the only one without a company name spelled out on the side.

Sitting on the edge of the open back compartment were three men in coveralls. They looked up at him as he approached, without a friendly expression among them.

"Help ya?" asked a lean, frowning man with salt-and-pepper hair favoring the salt.

"Just checking," said Cason. He looked into the back of the truck. "What are you delivering? Folding chairs?"

"Yeah."

"But the show's about to start. Shouldn't these chairs be inside?"

The deliveryman rubbed his bristly chin. "These are backup folding chairs. In case they run out. We're whatcha call Plan B."

The security guard shrugged. "I guess that makes sense."

$ $ $

It was eight o'clock. Dr. Oscar Hurley took a few deep breaths, then stepped from the wings, crossing slowly until he reached stage-center. He had toyed with the thought of making his customary entrance from the rear, but this hadn't been a good day. He wanted to get this over with as quickly as possible.

"Ladies and gentlemen," he said, and two thousand people fell silent. "Welcome to the opening night of the Virginia Cathedral of Love's new auditorium!" He waited for the applause to die down before continuing. "Tonight we have a special treat. Our musical director, Mr. Walter Pomeroy, has reimagined *The Sound of Music* for your listening—and spiritual—pleasure."

Again there was applause, this time spiking as Walter Pomeroy walked out of the opposite wing. Hurley's face dropped. He hadn't expected this, and he certainly didn't want to share the limelight with one of Merribaugh's experiments in sexual rehabilitation. Not on this day; not ever.

Pomeroy approached Hurley. Smiling. Offering his hand. And then…

Embracing him.

Hurley felt his stomach lurch, and yet Pomeroy held him tighter as the audience roared.

Finally, after it had gone on far too long, Hurley whispered in the musical director's ear. "Let me go, you sick fag."

Walter Pomeroy pulled back, wide-eyed. "Dr. Hurley, I…"

"Just smile and wave to the crowd and pretend everything is fine. Then, tomorrow, make sure you see Rev. Merribaugh to pick up your final paycheck."

The applause finally died off as Pomeroy, shaken, walked offstage.

"And now," said Hurley, as if nothing unpleasant had just happened onstage, "I'm proud to present *The Sound of Music*."

Walter Pomeroy reemerged in the orchestra pit and raised his baton, with one last, hurt look at the departing Hurley.

The overture began.

$ $ $

Lisa texted Grant to let him know Hurley was at the cathedral. They hadn't considered he wouldn't be in Washington, but it sort of made sense, since this was the grand opening of his five million dollar building.

They also knew his ex-gay conference had imploded, which probably lessened Washington's appeal.

Then she took a seat in the rear of the auditorium and kept a tight grip on her handbag.

$ $ $

An hour later, they figured it was dark enough, so Chase and Constance once again propped up the easel and foam core panel with the picture of the Great Cross, blocking the camera. This time, though, they were obstructing the view of the window.

Chase had resisted opening it because he didn't want to be distracted by *Sound of Music* earworms. Sure enough, the first thing he heard was the von Trapp kids singing.

"So long, farewell, *auf wiedersehen*, good-bye…"

He tried to ignore it, opening the black bag and extracting a rope ladder. Then he tied one end around the radiator under the window and stripped off his white shirt, revealing a back T-shirt underneath.

Constance's phone buzzed. She looked at Grant's incoming text message, then turned and talked at the rendition of the Great Cross of the Virginia Cathedral of Love.

"They're rolling, Chase."

"In that case," he said to the back of the panel, "I'm going down. Wish us luck."

She wished them a lot more than luck.

$ $ $

While they tried not to listen to *The Sound of Music*, Grant, Farraday, and Leonard had kept themselves busy. If Hurley was in the auditorium, there was a decent chance the Desk of Christ would have to be stolen if Grant couldn't quickly pick the locks.

First they'd unloaded the folding chairs, each one stenciled with "St. Agnes's Orphanage" on the back, in case they needed the room. Then they'd helped themselves to some equipment from the other delivery trucks: hand-trucks, dollies, straps, and a few tools that might prove useful.

Because this would be their last shot at seven million dollars, and none of them wanted to blow it.

Just after nine o'clock, Farraday got behind the wheel and began gently driving the half mile down the road to Cathedral House as the von Trapp kids wished them "So long, farewell..."

$ $ $

Chase unfurled the rope ladder, which stopped a few feet short of Hurley's terrace. He made his way down just as Grant, Farraday, and Leonard crept around the corner of the building, then whistled up to Constance.

She responded by untying the ladder from the radiator and letting it fall toward Chase. Then she slammed the window and busied herself putting away the easel and panel, and was almost out the door before remembering to take Chase's white shirt and black bag.

Two stories below the finance office, Chase dropped the rope from the terrace to the ground and secured it.

Grant began his climb.

$ $ $

Oscar Hurley, in the front row watching those damn von Trapp kids singing their insipid "So Long, Farewell" song, glanced at his watch. He'd try to tough it out until intermission, but *only* until intermission.

Lisa Cochrane, in the back row, didn't think the kids were too bad. Not pros, but not bad.

But now she had the song stuck in her head...

$ $ $

On her way out the front door of Cathedral House, Constance tossed the security guard a small wave and a "Good night."

"Good night, Ms. Brown," he said, followed quickly by: "Wait!"

She stopped and turned slowly. "Is there a problem?"

"Didn't a man go upstairs with you earlier?"

Constance affected a thoughtful look. "No, I was working alone tonight. No one was with me."

He didn't even try to hide his confusion. "But I'm sure…I mean, I think I'm sure…"

She gave him her most sympathetic smile. "It sounds like you've had a long day."

With that, she spun around, and tightly gripping Chase's bag containing Chase's shirt, walked out of the building.

$ $ $

"I was afraid of this," Grant said to the darkness. Somewhere in the room, pitch black since they'd closed the curtains to block out light that might reveal them to the security cameras, were his three companions. "I can barely find a lock, let alone pick one. I need some light."

"But we can't," said Chase.

"Yeah, I know." He sighed. "The desk has gotta go with us."

$ $ $

The Mother Abbess had now been Christianized into a preacher's wife, but she still sang "Climb Every Mountain," which always threatened to put Dr. Oscar Hurley to sleep. And for this version, Walter Pomeroy had written four additional verses.

Just one more reason tonight would be Walter Pomeroy's last night at the Cathedral.

If there was one bit of good news, it was that this was the last song in the first act. It would be followed immediately by intermission, which in turn would be followed by the departure of Dr. Oscar Hurley.

$ $ $

The Desk of Christ was heavy, and it had taken everything the four men had in them—as well as every piece of equipment they had with wheels—to move it.

But it was finally, slowly moving.

While Farraday and Leonard pushed, Grant and Chase pulled on straps wrapped around the desk's legs. With the help of a few well-placed dollies, they soon threw caution aside, opened the curtains and French doors, and had it on the terrace.

Chase looked at the ground below. "Now what?"

Grant sized up the situation. The good news was no one could really see them. The bad news was they were still ten feet above the ground.

"Back the truck up onto the grass," he told Farraday, and the driver hurriedly climbed over the railing and back down the rope ladder. When the truck was close, he turned to Chase and Leonard.

"And now…we push. And hope that ground's soft, 'cause otherwise we're gonna have a hell of a mess on our hands."

$ $ $

It was almost intermission when her phone buzzed. Lisa read the text message and excused herself from the seat she'd been occupying in the rear of the auditorium.

Constance was waiting outside.

"How's it going up there?" asked Lisa, nodding toward Cathedral House.

"Good on my end. As far as the rest of it, well…I know they made it as far as the terrace." She shook her head. "This is a damn crazy job. How are things here?"

"Great!" Lisa opened her handbag and showed off the offerings. "I figure about five grand."

"Nice. I should work that scam with you."

"You should." Lisa eyed Chase's bag in Constance's hands. "How about if I empty this into your bag? Mine is getting kind of full."

"Go ahead."

Lisa nudged her. "And I haven't even started working the right side of the room. We can tag-team them. Between intermission and the exit that could be worth ten grand!"

Constance smiled. "I like the way you talk numbers."

$ $ $

The Rev. Mr. Dennis Merribaugh had not been having a good day. He'd tried to watch the play, but was so distracted by all the things spinning out of control that he couldn't focus on it. Instead, he spent most of the first act pacing the cathedral's entrance hall, walking repeatedly from Adam and Eve past the Crucifixion to the Ten Commandments and back again.

He was outside, breathing the cool night air, when the auditorium doors banged open and people began to stream outside. That, he knew, would indicate intermission.

He almost disappeared again into the relative solitude of the cathedral when he saw perhaps the last person he expected to see standing on the edge of the crowd.

Sister Constance Brown.

Or rather, Constance *Price.* The *thief.*

He watched her as she talked to a tall woman with blond hair, and could only imagine what kind of scam she had up her sleeve. Well, she'd ripped them off once. He wouldn't allow it to happen again.

"Sister Constance!" Merribaugh hissed as he quickly approached. "Or whatever your name is!"

Constance wasn't used to being caught off guard…but she was. She'd assumed Merribaugh was somewhere in the dark theater with Hurley, not prowling around outside. Still, the FBI had given her their seal of approval. That should be good enough for Merribaugh.

It wasn't.

He pulled her to the side, unwilling to air dirty laundry in front of the tall, blond woman.

"I believe," he said, "that you somehow got into the safe and stole offerings to the cathedral before they could be banked."

"Who, me?"

He wagged a finger in her face. "Don't play innocent with me. I know your real name. I also know you have a criminal record." Merribaugh looked down at the bag she held. "What's in your bag."

She kept calm. "Just a shirt."

"I don't trust you. Open it."

"It's just…"

But he had already leaned over and was unzipping the bag, exposing an estimated five thousand dollars in cash. Before she could open her mouth in protest he had ripped the bag out of her hands.

"Shame on you, Ms. Price." Merribaugh wagged his finger again, and began walking away.

"Where you going with my money?" Constance asked in his wake.

"Somewhere safe. Somewhere you won't be able to get your hands on it."

When Merribaugh's back was turned, Lisa joined Constance and they watched him disappear into the crowd.

Lisa shrugged. "Easy come, easy go, I suppose."

"That pisses me off. He stole the money you stole fair and square. And Chase's shirt, too."

Lisa hiked her now almost-empty handbag. "At least he didn't get my favorite ashtray. That would have sucked."

$ $ $

The elderly security guard thought he heard the sound of wood splintering, followed by a thud.

First his mind was playing tricks on him, and now his ears. He wasn't going to report *this* and become a laughingstock. No sir…

He looked at the newspaper on his desk and went back to trying to solve the Jumble.

25

Farraday put the panel truck in neutral, and it slowly rolled down the slight slope back to the rear of the auditorium. As the unlit truck neared a Dumpster, he gently applied the brakes—waiting until the last moment because applying the brakes meant illuminating the brake lights—and glided to a stop behind two other trucks parked at the loading dock.

In the back, Grant worked under the dome light on the locks of the Desk of Christ, which had survived the ten-foot drop intact. It seemed to take forever, but finally—about the time Farraday was docking the truck—he heard a gentle click that told him the first one had opened. With a tug, he began to slide out a drawer…

A series of loud blows boomed against the back door.

Grant closed the drawer, threw a moving pad over the Desk of Christ, and told Chase, "Whoever it is, get rid of 'em."

Chase opened the back door eighteen inches and began to crawl out until he was blinded by a flashlight beam.

"You one of the movers?" asked an agitated voice from the other side of the light.

His eyes almost closed against the brightness, Chase slithered forward a few more feet until he was out of the truck, then stood. Only then did he answer. "Uh…yeah."

"Got any identification?"

"Depends. You are…?"

"Officer Cason. Cathedral security. You got ID?"

"It's in the truck," Chase bluffed, not really sure what he'd do next. "Want me to get it?"

The security guard kept the light fixed on Chase's eyes and didn't answer the question. Instead, he asked, "What were you doing up at Cathedral House?"

"You…you mean that building over there?" The flashlight wobbled with the guard's nod. "Uh…smoke break." Chase warmed to the idea. "I didn't want to smoke in the loading dock." And he warmed a bit more. "You know, because children might come back here. And I'd hate to set a bad example for the children."

Chase still couldn't see anything except the blinding light aimed at his eyes, but heard Farraday heave himself out from behind the wheel, step to the ground, and ask, "Is there a problem, Officer?"

The light shifted from Chase to Farraday. Chase blinked a few times and tried to see again, but his eyes were filled with spots.

In the meantime, the guard was interrogating Farraday. "Just checking on how come you took the truck up to Cathedral House. No one's supposed to have any business up there."

"We didn't know that," said Farraday. "No one said nothin' about that. This guy wanted a cigarette, is all."

Now the flashlight bounced back and forth between Chase and Farraday, then across the side of the truck.

"Weren't you carrying folding chairs?" the guard finally asked.

"Yeah," said Chase. "Turns out, they needed them."

Static from the security guard's radio interrupted him, followed by a tinny voice. "Post Two, come in."

The flashlight beam dropped to the ground as the security guard unclipped the radio from his belt. "Post Two."

"What's the situation with that truck?"

"Chair delivery for the play. Guy here says they drove over to Cathedral House for a cigarette, in order to get away from these premises."

"And not set a bad example for the children," Chase reminded him.

"And not set a bad example for the children."

"All right," was the response. "Tell 'em that area is strictly off-limits. Workers stay at the loading dock, 'kay?"

"I did, sir."

"All right."

There was a long pause as the security officer lowered his radio and began to clip it back on his belt, and Chase felt brief exhilaration that the cover story—flimsy as it was—had passed the test.

Until the tinny voice returned. "Post Two, better check the truck while you're there. After that, make an inspection of Cathedral House an' make sure everything's secure."

The security officer raised the radio back to his lips. "Roger that." He turned to Chase and said, "Mind opening it up for me?"

Chase said, "Not at all." What was going to happen next wasn't *his* fault. This security guard had asked for it. Hadn't he ever heard that story about curiosity and the cat?

He hoped that Grant and Leonard had heard every word of their encounter through the door, but—even if they hadn't—knew he had no choice. He stepped to the back of the truck, grabbed a handle, and lifted…

…and was relieved to see Grant, sitting alone among a jumble of moving pads. Somewhere underneath those pads were Leonard and the Desk of Christ, but you'd never know it from a cursory view.

"See? Just moving pads."

The flashlight darted across the interior, finally settling on Grant's eyes.

Grant squinted and frowned. "You mind getting that thing outta my eyes?"

"Just making sure everything's on the up-and-up, sir." Still, the guard moved the light from Grant's face and trained it on the mounds of pads. "Just you three fellas?"

"Yeah," said Grant. "Just the three of us."

The light moved around the back of the truck, then stopped. Chase followed it until he saw one exposed corner of the Desk of Christ Grant had missed in his rush to hide it.

"What's that?"

"Just furniture," said Chase, talking quickly. "Another job we picked up this afternoon. Delivery's scheduled for first thing in the morning, so we figured we'd keep it on the truck overnight."

The beam of light was now focused on the edge of the desk where the finish had worn off. The security guard blinked his eyes a few times, as if trying to reconcile this image with a familiar one from his time as a parishioner of the Virginia Cathedral of Love.

"Is that…?" he started to ask, then stopped.

"Just an old beat-up desk," said Chase. "It's nothing."

But the security guard was already climbing into the back of the truck. No one tried to stop him…until he tripped over Leonard, hidden on the floor under a moving pad, and they knew it was time for action.

Several minutes later, with Officer Chris Cason now bound with packing tape, muted with an old rag, and secreted under a dusty pad in the back of the truck, the radio squawked to life again.

"Post Two, come in."

"How do you work this thing?" Grant held the radio like it might explode.

"Let me." Chase took it from him and pushed a button, trying his best to mimic the guard's voice. "Post Two here."

"Everything check out with that truck?"

"Roger that."

"Ten-four."

The radio went silent and Chase handed it back to his partner.

"Close the door," Grant ordered. "And let's find out what's in this damn desk."

Farraday returned to the cab, closing the door behind him and turning off the rear dome light. As Leonard trained the guard's flashlight on the two open drawers, Grant rifled through them and found a lot of paperwork, although none of it was the shade of green they were looking for. He moved to the left side of the desk and began to work his magic on the lock.

$ $ $

Special Agents Patrick Waverly and Oliver Tolan sat in their SUV as it idled at the side of the road a half mile down Cathedral Boulevard from the Virginia Cathedral of Love. Waverly brushed a lock of hair off his forehead and glanced at his watch.

"Now they're fifteen minutes late."

Tolan, who was behind the wheel, tapped a few salted peanuts out of a packet into his palm. "Want to go in without them?"

"Yeah, right." Waverly chuckled. "Love you, Ollie, but you and I aren't *The Untouchables*." He took another look at his watch, then sat back in the less-comfortable-than-it-looked seat. "Let's give them five more minutes. Or ten. It's not like anyone's going anywhere."

$ $ $

"Nothing," said Grant, on his knees and surveying the contents of the remaining desk drawers as they lay strewn across the floor of the truck. "All of this for nothing."

"We got the Desk of Christ," said Leonard, hovering over his shoulder. "Maybe we could hold it for ransom."

Grant looked up at him. "You seriously think Hurley's gonna drop seven mil for a beat-up old desk?"

"Well, uh…I guess not."

"Then shut up."

"But he might pay a million."

Grant blinked twice, then looked back in the direction in which Leonard held the torch. "You been drinking? He could have a new one made for twenty bucks."

"You don't understand." Leonard nervously played with the zipper on his coveralls. "It's not the quality of the craftsmanship. The Desk of Christ has become iconic! People come from all over the world to touch the Desk of Christ. Hurley has it insured for…well, I can't really remember now, but at *least* a million dollars."

Grant motioned at the pile of moving pads covering the security guard. "Outside."

They climbed out of the truck and walked to a quiet area near the loading dock. When they had some privacy, Grant said, "That doesn't make sense."

"It makes sense," said Leonard. "It makes sense the same way the government pays all kinds of money to preserve and protect the original Declaration of Independence, which—when you think about it—is only an old, tattered piece of parchment. Same thing with this desk: its value exceeds the materials. The Desk of Christ is a symbol of the Virginia Cathedral of Love, and by extension, a symbol of Dr. Oscar Hurley's power and influence. Which is apparently worth a million dollars to him."

"So…you're saying without this desk, he loses his power and influence?"

Leonard shook his head. "No, not at all. But it's a symbol, and it means a lot. Enough that he insures it for a lot of money. Enough that I'd be willing to bet he'd pay a lot of ransom to get it back."

To Grant, that still didn't make sense, but, well…maybe it did. In a way.

Chase finally spoke, and Grant could forget about the concept of non-tangible value that had almost worked its way into his head.

"I'd still rather have the seven million."

"One million is better than nothing," said Leonard.

Grant muttered. “Everyone will have to take a lot less. But I guess we’d make a profit.”

“I’m willing to drop my share to a half million.” Leonard probably thought he was being magnanimous.

“You are, huh?” Leonard raised the flashlight and saw Grant fix him with a stare that made him instantly recalculate.

“I’m, uh, sure we’ll come up with a fair number.”

“That’s better.”

They walked a few yards to the truck and crawled back inside.

Grant turned to Chase, rubbing his hand against the rough grain of the desk. “Text the girls. It’s time to get out of here.” He looked at the bundle in the corner. “We’ll drop the guard out on Cathedral Boulevard. He’ll be fine. This’ll give him a story he can tell for the rest of his life.”

Farraday asked, “Should we take the chairs?”

“Nah. Consider them our contribution to the Virginia Cathedral of Love. Until St. Agnes’s Orphanage comes looking for ’em, at least.”

Grant and Leonard began sliding the drawers back into the desk, and Farraday slowly walked to the cab. As they did what they had to do, Chase took a few steps back into the parking lot and pulled out his cell phone.

Then he paused with one thumb over a button, unable to type.

True, one million dollars—if they could get that, which he doubted—would make for a nice payday. There’d still be a few hundred thou left after divvying the money with the rest of the gang. But he still couldn’t get past the belief—no, the *knowledge*—that they’d somehow managed to overlook a much bigger payday.

It wasn’t in the safe, and Merribaugh hadn’t taken it to DC, but Chase knew that somewhere in their immediate vicinity was hidden seven million dollars they’d managed to overlook. In crisp, easy-to-spend cash.

And if they left now with only the Desk of Christ, they’d never have the opportunity to get at it again.

Maybe the others had given up the idea they could get their hands on that money, but Chase didn’t want to give up. He *couldn’t* give up.

But where the hell could the money be? They had looked everywhere, and found nothing but trouble.

Where the hell *was* it?

He looked up at the 199-foot cross towering over their heads. If there was ever a time for divine intervention, he thought, it was now.

“Chase!” He jumped, then realized it was just Grant hollering at him from the truck. He heard the truck's rear door slide shut and latch. "Text those other guys. It's time to get out of here."

Chase's eyes traveled above the scaffolding to the top of the cross towering over him. He muttered an almost-silent prayer. "Give me a sign where the money is."

His answer came in the form of a memory…

Spirals.

"Chase! Let's go!"

Reluctantly, Chase began to type out a text message. Then, again, his thumbs stopped working.

He slowly turned and stared again at the Great Cross, and it was almost as if he could hear the Hallelujah Chorus.

"Grant…" His voice was a hoarse whisper as he backed up, slowly and steadily. "I think I know where it is."

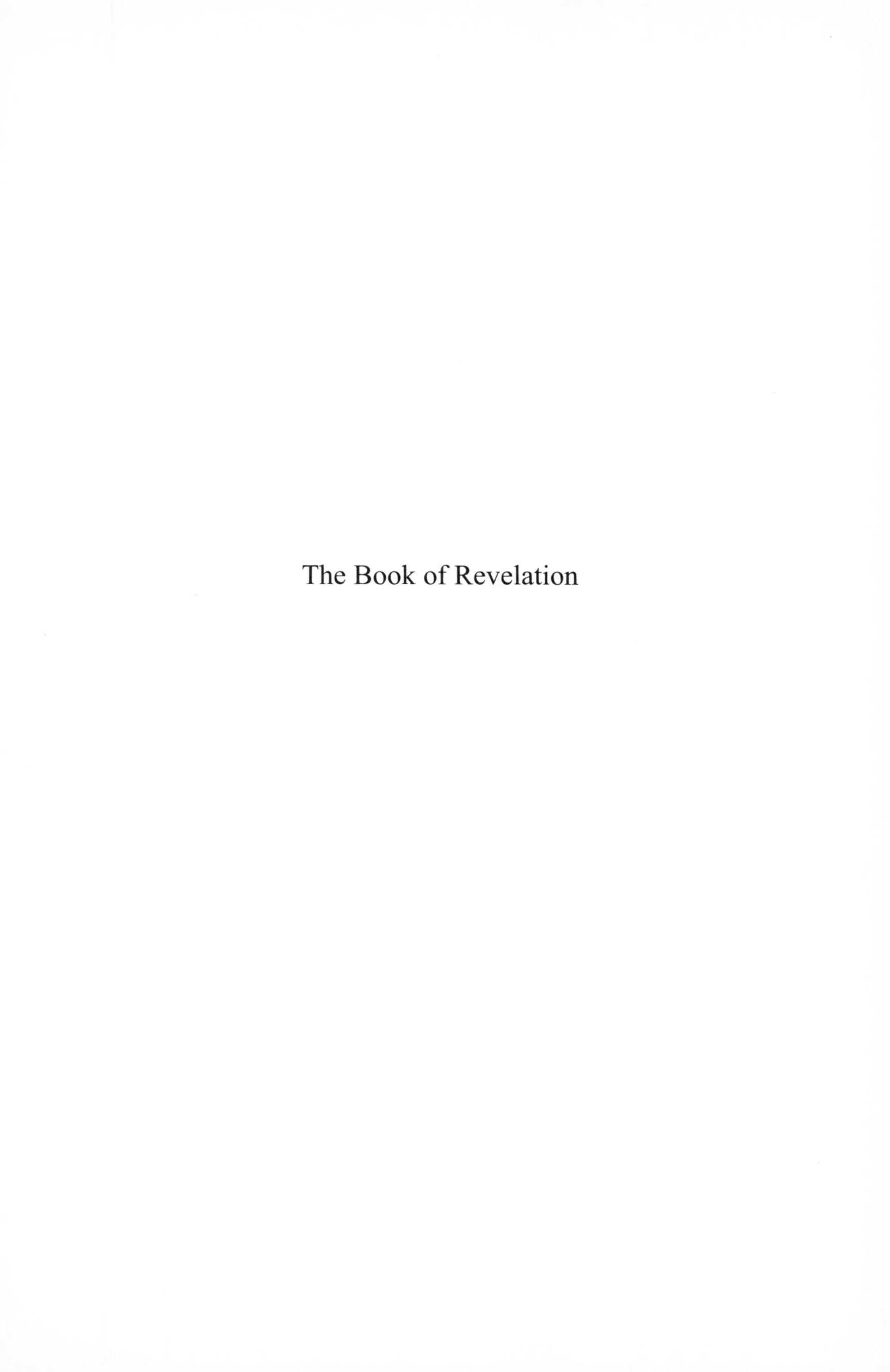

The Book of Revelation

26

The *cross*?" asked Grant, as he stood at the back of the truck with Chase and Leonard. "You want to go up in the *cross*?"

"I think so," said Chase, although—now that a half minute had passed since his divine inspiration—he wasn't quite as sure as he *had* been, and in any event he wasn't going to tell them about his moment of piety. They'd sense weakness.

Grant still couldn't grasp it. "Why the cross?"

"Why not? Who'd look there?"

"Lots of people."

"Not us."

Grant thought about that for a moment. Maybe Chase had a point.

"So what gave you this great idea, boyfriend?"

"The spirals on the drawing in the office. I just assumed someone had doodled…until I had this revelation they weren't doodles. Someone drew in a staircase."

"Inside the cross?"

"Yeah, inside the cross."

Leonard had been stammering since Chase announced his revelation, but now finally managed to speak in a more or less understandable sentence as he worked his zipper up and down. "But…but…there's nothing there! It's solid!"

"Says who?" asked Chase.

"Merribaugh." With that, his hands flew to his face. "Unless he lied!"

Grant couldn't look at him. "Now why would a crook lie about his hiding place? Jesus, Leonard, we could have been out of here a week ago."

"It…it…it just never occurred to me that the cross *wasn't* solid."

"That was the point," Chase said. "You can't blame Leonard. Why would someone lie about it? They tell everyone it's solid, everyone believes it's solid." He thought about it a bit more. "And that would also explain why there are no cameras around. Merribaugh and Hurley didn't want anyone to know what they were up to. Didn't want photographic proof that every now and then one or both of 'em were going inside a structure they'd been claiming couldn't be gone into."

Grant mulled that over. He was starting to warm to the idea, if not the fact that Chase stumbled upon it first.

"Hey, guys," said Farraday, who was now with them and staring into the back of the truck. "We should get this desk out of here."

"Hold on a second," said Grant. "We're taking one last look around. This might be a seven-million-dollar job after all."

"Eight," said Leonard, pointing to the Desk of Christ. "A million's a million, right?"

And Grant started to think that he might end up respecting Leonard after all.

Underneath the dirty moving pads, Chris Cason tried to follow what he could of the conversation. These thugs had stolen the Desk of Christ, they were discussing the Great Cross, one man called another man "boyfriend," and he'd even heard blasphemy.

None of this was good. Someone would have to stop them.

$ $ $

They left Leonard in the cab of the truck—figuring someone should guard the Desk of Christ and he'd be the most useless in the field—and made their way across the grounds, creeping behind the overgrown bushes lining the walkways and squeezing past one of the ground-mounted floodlights illuminating the Great Cross. The appearance of that security guard was a fresh reminder that even though they wouldn't be under surveillance by cameras, they might still be under surveillance by actual people.

"Where's the door?" Grant asked in a whisper as Chase and Farraday crouched beside him. "I don't see a door."

They skittered through the bushes to the other side of the cross, but still couldn't find a way in.

"Okay, this is ridiculous. If it's hollow there has to be—" He stopped, spotting movement in the shadows near the rear of the auditorium, not far from where Leonard sat in the truck. The men disappeared back into the bushes.

"Merribaugh," said Chase, as the Cathedral's chief operating officer passed under a light and crossed the loading dock before disappearing into the building.

"What was he doing out here?" Grant looked up the cross. "You think he was coming from the cross?"

Chase nodded. "Probably hiding the stash they raked in tonight."

Moments later they were creeping through dark bushes until they reached the spot where they'd seen Merribaugh emerge. It was Farraday, out from behind the wheel and therefore out of his comfort zone, who finally found the windowless door at the far end of the building. It was locked, but Grant dipped into his pocket, found what he needed, and had them past that obstacle in less than twenty seconds.

$ $ $

Tap tap tap.

Leonard was sitting nervously in the darkness, half-covered with a moving pad. He didn't like being left alone, so his thought upon hearing the taps against the side of the truck was that his partners in crime had returned. He felt great relief.

Until Captain Joseph Enright's face appeared in the window, just inches away. Leonard screamed and scrambled to push down the door lock but wasn't fast enough, and he half tumbled from the seat as Enright flung open the door.

"Hello, Mr. Platt. I figured we'd see you again one day. I just hadn't imagined it'd be so soon."

$ $ $

The windowless door led to a basement storage room. Above them, they heard applause as the curtain went up on the second act of *The Sound of Music.*

Grant pulled the flashlight from his rear pocket and ran the light once around the room before shutting it off. It was totally empty. He'd sort of hoped they'd find the money there and could forget that nonsense about the cross, but no.

"Okay, so we found a basement. Which isn't the same thing as finding a way into the cross. You sure about this?"

"No," Chase confessed. "But it's an idea, and we don't have any more of those."

Even in the darkness, Chase could feel Grant frowning. He distracted himself by blindly groping the nearest wall, hoping against hope that he'd somehow find a way into the cross.

"Maybe Merribaugh came from somewhere else," said Farraday's voice from the darkness. "Maybe he was out back takin' a leak."

"Maybe," Chase said. He might have said more if his hands hadn't suddenly found a handle sticking out of the wall. When he thumped it, he heard hollowness. "Grant, shine the flashlight over here!"

Once illuminated, Chase saw his hand was wrapped over a metal handle attached to a wooden door, both painted a cement-gray to match the cinderblock walls of the basement. It wasn't perfect camouflage, and maybe it wasn't supposed to be, but it served the purpose of visually blending the door to the wall.

He turned the handle, assuming it would be locked. It wasn't.

The door slowly swung open, and Grant followed its arc with the flashlight.

It was a tunnel, and it led out of the basement in the direction of the Great Cross of the Virginia Cathedral of Love.

"Huh," said Grant. "Maybe I should pay more attention to your hunches."

$ $ $

Captain Joseph Enright slapped the nightstick against his palm just hard enough to make the impressive wood-against-flesh noise, but not hard enough to hurt. As he'd hoped, Leonard Platt flinched and grew a shade paler.

"You need to start answerin' my questions, Platt. Otherwise, you gonna get an opportunity to feel this nightstick fo' yourself. Now, what'ja do with Officer Cason?"

By now, Leonard figured Cason was the security guard who was bound and gagged in the back of the panel truck. He wasn't about to give that up to Enright.

"I don't know this guy."

Whap went the nightstick into Enright's palm.

"Then tell me what you're doin' here. And who's with you?"

"I'm here alone. I just got…uh…nostalgic."

Whap! Enright winced; that one sort of hurt. He tried to shake the pain out of his hand without Leonard Platt noticing.

"What if I tell you I don't believe you, Platt? 'Cause I truly don't."

Leonard swallowed hard. "Are you going to call the cops?"

"That depends." Enright thought about whacking the nightstick into his palm again, then thought maybe he'd wait until the stinging stopped. "Depends on what Merribaugh wants me to do with you. Don't matter much to me. I could call the cops..." He leaned close to Leonard. "Or I could just take you back to the marsh, if you know what I mean."

A shudder swept through Leonard. He did indeed know what Enright meant.

$ $ $

At the end of the tunnel was a metal staircase heading in only one direction: up. Grant trained the flashlight above them, throwing light across a tightly wound circular stairway that wrapped around and around as it climbed through the center of the cross.

"There's your squiggle," said Grant.

"Spiral," said Chase.

Grant wasn't in the mood. "Squiggle or spiral, it's all the same thing. It was a drawing, not a doodle." He worked the flashlight up and down the metal stairs. "A drawing of this."

"Meaning I was right," said Chase.

"Yeah, you were right about the squiggle."

"Spiral."

Farraday, standing a few yards behind them, said, "I hate to interrupt your cute domestic argument, but you're burning the clock. And since we already know we don't have a lot of time..."

They started climbing.

They'd barely gotten under way when Grant heard Farraday's voice somewhere behind him in the dark. "Lambert, what the hell are you trying to do? Kill Me?"

"This cross is like two hundred feet high, and you're tired after twenty steps?"

Farraday took a few deep breaths. "I want to go back downstairs. I didn't sign up for stair-climbing."

"None of us did." Grant calculated in his head. "But it's only like climbing twenty stories in a building. Not too bad."

"I drive," Farraday panted. "I'm a ground-floor kind of guy."

Granted nodded, not that Farraday could see in the dark. "Tell you what. You stay behind and Chase and I will go up and look for the loot. If it's here, that is."

$ $ $

Security officer Chris Cason finally managed to spit out the gag and was gnawing at the packing tape binding his wrists.

He wasn't exactly sure what was going on, but he had a good guess. Dr. Hurley had long predicted that the forces of evil would try to silence the true believers. No doubt that was what was coming to fruition. These brutes had come to steal and…terrorize?

They had already stolen the Desk of Christ, and they had designs on the Great Cross. Both were the holiest symbols of the Cathedral. They had also blasphemed and exhibited homosexual tendencies. Those facts pointed in one direction, and only one direction.

Atheist homosexual terrorist criminals were attacking the Virginia Cathedral of Love. Maybe they were even planning to blow it up on this holiest of days, the day the True Christian version of *The Sound of Music* brought God's word to His people.

Chris Cason had been on the planet for thirty-eight years and had not yet lost his virginity, let alone become fruitful and multiplied, but he would give up all that—give up his life—to save the Cathedral and God's children. He would even postpone the completion of *Ant!* until the afterlife.

His teeth ripped into the tape and tore off a tiny piece. At this rate, it would only take two or three hundred more bites and he'd be a free man…

$ $ $

"And then there were four." Waverly took yet another glimpse at his watch and looked back at the two fresh-faced FBI agents who moments ago had pulled behind them and were now standing outside his window.

They were a half hour behind schedule. At some point soon, they'd have to move.

He looked back to Tolan. "Six more agents should be here, but I'm getting bored. You think we can handle it with four?"

Tolan popped some peanuts in to his mouth. "It's a church,

Patrick. And this is a financial crime. This won't be one of our tougher assignments."

Waverly nodded and looked out the window at the other agents. "Follow us."

$ $ $

The staircase was compact. Whoever had designed it—and Grant figured it had to be Merribaugh, since he did the planning around the cathedral—had made sure it was efficient, but unobtrusive. A dozen steps up, a yard-long landing in case you needed a rest, and then another dozen steps.

Grant and Chase had lost count of how many of those short landings they'd passed at some point around the twelfth. That was a problem; they had no idea how far they'd climbed, or how far they had to go, not to mention what they'd find when they got there.

At each landing, Grant would swing the flashlight around for a few seconds while they searched the concrete walls for a place Hurley and Merribaugh could hide seven million dollars. Not finding it, he'd turn it off and they'd continue their ascent through the core of the Great Cross. They had no idea what was going on outside. For all they knew, the cops were out there. Or worse, the entire congregation, armed with torches and pitchforks and determined to defend Hurley and Merribaugh to the death in the name of Jesus or whatever.

"How much more you figure we have to go?" Grant finally asked as the muscles in his legs cramped a bit.

Chase took a moment to find the words he wanted. "Near the perpendicular part, I think."

"The perp—You mean where the cross crosses?"

"I was trying to avoid the 'cross crosses' thing, but yes."

Grant rested one hand on the railing and took a deep breath as he massaged a thigh muscle. "Why there?"

"Remember the spirals on the drawing?"

"You mean the squiggles? Yeah."

Chase wasn't in the mood to revive that argument. "Those *squiggles* spilled into the cross-section. Meaning…"

Grant got it. "Meaning hiding place." He took another deep breath and said, "Okay, let's get climbing."

$ $ $

Two black SUVs turned off Cathedral Boulevard and swept past the guard shack, knocking down the sandwich signs telling playgoers where to park. They proceeded along the six-lane drive as it wound past the cathedral and auditorium before coming to a stop in front of Cathedral House. Waverly and Tolan, leather badge holders in hand, led the other agents up the front steps and into the building.

The elderly guard, still on post at the front desk, looked up at them, saw their badges, and nodded. He was beyond the point of questioning anything that happened around him.

Still, Waverly had to say it, so he did. "FBI. I'm Special Agent Waverly, this is Special Agent Tolan. And these are…" He forgot the names of the junior officers. "They're with us."

The guard nodded again. "I figured you'd be coming. Soon as Captain Enright caught Mr. Platt on the grounds, I knew the authorities would be getting involved."

"Mr. Platt? *Leonard* Platt?"

"Yessir. It's been a bit strange around here lately, what with the people I think I see and those noises I think I hear…"

Ignoring him, Waverly said, "Take us to Captain Enright."

$ $ $

Another landing. Grant trained the flashlight on the wall and—after the brief right/left sweep they'd perfected over the previous forty landings—both he and Chase gasped and simultaneously said, "This is it!"

On both sides were open passages. They had reached the point where the Great Cross *crossed.* Chase's hunch had been correct.

And, in fact, Chase waited a moment to hear Grant say those words of approval and appreciation. When it was clear he wasn't going to say them, Chase said it himself.

"Good job, Chase! You found seven million dollars!"

"Let's get to work," was the terse reply. "I'll be happy to celebrate when I actually see some cash."

$ $ $

In the security office, which took up significant space in the basement of Cathedral House, Patrick Waverly stared at the video monitor, watching one view cut to another for several long moments before he spoke.

"Nice setup they have here. Wouldn't you say this is a nice setup, Agent Tolan?"

"It is a nice setup," said Tolan.

Keeping his eyes on the monitor, Waverly said, "Don't *you* think this is a nice setup, Captain Enright?"

Enright, seated in a chair with his hands handcuffed securely behind his back and guarded by the junior agents, snarled sourly but said nothing.

"You don't feel like talking, Enright? That's a shame." He turned to Leonard. "And Mr. Platt! We meet at last."

"How do you know my name?" asked Leonard, one hand on the zipper of his coveralls. He was even more nervous than usual, but relieved that he—unlike Enright—hadn't been handcuffed.

Waverly smiled and his cheek dimpled. Leonard, despite his fear, couldn't help but be put at ease. "You're legendary, Mr. Platt. Isn't he, Agent Tolan?"

Tolan muttered something through a mouthful of peanuts.

Leonard didn't like any of this, but—as long as he wasn't handcuffed and didn't seem to be the person the FBI was looking for—tried his best to tolerate it.

Plus, he thought, this Agent Waverly was kind of cute. Leonard knew he was nothing special himself, but Waverly *had* called him legendary, so…

"Cool," said Leonard.

Waverly returned his attention to the monitor. "Hey, Enright, how do I change the channel on this thing? I want to lock it in so it's not jumping around on things that don't interest me."

Enright sat, stone-faced except for the sneer on his lips.

"Guess you got your answer, Waverly," said Tolan. "Captain Enright certainly isn't doing anything to make things easier on himself."

Waverly shook his head at Enright. "Well, I guess I can appreciate that. If we were in the Secret Service, we'd take a bullet for the president, right?" Tolan nodded. "So Enright here is willing to take one for a corrupt preacher. Which is almost the same thing in principle. Not in reality, but in principle."

Tolan sat on the chair in front of the monitor. "Let me see if I can figure out how to work this." He toggled a switch and the view was now the interior of the auditorium. There was no audio, but they saw Baptist Maria singing stage-center. "Look at that! I'm an electronic genius."

"You certainly are, Ollie." Waverly stared at the screen for a moment. "You get a lot of people here, don't you, Enright?"

Silence.

"I figured he was going to say that."

"And there's the Reverend Mr. Dennis Merribaugh." Tolan pointed to the monitor as Merribaugh's grainy black-and-white image appeared in the back of the auditorium.

"They say the camera adds ten pounds. Which in his case looks more like thirty." Waverly looked at Enright. "Sorry, Captain. Cheap shot." To Tolan, he said, "Now see if you can find Hurley."

Enright finally spoke. "You wanna tell me what this is about? Even though you're the FBI, there are rules. You can't bust in here and hold me hostage."

Not taking his eyes off the monitor as he cut to different cameras, Tolan said, "You are being temporarily detained, Enright."

"*Captain* Enright."

"Whatever. This way, when we arrest Hurley and Merribaugh—"

"What?!" Enright's face was purple. "I've never heard'a such a—"

Waverly talked over him. "This way, you can't warn them that we're here."

Enright's face turned from purple to plum. "This is an outrage! This is an attack on the church by the federal government!"

Waverly sized him up. "You see, Enright, these rage issues are why we had to handcuff you."

He might have said more if Tolan hadn't announced, "Found Hurley."

And Hurley was indeed on the screen, looking completely befuddled and more than a little bit angry.

"Captain Enright, where is this camera?"

Enright wouldn't answer.

But Leonard did. "That's Hurley's office. On the second floor."

"Of *this* building?"

"Yes."

Special Agent Patrick Waverly smiled. This was going to be too easy. Hurley would be detained within minutes. After just a few weeks. He and Tolan would have wrapped up a huge case…and made a lot of people on Capitol Hill very relieved and very happy.

So relieved and happy the Bureau wouldn't have to worry about full congressional funding for decades. Nothing would please the Director more than not having to testify before Congress.

Or that was his plan, until a disheveled man in a guard uniform, bits of brown packing tape stuck to his clothes and lips, burst through the door, screaming something about atheist homosexual terrorist criminals.

Waverly and Tolan exchanged glances. Nailing Hurley was important, but stopping a terrorist attack trumped it.

They knew what had to be done.

$ $ $

Gone!

How could it be…? But it was. It was *gone!*

Dr. Oscar Hurley had excused himself from *The Sound of Music*—a performance he was deeply, truly hating—and walked back to his office for no reason other than to get away from the show and his congregation for an hour or so. Maybe he'd shower…maybe take a nap…maybe even call his Francine. If she hadn't fallen into another sugar coma, she might want to chat for a while.

Whatever he'd do, it would be von Trapp-free, and that could be only a good thing.

But then he walked up the sweeping staircase to his office—the two black SUVs parked out front barely registering in his brain—and immediately noticed the void in the center of the room.

The Desk of Christ was gone.

First, he was confused. Had he walked into the wrong…?

No, of course not!

Then he was enraged, and became even angrier when he saw that the elegant wood railing enclosing his terrace had been destroyed.

Only then did he remember those black SUVs, and wondered what they had to do with this outrage.

He stepped out of his office and onto the landing, on his way downstairs to confront Enright, when a door burst open in the foyer below him. Hurley stepped back into the shadows and watched from above as two men—undoubtedly FBI, he thought, sizing up their clothes and shoes—filed out, followed by that Cason fellow they'd hired as a security guard and…

Is that Leonard Platt?

They didn't look in his direction, and he took advantage of that lapse to step closer to the polished oak railing and get a better look.

And, yes, that was indeed Leonard Platt.

What the hell was *he* doing there?

Hurley watched the quartet leave the building, and even with a largely obstructed view could tell that they'd walked past the black SUVs and out onto the campus. When they were gone, he scrambled down the stairs until he reached the elderly security guard, who was now so confused he was considering which no-good relative should get power of attorney, because all this craziness could *only* be taking place in his head.

"Is Enright down there?"

The guard judged his immediate mental condition to be passable. "Yessir."

Hurley stormed down the stairs without a thank-you and entered the Security Office without a hello.

"Enright, what the hell is—?" He stopped when he saw two unfamiliar faces, both also obviously FBI and both also obviously armed.

"Who's this?" one of the agents asked Enright.

"Mr. Smith," said Enright. "The choir director."

Hurley started to object, but noticed the strange way Enright was sitting in the chair, with his hands clasped behind his back. Whatever was going on, Hurley knew it wasn't a good thing. And he knew he had to play along.

"Yes, I'm the choir director. Mr.…uh…*Smith.* May I have a moment to speak to Captain Enright in private?"

"I'm afraid not," said the second agent. "Captain Enright stays here, and we stay with Captain Enright."

"Well…can we speak?"

The agents looked at each other and shrugged.

Hurley tried to pretend they weren't there. He wanted to ask about the Desk of Christ, but knew he couldn't. For some reason, Enright was trying to protect him by hiding his identity; it would do neither of them any good—and it especially wouldn't do *him* any good—if he acknowledged he was Hurley. If the FBI had confiscated his desk, it would be back soon enough.

But he had other questions.

"Did I just see Leonard Platt leave the building?"

Enright nodded. "He wouldn't say what he was doing here."

"Where did he and, uh, those *other* gentlemen go?"

"The Great Cross."

"The Great Cross?"

Another nod. "Officer Cason was abducted tonight. He thinks by militant atheist homosexual terrorists. When they had him taped up..."

"Taped up?"

"They bound him with packing tape. He had to chew his way out. Anyway, Cason overheard his captors talking about the cross."

Color drained from Hurley's face. "For...uh...what reason?"

"Cason got the impression they were gonna use it to commit a terroristic act." He shook his head slightly. "I wouldn't worry too much about it, Dr.—*Mr.* Smith. He's excitable."

Hurley looked heavenward, but knew his prayer wouldn't be answered. This was one of those times he hoped God was going to help someone who helped himself.

27

It took a while to find it in the dark, mostly using the sense of touch, but—when Chase finally felt that familiar crinkly combination of cotton and linen—he let out a loud shout. Grant stumbled through the blackness and soon they were both running their hands over the cash.

It was one thing—and a very nice thing, indeed—to finally touch it, but their eyes deserved to see it. Grant aimed the flashlight and then they were staring at pile upon pile of stacked bills. Singles, fives, tens, twenties…no doubt there were more than a few fifties and hundreds there, too.

"That look like seven million to you?" asked Chase, running the light over pile after pile.

Grant kissed Chase's cheek. "We can count it later. *After* we get it out of here." He paused. "But, yeah, that's gotta be the haul we've been looking for."

Chase returned Grant's kiss. "I found it! I mean, *we* found it!"

Grant pretended not to hear the dig, and taking the light from Chase, ran it over the cash one more time. "That's a lot of money. We'll have to make a lot of trips up and down those stairs."

"You up to it?"

"Not really. But I guess…" He rubbed his sore thigh, then shined the flashlight down the horizontal section of the cross. Besides the cash, which was in a box set on a pallet inches above the hard concrete, it looked mostly empty.

But then the light glimmered off something almost hidden by the darkness at the far end, and soon they were brushing off two large footlockers, lined side by side against the wall and rendered almost invisible by years of dust.

"What the hell are *these* doing up here?" asked Grant.

Chase shrugged. "Probably got left behind by whoever built the cross. And probably for the same reason we don't want to keep going up and down those damn stairs." He gently touched Grant's shoulder. "C'mon, I think I saw some plastic bags in the other section we can use."

To which Grant said, "I have a better idea."

$ $ $

Hurley stood in his dark office, pacing the empty space once occupied by the Desk of Christ and waiting for Merribaugh to answer his phone. It only took four rings, which felt like twenty, before the call was picked up.

"We've got problems," Hurley said before Merribaugh had a chance to say hello. In the background he heard nuns-who-were-no-longer-nuns singing, which made his body involuntarily shudder. "So many problems I don't even know where to begin. The FBI is here…and Leonard Platt…and some other characters. I don't know who they are, except they're going to the Great Cross."

Merribaugh gasped. "The cross? But no one knows…"

"*Someone* knows. Somehow, these *clowns* seem to know they can get inside the Great Cross."

"But I don't know how…"

"Dennis, I am not calling to have a conversation with you. I am calling to tell you that we need to act quickly. So get your ass to the damn cross and make sure no one gets inside!"

"What if someone's already inside?"

"Then make sure they don't get out." Hurley cut off the call.

Merribaugh looked at the silenced phone in his hand. He'd spent a lifetime lying, stealing, and—above all—improvising on the spur of the moment, but he had no idea how he was going to resolve this crisis.

But he was ready to rise to the challenge. Because he had seven million dollars on the line.

$ $ $

Flashlights blazing, Special Agents Waverly and Tolan made their third rotation around the base of the Great Cross and still saw nothing.

"Are you *sure* your abductors said they were going into the cross?" Tolan asked Chris Cason for the fourth time.

"They did, sir. Indeed they did. Absolutely. As God is my witness…"

"Okay, okay, okay."

Tolan kicked the dirt at the base. "I just don't see how…"

"The thing is solid," Leonard said, also for the fourth time. He'd been nervous when the FBI had arrived, but now he was starting to get bored. He wondered if this was how Cousin Paul and his confederates had grown so blasé. "Solid concrete. The only way someone's getting inside it is with a tunnel borer. I should know. I mean, I worked here for seven years."

"Maybe they've got one," said Cason. "You can't put anything past those terrorists. It'd be just like them to use a tunnel borer to get inside, and then blow us all to Kingdom Come!" He leaned into Waverly. "Like in my screenplay."

Waverly gently pushed him away.

"You wrote a screenplay?"

Chris Cason didn't pick up the skepticism. "A secret agent builds a tunnel borer and uses it to drill up from under the Earth's surface…"

Waverly shook his head. "You've been watching too many James Bond movies, kid."

"…and then he attacks the Ant-Women…"

Waverly looked back at the cross, then at his partner. "We're wasting our time, Ollie. Let's pick up Hurley and Merribaugh and get the hell out of here."

Chris Cason stopped babbling. "You're looking for the Rev. Mr. Merribaugh?" Waverly nodded and the man pointed to the back door of the auditorium. "There he is. Right over there!"

Waverly and Tolan followed his finger to where Merribaugh stood, staring back at them with a deer-in-the-headlights look in his eyes as he stood on the loading dock.

Like Hurley, he knew FBI when he saw it.

"Mr. Merribaugh?" Waverly took his leather shield holder out of his breast pocket and held it in the air. "Waverly, FBI. I'd like to ask you a few questions."

Merribaugh didn't wait for those questions. Instead, he broke into a wobbly run toward the windowless basement door.

$ $ $

"Hey, Farraday! Can you hear me?"

"Yeah." The faint answer from 160 feet below echoed off the cement walls and metal railings until it sounded like a small chorus of Farradays. "You find it?"

"Yup," Grant confirmed. "It's coming down now, and I need you to look out down there."

There was a long pause as Grant's voice echoed down through the center of the Great Cross.

Finally Farraday called back. "What?"

Grant turned to Chase. "Screw him. He either gets out of the way or he doesn't." The footlockers—heavy, rusty, but very useful now that they'd been cleared of discarded tools, rags, empty soda cans, a few old extension cords, a battered power drill, six losing lottery tickets, and a dozen plastic bottles of past-the-expiration-date motor oil—were now full of cash, and Chase pushed the closest one to the edge of the stairway.

"This is gonna be a pain in the ass," he said.

"Would you rather make twenty or thirty trips up and down these stairs?" Chase shook his head. "Anyway, this will be faster. Just shove a box and let it slide. When it gets stuck, get it unstuck and shove it again." He tapped his head. "I invented this gravity thing, and it's awesome."

"Yes, you're brilliant, Grant." Chase planted a kiss where Grant had tapped his head and said, "Ready?"

"Ready."

Chase pushed, and the footlocker rolled over the lip and began sliding down the spiral staircase. After grinding its way down a half dozen steps, it came to an abrupt stop.

$ $ $

Merribaugh locked the basement door behind him and, for extra measure, threw the deadbolt. That was the easy part; the hard part would be getting out.

He raced through the tunnel to the core of the Great Cross, trying to analyze the strange grinding—almost metal-on-metal—he heard from the stairwell. It had to be true; somehow, someone had breached his security.

For nine years no one had known about the hollow core of the Great Cross except himself and Hurley. Not even Enright had known. But now someone had not only discovered their secret, they'd found the way in, which Merribaugh always considered a double—maybe even triple—security measure.

And if they wanted to get into the cross that badly, that could only mean they knew what he and Hurley had been secreting there for almost a decade.

He stepped into the well at the base of the staircase and that grinding from above—accompanied by loud bangs, as if something heavy were being dragged down the metal staircase—became louder. He looked up, but could see nothing in the gloom. Still, he had a job to do…for himself, as well as Hurley.

"Who's there?" he yelled, knowing it was unlikely his voice would carry over the noise above him. Which is why he was surprised by a voice coming from above him, but not too far above.

"Who's *there*?" was the gruff answer.

Merribaugh swallowed. "I don't know what you're doing, but I demand you leave. Leave, or I'll call the police."

"No, you won't," growled the other man's voice.

Well, he was correct, after all. He wasn't going to call the police, and the man knew he wouldn't, because then Merribaugh would have to explain why approximately seven million dollars in United States currency was hidden in the Great Cross.

Point to the stranger.

Still, he had to get them out of there. His next bluff had better work.

$ $ $

They stood at the locked door to the basement for a few minutes, not quite sure what to do until Tolan shrugged and dryly said, "Want to shoot our way in?"

"You know," said Waverly, "Fifteen years on the job and I have *never* fired my service weapon. Isn't that something?"

"Never?" Tolan lifted an eyebrow. "I think I killed four people in my first couple of months alone."

Leonard, standing on the periphery, sighed. "You guys really don't have to put on an act for me. I believe you have guns, and I believe they work."

Tolan grinned. "Just toying with you, Platt. Want some peanuts?" Leonard shook his head. "Good. I'm out."

"So anyway," said Waverly, running a hand quickly along his

forehead, smoothing out his hair, "you're *sure* there's no other exit from the basement?"

"Pretty sure," Leonard said grimly. "It's been a while since I was down there, but to the best of my recollection it's just a storage room. Only one way in, and one way out. Not even any windows."

Waverly spotted Chris Cason running across the lawn toward them and said, "Guess we're about to find out how good your memory is. Oh, and before Cason gets here, are you working with those guys he says abducted him? The ones he thinks are atheist homosexual terrorists?"

Leonard shook his head. "I have no idea what he's talking about. But I highly doubt there are terrorists running around the Virginia Cathedral of Love."

"And why are *you* here, again?"

Now that he realized law enforcement was all about repetition, Leonard's nervousness was rapidly dissipating. No one knew repetition better than a bookkeeper, except maybe a CPA. "Again—for maybe the hundredth time—I missed the place. I spent a lot of time here over the years, and I figured tonight—"

"Would be a good time to visit, what with all the people around who came to see *The Sound of Music*."

"Exactly."

Waverly smiled. "Okay. Just checking. You see, we know you're gay, Leonard. And that's just great. Seriously, not a problem for us. But Cason talks about homosexual terrorists, and you're a homosexual. You don't look like the terrorist type to me, Leonard, but…"

"How *do* you know my name, anyway?" That still bothered him.

"You'd be surprised what I know." He turned and greeted Cason. "Did you get the keys?"

"Captain Enright told me that Mr. Merribaugh has the only set."

Waverly turned and ruffled his freshly neatened hair, deep in thought. "Okay, *now* we have a problem."

$ $ $

There was a long metal-on-metal squeal, and then a half dozen loud bangs, and Merribaugh found himself covering his ears. This madness had to come to an end.

"I'm coming up," he announced to the darkness. "And I have a gun."

"I'm here," said the other man. There was a brief pause before he added, "And I don't need no gun."

Which took a considerable amount of wind out of Dennis Merribaugh's sails. Still, he climbed a few steps.

Maybe *both* of them were bluffing. That's what he hoped, at least.

$ $ $

One hundred forty feet above Merribaugh—and maybe 130 feet above Farraday—Grant and Chase worked in near darkness to correct the angles of the heavy footlockers on the narrow staircase. When the loads were repositioned, first Chase and then Grant used their feet to encourage gravity, and the boxes groaned down another half dozen steps before coming to an abrupt stop, again wedged between the railing and wall.

"This is getting ridiculous," said Grant. "I'm starting to think two dozen trips up and down the stairs would have been a better idea."

"If there was only some way to…Wait a minute!"

"What?"

Chase thought his brainstorm through, and only when he was satisfied it was good said, "The oil!"

"Huh?"

"The motor oil we took out of the boxes!"

"What about it?"

"Maybe we spread it on the stairs and the toolboxes slide more smoothly."

"It's expired," said Grant. "Like, three years ago."

"For engines, maybe. But it can still lube the stairs."

Grant thought about that, then smiled. "I think you might've just saved us a lot of work and time. Good job."

"I'll go get it. Be right back."

$ $ $

A small caravan of black SUVs—identical in every detail to the vehicles that had brought Waverly, Tolan and the junior agents to the Virginia Cathedral of Love—finally turned off the highway and onto Cathedral Boulevard. If Waverly hadn't stopped checking his watch, he would have been annoyed to know they were more than a half hour late.

But the agents had another concern at the moment. Namely, should they shoot their way in to the Rev. Mr. Dennis Merribaugh's basement sanctuary? Or wait for him to come out voluntarily?

"You know what they should teach us at the academy?" asked Tolan, more to fill time than for any other reason. "Lock-picking."

"That would be a useful skill," Waverly agreed. "No one learns that anymore."

Leonard, standing near them but not quite with them, except for those times they wanted to ask him the same damn questions, had finally had enough. He was starting to not care much about the money, especially since it appeared his confederates had deserted him. Maybe they'd left the campus altogether. There was certainly no reason to think they'd found their way into the Great Cross, which Leonard was still mostly convinced was solid and impenetrable, no matter what Chase had said about spirals or squiggles or whatever.

He decided it was an appropriate time to ask, "Since we're all just standing around and I've got nothing to do, you think it'd be all right if I take off?"

Waverly smiled, but shook his head. "No, Mr. Platt, I don't see that happening."

$ $ $

Chase uncapped the bottles of motor oil, and starting at a point thirty steps or so below the spot where the footlockers had jammed, began liberally pouring it over the stairs, slowly backing up until he reached them.

"That should help," he said, tossing the last empty bottle over the railing.

$ $ $

"What the hell?!" Merribaugh was mid-step when a slick empty plastic bottle hit him in the head. It didn't really hurt; it was more of a surprise.

Although not quite as much of a surprise as the large man who suddenly loomed out of the darkness, knocking down his cocked index finger and thumb before he had a chance to react.

"A finger gun?" asked the man. "You were threatening me with a finger gun?"

Merribaugh hung his head in shame.

"Now," said the man, "I personally think it would be a smart idea for you to get out of here before someone gets hurt. And by someone, I mean you."

This, Merribaugh thought, as he slowly retraced his steps down the underground passage, was going to be extremely difficult and uncomfortable to explain to Dr. Oscar Hurley.

$ $ $

Chase kicked the first footlocker, then Grant kicked the second footlocker, and then gravity and past-its-expiration-date motor oil worked together to do their job. Just like they'd hoped.

Problem was, they worked together to do their job a little too well.

$ $ $

Unseen by anyone except the elderly security guard—who in any event no longer had full confidence in his faculties—Dr. Oscar Hurley left Cathedral House and hustled to his personal car, pausing only to throw a few armfuls of possessions into the trunk. He assumed he'd be back, and very soon, but with the FBI and other assorted unsavory types swarming through the Virginia Cathedral of Love that night, it was the last place he should be.

In the morning, when he could accurately assess the damage from a safe—and remote—vantage point, he'd be better able to handle things. It might take a lawyer, or maybe an entire firm, or maybe the entire Virginia Bar Association, but he had enough friends in high places that any damage would be neither permanent nor deep.

But in the meantime no one—not even Francine—would know where he was.

He started the car, pulled out of his parking space, and got almost one-tenth of a mile down the road before a black SUV cut him off, veering into his lane and forcing him to a stop.

$ $ $

Grant smiled and high-fived Chase in the darkened stairwell. "*Now* they're moving."

And they were. The two very heavy footlockers—weighted down further with seven million dollars in cash, give or take—moved effortlessly down the well-oiled staircase, picking up speed as they followed its spiral. Looking down from twenty—now thirty—feet above the racing boxes, Grant had an unsettling thought.

He hollered to be heard above the noise, even though Chase stood next to him. "Do you think maybe it's *too* slick?"

"Nah, listen to them go."

"I'm just worried about—" Grant started to say, but stopped at a new sound, a sound that could only be the deafening noise resulting from a violent collision between two very heavy footlockers and one not-as-strong-as-it-looked concrete wall.

"—runaways."

Forty feet below where they stood, a floodlight now illuminated the interior of the Great Cross. And their hearts sank.

$ $ $

The campus—which had been so silent for much of the evening, even as two thousand people watched Walter Pomeroy's version of *The Sound of Music* revision in all its born-again glory—was suddenly bustling with activity.

A dozen FBI agents—some guarding the handcuffed Dr. Oscar Hurley; Waverly and Tolan trying to figure out how to get Merribaugh out of the basement—stood with guns drawn.

Captain Joseph Enright—followed by the two junior agents, who'd just freed him on word that backup had arrived—stormed down the road from Cathedral House, but lost steam when he saw the black SUVs parked at all angles and Hurley in cuffs.

Chris Cason took in the chaos with confusion. If this was the end of the world, he knew God, at least, would appreciate *Ant!*

Leonard Platt took it in with the certainty that he would be the next to be cuffed, as soon as Waverly and Tolan were bored toying with him.

A few dozen curious bystanders—parishioners out for a smoke, ushers, deliverymen—who were drawn by the activity away from the shadows of the cathedral, auditorium, and loading dock, edged a bit closer to try to figure out what the H-E-double-hockey-sticks was going on. *Is that Dr. Hurley in handcuffs? They look like FBI; are they FBI?*

And then they thought, *What's that noise?!!*

That noise was the noise two footlockers stuffed with cash made as they burst through the crumbling concrete blocks in the center of the Great Cross.

They hit the safety railing on the scaffolding a few feet beneath them with enough speed and force to dislodge the harness that attached the metal structure to the Great Cross.

With enough speed and force to pop open the latches that ordinarily would have kept those footlockers closed…

And then the scaffolding started to buckle.

Hurley had to be tased by the FBI agents before he would calm down.

Twice.

$ $ $

"High on a hill was a lonely goatherd," sang the actress playing fundamentalist Maria onstage, who didn't even have an opportunity to follow the line with a yodel before one of the footlockers smashed through the skylight. She grabbed a von Trapp kid by the hand and they dove out of the way, inches from the spot where the box ripped through the wires holding the marionettes before it fell to the stage, in the process spewing maybe three-point-five million into the air.

The audience screamed, gasped, and then fell silent. Until, that is, a large amount of that three-point-five million—first hurled to the stage by God's hand, with the assistance of gravity and motor oil, and now borne by the auditorium's powerful HVAC system and a strong cross-wind blowing through the shattered skylight—began floating through the air.

"Praise the Lord!" a few people shouted.

"Jesus provides!" yelled others.

A frenzy began as more than two thousand good Christians forgot all about that squashed goatherd and his goat, crushed somewhere underneath a greased-up footlocker, but remembered they needed to fill the gas tank on the way home. Or for the luckier ones with faster reflexes, to buy a nicer TV to watch Dr. Oscar Hurley on those Sunday mornings when they didn't feel like driving to Nash Bog.

Two rather large piles of cash landed in the orchestra pit near Walter Pomeroy. He made sure no one was watching, then shoved the bills in his piano bench and dropped his ass back onto it. Not that he wasn't appreciative of everything Jesus had done for him, but he'd just been fired and was anxious to get back to New York—this ex-gay life was more depressing than his gay life had been—and this was as good a sign as any.

Maria and the von Trapp kid also found time to compensate themselves for their near-death experience. Although they both also knew they'd be suing, which was particularly precocious of the von Trapp kid, who was only six years old.

$ $ $

The second footlocker—the one that provided the momentum to send the first into the scaffolding with enough extra kick to plummet through the roof of the auditorium—made a less dramatic return to earth.

The box lay on its side, its monetary contents floating out into the night air, until the scaffold slowly collapsed toward the loading dock. As the structure fell forward, more bills flew, until the floodlights picked up little but green United States currency as it fluttered through the air.

Deliverymen scrambled out of the way as metal pipes crumpled toward them, running first in a direction away from the box that crashed through the auditorium skylight, then away from the second section moments before it fell over their trucks.

The second footlocker rode the scaffolding almost all the way down…

Until it plunged through the roof of a white panel truck and the loud sound of splintering wood filled the air.

Leonard Platt, standing not far away, heard that noise and immediately subtracted one million dollars from their hoped-for take. Then he looked up to the sky—at the thousands of pieces of currency floating through the air—and subtracted seven million more, just to keep it realistic.

He was a bookkeeper, after all. He had to keep accurate numbers.

$ $ $

Lisa and Constance had grabbed what they could in the auditorium before realizing the same scenario was unfolding outside. And there was a lot less competition out there.

"Looks like they found the money," said Constance, quickly moving through a parking lot, snatching bills from the air and scooping them off the pavement.

Lisa was right behind her, trying not to think about what they'd lost. What was done was done. But as she peeled a twenty off a car windshield, she couldn't help herself. "Only Lambert."

Constance rounded another row of cars and stopped. "They've got Hurley in handcuffs."

At her side, Lisa sized up the situation. "Looks like your friends from the FBI finally got their man."

"Yeah, and I'm keeping my head down in case they're out to get their *woman* again."

"This is bad," Lisa said, her eyes riveted on the agents guarding Hurley. She took out her phone and typed a warning to their colleagues, wherever they were.

$ $ $

Grant and Chase made their way as quickly as possible down the tightly winding spiral staircase—slipping in the motor oil even as they walked with care, feeling each whack of their tailbones on the slick, hard metal steps—but reached the hole that had been punched into the wall only when dust was rising from the loading dock, obscuring the view

"What…uh…What happened?" asked Chase.

A ten-spot hovered in the air near Grant like a butterfly. He grabbed it and jammed it into a pocket. "Nothing good."

Chase nodded at the hole, at the floodlights. "How are we gonna get out of here without being seen?"

Grant looked out the hole in the wall of the Great Cross. "Dust. Money blowing around. Confusion Panic. Greed. There's your answer." His phone buzzed and he pulled it out of a pocket. "Oh, sweet. The FBI is out there, too."

Chase looked at his partner. "You think we're gonna get out of here?"

"Not really." Grant's shoulders slumped. "But I guess we gotta try."

"Does anyone even know we're *in* here?"

Grant thought that over. "They probably figured it out after seven million dollars went flying into the air. Because who else but us…?"

$ $ $

Waverly and Tolan looked at the chaos and had the same thought.

"Remember how we were afraid this might be a wild goose chase?" asked Waverly. "I guess we didn't have to worry."

"Guess not," answered Tolan. He shook his head and his attention shifted to the hole in the cross. "They hid it in the cross. That was actually pretty ingenious."

"Until it wasn't."

"Well, yeah. That, too." Tolan sighed and rattled the door handle again. "So what do you want to do about Merribaugh?"

Waverly shrugged. "Wait him out, I guess."

"I guess." Tolan stared out into the closest thing he'd ever witnessed to a riot. "Wish I'd brought more peanuts."

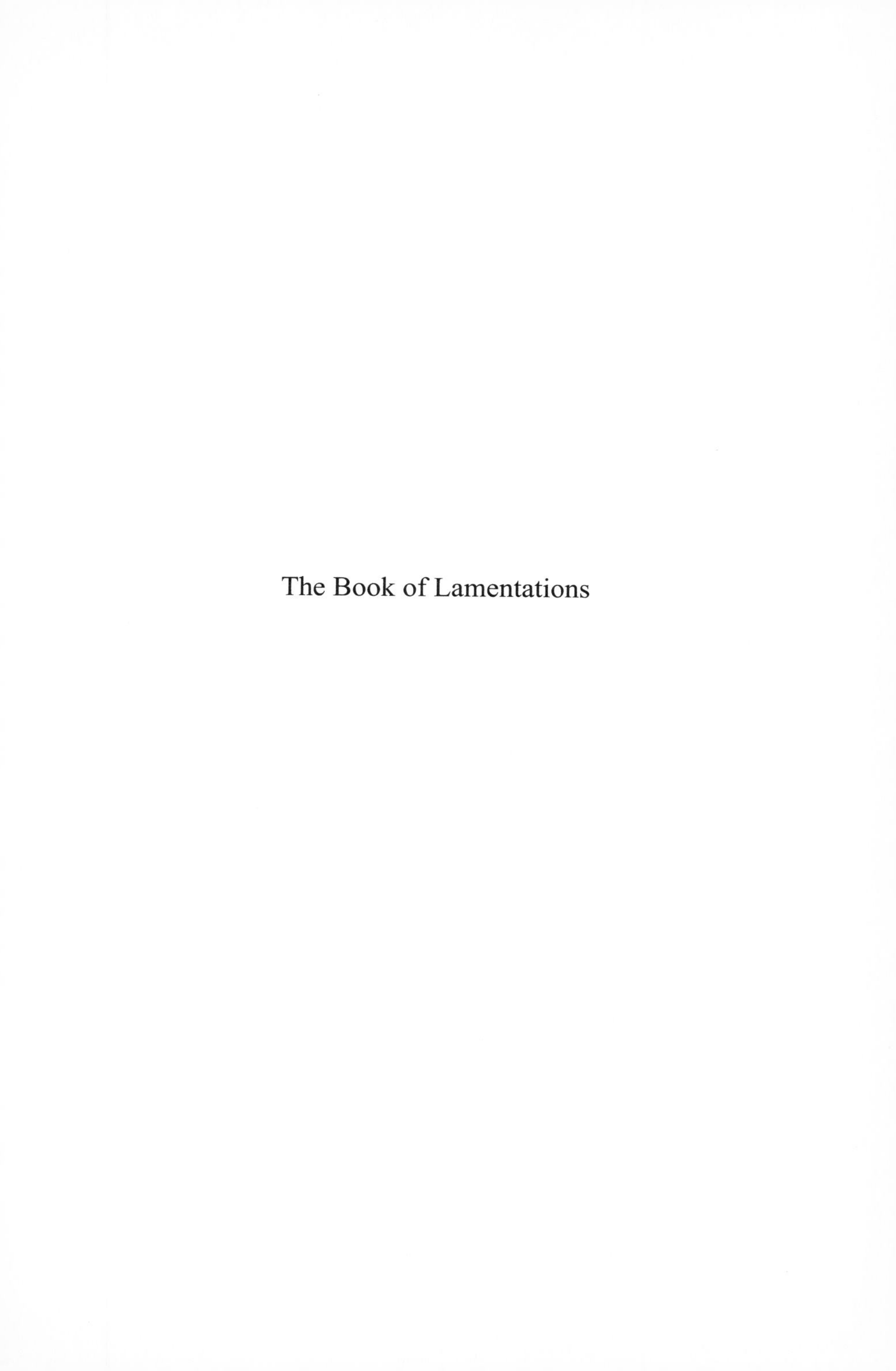

The Book of Lamentations

28

I have a thought," said Chase. Since they were nearing the bottom of the staircase and neither of them had come up with a decent escape route, Grant was willing to listen.

"Shoot."

"We already know the walls are weak, right? At least in certain places?"

"We certainly do *now*."

"How about we try to make a new hole?" Chase had a strange enthusiasm for his plan, which sounded to Grant like the least workable idea possible. His silence communicated that to Chase. "Just trying to help."

"I know you were." Grant's voice was melancholy. He was ready to face the inevitable. "But we've had a good run, and maybe prison ain't so bad. It's not like we won't know people."

Chase stopped mid-step. "I'm too pretty for prison. I am *not* going."

Grant continued his descent. "The situation says you are. But look, maybe we'll get sent to the same joint. Maybe we can even bunk together."

From not too far below them at the bottom of the staircase they heard Farraday's voice. "Nobody's goin' to prison, so stop talking like that. We'll work something out."

"I take it you know what happened," said Grant.

"Heard the noise, looked up, saw the hole, and figured it out." He made out their shapes in the darkness as they tromped down the last few steps.

"It's worse than you think. Lisa sent a text a while ago and the place is now crawling with FBI."

"Have you heard from her since?"

"No," Grant said, and reconfirmed with a glance at his cell phone. "Nothing."

"There's your answer," said Farraday. "We got people on the outside. Tell 'em to get us out."

"And how are they gonna do that? Supposing they haven't been picked up, that is."

"What, Lambert, you never heard of creating a diversion?" He cleared his throat. "It's like I gotta do all the thinking around here."

$ $ $

Lisa peered at her phone. "A diversion?"

Hiding next to her behind a parked car, Constance said, "Huh?"

"Those idiots are trapped inside the cross. They want us to attract attention so they can get out."

Constance looked at the money floating through the air, the collapsed scaffolding, the holes in the cross and the auditorium skylight, a thousand people moving back and forth, and, finally, at Dr. Oscar Hurley and the FBI agents.

"Should've figured they were inside it."

Lisa nodded. "This has their fingerprints all over it."

Constance leaned against a car, setting off the alarm. She ignored it. "Honey, I can't begin to think of how we'd attract attention in the middle of all this. Anything else is gonna look downright normal."

$ $ $

Security Officer Chris Cason heard the women before he saw them.

"I've been possessed by a demon!! Save me, Jesus!!"

And then she came into view, a tall, middle-aged woman spinning feverishly through the crowd, screaming over and over again that she'd been possessed.

A smaller black woman he recognized from the congregation ran next to her, also shouting.

"Someone help!" she hollered. "The demons of greed have taken control of her body!"

"Help me, Jesus! Save me from greed!" She spun into the lawn beneath the cross, scattering the throng of people who were still collecting the floating bills before falling to the ground.

Cason took a step toward her, but stopped as she rose up.

"Give the money back to the Cathedral! Don't let the demons steal your soul!"

"Yes! Praise the Lord!" The black woman turned to the crowd. "Give me the money so I can return it to its rightful place!"

"The demons!! They're burning my soul!"

Near Cason, a woman who'd felt guilty about the sixty-two dollars she'd gathered collapsed to the ground. "Help me, Jesus! I believe!" He was rushing to assist her when another woman fell. And then another.

Waverly and Tolan walked away from the door, trying to figure out what was happening. Something about demons and greed.

Leonard Platt saw his opportunity and slowly edged away.

$ $ $

Merribaugh knew what was waiting for him. The FBI knew where he was, and they wouldn't just shrug and walk away. Still, he'd put off the inevitable as long as possible, savoring his last moments of freedom in an empty basement.

But he heard the thieves approaching, and knew *that* wouldn't go well for him either. It was time to face the music.

He opened the door…

…and said, "What the hell?"

He thought he knew what to expect, but that didn't include hundreds of people running about and screaming. It didn't include mass hysteria. It didn't include collapsed scaffolding. And it certainly didn't include a night sky littered with thousands of pieces of paper.

It also didn't include a momentarily unguarded door, and—if there was one thing Dennis Merribaugh understood—it was that one should take every opportunity God provides.

He slipped out the door and made a dash for the closest marsh.

$ $ $

There were more than a dozen people on the ground when the wave of hysteria ended. Lisa, writhing on the lawn and screaming about the demons of greed, took a peek out of the corner of her eye to see if maybe it was time to end the charade, only to see Agent Waverly hovering above her.

Waverly turned to the agent standing next to him. "Ollie, I'd like you to meet Lisa Cochrane. She's the real estate agent I was telling you about." He pointed into the crowd. "And of course you remember Constance Price."

Lisa stopped writhing and said, "Oh, shit."

But then Waverly turned and said, "Damn it! The door's open." She didn't know what that meant, but if it delayed her arrest she was fine with it. Unfortunately, by the time she was in a seated position and found them again through the crowd, she knew it would be a short respite.

$ $ $

"Mr. LaMarca," said Agent Tolan as Chase emerged from the basement. "We meet again."

Chase bowed his head and held his hands out for the cuffs.

"Carrying any stolen cash on you, Charles?"

"No."

Tolan looked up at the bills that still fluttered through the air. "No, I guess you wouldn't be. So…see you around, LaMarca."

As Grant and Farraday emerged, Tolan and Waverly eyed them up and down, but made no effort to stop them. They were a few feet away when Waverly thought to ask, "Any of you fellows see Merribaugh in there?"

"Nah," said Farraday.

Waverly looked through the doorway, perplexed. "Okay, thanks, Farraday."

Farraday took a few more steps, then stopped.

"How do you know my name?"

"Because I'm good at what I do, Farraday. Very good. I'm about as good an agent as you were driving a cab."

"I don't know if I like you knowing so much about me."

Waverly smiled. "No one ever does."

When they were gone, taking Lisa and Constance with them, Tolan said, "I think we lost Merribaugh."

"He'll turn up, Ollie. Someday, he'll turn up. They always do."

29

"The first twenty thousand dollars," said Mary Beth, "Belongs to Lisa."

"Plus my expenses."

"Plus her expenses."

Grant pushed a carefully counted pile of money across the table. "That should cover everything." If he expected gratitude, he didn't get it.

"Nice try, Lambert." Lisa, put a bit more gravel into her voice. "The deal was the bank plus one-third."

He sighed and pushed another pile in her direction, subtracting a few fifties up his sleeve in the process. She wanted fair, she got as fair as she was going to get.

"See, honey?" said Lisa, who now radiated sweetness. "I told you there'd be a profit."

Mary Beth eyed the cash. "This ain't exactly gonna send Louboutin stock through the roof."

Farraday cleared his throat. "The way I understood this job, I was getting a hundred Gs and Leonard was getting a million-five."

Grant nodded. "Up until all the money flew away, that's exactly what you were getting. But now…" He looked at the remaining cash on the kitchen table which would have looked like a lot of money at any other time. "You know how this business works, Farraday. Now Cousin Leonard does, too."

Farraday did something with his face that could've been intended as a smile. "A guy's gotta try, right?"

"Here's what I think," said Chase. "We've got about ninety thousand, and six people left to pay off. Meaning we each get…" He divided in his head. "Roughly fifteen grand."

“No way!” Jared was outraged. He was not about to be short-changed, and he showed it by giving them Outraged Look Number Seven, which he knew was his best. “I was *guaranteed* ten thousand dollars.”

They all looked at each other, but no one said a word.

Finally, Grant slid two piles of bills to Jared, ruefully adding, “I should never try to bluff a pro.”

Leonard started to say, “So that means the rest of us get part of his…” but Farraday shut him up.

Then Farraday took a swig from a bottle of scotch and looked at Jared. “Looks like you did all right for yourself, kid.”

$ $ $

In their bedroom, Lisa pulled her top down, exposing a little bit of black bra.

Mary Beth squealed. “*Lisa!* Please! We’ll be back in New York tomorrow.”

“No, you don’t understand.” She pulled her bra away from her right breast and Mary Beth could see cash stuffed inside, which she did her best to count with a breast jiggling in front of her.

“That looks like five, six thousand dollars,” she finally gasped.

Lisa winked. “Mama provides.”

That night, they had the best sex they’d had in years.

$ $ $

Constance didn’t have hot sex that night—she’d wait until she was back with her girlfriend—but she’d managed to grab a few thousand herself as it fell from the sky, so she considered it a good night.

$ $ $

Leonard smiled. He’d managed to grab *forty dollars* when Waverly and Tolan weren’t looking. *Score!*

He hid his ill-gotten gains beneath his Odor Eaters and prayed no one would find it.

$ $ $

Grant and Chase slept fitfully.

There was nothing worse than working a job when their confederates made no money. It was the sort of thing that haunted a professional.

$ $ $

Early the next morning—far earlier than he was used to rising, but ten thousand dollars in cash excited him—Jared walked out to the front porch.

Lisa was there, already on her third cigarette of the morning.

"What are you doing up this early?" he asked.

She glanced at her watch. "It's eight."

"I *know*! Up with the chickens!"

"Roosters."

"Whatever."

Lisa shook her head. "I cannot wait to see you in thirty years…"

He bounced. "The rest of you will probably be dead by then."

"Shut *up*, Jared!"

Across the street, Tish and Malcolm walked out their front door. They looked and saw Lisa and Jared. Tish wrinkled her nose.

"I hate that bitch," said Lisa as Tish got in her BMW and Malcolm kissed her good-bye.

"Wanna give the neighbors a final 'screw you'?" Jared asked.

Lisa flicked her dead cigarette onto the lawn and lit another. "That depends on what you mean."

Tish backed her car onto Old Stone Fence Post Road, threw it into gear, and sped down the street.

"I'll be back when I'm back," he said. He took a few steps off the porch and turned to her. "Call Tish in ten minutes and tell her the house is on fire." He paused and winked. "Because it will be."

Twenty minutes later—ten minutes for Tish to drive out; ten more for her to drive back—the neighborhood exploded.

Lisa, taking a break from smoking, nodded approvingly as Jared raced home to safety wearing only a pair of briefs, the rest of his clothes in one hand and his sneakers in the other.

The entire neighborhood could hear the screams. "I'll kill you, Malcolm! I'll kill you, you faggot!"

Ms. Jarvis was a few doors down in one direction, Mr. Scribner a few in the other. They pulled out their cell phones and dialed.

Chase LaMarca stepped out onto the front porch and stretched. He noticed that Jared was virtually naked, but Jared did little that surprised him.

"What's going on?" he asked mid-stretch.

"Mmmm…nothing," said Jared. Innocent Angelic Look Number Two was on his face.

$ $ $

"I kind of feel bad," said Lisa, looking out the front window with Grant. Some people were still packing, but it wasn't her fault they were inefficient. She'd been packed for hours.

Grant held one lacy curtain to the side. "Faggots are your neighbors."

"Huh?" asked Chase, somewhere behind them.

"That's what it says on the sign one of 'em's holding. Scribs, I think. And Herren and Ford are…" He peered through the glass. "Looks like they're peeing on Tish's lawn."

Farraday shook his head. "Frat boys."

They heard the *whump-whump-whump* of luggage bouncing off steps and soon Mary Beth and her heavy suitcases were in the foyer.

"Ready to go, princess?" asked Lisa.

To which Mary Beth said, "Get me the fuck out of Deliverance Country *now*."

Another *whump-whump-whump*. It was Jared. He shrugged when he saw the near riot outside.

"Sorry. Not my fault."

Lisa agreed. "Nope. Not at all."

Grant stepped away from the window. "Okay, then. It seems our work in Nash Bog, Virginia, is done."

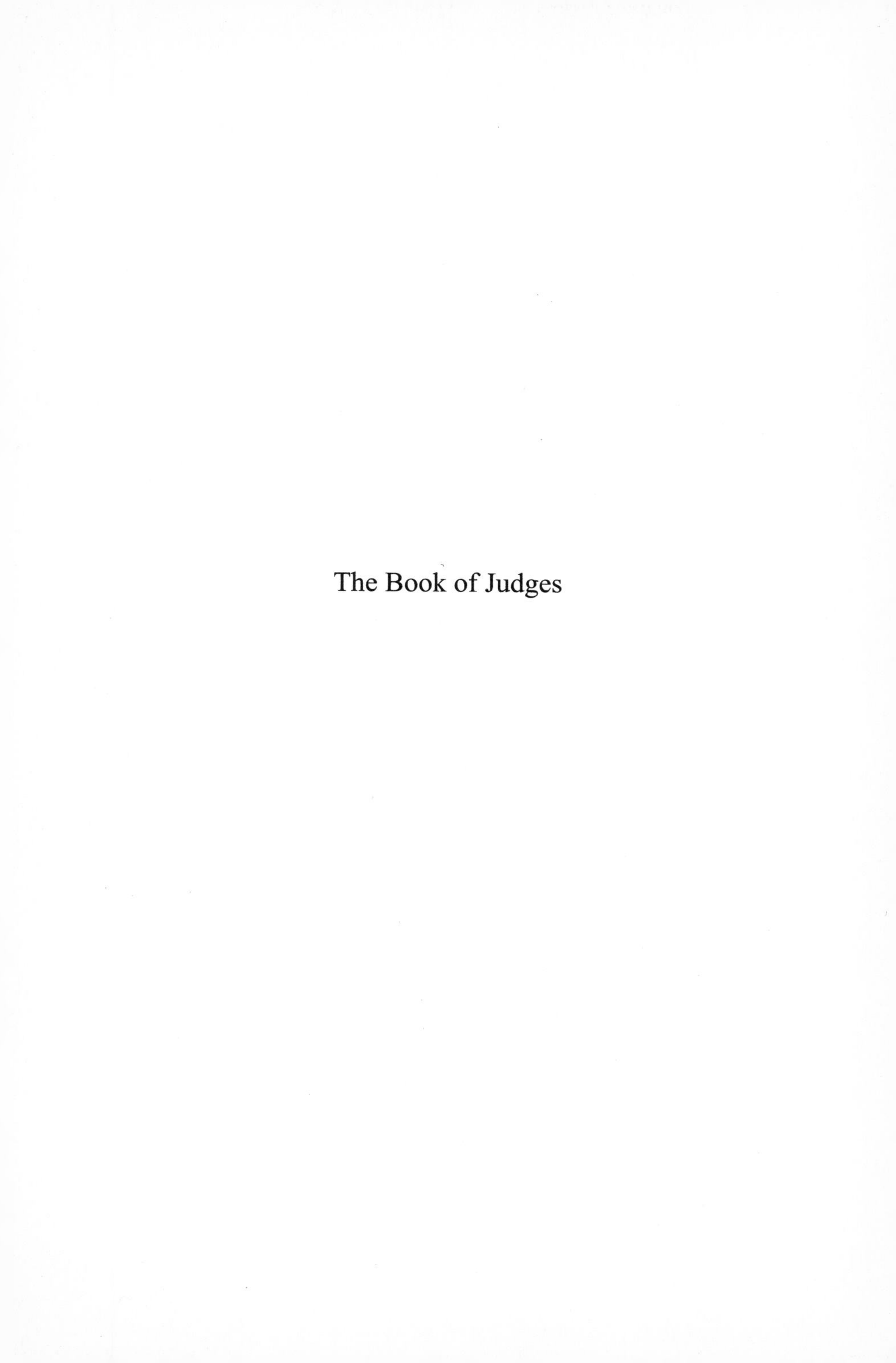

The Book of Judges

30

The newscaster read soberly from his script.

"Sources say United States Congressman Donald Skinner of New Hampshire is under investigation by the FBI for his role in the financial corruption scandal centered on religious powerhouse Dr. Oscar Hurley and his Virginia Cathedral of Love. Skinner is a prominent member of the House leadership and has recently been mentioned as a possible vice-presidential candidate.

"You may also recall that Skinner was in the news just last week when his car was stolen from a hotel valet queue, where he was attending an ex-gay conference sponsored by Hurley's ministry…"

$ $ $

"My name is Daniel Michael Rowell. I am employed as press secretary to United States Senator Gordon Cobey of Ohio."

They'd never watched C-SPAN. Never even knew C-SPAN existed, for that matter. But ever since the debacle at the Virginia Cathedral of Love—which was followed by the revelation that the FBI and IRS had been investigating Hurley, which was followed in turn by the revelation that one shaken-down U.S. senator from Ohio had finally had it and launched his own personal investigation of Hurley—they'd been hooked.

"There's a familiar face," said Grant, lying in bed next to Chase as they watched DVR'ed testimony on TV that night. "First time I've ever seen someone on TV I've already seen naked."

Chase pulled the sheets close around him and studied Dan Rowell's image on the screen. "He doesn't seem like Jared's type. He looks fat."

Grant cast a sidelong glance at Chase. "Jealous?"

"Of course not. Why would I be jealous? Especially of a fatty."

Grant kept his smile to himself.

Dan Rowell's congressional testimony that day was a follow-up to Senator Gordon Cobey's exhaustive narrative—backed up with documents and recordings—of the long history of blackmail and extortion undertaken by Dr. Oscar Hurley and the Rev. Mr. Dennis Merribaugh. Dan's role was to flesh out the evils of Project Rectitude and the Beyond Sin conference. It was all mostly irrelevant, if prurient. He *claimed* Merribaugh sought sex from participants at his ex-gay conferences, but couldn't prove it. He refused to name names, except—at Jared's insistence—that of Louis Lombardo, who promptly denied everything. And the allegedly molested possibly ex-gays had refused to come forward.

Finally, the senator from Mississippi who'd been chairing the hearing with a decidedly pro-Hurley bias gaveled Dan Rowell right out of the witness seat.

"Good," said Chase, when the gavel rapped.

Another sidelong glance. "Still jealous?"

Chase gave Grant a reassuring smile and a kiss on the lips. "I have nothing to be jealous about. I just thought the fat guy was a waste of time, is all."

"Mmm-hmm."

Not that Senator Cobey himself had a lot to offer a few days earlier. Yes, he had dates and times and recordings and documents, but it was almost beside the point. The FBI and IRS already had their hooks in Dr. Hurley and the Rev. Mr. Merribaugh, so anything Cobey could add would be icing on the cake.

And that cake had already been baked and was ready to be served.

$ $ $

The man on the treadmill had been watching the pudgy, bearded man desperately puffing away on the stationary bike in the mirrored wall of Dick's Maxi-Fitness, one of the less popular health clubs in Cedar Rapids, Iowa. He'd started watching to see how long the guy would hang in there; after a half hour, he admired his commitment.

But now eighty minutes had passed, and the man on the treadmill was starting to think the guy on the bike might be crazy. Was he one of those people who thought he could lose all kinds of weight almost instantly? On a *stationary bike*?

After another twenty minutes that was exactly what he thought. The man on the bike was drenched with sweat, gasping…and, sadly, would no doubt reclaim those lost calories with the next tuna fish sandwich. Even though he was himself maxing out his own cardio session, as the Dick in Dick's Maxi-Fitness, he should know.

He looked up at the television mounted on the wall. He didn't want to witness the inevitable heart attack.

A man's face flashed on the screen. The caption underneath read DENNIS MERRIBAUGH: SOUGHT IN MULTIMILLION-DOLLAR SCAM.

Through the music from his ear buds, Dick heard a groan. When he turned, ready to perform CPR, the pudgy man was heaving himself off the stationary bike, trying his best to move on jelly-like legs. He bounced off a pillar and another bike before he made it to the locker room door.

Dick unhappily noted he hadn't wiped down the equipment.

His eyes went back to the TV moments before Merribaugh's face disappeared…and then he turned off the treadmill.

If that guy had a beard and mustache… He looked back to the door of the locker room, catching a glimpse of a wide, sweaty posterior before it vanished around the corner.

The nightly news would again use that photo of Merribaugh just twenty-four hours later. Only this time the caption would read: VIRGINIA FUGITIVE CAPTURED IN IOWA.

$ $ $

"Wait a minute," said Constance, who was sitting in her Harlem living room and holding a mug of hot coffee inches from her lips, because if she'd really heard what she thought she'd heard, she knew she'd spit the coffee all over her couch. "Did you just offer me a job?"

Special Agent Patrick Waverly brushed a forelock off his brow. "I've seen you in action, and you're good. Not as good as me, but good."

"You realize I'm a criminal, right?"

"Yep. Ran your record, saw you in action…Everything looked pretty criminal to me."

She set the coffee cup down and sized him up. "So what's the job pay?"

"Don't you want to know what the Bureau wants you to do?"

Constance Price folded her arms. "I *asked*, what's the job pay?"

Waverly laughed. "I love you criminals. Sometimes you're so *honest*."

$ $ $

Paul Farraday walked out of the McDonald's on Route 46 in Little Ferry, New Jersey. His bag contained a Big Mac and large order of fries; he'd ditched the large soda in the trash can out front because he didn't want to gain weight.

A few miles down the road he pulled the car he'd borrowed without permission into the lot of a strip mall and parked. Then, still carrying the McDonald's bag, he walked a few hundred feet down the road.

He looked across Route 46 toward Teterboro Airport and thought, *Yeah.*

Farraday was a firm believer in developing one's skills. That was how he'd become a legendary driver…a deft car thief…a great chef…a memorable alcoholic…

And now he was ready for a new challenge.

He took a deep breath of Route 46 exhaust, watched a small plane launch into the air, and smiled.

"Yeah."

$ $ $

"Five-point-one, David!"

She'd phoned ahead to tell him she had great news, and she did. She'd managed to squeeze an extra hundred thousand dollars out of a buyer above the five million they'd *almost* accepted for his beach-adjacent home in Southampton. But Lisa Cochrane had wanted to personally deliver that news to David R. Carlyle IV, which was how she and Mary Beth found themselves in his Midtown Manhattan office a few hours later.

"That's wonderful news," said David. He stared out the window overlooking Sixth Avenue. "Except…"

"Except?" Lisa raised one eyebrow. She liked the word "accept." The word he had used? Not so much.

He looked everywhere but at her. "Except now I'm not so sure I want to sell."

Lisa had wanted Mary Beth to witness the triumphant moment when David R. Carlyle IV clapped his hands with joy at a five-point-one-million-dollar offer on his financial albatross. Not this.

But her girlfriend made her own entertainment.

Mary Beth walked up to him, grabbed his collar, and said, "I will kill you with my bare hands if you don't take the deal."

"Oh, my!" David took a step back.

And then he thought, *Five million, one hundred thousand dollars isn't a bad deal. Not bad at all…*

It was an unorthodox negotiating strategy, but it worked. Better yet, he still wanted to write some real estate porn.

Not a bad afternoon.

$ $ $

Leonard Platt's fifteen thousand dollars—correction: fifteen thousand *forty* dollars!—would be just enough to get him through seventeen weeks, according to calculations he'd done over and over since the night most of the seven million dollars flew into the darkness and the pockets of the devout.

One-third of a year. Better than the average termination settlement—*much* better than the zero dollars he'd received from the Cathedral—so maybe, he thought, he shouldn't dwell on it.

And if he banked it, well…he'd almost have enough cash to bankroll a future job one day. He could be the Lisa!

Then Leonard thought, *Bankroll a job? I've become one of them!*

When the thought first crossed his mind he was horrified. For maybe five seconds. Then he was giddy for the rest of the night.

$ $ $

"I ever tell you about Devin Hannerty?" Grant asked one night.

Chase rolled over to face him, although he was tempted to feign sleep. "The one who owns the gay clubs, right?"

"That's the guy."

"And he treated you like shit when you moved to New York, so now you hate him, right?"

"That's the guy."

Chase yawned. "Yeah, you told me about him. So?"

"Heard today he's hiring."

Chase rolled away. "That's nice."

Grant pretended not to notice. "*Really* hiring. Word on the street is he fired almost his entire staff. The only ones left are incompetent ass-kissers."

Chase rolled back to face him. "Are you talking…a job?"

"Maybe. If we can find the right bait. Devin likes 'em young." Now it was Grant's turn to roll away.

They lay in the darkness for a few minutes.

Chase cracked first.

"Jared?"

Grant rolled back until their noses touched. "Maybe."

"I'll call him right now." Chase wasn't surprised by Grant's exaggerated sigh in the darkness as he grabbed his phone from the charger and dialed, but he *was* surprised when Jared answered at that hour. And without pounding dance music in the background, at that.

"Hi, Chase!"

"Uh…Hi. Listen, you got a half hour tomorrow to talk about some work we might have?"

"Sorry, I can't."

Chase turned on his Barry White voice. "Are you sure you don't want to work with me?" That earned him a physical slap from Grant, and a verbal one from Jared.

"I'm in Washington now."

Chase scratched his head. "Washington state? Or Washington, DC?"

"DC, of course!" Jared squealed. "Dan and I are boyfriends now! Isn't that—?"

Chase clicked off the phone and said, "Jared can't do the job."

Grant, who'd heard Jared's side of the conversation, laughed himself to sleep.

About the Author

Rob Byrnes is the author of five novels, including the 2006 Lambda Literary Award–winning *When the Stars Come Out* and 2009 Lammy finalist *Straight Lies*. His short stories have also appeared in several anthologies, including *Men of the Mean Streets* (Bold Strokes Books, 2011).

A native of upstate New York, Byrnes was born and raised in Rochester and graduated from Union College in Schenectady before moving to Manhattan. He now resides in West New York, New Jersey, with his partner, Brady Allen.

Books Available From Bold Strokes Books

Sheltering Dunes by Radclyffe. The seventh in the award-winning Provincetown Tales. The pasts, presents, and futures of three women collide in a single moment that will alter all their lives forever. (978-1-60282-573-4)

Holy Rollers by Rob Byrnes. Partners in life and crime Grant Lambert and Chase LaMarca assemble a team of gay and lesbian criminals to steal millions from a right-wing mega-church, but the gang's plans are complicated by an "ex-gay" conference, the FBI, and a corrupt reverend with his own plans for the cash. (978-1-60282-578-9)

History's Passion: Stories of Sex Before Stonewall, edited by Richard Labonté. Four acclaimed erotic authors re-imagine the past…Welcome to the hidden queer history of men loving men not so very long—and centuries—ago. (978-1-60282-576-5)

Lucky Loser by Yolanda Wallace. Top tennis pros Sinjin Smythe and Laure Fortescue reach Wimbledon desperate to claim tennis's crown jewel, but will their feelings for each other get in the way? (978-1-60282-575-8)

Mystery of The Tempest: A Fisher Key Adventure by Sam Cameron. Twin brothers Denny and Steven Anderson love helping people and fighting crime alongside their sheriff dad on sun-drenched Fisher Key, Florida, but Denny doesn't dare tell anyone he's gay, and Steven has secrets of his own to keep. (978-1-60282-579-6)

Better Off Red: Vampire Sorority Sisters Book 1 by Rebekah Weatherspoon. Every sorority has its secrets, and college freshman Ginger Carmichael soon discovers that her pledge is more than a bond of sisterhood—it's a lifelong pact to serve six bloodthirsty demons with a lot more than nutritional needs. (978-1-60282-574-1)

Detours by Jeffrey Ricker. Joel Patterson is heading to Maine for his mother's funeral, and his high school friend Lincoln has invited himself along on the ride—and into Joel's bed—but when the ghost of Joel's mother joins the trip, the route is likely to be anything but straight. (978-1-60282-577-2)

Three Days by L.T. Marie. In a town like Vegas where anything can happen, Shawn and Dakota find that the stakes are love at all costs, and it's a gamble neither can afford to lose. (978-1-60282-569-7)

Swimming to Chicago by David-Matthew Barnes. As the lives of the adults around them unravel, high school students Alex and Robby form an unbreakable bond, vowing to do anything to stay together—even if it means leaving everything behind.(978-1-60282-572-7)

Hostage Moon by AJ Quinn. Hunter Roswell thought she had left her past behind, until a serial killer begins stalking her. Can FBI profiler Sara Wilder help her find her connection to the killer before he strikes on blood moon? (978-1-60282-568-0)

Erotica Exotica: Tales of Sex, Magic, and the Supernatural, edited by Richard Labonté. Today's top gay erotica authors offer sexual thrills and perverse arousal, spooky chills, and magical orgasms in these stories exploring arcane mystery, supernatural seduction, and sex that haunts in a manner both weird and wondrous. (978-1-60282-570-3)

Blue by Russ Gregory. Matt and Thatcher find themselves in the crosshairs of a psychotic killer stalking gay men in the streets of Austin, and only a 103-year-old nursing home resident holds the key to solving the murders—but can she give up her secrets in time to save them? (978-1-60282-571-0)

Balance of Forces: Toujours Ici by Ali Vali. Immortal Kendal Richoux's life began during the reign of Egypt's only female pharaoh, and history has taught her the dangers of getting too close to anyone who hasn't harnessed the power of time, but as she prepares for the most important battle of her long life, can she resist her attraction to Piper Marmande? (978-1-60282-567-3)

Wings: Subversive Gay Angel Erotica, edited by Todd Gregory. A collection of powerfully written tales of passion and desire centered on the aching beauty of angels. (978-1-60282-565-9)

Contemporary Gay Romances by Felice Picano. These works of short fiction from legendary novelist and memoirist Felice Picano are as different from any standard "romances" as you can get, but they will linger in the mind and memory. (978-1-60282-639-7)